Tethered

Eleanor Bertin

Leaf & BLADE

TETHERED

Published by Leaf & Blade, Big Valley, Canada

ISBN 978-1-7771825-1-9

Author photo by Alyssa Raeanne Photography, alyssaraeanne.ca

Cover design by Roseanna White Designs. Cover images from Shutterstock.
Formatting by Polgarus Studio

To my sister, Becky, with love and gratitude

Welcome to

THE MOSAIC COLLECTION

We are sisters, a beautiful mosaic united by the love of God through the blood of Christ.

Each month The Mosaic Collection releases one faith-based novel or anthology exploring our theme, Family by His Design, and sharing stories that feature diverse, God-designed families. All are contemporary stories ranging from mystery and women's fiction to comedic and literary fiction. We hope you'll join our Mosaic family as we explore together what truly defines a family.

If you're like us, loneliness and suffering have touched your life in ways you never imagined; but Dear One, while you may feel alone in your suffering—whatever it is—you are never alone!

Subscribe to *Grace & Glory*, the official newsletter of The Mosaic Collection, to receive monthly encouragement from Mosaic authors, as well as timely updates about events, new releases, and giveaways.

Learn more about The Mosaic Collection at
www.mosaiccollectionbooks.com

Join our Reader Community, too!
www.facebook.com/groups/TheMosaicCollection

Books in

THE MOSAIC COLLECTION

When Mountains Sing by Stacy Monson

Unbound by Eleanor Bertin

The Red Journal by Deb Elkink

A Beautiful Mess by Brenda S. Anderson

Hope is Born: A Mosaic Christmas Anthology

More Than Enough by Lorna Seilstad

The Road to Happenstance by Janice L. Dick

This Side of Yesterday by Angela D. Meyer

Lost Down Deep by Sara Davison

The Mischief Thief by Johnnie Alexander

Before Summer's End: A Mosaic Summer Anthology

Tethered by Eleanor Bertin

Learn more at www.mosaiccollectionbooks.com/books

"...rooted and grounded in Him..."

Ephesians 3:17

CHAPTER 1

Downstairs, the front door opened. Jacqui held her breath, listening. Not until it closed, did she creep from her bed to the window. Keeping out of sight, she slid a finger down the silky length of the imported drapes, moving them ever so slightly to watch the two figures below leaving the house. Geoff's hand wandered down Dale's back as they headed to the street where Geoff's convertible waited. Together they stowed their weekend bags and a picnic hamper in the trunk, laughing at some private joke, though Jacqui couldn't make out their words. What she did hear was the muffled thud of each door muttering goodbye.

When Geoff's taillights disappeared left toward the highway out of the city, Jacqui let out a long-held, steadying breath. A breath she must have been holding for how long? Weeks? Months? She cleared her throat hard, not allowing the exhale to end in a sob. Then she sprang into action.

To fend off the unspeakable, she worked at fever-pitch to pack and leave before their return tomorrow. She flew through the house with a nervous energy, forcing herself to stick with her prepared lists, filling the boxes she had sequestered under her bed in preparation, dragging furniture and wrapping household items for the movers. In arranging storage for the bulk of her belongings, she was scrupulous about taking only what she had paid for herself plus half of what she and Geoff had purchased together. He would not return to a condo stripped bare. She would take the high ground, which was more than could be said of him. Or was it? She paused with her hand on a sculpture by a local artist. Who was to say Geoff wasn't right?

But that line of thinking only ended in a stomachache. Dread of confrontation compelled her to act now, during Geoff's two days away. What, after all, could she possibly say to him? His was no ordinary betrayal. The new lover left Jacqui aghast, yet Geoff expected she would be pleased for him? She settled for leaving him a note of a few terse lines.

All morning and well into the afternoon, she sweated and lugged and packaged. While making her lists, she'd had to decide which of her belongings were essential, requiring much paring down punctuated by moments of painful nostalgia. But by midday, nearly twenty years of her life with Geoff were jammed into a few cubic meters of her mid-size, fuel-efficient vehicle. Well, not jammed exactly. Despite her hurry, like a game of Tetris, each cubbyhole and centimetre was wedged full of her belongings. The items she would need on the trip she kept near the front for easy access.

When the movers arrived at four, she supervised their every turn lest they bash and ding her beautiful home. After they finished, she rearranged the furniture that was left, vacuumed, and scrubbed. At last she leaned against the kitchen island, exhausted and famished. She allowed herself one final act of spite. She barbequed and devoured both tenderloins that Geoff and Dale had earmarked for a special dinner on their return.

The next morning, before the sun rose above the rooftops on the opposite side of the street, Jacqui slammed the hatchback of her car against its bulging contents. This thud and click muttered goodbye, too. Or more like good riddance.

She slid behind the steering wheel and shut the car door, resisting the urge to turn back, to mourn for what was lost and to long for what might have been.

To arrive at her inherited land, her own piece of the earth, on the day of her fortieth birthday would be perfect. *Bury that day in oblivion.* Not a soul knew her there in central Alberta, so she could have no expectations and no disappointment. Jacqui calculated it would take precisely thirty-four hours to cross the Canadian Shield and most of the Prairies, which, allowing stops for food, sleep, and breaks, would put her at her new place about the middle of the first week of July. Of course, she was entirely free to prolong the trip as long as she wished. And unlike the precise travel plans she and Geoff had always made when they travelled, she had no return date. This was to be an adventure, after all. But the long habit of deadlines and goal setting didn't die easily. *Go west, young—er—middle-aged woman!*

And so, she drove north from Hamilton heading for the TransCanada highway, a more circuitous yet more scenic route than going through the US. Who knew, after all, what American Customs might have done with her—no job, no permanent address, no clear plan of action?

Scanning the view through her windshield, she was astounded at the vast wilderness. It truly was beautiful country. Why had they never camped up here? *Oh right.* They never camped anywhere. Geoff favoured luxury hotels and night life. She pushed that line of thought firmly behind her. The thick forest encroaching on the highway recalled the 19th-century Canadian novel, *Roughing it in the Bush.* At the thought of the tooth-jarring, bone-jolting travel over the corduroy roads of Susannah Moodie's day, Jacqui gave the steering wheel of her faithful steed a grateful pat.

Farther on, sporadic radio and Internet signals tested her endurance. *Ah, a road sign ahead.* She was starved for the written word. That brought to mind her precious collection of classic books left behind in storage. The thought of being forced out of her spacious home brought a fresh wave of resentment. *Focus, Jacqui!*

Waubamik, the sign read. *Waubamik-mik-mik-mik.* It had a certain rhythm. Down the road, another town: Shawanaga. She sang the musical names together keeping time with her thumbs on the steering wheel. Geoff would have sung variations—a calypso beat, an Italian oratorio, a jazz rendition. But no more Geoff, came the stern reminder.

Hours later, a road sign pointed north to Kapuskasing. For a few kilometres, mispronouncing and redefining the unfamiliar town name provided entertainment. Kapus*kas*ing—a drapery technique for enclosing a curtain rod. *Enough with the home decor allusions, already*. Alternately, Ka*pus*kasing—the sudden emergence of bodily fluid from an infected sliver. *Obtained while helping your mate with renovations. For nineteen years. Boo hoo*. Or possibly, Ka*poos*kas*ing*—a northern Ontario karaoke event celebrating outhouses. *Oh yeah, that's more like it, Jacqui.* The smile she cracked felt foreign to her unaccustomed cheeks. How long had it been since anything made her laugh?

But really, what was with all the trees? And rocks. And rocks and trees, interrupted only by an occasional deer-crossing sign.

To keep from being lulled to sleep by the repetitive scenery she had to pull over at times, get out and walk around breathing in great gulps of the pine-scented summer air, and a few black flies too, if the truth was told.

And yet, what was the rush? Why make a mad drive across the country for the false deadline of her birthday? It wasn't as though she had anyone waiting for her there. Like she had no one waiting for her to return. She was under no obligations, completely independent, set free.

Then why does it feel so much like I've been cut loose? Adrift was exactly how Jacqui had felt at eight years old when her mother had stuffed her and a couple of suitcases into the car to leave her father—rootless, tossed about by the erratic winds of her mother's whims.

Today she had nothing and no one to tie her down, no partner, no dependents, no family. Well, except Pops. But as infrequently as she saw him, even living in the same city, the distance would make little difference, as long as she called once in a while. She quelled a pang of guilt at not making the time to see him once more before she left.

Maybe she should take it easy, drive at a leisurely pace, stop at all the points of interest along the way. *Who decides what makes a point interesting, anyway?* The trip could be a sort of personal Discover Canada odyssey. *Yeah, that ought to be a real You-tube winner. Inept photographer searches motherland to find herself. And then what?*

No, Jacqui couldn't imagine dragging the trip on any longer than necessary. At least covering the distance felt like some kind of progress. So, she drove on, north, then west, skirting Georgian Bay off Lake Huron. More trees, more rocks, more road curves flew by, and fewer and fewer towns appeared as she topped Lake Superior. The shadows lengthened as evening drew on. Her headlights groped through heavy fog that crept in menacing wisps across the road. She'd had grand intentions of reaching Thunder Bay the first night, but after all these hours, her hands cleaved to the steering wheel.

Is cleaved the past tense? Clove? Cleft? Weird that the word can mean "adhered to" or its exact opposite, "split or broken apart." Like Geoff and Jacqui, split apart. No, don't go there. Her mind, weakened by weariness, was drifting into the bizarre.

The monotony of highway-hugging forest and endless yellow painted lines enticed her to slumber. A sudden rumble of her tires on the grooved centre line jerked Jacqui alert. She pulled to the right, corrected the steering wheel and was instantly wide awake. Fear of falling asleep while driving, combined with her cramped lower back finally forced her to stop short of her destination goal.

A small, vacant picnic site overlooking a tree-crowded ravine became Jacqui's first camping spot, if it could be called that. She pulled her sleeping bag and pillow from behind the driver's seat, flattening the seat to lay out the bedding. Before settling in for the night, she grabbed a towel and her toiletries bag and climbed out of the car, intending to use the outhouse. An army of bloodthirsty mosquitoes ambushed her. She fought the attack with flailing arms, dashing to the cobwebby, smelly wooden shack.

The only running water was an outdoor spigot. In a spastic dance of continual bug-swatting, Jacqui wiped down her face and neck with the icy water, brushed her teeth and raced back to her car, slamming the door against the hungry horde. She spent the next few minutes in a bloody massacre of anything that buzzed or fluttered. Finally, she slid down into the sleeping bag. It wasn't an ideal bed, with the seatbelt buckle digging into her hip on one side and the arm rest pressing in on the other. Had it been this uncomfortable when she and her college girlfriend travelled this way? *But I wasn't forty then.* She squirmed for a more comfortable position. *So, this is what it's like to be homeless.* No doubt about it, tomorrow night would be a hotel night.

Darkness fell suddenly, with the close-pressing evergreens blotting the light in a blackness deeper than night ever was in the city. On the highway behind her, traffic was reduced to the swelling and fading of the occasional semi-truck, accentuating her aloneness. The quiet was by far the worst part. Thoughts and memories buzzed around her brain like the last persistent mosquitoes that plagued her through the night.

CHAPTER 2

Two sharp raps on her window startled Jacqui into awareness the next morning. She jerked upright, trying to shrug off the sleeping bag that bound her arm. Fumbling with the key in the ignition, she cracked open the window to a man in a brown uniform beside her door.

"Picnic only, lady." The ranger with the gravelly voice pointed to the edge of the parking lot. "Didn't you see the sign? No overnight camping. Better move on." Without waiting for a response, he clumped back to his pick-up and roared out of the parking lot.

Yes, sir! Right away, sir! Jacqui grumbled some choice epithets, then shimmied out of the sleeping bag. She peeked in the visor mirror. Her hair was in a ghastly state and a vicious crease from the upholstery welting scored one cheek. Bracing herself against the insect onslaught, she dashed out of the car but found the morning sun had driven them away, leaving a pleasant pine-freshened morning. She braved the outhouse then did what she could to untangle her curls and shake out her stiff limbs in a short walk around the picnic area before heading back to the car to repack her bedding. Little was left of her stash of travel food after three meals on the road yesterday. She resigned herself to a breakfast of the last two slices of cheese and a granola bar. Even for that, she'd overestimated her appetite.

Swigging a gulp of tepid water, she forced down the paper-dry bar then set the GPS for the Manitoba border, another eight hours of driving ahead. *Ontario is way too big.* Hour after hour of rocks and trees crept by, more than once drawing Jacqui's mind back with regretful longing to the large audio book collection at the library where she worked, or rather, used to work. She snuffled, fiddling with the radio dial with unsatisfactory results. She settled for one of the downloaded books on her phone.

Lunch was a gas station diner where she eavesdropped on two guys in hardhats engaged in a fervent interchange over which brand of boat engine was superior. The earnest conversation was still going on when Jacqui finished her soup and rose to leave. Miles later, she stopped for a break in a larger centre with a Tim Horton's. In the two-cubicle restroom, a deep voice suddenly made her jump.

"Everything come out OK, then?" the voice asked.

Of all the—! It took a second before Jacqui realized the voice in the next cubicle was a woman on a cell phone and not a man. *Glad I didn't answer.* Increasingly, Jacqui felt like a mere spectator in the world. She washed up in a hurry and fled.

At Thunder Bay, Jacqui stocked up on fresh vegetables and fruit then searched for other healthy snack options. In her loneliness she found herself hungry for conversation. She eavesdropped shamelessly in the supermarket check-out line.

"Yeah, she's converted to Buddhism," a woman told her friend.

"Well, good on her," the acquaintance responded. "I always say, doesn't matter what you believe, as long as you believe."

You always say that, do you? Jacqui bit back a caustic reply, keeping her gaze on the woman's grocery items as they rode towards the cashier. *Does it matter if you believe toilet cleaner is medicine and take a big swig? How would that work out for you?* Now she sounded like Geoff.

Back in her car, Jacqui surveyed the nearby hotels, itching for a shower. But she decided to drive on, taking her chances on finding a vacancy later in the day. As tired and stiff as she was, she didn't want tomorrow, her last day of driving, to be the longest.

Across the Manitoba border, she soon emerged out of forest into prairie farmland. She'd never been this far west. The open country and stubby trees exposed her to the wind. She closed the sunroof. By now, too, the low sun was dazzling her eyes. In Winnipeg, she craved a hot meal and a little human interaction, and decided to try a restaurant called Salisbury House. Seated in a capacious booth inside, she scanned the menu for salad rolling her eyes at some sort of burger ridiculously named "nip and chips."

From the booth behind her, a woman with a heavy accent chatted on her cell phone. "I'm just here for something to bite."

Jacqui snickered. Still, she pulled her collar more snugly around her neck.

She reached Brandon after ten that night, though the western sky still glowed bright. City lights spread out on her left, but she could see open highway not much farther ahead. *Better pick the first hotel I see.* She pulled into Barney's Motel, breathing a relieved sigh when the desk clerk handed her the key card. After a welcome shower, she stretched out on the bed, withdrawing the familiar file with the title deed to her new property.

When she was first notified two years before about her inheritance of this piece of central Alberta farmland from her bachelor uncle, she hadn't paid it much attention other than a faint curiosity about relatives her father had long ago disowned. Pops had given only a brief snort of disgust when she told him about it. Soon, her initial mild interest had faded. She was busy with her career at the library and her after-hours business with Geoff, renovating and flipping houses. She'd always meant to investigate the prospect of selling the land out west, but the thought of the tax hit was daunting. At the time, she simply appreciated receiving the extra land rental income. She'd shoved the deed into a file and left it at that.

But recently, as everyday encounters at work with Geoff's new flame became intolerable and Jacqui increasingly became an alien in her own home, the thought of somewhere to go grew urgent. And she found a tenuous comfort in this tie to a family she'd never known. When she received the title deed or the brief notes from the tenant that came with the annual cheques, she'd had to rely on Google to explain the unfamiliar terms. What is a half-section? What did "in crop" or "feed crop" mean? But the residence—now, that caught her interest.

As she had done repeatedly during the past few weeks, Jacqui scanned the legal description, trying to squeeze out more details than it offered. At nine hundred square feet, the house would be small. When she'd searched for an online satellite image, trees had obscured the home. She pictured a country cottage, maybe of stone, surrounded by a colourful English-style garden. She was hoping for a fireplace and original millwork, perhaps a view of the Rockies. Outbuildings showed up on the image, too. Maybe a garage, a greenhouse, and a red, hip-roofed barn? She especially hoped for a greenhouse. Without a doubt, the property would be a project, having been uninhabited for two years. For that reason, Jacqui had claimed more tools than household items as she separated her belongings from Geoff's and packed the car.

She was up early the next morning, the sun at her back and open farmland on every side. West of the Saskatchewan border, the land got flatter if that was possible, and virtually treeless. Where the Manitoba wildlife-crossing signs showed a deer gracefully leaping nearly vertically, here the deer silhouetted on the yellow sign appeared to charge madly headlong.

A green road sign ahead indicated just forty kilometres to Moose Jaw. *To think I believed it when a novel I read was set in a cabin in the forests of Moose Jaw. Ha! I can probably see the town from here and I can count the trees on one hand.*

That afternoon, heading northwest from Regina, Jacqui fought the wind with her steering wheel and battled drowsiness with snacks, letting in the stiff breeze through open windows and surfing the radio dial. She'd never seen flat land like this. *The government should simply fold up Saskatchewan—nothing to see here, folks.* A *tick-a-tick* sound on the windshield that at first, Jacqui thought was rain turned out to be a splattering of bugs. And the wind! *Alberta better not be more of this.*

But Alberta was worse. Her GPS took her through monotonous miles of barren, uninhabited land that the map on her phone optimistically labelled "Special Area," whatever that meant. *Nothing special about it as far as I can see.* The signs here warning of deer showed the animal veering awkwardly toward traffic, its front legs stiffly straight in a stubborn challenge, much like everything she'd read about the western province itself.

At Hanna, she stopped to refuel, noting a sign on the back of a truck reading "Now Hiring Crude Transport Drivers."

They specifically want crude ones? She laughed to herself. *I'm getting punchy.*

She stepped inside the restaurant for soup and a sandwich. Seniors at a table nearby were shaking their heads, clucking about news Jacqui had missed—an earthquake had devastated Central America that morning, killing hundreds, with many more missing.

"Well, you know, those folks likely needed thinning out," one of the men said.

Jacqui shot an incredulous glance at the speaker, a decrepit old man flanked by an oxygen tank, with tubes running from it to his nose. *Seriously? As long as we're thinning folks out, shouldn't the old, weak and sick go first?* So, this was the racist redneck country her friend Bree had warned her about. *What have I got myself into?* Jacqui rose to leave, letting her chair give a loud scrape back from the table to signal her disgust.

Along the bald prairie, the shadows of hydro poles grew long. How could anyone live out here in the middle of nowhere? She was seeing more farms now, but an uneasiness began to gnaw at her. *How am I going to find my place?* For all Jacqui's planning, she'd neglected this vital detail. She had no clear address. The title deed bore a numbered land location, but Jacqui didn't know what the series of three numbers meant and had no idea how to navigate to it. Should she go back to town for the night and start fresh tomorrow? But that would blow her strict budget for the trip.

Anxiety coiled around her neck, constricting her throat. Road signs were sparse, and the light was waning. A lone, oncoming vehicle's lights blurred against the thick insect smears on her windshield. Jacqui strained forward to see each intersection's blue numbered sign. At last she began to notice a predictable pattern. She turned north on pavement, hoping it would bring her closer to her destination, but as the empty miles flew by, her confidence ebbed, too. Passing a farmyard near the road, she glimpsed a man helping a couple of young children out of a truck. Perhaps the time had come to admit defeat and ask for help. She slowed, backed up, and crept into the driveway. The man straightened and sauntered towards her as she opened her window.

"I'm afraid I'm a bit lost." Jacqui held up the legal page with its vague address.

"C'mon in," the man said. "We'll check it on the county map."

Jacqui hesitated to follow him. Any number of true crime stories flooded her mind. Finally, one of his young sons beckoned to her and led her into the house. Without his cap, the man's forehead gleamed snowy white in contrast to the rest of his deeply tanned face. He spread a map on the large kitchen table. Before she could orient herself, he jabbed his thumb on a square on the page, traced a series of turns with his finger, and began scribbling directions on a sticky note.

Eyes twinkling, he handed her the note. “You can just about see it from here.”

“Really?”

“Nah. But it looks like about twenty-five miles or so.” He tilted his head, appraising her. “You visiting someone out here?”

Jacqui took a step back, anxious to get going. “Sort of. My dad grew up here. It's my family's land.” *Now why did I put it that way?*

On the road again, she gripped the steering wheel with sweaty hands, following the farmer's scrawled directions. Her lights punched a narrow tunnel down the dark gravel roads. *I'm in a dystopian novel, the last human being alive.* After an eternity, she caught sight of the road address she'd been searching for. She pulled up the driveway overarched by large trees. On either side, tall grass stood sentry in the night-blackened yard. She couldn't make out any buildings. Jacqui opened the car door, intending to get out and stretch her cramped legs, but the hum and tickle of mosquitoes drove her back inside.

And now, a wave of weariness swept over her. She groped for her bedding and settled in for the night. Like Scarlett O'Hara in *Gone with the Wind*, she decided, *I'll deal with it in the morning.*

CHAPTER 3

Parked in the driveway of her country property, Jacqui opened her eyes to a green-filtered sunlight flickering across her face. She slowly woke to an intense need for the washroom. Rolling her stiff neck and shoulders, she surveyed the overgrown yard. *So, this is me. This is home.*

To her left, the house, sleepy-eaved under a cottage roof, hid coyly behind two massive evergreen trees. Ahead, a narrow track was cut in the overgrown yard leaving a stiff brush of coarse stalks that led to a distant gate. Beyond it lay an open mowed field dotted with what appeared to be huge marshmallows. The rest of the yard was overtaken by a sea of grass sparkling with dew, dotted with an assortment of derelict outbuildings. So, this was the scene of Pops' miserable upbringing, his humiliating slave-labour, and the roots of his late-night outbursts of anger, rare now, but still occurring often enough to keep Jacqui wary. Here he had received years of abuse at the hands of his father.

And now it's mine. My roots, and now my own place. Curiosity narrowed Jacqui's eyes, but more than anything, an intense disappointment. No English country garden, no greenhouse, no red hip-roofed barn, and likely no fireplace or original mill work inside the house, either. Not for the first time, she wondered what she had gotten herself into. Yet what choice had she had? Her lips firmed. She pulled on her socks and shoes. *It's got to at least have plumbing.*

With a sinking heart she opened the car door, fishing in the pocket of her purse for the pair of house keys the lawyer had sent. What a relief that the mosquitoes had gone into hiding. She waded through the waving grass, letting her feet make cautious sweeps of the unseen ground ahead, fearing hidden vermin. The house door lurked behind the bushy branches of a shrub with lacy white flowers.

"Well, you don't look like much," she said, scanning the gray faux-brick asphalt siding, the paint-peeled door, and flimsy windows. As if the place were returning the compliment, Jacqui caught sight of herself in the glass of the porch door. *Touché.* She smoothed her rumpled T-shirt, running her fingers through her tangled hair.

The door came unstuck on her second stout thrust against it. A smell of mothballs, must, dust, and something else rushed up her nostrils. Like entering a second-hand store. She found herself in a porch with a double row of coat hooks on her left and on the opposite wall, a plywood shelf of dust-filmed boots beneath three double-hung windows. At this point, Geoff would have tapped the sloping, outdated linoleum floor with his shiny, realtor's shoe and said, "What this place needs most is a lighter." *But you aren't here, Geoff. You lost interest in our renovations, our life, and in me, remember? So, I'm on my own here. I can't burn down the only option I have.*

The door to the main part of the house squeaked at her push, opening to the kitchen. Jacqui took one look and tipped her head in chagrin. Resplendent with bold orange and brown mushroom wallpaper, the room sported an orange-painted tile back-splash above brown, metal-edged counters strewn with beer cans, blackened spoons, and filth.

Her sibling uncle and aunt might have been responsible for the decorating disaster, but it was hard to believe they had made such a mess. Had her place become a local teen party house?

The cabinets were varnished plywood with grubby spots circling the round, flat chrome handles. Light streamed past the flyspecks on a small window above the sink. Next to that stood a chubby old-style refrigerator, and in the centre of the room sat a chrome and Arborite table flanked by two vinyl-covered chairs. Plenty of character, though not from the era she'd had in mind. Ignoring her sinking hopes, she tried a narrow door off the kitchen and found a tiny bathroom. Icky, but it would have to do. She hovered rather than sitting on the brittle-looking pink seat. When she turned on the faucet to wash her hands, nothing happened. Of course, the water would be turned off. Rust stains on the pink porcelain basin gave Jacqui misgivings about water purity. The Pepto Bismol-pink tub shared the malady with a dark brown stain below the faucet. *Charming.*

Lacking water, Jacqui used the antibacterial gel in her purse. She wiped her hands on her jeans, then gripped her knees and hung her head in despair. Every euphemistic real estate description she'd ever read paraded through her mind, followed by Geoff's interpretation of their actual meaning. "Cute cottage"—no room to swing a cat. "Just needs a little TLC"—it's a money pit. "Hurry! This one won't last"—literally. Because its foundation is rotten.

She straightened, took a deep breath, and ventured through to the living room, bracing herself for further horrors. The unidentified smell grew stronger. Urine. She covered her nose. One of the windows to the right was boarded up with new wood. On the far wall, a green metal furnace or heater spilled ashes and half-burned sticks from its opening. It stood between two doors which likely led to her uncle's and aunt's bedrooms.

Jacqui thought of the past. How on earth had the place ever housed a family of five children? Pops had never mentioned how small the house was. His father might have been driven to his perpetual rage by sheer overcrowding.

A bold green-and-gold wallpaper striped the walls of the fully furnished living room. Beside the doorway where she stood, a built-in china cabinet imprisoned a mob of figurines, salt-and-pepper shakers, and china teacups. Many were broken and the figurines were coupled in obscene poses. She couldn't imagine an aunt by the name of Priscilla allowing such desecration. Must have been the partiers.

Everything else in the room, couch and chairs to tables, wore a uniform, gray mantle of dust, except for the host of crushed beer cans. The morning sun streaming through the windows highlighted dust motes cascading through the air and small puffs rose and fell with each step Jacqui took on the green carpet as she moved across the room. The source of the disgusting smell was evident in a large darkened stain in the far corner of the carpet.

I left a completely re-done, high-end condo with granite countertops and imported Italian floor tile for this? Jacqui fumed, mourning her custom kitchen cabinetry and spacious storage. The thought of the sweat-equity she still had in that place brought back her worry over whether Geoff and his new lover would do right by her when the condo finally sold. As she surveyed what lay before her, she couldn't help but long for those gleaming surfaces and the pristine freshness of the place. And yet, the last eight months of vague unease, then nameless dread, and finally her belated realization of the stunning betrayal now stained her memory of the place. No. A beautiful home alone could never negate the misery of its occupants.

What had Bree said as they parted ways after their final lunch together last week? "I'm expecting to hear all about it, Jac. Be strong." But what did it mean to be strong? *Ah, Bree. I could use one of your proverbial kicks in the butt right about now.*

Jacqui forced herself to open each interior door. The one to the left of the living room heater opened to a bedroom, painted blue and sparsely furnished. *Must have been Uncle Russell's.* The one to the right would have to be Aunt Priscilla's, who evidently had a fondness for mauve. And lacy pillows. At every turn, from the cramped bedroom closets where clothes still hung inside, to the narrow stairways to attic or cellar, she heard Geoff's gentle mocking. Worthless, functionally obsolete, unsaleable. She banished the damning words. What if "strong" meant carrying on when you felt like giving up? Is that what Bree had meant?

She stopped in the kitchen again, squaring her shoulders. *OK. I know it's bad.* She reached for the notepad in her purse. *But how bad?* After another round of the house, inside and out, mentally tallying, she made notes of the work to be done, trying to prioritize.

Gut the kitchen.

Ditto the bathroom.

New windows, doors, paint and trim.

Pull up gross carpet.

Nothing that a few grand couldn't fix. But no doubt more complex, pricier projects would arise. From experience, she knew they always did. *Hmph.* Geoff had better hustle with selling their place.

What about the furnace, plumbing, roof, insulation, electrical, exterior finishing? The list was overwhelming. But to cave now was what Jacqui's mother would have done. Sylvie would have turned tail and run to the nearest bar, letting the whole mess somehow sort itself out, which too often had meant Jacqui cleaned up the mess. She thrust out her chin. *Good thing I know Mom's playbook so well. That way, I always know what not to do.*

Returning to her car, she pulled her oldest jeans and T-shirt out of her bag, wiggling into them in the front seat. She sat for a while longer, making her beloved lists, narrowing the daunting tasks into manageable bites. Cleaning was the first priority. She could function in old if at least it was clean. But that meant turning the water back on, which also meant braving that scary-looking cellar.

Jacqui paused to lean on the steering wheel, considering the house for a long moment. Something indefinable about it stirred her resolve. She opened the door again and appraised the building, declaring war. This place had defeated her father, forcing him to flee, enslaving him to a perpetual resentment that even half a century and a thousand beer-numbed Friday nights had been unable to uproot. She squared herself to face the slouching building.

You won't do that to me. I may not be here for very long, but you won't beat me. I won't let you.

CHAPTER 4

The plumbing pipes engaged in a loud throat clearing as Jacqui hurried up the steep, narrow stairs from the basement. *Like the Count of Monte Cristo arising from his dungeon.* She shuddered with relief as she emerged into the living room. And more than relief, she felt a triumphant pride. Not only had she defied the cellar's damp mustiness and cobwebs, but she had succeeded in locating and turning on the water valve. Yet when she twisted the kitchen faucet, it only coughed up a disappointing spasm of brownish water before falling silent. *Now what? That's the end of my bag of tricks.* She had never moved to a country property before. She perched gingerly on the edge of one of the dusty kitchen chairs. *Think, Jacqui, think.*

Without water, she couldn't begin a single project toward making the place habitable. She'd have to go to town. Her stomach, now hollow after only a light supper the night before and no breakfast this morning, growled in agreement. Maybe a plumbing business in town could solve the problem.

"Duh! No electricity, no plumbing." Her own voice, loud in the quiet, startled her. Flipping the switch near the door confirmed there was no power. No question, she would have to head to town. Besides, she was ravenous.

Jacqui waded to her car through the tall grasses and weeds, dry now and buzzing with insects. She smelled greenery growing, and earth, and surprisingly on this prairie land, stagnant water. From somewhere farther away, she caught a whiff of cow. Since crossing into this province, she'd seen more than one bumper sticker with the rebus *I Heart Alberta Beef.* So, this was the smell of it. Did these proud Albertans love its pungent pong, too?

The insect buzz grew louder, along with a snapping and crackling coming from a row of shrubs screening the house from the gravel road in front. Sounds swirled to surround her. She was startled by a sudden rustle and flapping that jerked her attention to the opening between the trees and the field beyond. From the clearing, a hawk rose on powerful wings with its beak clamped on something thick and furry. A cry escaped her at the sight. Jacqui intuitively felt the pattering of the small animal's heart at its sudden flight, the razor vise that gripped its soft belly. She sensed its terror at being yanked from all it had ever known, its panic at the panorama now spread before myopic eyes meant only for its tiny world. Did it long for the security of solid ground? Was its feeling of being torn in half anything like what she had experienced the morning Geoff and his new lover had declared their love for each other, right at her own breakfast table? She was that creature—frantic with pain, flying far from the known, without foundation or future. She sucked in a great gulp of air to calm herself.

Jacqui hurried to the car and jumped inside, shutting out the overwhelming sights and sounds and smells of this harsh and wild country. The interior of her car, as stuffed full as it was, at least offered a controlled safety in its orderly, familiar confines. She closed her eyes, deliberately slowing her hammering heart. Backing out the curving driveway, she noticed a pond below the house that she hadn't seen late last night when she arrived. That must be the source of the water odour. *Why are people always eager to get out in nature? Everything is either itchy, stinky, or annoying. Or cruel.* But then, city life had proved cruel to her as well.

She followed the gravel road away from her place, her GPS

navigating "off-road" until she found the pavement that took her to civilization. *If you could call it that.* On the way into town, the drivers of the only two vehicles she met lifted their hands in greeting. She felt violated. The gesture was an unheard-of intimacy for Jacqui who had never even struck up a conversation with a city bus seatmate.

Town was a letdown. *What was I expecting?* Whatever she thought she would find, this wasn't it. Could there be a more stodgy, nondescript collection of businesses and buildings? What she did notice was the multitude of big, gas-guzzling pick-up trucks. *Hasn't anyone here heard of climate change?* And the willy-nilly liquor shops. Unlike Ontario with its staid and respectable government liquor outlets, here booze shops bubbled up on nearly every street. *Casey's Sunshine and Spirits? Seriously?*

Jacqui pulled into a Tim Horton's for a breakfast sandwich. Ahead of her in the line-up stood two men and a woman in full cowboy regalia—boots, bandanas, the whole shebang. They had nerve, appearing in costume publicly. Of course, by the greasy ring around their hats, the curled leather of their chaps and the dirt on their boots, these weren't mere costumes.

Oh Bree! If only you could see this. Jacqui's friend would be more convinced than ever in her judgment of westerners as rednecks, and would take the first flight back east in fear of being lynched. But that was Bree, who had reason, with her southern US heritage, to be conscious of racism. Jacqui herself had already noticed the lack of diversity here compared to the east.

With something to fill her belly at last, some of Jacqui's flagging confidence was renewed. She drove down what appeared to be the main street and found a hardware store. Wandering through the aisles, she scanned the merchandise, mindful of her extensive project list. The colorful paint sample display called out to her, bringing to mind the ghastly orange walls of her kitchen and the purple of the bedroom. But so much preliminary work had to be done before she could paint. For now, she picked up rubber gloves, garbage bags, ammonia, a bucket and mop.

Jacqui tapped the shoulder of a short woman in a red shirt with a name tag marked “Francie.”

“I'm wondering if you can answer a question for me.”

Francie turned to her with raised eyebrows. “Uh-huh?”

“How do I go about getting the electricity restored to a home that's been vacant for a few years?”

“You've got no power?” Francie went through her pants' pockets. “I'll find you a card for the utility company. You won't get far without power.” She hurried away, returning soon to hand Jacqui several business cards and a sheaf of brochures. “Looks like you're new to the area. I figured you could use some of this info.”

“Thanks.”

“Is your new place in town?” the clerk asked.

“No.” Jacqui poked her chin down the garden tool aisle where they stood. “I do have another question though. What's the best way to handle an overgrown yard? I don't think a regular lawn mower is going to get through it at this stage.”

Francie eyed Jacqui with keen interest. “How big a yard?”

“Fairly big,” Jacqui said, following Francie toward the rakes and spades.

The tubby woman snatched a wooden-handled tool from the peg board and thrust it at Jacqui. “You could start with this grass whip, but it'll be slow going unless you're used to hard work. If you go that route, better pick up some good leather work gloves—aisle five. Or you could use a heavy-duty trimmer. We've got them for fifty bucks off, aisle twelve. But for a farm or acreage, your best bet would likely be to bring in a brush cutter.” Francie turned and hurried away, abandoning her.

Jacqui hesitated a few moments, then rattled to the check-out with her unwieldy purchases. As she was paying for the items, Francie reappeared offering an additional business card.

"Call my son, Tim. He'll get the job done for you." She flashed Jacqui another warm smile, leaning against the railing parallel to the check-out counter. This first genuinely personal contact Jacqui had received since leaving Hamilton brought an embarrassing moisture to her eyes. Turning back to the cashier to avoid Francie's curiosity, Jacqui made an impatient swipe of the back of her hand across her face. She gathered her awkward supplies and turned toward the door only to find Francie at her side, waiting for her.

Jacqui felt her grip on the grass whip slipping.

Francie caught the implement before it clattered to the floor. "Here, I'll walk you out to your car." She followed Jacqui to the parking lot, pausing while she unlocked the rear door. "Whoa! Everything in here but the kitchen sink."

She eyeballed the purchases in Jacqui's arms. "No worries. We'll make 'em fit."

"It's okay. I can manage."

But Francie wiggled and slid the long-handled whip down one side of the car while Jacqui squeezed in the cleaning supplies.

"So, whereabouts is your acreage?"

Jacqui slammed the door and scanned the area. "I'm out of town. That way." She jabbed a thumb in what she hoped was the general direction. She was honestly unsure of her exact whereabouts and was relying solely on GPS to get her back when the time came. As Francie pressed for a more exact location, Jacqui shifted from one foot to another. Friendly was one thing, but why did this stranger take such an interest?

"You're not talking about the old Penner homestead, are you? 'Cause if you're where I'm thinking you are, just a few miles south and a bit west of the highway, chances are we're neighbours," Francie grinned and stuck out her hand. "I'm Francie Barry. All of us in that corner of the country have been hoping someone would move in that place."

"How come?" Jacqui withdrew her hand, dug her car keys out of her bag and reached for the handle of the driver's door.

"Empty houses are a favourite spot for town kids on the prowl." Francie's eyebrows formed a V. "You notice any evidence of parties?"

"Yeah. They must have broken in through a window." Jacqui sidled into the driver's seat, leaving her door open. "It's a disgusting mess."

Francie murmured her sympathy. "By the way, I didn't catch your name?"

"I'm Jacqui."

The woman seemed to be waiting for more.

"Jacqui Penn," she said, relenting. Francie had been more than friendly, after all.

"You mean Penner." She nodded confidently.

"No, just Penn."

But Francie breezed on. "So, you're the niece who inherited Russ and Priscilla's place. Well now I'm really glad we met up. My folks grew up with the Penners. It's going to be great being neighbours."

"Thanks for the help and all the information. I've really got to get over to the grocery store." It would raise too many questions and take too much valuable time to explain Pops having changed his surname. Instead, she smiled her thanks, closed the door and started the car. The discomfort of having strangers know so much about her warred with a welcome sense of support. She wasn't alone.

Francie tapped on her window. "Hubby and me'll be over with the Welcome Wagon as soon as we can!"

Alrighty then.

From the supermarket parking lot, Jacqui used Francie's

information to call the utility company. They promised to send someone out to do the hook up that afternoon. By the time she was ready to leave town, her car was more tightly packed than ever with the addition of tools, cleaners and groceries. Would everyone in town now know who she was and where she lived?

CHAPTER 5

The mauve bedroom was first on Jacqui's cleaning list. She opened both windows to the gentle July breeze then set to work dusting and wiping down furniture, scrubbing walls, washing and boxing up knick-knacks, and laundering bedding, including the lacy covers of at least a dozen bed cushions. The worn and mended sheets and blankets would make dandy drop cloths when she was ready to paint.

What a relief to have water and power. It allowed her to operate the surprisingly high-end vacuum cleaner she found in a crammed closet outside the bathroom. Uncle and Aunt had odd priorities, it seemed.

The filth of the living room clamored for attention, and it took everything in her to stick to her priority of essential spaces first. Moving to the next on her list, she wiped and scrubbed and scoured in the kitchen, emptying cupboards of expired spices, canned foods and stained dishes. Two cleaning rags became ribbons in her frenzy, and Jacqui's fingernails broke or wore down to nubbins. Pulling out a now-shiny kitchen chair, she sat down, satisfied but bone weary. Her stomach told her she'd missed dinnertime. She consulted the fridge, which now hummed pleasingly clean and cool inside and dug out an assortment of vegetables, cheese and a couple of wraps she'd purchased that morning.

While she munched, she sized up her work. The bathroom was an absolute must-do tonight. And she should bring in as much from her car as she possibly could to make room in the vehicle for bags and boxes of stuff left by the last owners. Clothing and shoes, magazines and tchotchkes—it would be a wonderful feeling to get rid of it all. After that, the living room.

But as the ache in her muscles grew, she knew she'd never get to most of her ambitious plans. She checked her phone. A message from Bree:

> "Hey girl! How goes it? Have you had a showdown with any redneck cowboys yet? Ha ha. Hope everything's sorting itself out for you way out there in Albertistan. It's bleak at work without you. You-know-who arrives every morning with an in-love glow. I figure that'll wear off soon enough. At least, I hope so. It's a bit much. The manager hasn't hired anybody to replace you in Interlibrary Loans, yet. Waiting for budget confirmation, I guess.
>
> "At my house, the ladies miss you, or at least, the treats you always used to spoil them with. I guess I'm chopped liver by comparison. But you'd think cats would love chopped liver. Hey, now that you're free of the tyrant Geoff and his ailurophobia I'll be expecting to hear you've acquired a couple of kitties of your own. Or maybe a horse! (Gotta ride with the cowboys, right?)
>
> "So, message me sometime, OK?"

Ah, Bree. If you could see me now. Doing all this degrading menial work.

A stalk of celery in her mouth, Jacqui stopped crunching and cocked her ear toward the driveway. Had she heard bells? She tossed the celery onto her plate and went to the window. Two large horses, the kind with hairy bell-bottom feet, rose high above the tall grass.

They were harnessed to a white wagon from which laughing, chattering people were descending. In the lead was short and stubby Francie from the hardware store, followed by a lanky bald man with a white mustache.

Jacqui poked her head in the bathroom to check her hair in the mirror. She used a squirt of gel to define the curls, then raced to the bedroom for her plaid shirt to cover her braless tank top. Someone rapped loudly on the glass in the front door.

"Wow! You weren't kidding about the Welcome Wagon." Jacqui counted six grinning adults and two youngsters standing on the front step.

They chuckled far out of proportion to her mention of their unofficial name.

"We like an excuse to hitch up the Clydes." Francie grinned. "Folks," she said, turning to address the group, "this is Jacqui, the new generation of Penners to live on this homestead and join our community." She introduced her husband Al, their daughter and her husband and kids, and a neighbour woman whose farm lay between Jacqui's place and the Barrys'.

"You got the coffee on? Better still, we brought our own refreshment." Al hoisted a case of twenty-four so she could see. "'Cause our Tim'll be thirsty once he finishes with the mowing."

They plan on coming in? This was more than Jacqui had bargained for. She still had a long list to accomplish.

Al made a sweeping gesture across the unruly grass with the long tube of rolled paper he carried then craned his neck to check down the driveway. A putt-putting sound came from the lane.

"He's coming tonight?" Jacqui glanced from Francie to the other visitors, incredulous. "I haven't even called him yet."

Francie was exultant. "I told you we were the Welcome Wagon. And that's not all. We're here to give you a leg up on the cleaning, too.

Just point us ladies in the right direction," she bobbed and leaned, trying to see past Jacqui into the house, "and we'll get everything ship-shape for you in no time."

The thought of a crowd in her house this evening when she was dog-tired was intimidating, yet the offer of help tempted strongly. She managed a smile and pulled the door wide to invite them in.

The women followed her into the house leaving small gifts on the kitchen counter—jars of jam, muffins, a new kitchen towel, and set of crocheted potholders that unfortunately matched the current decor. Jacqui thanked them and led them into the living room.

"Here's where I left off before dinner," she told them. "I have no idea what to do about that." She pointed to the dark urine patch in the corner of the carpet.

Francie walked over to inspect it, sniffing. "A good spritzing with hydrogen peroxide should mask the smell. At least until you can get it shampooed." In no time, the three women were attacking the accumulated dust and grime, while the men unpacked every last item from her car, stacking tools in the porch and stashing the rest wherever Jacqui directed.

On his way through, Al commended her on the living room heater. "That'll keep you toasty in winter. Maybe we'll get around to bringing you a load of firewood come fall."

The work all happened with bewildering speed. When Jacqui peeked out the kitchen window, she found the yard's bushy grass shorn away by the mower, allowing a new landscape to emerge. She was encouraged to see the mower had skirted around overgrown areas that might well be flowerbeds with shrubs.

Finally, everyone including Tractor Tim gathered in the kitchen, either to take a chair or lean against the counters. Jacqui found mugs and glasses, but most helped themselves to a beer and one of the cream-cheese-frosted carrot muffins. Jacqui offered the kids a bottle of sparkling water, which they both hesitantly accepted. Al then unrolled his county map, showing Jacqui where her property lay in relation to those of the neighbours present. The others offered tidbits of area history as well as their opinions of the locals.

"Every corner of the country's got their eccentrics and we're no exception. Take Dorlan and Orville Tapp, for instance." Al pointed to a square on the map marked D. and O. Tapp. "They're what you might call the cutting-corners type." Knowing laughter rippled around the circle. "Plenty of enthusiasm, though. Never met a type of animal they wouldn't try raising. That chinchilla venture never lasted too long, though." More chuckling.

The group was eager to educate her in local ways. They explained the land grid with its range roads running north-south and township roads east-west, which made all kinds of sense. They gave solemn advice about moving to the right in case of oncoming traffic when approaching a hill on the local gravel roads.

Ya think?

Some of Jacqui's earlier questions found answers in their talk. She learned that a section was a square mile of land, 640 acres, and that some of the lakes in the region dried up completely in drought years as there had been a few years back. "That's when we found out we could grow crops on three inches of rain," Al said with grim recall.

They explained the countryside was dotted with Hutterite colonies, a communal-living sect, and that many of the neighbouring farmers were Mennonite.

"The Mennonites are the ones with the picture-perfect landscaping," Francie's daughter said. "That's what they do instead of watching TV."

"Acrosst the road from you here," Al tapped another square on the map, "you've got Seaitch and Roslyn."

Huh? Seaitch? What kind of parents give their kid a name like—wait, could that be C.H.? C.H. Legrand, her tenant?

The room went silent. Jacqui looked up from the map. Had someone asked her a question?

Before she could form an answer, Al continued. "C.H. came up from the States to marry Roz and ended up staying to farm her parents' land. We've made a pretty good Canuck out of him. Too bad Roz has the cancer. It's eaten her up pretty bad, by now."

Francie's daughter shook her head dolefully. "She's been fighting it off and on for at least twelve or thirteen years."

"Great neighbours to have, though. They're also part of our church."

Jacqui's eyes were growing sticky with fatigue and she was starting to lose track of who was who in the local genealogies. She picked up on the pattern, though. Name, social commentary, church affiliation.

Is everyone out here religious? How will they categorize me? And why does it matter? She bit off a yawn, wondering when the wagon load might clear out and let her get to bed. Glancing around, she saw no sign of them leaving, though the kids had slid down the cabinetry to sit on the floor. To Jacqui's distaste, she noticed muffin crumbs were accumulating around the youngsters.

"Over here," Francie drew attention to another region on the map, "just east of the highway, is the Adrians." She scrutinized Jacqui's reaction to the name, evidently waiting for a response. When Jacqui shrugged, the shorter woman continued. "They go to our church. You're related, you know. Naomi is your aunt, the younger sister of Russell and Priscilla who lived here. Both of Eli and Naomi's sons—your cousins, Mac and Chet—married city girls."

"One hates country life, the other's into it like she was born on a tractor," someone put in.

With the mention of her relations, Jacqui came awake. She sensed a reproach at knowing so little about her family. It had never seemed important before, only a boring refrain when Pops was in his cups, an excuse for him to drink. But with the trip out here and settling into her father's childhood home, curiosity had also grown. Suddenly, she wanted to hear about his family, find out what gave him his embittered perspective.

"Did you know my aunt and uncle, the ones who lived here?"

The older couple seated at the table nodded. "Russ took over the farm when your grandpa died. Priscilla took care of their mother until the old lady passed, then stayed on with her brother. They didn't get out much but were friendly enough. I think they socialized with the McCallums some."

The woman cocked her head toward the door. "Priscilla would be ashamed if she could see how her yard's gone to wrack and ruin since she's been gone. It used to be her pride and joy. But I guess Russ wasn't much interested in flowers."

"Got any plans for the Bel Air you got in the machine shed out past them trees?" Tractor Tim asked, eying her with interest.

"The what?" Jacqui hadn't quite caught his garbled speech.

Francie swatted him, perhaps for his obvious personal plans for whatever it was. "It's an antique car your uncle Russ kept locked up in there."

"Lotta guys around here would be interested if you ever decide to sell," the stocky young man told her.

Talk around the table drifted away to weather and the current dry spell but Jacqui wanted to tap the family tree further. *How do I find out what Pops' dad was really like without bringing up his history and the embarrassing state he's now in?*

"So, tell me, what would farming have been like in the late 50s, early 60s? Pretty hard work back then?" This question led to animated descriptions of apparently outdated agricultural practices that were unintelligible to Jacqui. It failed, however, to produce any opening into the more personal matter of her grandparents' family. She was relieved when her guests finally rose to leave.

CHAPTER 6

A thunderous bellow from just outside Jacqui's bedroom window rocketed her out of bed the next morning with pounding pulse and shaky limbs. Was it the partying teens, angry at being displaced? Or were her neighbours back again, this time in force? More sonorous bawling echoed outside, mingled with the sound of heavy footfalls and jostling bodies.

Jacqui snatched up her housecoat. She flattened herself against the wall to peer out the curtainless glass. What she saw stiffened her back and constricted her jaw. *Cows! All over my yard.*

The animals were milling about, tearing up the turf with their great hooves, raising clods of mud in the flowerbeds newly revealed after last night's mowing. The wretched creatures were even defecating in great steaming piles on her lawn. She jammed her feet into runners and raced out to the porch. Poised to open the door, she paused. A thick-muscled brute stood at the bottom of her step, waggling a set of wicked-looking horns and showing the whites of its huge eyes. The bovine Arnold Schwarzenegger was a case of steroids gone awry. Like some monstrous diva with a sprig of white flowers dangling out of the corner of its mouth, it chewed in a graceless circular motion, a string of spittle spiraling downward. Jacqui slid open the door's glass pane.

From the dubious safety of her wooden front door that now seemed flimsy as cardboard, she screamed, "Go away!"

The creature gave a small start, sidling to the left, then resumed munching on Jacqui's spirea leaves.

"Go! Get away! Shoo!" she hollered, her eyes making a frantic search around the porch for her broom.

Ever so slowly, the creature ambled away. Emboldened by this success, Jacqui cinched the belt of her robe and edged out the door with her broom thrust before her. But the power of that much muscle in an animal was daunting. Jacqui still clung to the doorknob ready to rush inside at the first sign of aggression from the beast. As if the intimidating Muscle-Cow to her left wasn't enough, to her right Jacqui caught sight of a group of cows munching on what must have been peonies once. The voluptuous blooms were in tatters. She'd never even had a chance to inspect them.

"Begone evil beasts! Shoo, shoo, shoo!" She screamed every possible obscenity at them, at full volume, with no effect. In a burst of fury, she charged at them, waving her broom, her hair and housecoat streaming behind her. "Raahh!"

The cows rolled their eyes at her, raising their tails and galumphing away, clear through a patch of yellow day lilies. And directly into the path of a small vehicle careening around the bend of her driveway. The driver of the ATV swerved to miss the animals, but its wide wheels tamped a path right over the already bedraggled lilies.

"Hey, watch where you're going! You're as bad as the cows."

Both the man and the boy on the vehicle turned to stare at her, open-mouthed.

Jacqui pulled the flapping sides of her bathrobe more snugly over her thin nightgown, crossing her arms and holding tight to her broom. "Are these your cows?"

The drone of the ATV motor lowered to a hum as the driver swung his leg over and sauntered toward Jacqui, his hand outstretched.

"C.H. Legrand," he said with a friendly twinkle in his clear green eyes. "Glad to finally meet my landlord." He dropped his hand when she maintained a stubborn grip on her broom, then nodded in the direction of his vehicle. “My son Lewis.” On the seat, the skinny teenage boy in the over-sized ball cap stared ahead at the cattle, giving no sign that he heard his father. Abruptly, he reached his stick-like arms forward to grasp the handlebars, revved the motor and lurched ahead after a cluster of the beasts. Dodging in an out, charging the animals, to Jacqui's chagrin, the kid seemed to be creating nothing but more chaos. In their frenzy to escape the buzzing nuisance among them, cows tore up the grass, trampled plants and broke branches of shrubs. She almost screamed watching a few delphinium wands break off to give way for the lumbering animals.

“Don't worry, he knows what he's doing. He'll have them out of your hair in no time.” Traces of a southern drawl came with his reassuring smile. “Even Big Boy over there.” C.H. jutted his chin at Muscle-Cow. “He's docile as a pussy-cat.”

So, it's a male. Like I care about his disposition.

Before long, Jacqui could see Lewis had managed to gather the beasts into a single herd and was slowly following them as they trotted obediently out the driveway.

Frowning, Jacqui turned to face the man beside her. “Are they your cows? “

“Yeah. Must have breached a fence.” He ran a hand over the stubble on his jaw. “Looks like I've got some repairs to do.”

“It would appear so.” Jacqui tightened her lips to keep from saying more. She moved through the ankle-deep grass bristles toward the nearest flowerbed, anger welling in her chest as she surveyed the carnage. Leaves and stalks and petals littered the ground, some thrust deep into the earth by heavy hoof prints. The other beds, several rimming the yard, others encircling trees, had suffered damage as well. She shook her head in frustration.

“Hey, it's just a bit of a setback.” C.H. knelt beside her and began clearing plant debris. “It's early enough in the season that these'll come back.” Using his bare hands, he pushed soil, filling holes and propping up bent stems. “See? There's still a bunch of buds. Have a little patience. Life wants to live.” He smiled up at her, the dark stubble on his cheeks collecting in a dimple on each side.

“Right. Well, I can see I've got my work cut out for me today.” Jacqui turned, heading for the house. “From here on, please try to keep your animals on your own property.”

“Hey,” C.H. caught up with her, “it's not like I got up this morning plotting to send my cattle out to annoy you. Out here in ranch country, stuff happens. Cattle get out. Sometimes they get hit by traffic and I lose my investment. Sometimes they're the ones causing the harm. And if it's not cattle, it might be coyotes or skunks or deer. Heck, you'll be lucky if your shrubs survive one nighttime visit from a swamp donkey. Trust me, your flowers will be fine. But if it'll do any good, I offer my sincere apologies, okay?” He thrust his hand out to her.

Swamp donkey sounded grotesque, but Jacqui refused to admit her ignorance of the local fauna, whatever it was. Grudgingly, she stopped to shake his hand.

“And Lewis and I can come back to help you fix things.”

“Never mind. It was a bit of a shock to wake up to, that's all. You don't have to fix anything here, but it seems your fence could use your attention. And I'm certain a teenage boy has better stuff to do.”

“You sure, Jacqui? 'Cause it's no trouble.”

Feeling invaded by his familiarity, Jacqui shook her head at his offer and resumed walking, but he followed her.

“Actually, I'm in a bit of a bind here.”

She stopped, looking askance at him.

“See, Lewis isn't like most teenage boys. He'll drive the cows home and hopefully even remember to shut the gate behind them. But he'll go into the house and get busy with his books and not give me a second thought. He's a bit like the lilies," he paused to give a bemused shake of his head, "he 'neither toils nor spins.'"

Jacqui raised her eyebrows at him, not understanding. "But you offered his help in repairing the damage."

"Oh, he can work sometimes. But it's no use phoning to ask him to come back and get me; he doesn't answer phone calls."

Maybe you should teach your kid a few basic life skills. "What are you saying?"

C.H. gave a sheepish look. "I need a lift home."

Jacqui exhaled loudly. "Let me get dressed first. You'll have to excuse the mess in my car. I haven't had a chance to vacuum it out yet."

C.H. pulled off his cowboy hat and wedged himself into the passenger seat of his new neighbour's car. She called this a mess? There were all of five crumbs on the seat and a slight drink stain on the console. Bit of a clean freak.

He adjusted the seat for more leg room, chuckling to himself. She sure was a knockout but that wild broom charge at his cows had been quite the introduction. When Jacqui returned and slid behind the wheel, she wore a pair of white jeans that fit in all the right places and a blue shirt the same colour as her eyes. He forced his eyes to focus on the road ahead.

"This way," C.H. said, thumbing right at the end of her driveway. "And turn north at the next road, then I'm the first farm on the left."

Jacqui silently turned right and crept down the gravel road at a snail's pace. Was she scared of getting a rock chip in her windshield? She'd have to get used to such hazards if she was going to live around here.

At the intersection, she slowed nearly to a stop and gave him a disgruntled glance. "OK. You've got me. Which way is north?"

C.H. laughed and pointed left. "City girl, huh?"

"Where I come from, there are street signs." She said it kind of snippy-like. The woman seemed a bit high-strung and C.H. wondered again what brought her to this part of the country.

"You'll catch on," he said. "I was the same way when I first moved here, and I figured it out."

"I thought I detected an accent. Where are you from?"

"Ha, I thought I'd lost that. I grew up in Oklahoma. My wife and I met at college in the US and I came up here to marry her. Long story short, we ended up staying to farm her folks' place. This is the place." C.H. pointed to his lane shaded by large cottonwoods.

She putzed up the driveway and he tried to picture what a city girl would think of his simple ranch house overlooking a scattering of corrals and outbuildings.

Although there was no sign of Lewis, C.H. was glad to see his animals back in the pasture where they belonged. The kid always had trouble with those barbed wire gates. But at least he had thought to park the ATV across the opening against further escapes.

C.H. opened the door and turned to Jacqui. "Good to finally put a face to the J. Penn from Hamilton, Ontario I've been sending those cheques to." He unfolded himself to step out of the car. "As long as you're OK with the arrangement, I hope to continue renting the land."

"I don't see why not." Something about the way she said it told him she had learned to keep any enthusiasm under strict control. Except where wayward cows were concerned.

C.H. leaned back into the car. "Remember, don't worry about your flowers." He grinned, hoping to coax a smile from her serious face. "Life wants to live."

CHAPTER 7

When Jacqui rounded the curve of her own driveway on her return, she scanned the place now that it was mown. What a difference. Though the grass bristled with stalks and the edges remained shaggy with weeds, simply clearing the jungle lent an air of civilization to the yard. She sat in her car for a few moments, pondering the breadth of the project. *Some English country garden.* Still, the patches of perennial peonies, delphiniums and lilies were a start. She could find out what did well here, add some roses. The garden had good bones, edged by evergreens most of which were wisely set back from the house by an expanse of lawn softened here and there by groupings of shrubs and trees. Aunt Priscilla had made a good beginning.

She sighed and got out of the car. The interior was what daunted her. Entering the house, no matter which way she turned, ugliness glowered in every direction. *At least the coating of dust is gone and it's mostly clean ugliness now.* But that was as much positivity as she could muster. Despite the neighbour women's scrubbing, a faint whiff of urine was still detectable from the carpet. The work ahead loomed monumentally. What to tackle first? Flesh-and-blood-coloured bathroom? Vomit kitchen? Or diarrhea living room?

Peeling the striped wallpaper off the far living room wall would be the quickest and least disruptive. Jacqui shoved furniture out of the way and hunted for a corner where the paper might give way. The work was satisfying, if messy, and she wasn't surprised to find a series of wallcoverings under the first. Like an archaeological dig, the paper marked style trends through the decades, right down to the bottom layer, a 1930s tiny yellowed print. As she worked left to right, stripping the walls like she'd done with any number of the houses she and Geoff had flipped over the years, she couldn't help examining the decades of her own life, now papered over with rejection and loss.

How could you, Geoff? Was every word, every compliment, every promise you ever made to me a lie?

Great sheets were shed from the walls, like blinders that fell and were still falling from Jacqui's eyes.

Oh, Geoff! We learned so much together, worked so well together. Remember racing the clock, getting as much demolition done in a day as we could before showering and going out for a late dinner at one of our favourite restaurants? And we loved well together, too. Remember the time we made love in an empty house, and afterward the awkwardness of the pizza delivery guy when you answered the door in your underwear? You found me ravishing then, I know you did.

And now? What did it say about Jacqui that he could replace her with someone so vastly different from her? Was their entire history together a sham? And what did it make her, that she had believed in him and in what they had together for all these years?

Inner turmoil propelled her onward. The final layer of ancient paper was still bonded stubbornly to the wall. It came away in frustratingly small pieces that clung to her clothes and gummed up her fingernails. The chore seemed to take an eternity, making her wonder if recovering from Geoff would be the same. At last, she resorted to using a spray bottle to dampen the final residue, scraping it away with her trowel in giant strokes. What was left was a bare, dingy green wall that still needed a wash and a fresh coat of paint, but already the room seemed cleaner, more spacious.

Jacqui dropped to the floor in a corner of the room, rubbing her right shoulder in weariness. She hadn't yet cried about any of it. Not the slow-growing distance between her and Geoff, not his puzzling disinterest, or even her co-worker's frequent visits to their home. How stupid could she have been? Or had she known, deep down, that something was going on between them and it was too devastating, or she was too afraid to name it for what it was? Whatever the case, when Geoff finally sat down with her to give his calm, reasonable explanation that his relationship with her was, as he put it, "a thing of the past" it took two repetitions to sink in.

"I was pretty sure you'd understand," he'd said with his winsome smile, mistaking her stunned silence for acceptance. "It's who I am now." And how, after all, could she possibly argue with that?

"Don't waste time crying over any man," Bree had warned her when Jacqui dully broke the news. "They're not worth it." And Bree would know. She'd stayed stoic and strong through what Jacqui considered unimaginable devastation. When Bree gave her husband Lonzo the ultimatum, he had chosen his precious computer gaming over their marriage. With astounding courage, Bree had left him, supporting herself and her two kids while she went back to school and established a career. By the time Jacqui had met her in college, she could see firsthand what a strain her friend was under with work, course load, and children. Now, that was strong. Bree's sheer willpower had always inspired Jacqui, so that ever since her own break-up, Jacqui had fought to keep her emotional control. But she was perilously close to losing it now. She forced herself to exhale slowly in a low hum.

Sitting on the floor, she noticed a corner of the carpet at her knee was flipped up from beneath the baseboard. She tugged at it without result then yanked harder. A loud ripping sound came as Jacqui pulled up the rug and she sprawled back on her rear end. She rose and gave another yank, then continued wrenching the carpet free from its tacks. Underneath the broadloom, she brushed aside decades of fine silt along with a layer of crumbling underlay, and discovered wood flooring, possibly hardwood. Experience told her the wood might still be in good condition.

What was with those stupid 70s people and their penchant for covering everything with carpet?

An irrational anger welled up in her at fools who blindly followed the decor trends of the past. *And how about idiots that follow current trends in relationships?* The rage gave her new strength. She shoved the furniture to the other half of the room, then heaved and rolled the foul-smelling carpet to the middle. The bare floor needed a thorough cleaning. Coughing at the dust this raised, she swept, vacuumed, and scrubbed with a vengeance. Then she transferred furniture back to the other end of the room so she could drag the heavy rug outside and repeat the cleaning on the rest of the room.

Hours later, hollow with hunger and arms aching with fatigue, Jacqui finally got the room put back together. She shed her filthy clothes, showered and limply foraged for whatever the fridge offered that required no effort. Munching a chunk of cheese, she scanned her day's work in the living room. Getting rid of the urine-stained carpet went a long way toward freshening the house. Its walls and floor were clean and free of their past.

If only it were that easy with my own.

CHAPTER 8

Jacqui gave a start when the woman with bobbing blonde curls answered the door of Aunt Anna's home in Red Deer. Looking into such familiar blue eyes was disconcerting. These were the eyes reflected in Jacqui's own mirror every morning, except these held a helpful light, and were pulled upward by a welcoming, if questioning smile.

Is this my cousin?

Behind the blondie stood a freckled young man with Down syndrome and clinging to the young woman's leg was a small boy watching Jacqui with grave brown eyes.

"Welcome here!" the suspected cousin smiled. "I know Mom was thrilled that you got in touch. It's just that she hasn't really been herself since she was injured last year." Her eyes dropped downward. But the smile quickly returned and she stretched out a hand. "I'm Beth, her daughter, which I guess makes us cousins. It's great to meet you. Come in." She backed up to make room, only to step on the silent young man's toes.

"Ow!" he howled.

Beth ducked her head. "Oops, sorry Jesse. Practicing the art of invisibility again, were you?" She gestured toward him and said to Jacqui. "This is my baby brother Jesse."

"Not a baby," Jesse murmured.

Mussing the young man's buzz cut, Beth laughed. Jesse immediately made an elaborate show of smoothing down the unruffled hair.

"And this is my youngest, Dusty." Beth pulled the child at her leg into her arms.

Jacqui followed her cousin into the warm interior of the small duplex, taking the living room chair the young woman indicated.

"I'll go wake Mom. I know she won't want to miss you." Beth paused, meeting Jacqui's eyes and frowning. She leaned towards Jacqui and, with a glance at Jesse, lowered her voice. "I hope you'll understand if my mom isn't very talkative. She's been through a lot in the past year or so. A couple of thugs assaulted her right here in her own home last year and threw her down the basement stairs. She broke some ribs and her knee, and on top of all that, the trauma and stress brought on a heart attack. It's left her, uh, different than she used to be."

Jacqui shook her head, dismayed by the crime, but even more, disappointed that her questions might go unanswered. "That's awful."

"Yeah, it really has been. She barely speaks at all. But as long as you don't expect her to answer any questions, we'll be fine. You and I will have to keep the conversation going ourselves."

As Beth left the room, tailed by her son, Jacqui puzzled over the silence Aunt Anna kept. *How do a heart attack and broken bones cause an inability to speak?* Her main aim in coming was to quiz her aunt about Pops' upbringing. Why had Jacqui's grandfather been such a tyrant? Why hadn't anyone done anything about it? And how had the other children survived it? To hear Pops tell it, he was the only one with the nerve to defy his father. His mother and siblings had all kowtowed to the old man's whims. Jacqui had to admit she'd arrived with her own resentments against the family. Weren't they the cause of her father's bitterness, his poor choice of a wife, and his current growing addiction?

Jacqui soon grew conscious of the intent gaze of the young man in the room with her. She'd always enjoyed the people with Down syndrome or other special needs who volunteered at the library, dusting shelves or performing other chores. She'd especially grown fond of Harmony, the young woman employed to help with children's programming. Her enthusiasm for everything they planned never failed to cheer Jacqui. And a couple of weeks before, when Harmony had found her in the staff room after hearing of Jacqui's resignation, the young woman had broken down bawling, enfolding her in a lingering hug.

Glancing around for a topic to escape melancholy thoughts, Jacqui caught sight of a deck of cards on the coffee table. “You know any good card games?”

Jesse plopped himself on the floor opposite her chair and handed her the cards. “Go Fish.”

Apparently, the game was on. Jacqui scooted forward in her chair to shuffle the cards, conscious of the young fellow's intent gaze on her hands.

“You shuffle good.”

“My dad taught me.” She considered Jesse, rocking back and forth in anticipation of the game. “Have you ever tried?”

His face opened to her in a crinkly-eyed smile. Jacqui worked with him a bit, splitting the deck in two, letting him flip the halves to mingle. His mild touch wasn't forceful enough to do the job. Jesse handed back the cards.

Jacqui dealt, watching Jesse slide each card into a plastic holder that fanned his hand out in front of him. As the young man pondered the cards, Dusty and Beth descended the stairs from above followed by a small woman keeping a tight grip on the railing. Jacqui stifled a gasp of surprise. Here was the female version of Pops, only the droop of her eyes hinted at gentle humour rather than cynicism, and the set of her generous mouth was kindly, not grim. Her Aunt Anna focused on each slow step, arriving on the main floor several paces behind her daughter.

"Mom, this is Jacqui," Beth said, seating her mother in an armchair adjacent to the one where Jacqui sat. The young mom took a hassock near Anna, her toddler wandering to a box of toys beneath the front window.

Jacqui rose to to shake Anna's thin, limp hand. Meeting the older woman's steady blue gaze above her faint smile, Jacqui found herself wanting to impress her, maybe even be the one to draw her out of her strange silence.

"It's good to meet you." She realized she was blaring and lowered her volume, reminding herself her aunt was mute, not deaf. "I'm sure Beth already told you that I've moved to the area now. I'm living in your childhood home in the country." Was that a flicker of interest in Anna's eyes at the mention of her childhood? It was hard to tell. Without a response from her aunt, Jacqui quickly ran out of steam. She shot an appealing glance at Beth then returned to her seat on the sofa, angling toward the older woman.

"Your turn," Jesse murmured, prodding Jacqui to resume their game.

"There's a lot of cleaning to do out at Uncle Russell and Aunt Priscilla's place, isn't there?" Beth offered a sympathetic look.

"You've got that right," Jacqui said.

"After Uncle Russell died two years ago, Mom and Aunt Naomi went over to clean and try sorting through the belongings." Beth glanced at her mother. "But then they realized they weren't sure what the new owner—you—might want to keep and maybe they shouldn't really be doing it."

Jacqui gave half a laugh. "You could have helped yourself to all the salt and pepper shakers and porcelain figurines you wanted."

Beth chuckled and squeezed her mother's hand. "Aunt Priscilla was a great collector, that's for sure."

The older woman offered another fleeting smile, made eating motions to her daughter, then pointed to the dining room wall behind them.

Beth took the hint. "C'mon over here. I'll introduce you to the family and then we can sit down with some pie," she said, leading the way to the gallery of framed portraits on the wall.

"Mm. I like pie!" Jesse rubbed his middle.

Starting at the top with a Depression era wedding photo, Beth gave a detailed run-down of the family tree. Jacqui already knew the birth order; Russell, her father John, Priscilla, Naomi, Anna, and the youngest, Helen, who had drowned as a three year old. But beyond that, she knew nothing.

"I'm afraid you lost me at about 1940," Jacqui finally said. "But I'm intrigued by the pictures of my dad. I've never seen any from when he was a boy." She examined them, lingering over one particular photo. Before Beth passed by on her way to the kitchen for pie, Jacqui asked her to confirm the identity of the picture's subjects. In it, Pops' parents stood in front of an old car, the father smiling proudly at his baby son on one strong arm while the other arm curled around his shyly smiling young wife. His forehead gleamed above the rest of his sun-ripened face, but he didn't look like an abuser. It only went to show you never knew what went on behind closed doors.

What could have happened in the intervening years to create such a monster?

The next picture caused Jacqui a moment of doubt about Pops' version of history. In this later family portrait, five stair-step smiling children surrounded their seated parents, but the second son, unmistakably her own Pops, stood apart from the rest of the group, scowling sullenly. Was it teenage awkwardness, or was this a reflection of the relationship between Pops and his family? And what was the truth about their family life? Harsh and over-bearing father, who made life difficult for all but insisted everyone uphold a happy facade? Or bitter young man, sowing seeds of discord? Was it even fair to glean this many conclusions from a single snapshot in time? The gallery was an unexpected glimpse into the past, shaking her assumptions about how her father had grown up.

Beth returned with a piece of pie for each of them, seating herself at the coffee table to feed her son.

Jacqui sat down near the older woman and tasted a bite of the golden, pastry-wrapped cherries. "It's marvelous pie," she said, glancing from one woman to the other. "So flaky. And I've never had cherry filling this flavourful."

Beth smiled at her mother. "Mom's nearly famous for her pie."

"I've never had much success with pastry. I'd like to learn her technique sometime."

"You'd love that, wouldn't you, Mom?"

Her mother reached over and patted Jacqui's arm, giving a slight nod.

"Aunt Anna," Jacqui said, liking the sound of the title, "my dad has talked about you over the years."

This time, Anna's eyes registered unmistakable surprise. Rejoining them, Beth stroked her hand. "Do you remember how old you were when Uncle John left home?" Beth asked her mother, then reformed the question for a yes-no response. "I think you once told me he was sixteen when he left, so that would have made you about eight, right?"

Anna gave a slight nod, eyeing Jacqui with interest.

"He told me he saved you from drowning once." Jacqui met her frank blue gaze, pleased to have been able to elicit another smile and nod from the older woman.

How do I reach her, find out what I need to know?

"My dad hasn't spoken of his family or his growing up very much."

She struggled with the years-old habit of covering up her family's dysfunction. “But when he does, it isn't very...” The eyes still watched keenly. Jacqui glanced at Beth, wondering if questions on the topic would make Anna's strange condition worse. Beth nodded encouragement.

“I've gotten the impression it wasn't a happy home.”

Anna's chin pulled back as though affronted. Almost imperceptibly, she shook her head, dropping her gaze to Jacqui's knee. After an awkward silence, Jacqui watched Beth for a clue on how to proceed. But the young woman had rushed to keep the contents of her purse out of Dusty's chubby reach.

“I take it you don't agree?” Jacqui asked her aunt.

Unmistakably, Anna shook her head.

“But you were one of the younger ones. Maybe your father had mellowed some by the time you were growing up?”

The older woman sat silent for a moment, then reached across to the hole in the knee of Jacqui's jeans and began gathering up the dangling threads. *How strange.* Her cool fingertips slowly and carefully wove the hanging fibers in and out between the cross-weave. It tickled.

Beth laughed when she caught sight of the effort. “My grandmother taught her girls to mend everything. Aunt Naomi is an absolute whiz at it.”

Here Anna nodded again. Then she pointed at the wall of photos. Beth watched, obviously as puzzled as Jacqui was. Anna half rose, pointing at the pictures again. She wove her fingers together in front of her and shook them with a firm motion at the watching young women.

“Oh, I think I get it,” Beth said, turning to Jacqui. “Mom used to tell us that families are knit together. She's saying that's how her family was. Am I right?”

With a nod, Anna said yes. But that didn't answer Jacqui's question. Did her aunt mean their family was tightly knit, or was this simply a general statement of how families should be? In which case, it seemed like more cover-up, more denial of a very real problem.

Anna sighed deeply and leaned back in the armchair, closing her eyes. It appeared the visit was over.

CHAPTER 9

Midmorning a few days later, Jacqui put up her feet, exhausted from the day's early start on coaxing the kitchen walls to shed their thick hide of orange and brown mushroom wallpaper. She decided to use the break to do some online banking at the kitchen table.

A message just then from Bree back east informed her that a For Sale sign had still not gone up at Geoff and Jacqui's condo. She could tell Bree suspected the worst, that Jacqui's ex had no intention of selling. But lack of a sign didn't mean Geoff wasn't showing the property. As a realtor, he could do that. Though he should have at least put it up on multiple listings for the best chance at selling. Easy enough to check that online.

Nope, not listed yet. She frowned then checked her bank statement, which only deepened her frown. Her money would dwindle fast without an income. She'd been counting on her half of the equity from the home. She was beginning to regret renting the storage unit in Hamilton for her larger items. But having already paid for six months, it was too late to back out.

In the morning quiet, she heard a vehicle pull up in front of the house. She resisted rising from her chair. The intense summer heat had forced her to open all the windows and she was clad only in her underwear. Whoever it was didn't come to the door. Then she heard the high-pitched whine of a power tool shrilling outdoors. Duck-walking below the low living room windows to keep out of sight,

Jacqui grabbed her robe from the bedroom and peeked outside.

C.H. wielded a weed whacker, trimming the edges of her lawn. At the shaggy flowerbed in the foreground, his son Lewis stomped a garden fork into the soil and turned over a chunk of grass-root-riddled earth. Nice gesture, but she didn't trust a kid to know the difference between a lily stem and quack grass. She hurriedly pulled on shorts and a T-shirt and dashed out.

But when she jogged up behind the kid and began offering weeding advice, the skinny boy gave an exaggerated leap away, hunkering down behind the fork tines as though she were a malevolent zoo animal on the lam.

"I just wanted to remind you to be careful around anything that looks like it's supposed to be planted here," she said, raising her voice to be heard above the approach of C.H. and his buzzing trimmer. The lad crept farther away until his back touched a tree trunk.

Hmm, no eye contact, body rocking back and forth, unintelligible murmuring. She'd seen this before. Now it made sense that C.H. had said the boy didn't answer the phone. Perhaps Lewis had autism.

The motor noise died, relieving Jacqui of the need to shout. She knelt in front of the newly dug earth, loosening the soil and unthreading the tangled root system.

"It's good you've brought that fork, Lewis. That's the only way to get deep enough to get at the whole grass plant." She avoided eye contact with him, calmly talking through her every action. Out of the corner of her eye, she saw with satisfaction that the boy was inching his way back to the flowerbed. He rose slowly, then plunged the fork into the soil an arms' length to Jacqui's right.

"Over there," she said, waving her hand at a low-growing mound, "I think I've got pinks, so we'll have to be extra careful digging around them."

The lad got about half-way around the oval flower bed then bent to pull at two tall clumps of a wildflower with pretty purple buds that

Jacqui had transplanted from the ditch in front of her place.

She lunged toward him. “Not those! I just planted them.”

Lewis jumped back in alarm. He dropped the pitchfork and ran off in the direction of some lilac bushes.

Now what have I done? Jacqui stared after him, hoping she hadn't caused a full-scale meltdown. She'd witnessed a couple of those fearsome scenes in the library back east. Sighing, she went on removing weeds from the clods of earth Lewis had dug up. In a moment, she grew conscious of C.H. approaching from behind.

“Don't worry,” C.H. reassured her. “He'll be back. He's like that. Works in fits and snatches. But he does work.”

Jacqui gave a guilty start, glancing up from the soil under her hands. “Well, I probably shouldn't have jumped at him like that.” She motioned toward her transplants. “But I've been babying these, and he was about to uproot them.”

C.H. looked from the flowers to Jacqui's face then guffawed. “The boy knew what he was doing. Those are purple loosestrife, a noxious weed. You give them TLC and they'll multiply like a math teacher. They choke out everything else. Here, let me help you.”

Before Jacqui could stop him, he yanked the plants up by the roots and shook off the soil. He sauntered over to the burning barrel at the far end of the yard and returned wiping his hands on his jeans.

Embarrassed, Jacqui averted her gaze. He seemed to be hovering over her. *What? Does he think I'm going to retrieve the weeds and replant them?* “Well, I appreciate your help with the yard work today. I thought you said Lewis neither toils nor spins?”

C.H. grinned. “Sometimes it seems like it.”

“I take it he has autism?”

“Yeah.” C.H. flopped down on the grass beside her, laying his trimmer alongside him and leaning back on his elbows. “Diagnosed at about three.”

"Does he talk at all?"

"Ha! Does Lewis talk? Do bees buzz?" He threw back his head showing a big white grin and causing his cowboy hat to fall into the grass. His thick sandy hair was dented where the hat had been. "Yeah, he talks. More than you'd want to hear, most of the time," he said, picking up the hat and dusting the grass clippings off it. "He's in his quiet phase right now. A couple of years ago, my wife started tracking it and figured out there's a pattern, almost to the hour. Every twenty-one days, Lewis goes quiet for about three days then starts talking again. When he's in that silent mode, nothing you can do will get a word out of him."

"I've never heard of that before."

"Yeah. It's kind of weird, but you get used to it." C.H. eyed her. "I watched how you worked with him. How did you know not to say, 'Is he autistic'? Seems like you know a bit about autism."

"Through work." She returned to drawing the grass roots out of the warm dirt with her fingers. "I've taken some awareness training. The library where I come from has a lot of people with special needs using it and even a few working there."

"Library, huh?" He peered at her through slitted eyes. "Yeah, I can see that."

"What do you mean?" Jacqui had heard every librarian stereotype.

"There's a bookish look to you."

"Well, thanks. I think." She turned her head to hide a smile.

"It's a good thing. I'm rather partial to books myself." C.H. stood, clapped his hat back on his head and grabbed the trimmer again. "You planning on getting work at one of the libraries around here?"

"I'm not sure. Are they hiring?"

"It's worth a try. You never know. The local one could sure use someone who knows what they're doing. Have you explored Broad Valley yet?"

"I wasn't planning to be here all that long." She straightened, rubbing the small of her back then realized she must have left a smudge of mud on her shirt. Her hands were filthy.

"I got the impression you were here to stay. Figured you'd be baling your own hay on the back forty there by next year at this time." C.H. smiled wryly.

Next year at this time? Why did being here that long seem such a fearsome prospect? Yet where else did she belong? "I don't know what my plans are yet." Jacqui left it at that, not wanting to share her uncertainties.

He rose to his feet then paused. "What are you planning to do with that car in the shed behind those trees?"

"I have no idea. I only heard about it when the neighbours came over the other day."

"Yeah, it's a classic Bel Air convertible, '61 or '62, I think. Haven't seen it in quite a while, but your uncle used to lend it out once in a while to nonprofit groups for the Sports Day parade. Mint condition and really low mileage. Might be worth a potful by now. You haven't scoped it out yet?"

"No. I've had more pressing matters to deal with."

"Oh yeah, I guess. But you'll definitely be wanting to take that beauty for a spin before winter sets in. And if you decide to sell it, there'll be a line-up of local guys making offers." C.H. took a few steps toward the edges of the lawn where he'd been working, then turned back to her. "Back to what you said about folks with handicaps working at that library—did you mean they get paid?"

"Some volunteer, some are actually employed. The rest of the staff had training for working with special-needs individuals. I got to like them."

"Interesting." He paused. "Some people find it difficult to be around folks with disabilities."

"Fear of the unpredictable, I guess?"

"Or fear of their own possible future. There's a handicapped person in nearly everyone's future, for one reason or another. Accident, aging, disease or what have you."

"Kind of a bleak way of thinking about life."

"Could be. Or maybe it's being realistic. Everybody's likely to get old and disabled eventually. And the death rate is one per person. Kinda puts life in perspective, doesn't it?"

"I always enjoyed working with our special needs people." C.H.'s easy manner almost led her to mention her infant brother, but she reminded herself not to overshare. "One of my friends used to call them 'the happy people.' Sometimes they were hilarious."

"What I've found is, some folks gravitate to the disabled because they like a project while others do it because it's easier to be with people that don't make the kind of demands regular folks make. But it takes a special kind of person to truly enjoy them." He touched the brim of his hat at her. "I'll be getting on with my work now. C'mon buddy, gird up your loins and get at it," he called to his son, who ambled back to the flowerbed. Turning back to Jacqui, C.H. said, "You have a great day, now."

When C.H.'s trimming was finished and Lewis had dug up the rest of the flower bed, Jacqui watched the two of them speed out her driveway on their ATV. She pondered her neighbour's complacent musing that there's a disability in everyone's future. This new idea seemed obvious, yet alarming. She thought guiltily of Pops and his long silence when she'd called to tell him she was moving out west. *But his condition is hardly in the category of special needs. He's quite capable of taking care of himself.* Jacqui recalled the tender care her new-found cousin Beth was providing for her mother, Anna. But who would care for Jacqui when she became decrepit and infirm?

CHAPTER 10

Exploring Broad Valley sounded a lot more glamorous than it turned out to be. Jacqui drove the single main street past a credit union and Velvet's Tea Room on one side, and a hotel and leather shop on the other. Her eye skimmed past the few other nondescript shops and businesses searching for the library when she noticed an antique shop called Days of Your. *Seriously?* Somebody thought he was clever.

She finally spotted a small stucco building bearing the sign *Library* and pulled to a stop in front. Through trickles of moisture on her car window, she found herself critiquing the facility with its narrow steps, perpendicular to the door, making access possible from only one direction and impossible for those in wheelchairs. The only parking available was along the street. The upper half of the squat stucco building appeared to be a residence, judging by the frilly curtains in the front window and the child's tricycle on the wet sidewalk.

What, the librarian lives on site? I suppose that would make it easier to nab vandals who throw firecrackers into the book drop. That had actually happened in Hamilton. Jacqui herself had been the one to discover the stinking, smoldering mess of melted DVDs and blackened books. It could have been far worse, of course, but what was wrong with some people? And there had been other disgusting discoveries in the book deposit involving bodily fluids and rotten poultry.

This library appeared to have no after-hours book drop at all. Speaking of hours, Jacqui had to brave the drizzle by getting out of her car and mounting the steps before she could read the tiny hours of operation sign. Odd. On two weekdays the library was open during two separate periods and on two other days, the open hours were only over the lunch hour. They certainly functioned differently out here. But then, maybe cowboys didn't read books besides the odd Louis L'Amour western. She shivered under her now-damp hoodie. Back east the summer rain was warm, here it was icy.

She'd lucked out. The library was open now. A bell above the door tinkled as she entered, drawing all eyes in her direction. Inside, the smell of old books and wet jackets and a general hum of subdued activity caused her a twinge of homesickness. She'd always felt a sense of belonging and safety in a library.

A pair of teenage girls standing by the left wall were tittering over some magazine. To Jacqui's right, a couple of boys were competing loudly at a game on one computer, while at the computer beside them a woman reached across to shush them. At least the place was well used. But the circulation desk was vacant. A bald man in a dapper bowtie stood in front of it, swivelling his head in a futile search for someone to check out his books.

"Ahem," he ventured, craning his head to see down the aisles. "Miss Mueller!" he called, somewhat louder. No one responded.

What a disgraceful way to run a public service.

At this point, the gentleman gave Jacqui a nod that was half apologetic, half annoyed. "Perhaps our trusty librarian has had an emergency." A trace of British accent tinged his words. He cleared his throat and addressed the entire room. "Does anyone know the whereabouts of Miss Mueller?"

The hum of activity paused long enough for a few of the others present to shake their heads. The gentleman frowned down at the two thick books and National Geographic magazines in his hand. “I had hoped to be well stocked with reading material for the weekend.” He hesitated, then laid the items on the cluttered desk and turned to leave, a picture of exasperated disappointment.

Jacqui scanned the room one more time, disgusted at this breach of service. Still no library employee in evidence.

“Wait,” she said, catching his arm as he aimed for the door. “I may be able to help.” She circled the desk nervously, woke the blackened screen of the computer and was relieved to find the same familiar library circulation program she knew so well.

He returned to the desk, raising his eyebrows at her. “If you could, I’d be most grateful.”

“No trouble at all, sir,” she said, taking his card and checking out his material.

“Thank you very much, Miss...?”

“I'm Jacqui Penn,” she said, shaking the sinewy hand he offered.

“I wasn't aware there was another qualified person on staff here.” A twinkle sparked in his eyes briefly.

Jacqui smiled. “Not on staff, no. But I do have a degree in library science.”

“Ah,” he said. “A fellow bibliophile.”

Just then, a door opened in the back of the building and a puff of wind swept in. A short, plump woman—or rather, a woman who would have been short without her red suede spike-heeled platform shoes—tottered up the aisle and stopped when she saw Jacqui at the desk. The flowing fabric of her short navy polka-dot dress was still swinging when she arrived, opening her mouth, closing it, and glancing from the patron to Jacqui. With an officious air, she bustled to the desk. Jacqui freed up the chair as quickly as she could.

“Now, Mr. Fanshawe,” Miss Mueller said, typing rapidly. “Let me help you.” The red silk flower in her blonde hair quivered while the lips that matched her shoes turned up in a cherubic smile as she held out her hand for his books.

Shifting his uncertain gaze from her to Jacqui, Mr. Fanshawe returned his items to the desk. Jacqui made a discreet escape, gliding down one of the aisles with a smirk as she peeked above the books on a shelf, anticipating the pop-up message the Mueller woman was about to receive.

"Hmm." The woman frowned, then giggled. "I guess these are all checked out and good to go, then. Have a great day!" Once Fanshawe was out the door, Jacqui heard Miss Mueller leave her desk and strike up a conversation with the woman at the public computer. Fragments of their gossip about local residents were plain to be heard around the small building. Miss Mueller used laughter as punctuation. Jacqui was appalled at the unprofessionalism and the poor example to the young people present.

Meanwhile, she took stock of the library. All the usual collections were here, even a surprisingly extensive large print selection. *Must have a lot of senior clientele.* Predictably, the shelves held a plethora of westerns. But judging by the number of shabby books and outdated volumes, the whole library needed a good weeding.

Miss Mueller's tripping footsteps made their way back to the circulation desk.

"What was it you were needing help with?" she asked her gossip companion.

Jacqui couldn't make out the woman's soft response.

"Let me check for it," Miss Mueller said, then added almost immediately, "Nope, sorry, that one's not in the system." Another title must have been requested because Miss Mueller offered the same lack of results.

Why doesn't she order them from outside the system? Curious at this glitch in service, Jacqui ventured closer to the front. The third book was found and ordered. From where Jacqui now stood at an oblique angle from the circulation computer, she could follow the librarian's procedure. Miss M's cherry acrylic fingernails tap-tapped against the keys. *She's making no attempt to find the books outside the local region.* Twice more, the woman turned down the patron's requests. This was too much for Jacqui.

"Excuse me," she said, approaching Mueller as diplomatically as she could. "Maybe you could try a wider search?"

Miss Mueller's precisely defined eyebrows drew together in a frown. "Oh, they have to go to the city for that."

"Surely not." Jacqui reached for the mouse. "Do you mind...?"

"You think you know better than me? Be my guest," Miss Mueller swept out of the chair. "You'll see."

Jacqui sat in the warmed chair, feeling certain she had just made an enemy. With some technological maneuvering, she found the appropriate website, and successfully ordered each of the books the patron asked for.

"Thanks so much!" the woman said with a relieved smile. Calling her two boys away from the computers, she reached for the door handle, then turned. "I really need those books."

At least someone's happy.

Clip, clip, clip. The librarian's heels signalled her return to the desk. She settled in the seat Jacqui had again hastily vacated.

"Now, show me how you did that." Mueller waited without a trace of animosity.

Startled at the woman's demand but relieved that she appeared to harbor no ill feelings, Jacqui reached over to demonstrate the steps.

Miss Mueller barely glanced at the screen before tossing her head back with a laugh. "I'll never be able to remember any of that. As they say, 'Ain't nobody got time for that!'"

"But—"

"Tell you what, though. It seems like you've got library experience. You want a job?"

Jacqui stared into Miss Mueller's blue-shadowed eyes in surprise.

"I'm serious. I only took this job because I live upstairs and it saved me commuting. I've been hoping someone would come along to take over the boring parts of the work." She grinned, showing a fleck of lipstick on one front tooth. "Me, I don't want the bother of worrying about all those technical details. I'd much rather spend time on what's really important in life—the people." She waved a dismissive hand toward a second desk set back from hers. "You can have that desk and work whatever days you want. I could do with some time away from here."

An hour later, Jacqui exited the building as an employee of the Town of Broad Valley. She'd be working at the library any time they were open, which admittedly made for an erratic schedule. Still, it left her with time to pursue renovations at home yet still earn an income. Of course, how long she would be here remained uncertain, but a job was a job. She drove home enumerating a list of changes she intended to make in the small library. Pleased with herself despite the step down her career had taken, she felt a smile of satisfaction lift the corners of her mouth. Someone wanted her.

CHAPTER 11

This has got to be the last of it. Jacqui scraped and tore a final sheet of the ghastly giant mushrooms covering the kitchen wall. They were the stuff of nightmares. But now they lay vanquished in limp piles on the floor and the walls were bare.

She plunked herself onto a chair to judge the effect of her morning's efforts. The strong grain of the plywood cupboards and the deep brown of the counter tops and orange-painted back splash still overpowered the room. *But how far do I want to go with this sow's ear of a project?* Whenever she and Geoff had planned a reno, they'd had a clear end in mind. Purchase a house, gut, rebuild, update, stage and sell. They'd always had a timeline and a price point to meet, and they'd usually met both, give or take a few weeks or a couple thousand dollars. Their buy-flip-sell strategy had brought them to mortgage-free status in twelve years and the next step was to move up in house, perhaps to an acreage or maybe adding a vacation home. *At least, that was supposed to have been the next step.*

Here, it was a different story. Without a good income and with only her existing savings, Jacqui had next to nothing for a budget and she hadn't the least notion how long she would be here. That was partly dependent on the sale of the condo in Hamilton. Bree had promised to alert her when the place was listed and sold because Jacqui couldn't bear to contact Geoff directly. Not only that, but when she did receive her payout, could she simply move back east and take up where she left off? The idea of returning to work with the very interloper who had replaced her in Geoff's heart and life was insufferable.

And not only that, now I've got a personal battle with this house going on.

She straightened her spine, narrowing her eyes at the walls around her.

Here's the plan, house. I'm going to throw every skill I've got at you with the least money I can get by on. So, take that! And don't even dream of tossing some stupid structural issue back at me.

She glared at the cabinets with a sinking heart, fighting to keep up her flagging bravado. Not only were they ugly, the way the inside shelves were configured defied logic. There were no shelves at all behind the lower doors, only cavernous holes, while the upper cupboards weren't deep enough for a dinner plate to fit on the shelf without the door sticking open partway. She envisioned the sleek modern cabinetry she'd left behind in Hamilton, then forced her thoughts to the problems at hand. What would be adorable here would be new cupboards that reflected the home's farmhouse persona, perhaps a couple with glass fronts to break up the uppers. She drew a deep sigh of disappointment. The room cried out for a thorough reno, done the right way.

But no. Paint and new hardware would have to be enough to transform the cupboards, given her skimpy finances.

Now, that gross back splash had to go. And yet, removing tile always risked major wall repair. *I wonder...* Jacqui grabbed the trowel she'd been using and thoughtfully approached the backsplash where it crept across the wall hidden by the stove. She wedged herself between the stove and lower cupboard to try prying the tile. With a sharp pop, a large square of the stuff skittered onto the counter. It was plastic, the underside of which showed it had originally been pink.

Seriously, Grandma? You thought citrus orange was an

improvement on peppermint pink? Or maybe Jacqui would have called her Granny? *Granny. I like that.*

The wall behind the faux tile wore brown squiggles of dried glue that mostly broke off in short, dry sticks when she plowed through with the trowel. Re-energized, she set to work removing it all and cleaning the surface. This success led to the ambitious plan of slathering walls and cabinets with white primer. The whole room became lighter and airier the more progress she made, despite the streakiness of the undercoat and the floor trash she had to tramp through. It was nearly dinner time when Jacqui wrapped up the roller and brush to store them in the fridge. Having missed lunch, she was starving. Calling for takeout or delivery wasn't an option out here in the sticks. She needed a maid.

Obviously, I'll have to plan for convenience foods for days like this, no matter how much of a food snob I am. Living in the country meant more adjustments than she'd anticipated.

With her right foot, she stepped on and pulled off a strip of wallpaper stuck by a drop of paint to the bottom of her other shoe. Where, for example, was she to dispose of all this renovation debris? She'd burned the wallpaper torn from the living room walls in a rusty barrel behind the house, but these plastic tile panels, she realized with a sense of helpless guilt, would have to go to a landfill. *Renovations are a net waste-producer, no doubt about it.* All those shelter magazines featuring stories of "green renovations" were a crock. The true environmentalist would have kept everything unchanged and simply lived with the ugliness. *Blech.* Unwilling to make such an extreme sacrifice, Jacqui switched off her inner guilt about climate change.

She poached two eggs, slid them onto a slice of rye toast and ate them between sips of green tea. A granny meal.

Speaking of Granny, I wonder what she was like? A bit like Aunt Anna, maybe?

The thought of her aunt's cool fingers, weaving the threads of the rip in the knee of Jacqui's jeans as though to mend the tear, made her eyes water. Even as a young child, she couldn't remember being so carefully tended or feeling so tenderly cared for. What would it have been like to have a mother like that? Solicitous, cherishing, nurturing. And where had Anna learned such ways if not from her mother before her? Pops had never had much to say about his mother, only that she was fearful and weak and under the thumb of his demanding father. But she had been "frivolous" enough to want to redecorate her kitchen. And she'd likely been ambitious enough to do the work herself. *Do I get my interest in all things home from you, Granny?*

Jacqui finished the last bite of toast, downed the tea, and left the table. She headed for the narrow door in the living room next to the kitchen entrance. She had opened it briefly when she'd first arrived, enough to know it led to the attic. The close, hot air intensified as she climbed the creaky, steep, and narrow stairs. Sloping walls of the single large room were panelled in plywood, while the gable in each end wall bore a single narrow window. On the paisley linoleum floor, stacks of cardboard boxes lined the pony walls along with a family history of items from metal farm toys to a pair of roller skates and a swaybacked rack of clothing. She stooped to examine the labels on boxes. Priscilla's schoolwork, baby clothes, Christmas decorations, farm ledgers.

At the bottom of one stack Jacqui found a box marked John's keepsakes. *That would be Pops.* Her pulse quickened as she set the upper box aside, blew the dust away and opened the flaps. Inside lay a stack of school notebooks, from early printing to high school essays to simple primary art projects and one labelled "My Bible Verses 1954" entirely filled with childish writing. "My son, hear the instruction of your father, and do not forsake the law of your mother..." In bitter tones, Pops had once told her of being forced to write out Bible verses. She snapped the notebook shut.

The box also contained a Meccano building set, a pair of black leather skates with floppy ankles, a small Roger's syrup can filled with marbles. Near the bottom was an aged toy tractor, hand carved of wood and unvarnished but with the patina of much use by small hands. Its wooden wheels still rolled. On its seat was a tiny wooden farmer missing the lower half of one arm. Carved on the underside were the words, For John, Christmas 1948. *Pops would have been two and a half.*

Jacqui ran her hands over the smooth-worn wood of the toy for a long time, rolling its wheels back and forth and thinking. A father had spent hours making this for his son, eager to see the pleasure on the child's face. Perhaps he was a father who had no money for store-bought toys, but surely the time and the detail showed he was a father who loved his son.

So, then, what happened? Again, she asked herself, what changed a devoted father into a tyrant? Was it the pressures of farm and family life? Was it the fault of religion, as Pops insisted? Or was it something darker, something in the nature of the son himself? The photo on Aunt Anna's wall where her father was a belligerent teen had led to doubts about his side of the story. But no matter how many whirls Jacqui gave the narrow front wheels of the toy tractor, they refused to yield an answer.

CHAPTER 12

In the ambient lighting of the local grocery store's produce section, Jacqui jerked her hand back from a package of organic tomatoes when she caught sight of the price.

Seriously? That's outrageous! She couldn't remember ever paying that much back east. Were tomatoes so rare in this dry land that they sold for the price of gold? Then again, she'd never paid much attention to prices. There'd been no need to watch pennies this meticulously back then. Biting her lip in doubt, she cast a reluctant glance at the non-organics, larger, smoother, but less ripe. She bagged a couple and carried on travelling through the store, crossing items off her list.

At the hardware store, Francie was only too eager to mix paint colours for Jacqui.

"Making progress on the house then, are you?" She took the paint chips Jacqui offered and raised her eyebrows. "That's a lot of white. You sure you don't want a bit more colour? We've got six months of white out our windows as it is."

Jacqui smiled. "I'm sure."

"Up to you." While the tandem paint cans rumbled and shook in the mixer, Francie chattered. "Harvest is earlier this year, but the crops haven't had enough moisture or what we've had, came too late. And don't even start asking about hay."

Jacqui hadn't planned to.

The early dry season meant a hay shortage again, Francie

continued. Last year's crop had been great, but nobody loved feeding cattle last season's feed. She planned on attending her grandkids' 4-H riding club on Saturday at so-and-so's indoor riding arena.

"Brings tears to my eyes to see those sweet kids up in the saddle." On cue, Francie's eyes grew watery. "Fourth generation riders." She dabbed with her thumb and forefinger to staunch the waterworks.

C.H. parked his truck and trailer loaded with large round hay bales from Jacqui's south field in front of her house, waiting for her to arrive home so he could drop off his payment. He'd seen her car raising dust up the road moments earlier. When she turned in the driveway, she stopped and backed her car as though allowing him room to pass.

He climbed out of his rig. "I came to bring your land rental cheque," C.H. called, holding it out to her.

Jacqui had switched off the ignition and was filling her arms with grocery bags when he approached.

"But I can bring it to the house for you." He nodded at her bags. "Is that it or can I carry something?"

"There's a couple of cans of paint on the rear floor, if you don't mind."

He fetched them and followed Jacqui to her door.

She set her shopping on the kitchen table. "Thanks. If you could put the paint on the porch floor next to my drill, that would be fine."

C.H. set them down next to a tidy array of tools then returned to scan the kitchen and what could be seen of the living room from where he stood. "Impressive. You've been hard at it, I see. Big improvement already."

"I've still got a long way to go." Jacqui nodded toward the detailed renovation to-do list posted on the kitchen wall.

Leaning against the doorway, he craned his neck to scan it. It was detailed and colour-coded and already had a couple of ruler-straight lines through the entries. Some of the jobs listed would be tough to accomplish alone. “You planning to do all this yourself? I could probably find time to help. I always intended to repair that broken window I boarded up.”

“I’ll manage,” she said, emptying the grocery bags, piece by piece. “Google is my friend.”

“Well, call if you need some muscle on any of it.”

“As the saying goes, 'A woman needs a man like a fish needs a bicycle.'“

Did she mean to be funny with the old feminist slogan? He knew where it came from and he wasn’t a fan of the source but he said nothing.

As though needing to change the subject, she pulled pinkish tomatoes out of the bag and held them up. “I'm reduced to buying regular, chemical-laden produce. I couldn't believe the price of organic.” She removed them from their bag and placed them in a basket on the counter.

“Everything is chemical,” C.H. said.

Jacqui lifted an eyebrow at him.

“What did you mean by 'chemical-laden'?” he asked.

“I've watched a few documentaries and done some reading on what's in the food we eat.”

“What was the source?” C.H. leaned forward with interest. People were far too gullible when it came to media representations of food production. He tried not to hit anyone over the head with the facts, but he couldn’t help defending his industry.

“Hey, I just thought the organic price was way too much for a couple of vegetables.” She placed the last of the packages in the cupboard and folded the grocery bags.

“Fruit.”

"What?"

"Tomatoes are fruit."

Jacqui tightened her lips. "You know what I meant."

He only laughed. "Tell you what," he said, backing out slowly through the porch. "I've got to deliver these bales to someone before five today, but I want to show you something while there's still daylight. Lewis and I'll swing around as soon as I'm done, OK?"

Jacqui shrugged and smiled.

After he'd dropped off his load, C.H. drove home, met Lewis with a snack when the school bus let him off, and got to Jacqui's shortly before four-thirty. Lewis hopped out of the truck to open the door for her then folded his long thin legs into the back seat.

"Where are we going?" Jacqui asked, groping for the seatbelt.

"Out checking crops."

"That's funny. When I was young, my dad used to say that when he took me for a drive. I never knew anyone else's dad who used that term for 'going for a drive.'"

"That's right. Your father grew up in this area didn't he? You can take the boy off the farm..." He glanced at Jacqui but she gave no indication of wanting to finish the cliché.

Instead she watched the rolling stretches of cropland pass by without comment.

"Lewis, tell Miss Jacqui the name of each of these crops," C.H. said, not wanting to insult her intelligence.

"Make way for the ignorant city girl," Jacqui murmured with a wry look.

C.H. gave an apologetic smile. Lewis solemnly named the patchwork of thick green brushes—barley, durum wheat, or canola—to which C.H. added his own commentary on the condition of the field in question. This one had a lot of wild oats, that one was top grade.

"Sunflowers," Jacqui blurted when she spotted a field of the yellow flowers, as though she was determined to prove she recognized something.

They rolled past an expanse of rolling pasture, dotted with brown cattle. "Hereford," Lewis piped up then tapped Jacqui on the shoulder. "A crop of Herefords!" He cackled uproariously.

"I've always wondered what the difference between Herefords and heifers was," Jacqui said.

From the back seat came another of Lewis's snorting laughs while C.H. stared at her incredulously. "Hereford is a breed of cattle," he explained, trying to suppress a grin. "Now if we were cattle, heifer is what you might be called if you've never had a child. Or have you?"

"Have I what?"

"Had a child?"

"No."

Probably shouldn't have pried, but it seemed odd at her age—somewhere in her 30s—not to have a husband or kids. "No offense meant."

"None taken." She watched the passing scenery. "So, I'd be a heifer, as opposed to a cow."

"Right."

She slapped her knee, laughing. "Gotcha!"

He startled. "What?"

"You seriously believed I didn't know what a heifer was?"

Uncertain about her, he gave a sheepish shrug. "Oops. Sorry."

"I came across it in a Garfield comic," Jacqui googled her eyes at him, "at *six years old.* I did have to look up swamp donkey when I heard you mention that, though. At first, I was a bit shocked that sleazy women roamed the countryside," she shot him a sly glance, "but then I figured you were referring to the second meaning, moose. Never heard them called that before."

He was relieved to find she had a sense of humour.

“So, the point of this drive was to educate me on the local flora and fauna?” she asked.

“Not entirely.” He pointed ahead to the right. “We're almost there.” He pulled to a stop on the side of the road next to a field noticeably different from the previous ones then swung his arm wide to take in the piece of land with its thinner, sparser, less even crop.

“See how it's not as deep green or as tall as the other crops, and way weedier? That's organic wheat, right there.” He gazed at it for a few moments then at Jacqui. “That's why organics cost more in the grocery store. With your tomatoes or other vegetables, they're usually smaller and not as attractive. And with grain, there's less yield per acre, it's more labor-intensive because there's more cleaning of the seed to be done after harvest, and there are additional costs due to more regulation and inspection.”

“But surely that's balanced by the cost-saving of not using chemicals.”

“You’d think so,” C.H. said, nodding. “But don't make the mistake of thinking organic farmers aren't using weed and pest control substances or techniques. Some of what they use is even more expensive than what the rest of us use because it's specialty stuff that has to pass through a lot of bureaucratic approval. It’s a tough way to try to make a living.”

“And I suppose if everybody farmed this way, the world would starve?”

C.H. frowned at the irony in her tone. “Well, actually, yeah. Organics only account for about two percent of all food production.” He paused, searching her face. “Something social media doesn't tell people is what the miracle of modern agriculture really means for the world's population. My father-in-law could tell you about how grain production levels they only dreamed of in the early 80s have been far surpassed now. They have to be, to meet humanity's growing demand. World hunger is dropping all the time.”

"That's not what I've heard."

"Might depend on who you listen to. United Nations stats say world hunger has dropped from the 90s when one in five people were malnourished. Now it's about one in nine. Still too many." The thought of starvation always bothered him. "But world hunger isn't as much about food shortages as it is about war and bad governments." His phone interrupted with a jazz tune ring. "Sorry, I need to take this call."

His mother-in-law was on the line. He pulled the phone from his ear slightly at the sound of her loud voice. She told him she and Dad would not be home tonight, after all, which left him without a place for Lewis to stay tomorrow while he was with Roslyn. C.H. let out a slow exhale.

Lewis must have heard his Grandma. He leaned his chin on his dad's shoulder. "I can stay with Miss Jacqui." He settled back in his seat with a satisfied air.

C.H. grimaced and rubbed the back of his neck, avoiding Jacqui's eyes.

"He can, you know," she offered. "I'm not working tomorrow, except around the house. Although it'll be kind of boring."

Her suggestion surprised him, seeming out of character for the independent, self-sufficient woman he took her for. "Look," C.H. said in a low tone, "you don't have to do this. I can probably find someone..."

Jacqui glanced back at Lewis. "No, really. I don't mind."

"Well, if you're sure, that'd be great." C.H. shifted in his seat, then put the truck in gear. "I would take him with me, but my wife," he lowered his voice even further, "will be having a procedure tomorrow that'll be painful. Lewis can't handle that."

CHAPTER 13

The weather turned chilly suddenly. Frost on the pumpkin, Jacqui had heard someone say in the lumber store the other day. She pulled on a thick hoodie, stepped into her floppy old runners, grabbed work gloves and tramped outdoors to rake leaves.

In the flowerbed, a lone desiccated orange lily clung to its stem, as well as a few roses still in bloom on Aunt Priscilla's rosebushes, pale and crepey like the old lady's skin might have been. But most of the trees' leaves had already fallen, burying the low-growing plants in the flowerbeds, and covering the grass in yellow. Why had they dropped this early? In Hamilton right about now, the brilliant scarlet sumac and crimson maples would be lighting the escarpment afire. Orange and bronze and golden trees would mingle their colours, too, and the show would last for weeks. Here, yellow and brown were all there seemed to be. A week, and then gone. So much for Jacqui's favourite season.

The exception in her yard was a small shrub anchoring one end of the front flowerbed. Burning bush, Francie had called it. It still held its brilliant foliage, and when it caught the sun, it truly flamed. But not today. The stubborn sun sulked behind a sky of steel gray.

She wanted to get a head start on raking before Lewis arrived. It shouldn't take too long; she had indoor plans for the afternoon. Starting close to the house, she heaped up piles of poplar leaves, shimmering gold under a momentary shaft of sun like a pirate's doubloons. *If only each of these were a loonie, this small pile in one-dollar coins would be worth a fortune.* Ha! She hadn't indulged in that childhood fantasy in forever. There'd been no need, with Geoff's big realty commissions and her own growing salary. She released a bitter grunt, letting her anger fuel even harder strokes of the rake.

Soon a throbbing ache from her upper arms clamoured for her to stop. It usually pleased her to push through muscle fatigue but glancing around the yard at all that remained to be raked was discouraging. She stopped to lean on the wooden handle. The heaps she'd made would need to be bagged lest one of these prairie winds suddenly whip up and undo all her work. But why bag and discard them? A better plan would be to compost them.

More than anything, she needed another pair of hands.

C.H.'s truck pulled up her driveway. *Hm, Lewis seems capable enough.* He'd helped in the past.

Jacqui approached the driver's window. Lewis's eyes were set ahead, while he muttered his stream of consciousness.

"I know you said Lewis doesn't toil or spin," she said to C.H., "but do you think he'd like to make some cash raking leaves with me? I'm about fed up with this. He could name his price."

This brought a chuckle. "Considering Lewis' concept of money, you could either get by with paying him slave wages, or you might have to sell a kidney to afford him."

"So, what would be more meaningful to him than money?"

"Ha! Food, a new nature documentary, dinosaur books, a ride on the quad, almost about anything but money."

"I could probably handle that. But do you think he could do the work?"

"For a while. I can't guarantee how long."

"Good enough. Even if it's only for an hour, I could use the help." Jacqui paused, realizing something. "And I wouldn't mind the company."

"That'd be good 'cause I'll be at the hospital most of today. I should warn you though—he's in his talkative phase."

"All right then. Take as long as you need. He and I will be fine."

Watching Lewis at work was a study in deductive reasoning. There had to be some explanation for why he started raking from the edge of the driveway, made a small pile, then raked the next sections into heaps in an oblique angle from the first. Gradually, Jacqui caught on to the pattern. He was clearing a trail diagonally to the far corner of the lawn. She followed his lead, raking a path parallel to his.

The kid talked without stopping for breath, it seemed, and Jacqui gradually understood no response was required from her. Excerpts from the boy's monologue floated across the still, chill air. "What killed them then? If the dinosaurs were all over the earth, it couldn't have been just a meteorite. That would only be in one spot. But there are dino skeletons in China and England and Alberta." Lewis leaned on his rake cocking his head as though listening for the earth to give up its ancient secrets. So rapt was his expression, Jacqui half-expected it to respond.

Meanwhile the distance between them was widening. "I'm getting ahead of you, buddy."

Lewis absently put his rake to work again. "Were they too stupid to survive? T. Rex had such useless arms. And brachiosaurus with his brain too small. Too slow and too big to escape from predators." He reached the trees, circled past Jacqui who was nearly to the end of her section and started working his way back on the next parallel strip of grass.

"Hey Lewis, why don't we get rid of the piles we've already made before the wind takes them?"

But Lewis was cogitating on the problems of extinction, his arms moving more and more slowly. Jacqui swiftly stuffed the leaves into her wheelbarrow, carting them to a pile in the far trees that screened the yard from the pond.

When she returned, Lewis was still absorbed in his thoughts. "And why have they just recently found a dino skeleton with skin still on? That should have rotted away pretty quick. The article Dad read said the dinosaur was likely swept away by water. But fish that die don't keep their skin on. They fall all to pieces. It must have been squeezed under a lot of pressure. Like maybe a huge flood of a lot of water."

She was losing him, his progress slowed by the prehistoric puzzlement. Jacqui watched him come to a halt, staring into the gray sky again, still murmuring. She had reached the trees and was preparing to start on another swath of lawn when she heard a small sound from the lilacs edging the yard. She froze, listening.

"Lewis," she said in a loud whisper.

He kept up his soliloquy.

"Shh, Lewis. Something's in there." Pointing to the shrubbery, she finally got his attention.

He joined her at the bushes, crouching down to peer beneath them. He reached a long arm into the drifted leaves, the low branches bunching the sleeve of his jacket. When he pulled out his hand, he was grasping a handful of leaves... and something else.

"Aaa! It moved!" He dropped the clump to the ground.

"Get away from it!" Jacqui pushed Lewis behind her, holding her rake tines in front of her like a shield. An ineffectual shield, she realized, if this turned out to be some rabid beast. But the clump had gone still, with only a small patch of tawny fur peeking from under the leaves. She prodded at it gingerly with her rake. No sign of life, but leaves fell away to uncover the form of a small animal. A groundhog? A weasel?

Dropping his rake, Lewis strained forward to inspect it.

"Watch out!" she warned, but nothing moved when he poked with his gloved hand. "Is it a rat?"

"There are no rats in Alberta."

"What do you mean, no rats? There are rats all over the world."

"Not in Alberta. We have a Rat Patrol."

Jacqui laughed. "Yeah, right."

"We do." Lewis turned a grave face toward her. "Dad read to me about it. The Rat Patrol guys search along the borders, making sure no rats get into Alberta."

Sounds like fantasy. But she wouldn't argue with Lewis. *Something to Google later.*

Venturing closer to the lump, Jacqui knelt and cleared leaves from around the animal. Or two, as it turned out.

"Kittens." Lewis said. "They're dead." He straightened abruptly and backed off in disgust. "Let's go. I don't like dead. I hate dead." His face was contorting, mobile with consternation, before he turned and ran for the house.

Jacqui turned her attention back to the creatures in the grass. One was orange, its glassy, vacant eyes open, the other a pinkish beige with eyes closed. With such large ears, they clearly weren't newborn. But what could have happened to them? She scanned the undergrowth for signs of a mother. Nothing. Pulling off her gloves, she stroked the soft fur of first one, then the other with her finger. They were frigid. Life wants to live, C.H. had said. *But not these, I guess.*

Her head had begun to shift back to the work at hand when something caught her attention. She could have sworn she saw a slight movement of a tiny chest. But it couldn't be. The kittens were already cold. And yet almost imperceptibly, it rose again. No doubt about it. The tawny one was still alive. She scooped it up, tucking it into the front neckline of her jacket, racing past Lewis to the house. She beckoned to him to follow.

Inside, she unzipped, easing the creature into her hands to show Lewis.

He turned away in distaste. "Dead."

"But Lewis, it's not dead. I saw it breathe."

For the first time ever, Lewis met Jacqui's eyes. Abruptly he turned away. "We should get the fire going."

Jacqui stared at him. "You're right. But you'll have to do it. I'm going to try to keep this little guy warm inside my shirt." Jacqui had read about skin-to-skin contact for newborns. Surely that would be good for a kitten too, wouldn't it? She slid the creature against her belly, its cool fur raising goosebumps on her flesh. Not just cool, it pressed a deep cold, like a frozen sausage, against her body. For a moment she doubted the wisdom of bringing something near death into the house where Lewis would be forced to confront it.

Lewis, however, was at the wood heater, intent on building a tepee of kindling and crumpling newspaper inside it. Then he turned to hand her the matchbox. "I can't play with matches," he said, shaking his head vigorously and backing away.

Okay. There must be a story behind that. Jacqui struck a match and watched it eat away at the curling paper. "Let's keep feeding it more wood. We need it nice and hot for the kitten." The cold lump in her shirt pressing against her midriff, however, felt as cold as it had at the first. She moved it to a warmer patch of skin, cringing again. She began to stroke the small being under her shirt, hoping massage might stimulate its heart. Lewis's jaw under the thin skin of his cheek was working rhythmically, but he cast his eyes away from her. She thought of his earlier outburst.

Of course he hated "dead." His mother was dying. Had he heard talk about it from C.H.? Or neighbours? Or nurses? She knew how that could be. She'd heard snatches of such fearsome talk when her baby brother lay limp and weak in his incubator.

All at once, she felt an urgency to keep the creature alive. She had to. Lewis needed to see life. And hope. *Life wants to live!* Under her breath, she chanted the words to the wee thing, willing it to come alive. She moved closer to the heater, adding thicker lengths of wood. Leaving its front door open, she could feel its heat searing her cheeks. Lewis had retreated to an armchair and resumed muttering to himself. She couldn't hear whether he was still going on about dinosaurs or had switched topics.

She palpated the limp form against her ribs. Limp, not stiff. Her heart leaped in hope. Was it not quite as cool as it had been? She shifted it to warmer skin. Undoing two buttons of her shirt to hold her hand against the kitten, she felt for vitals. The furry chest was expanding.

She crooked a finger at Lewis. “He's alive! Come here and see.”

The boy held back, but Jacqui reached for his hand. He pulled it away yet moved toward her. Jacqui withdrew the kitty, laying it across her thigh. On his knees, Lewis stared in wonder. Again, he was working his jaw, but this time, she suspected, to swallow the knot in his throat.

He turned brimming eyes directly to hers. “You did it! You brought it back to life. Thank you.”

A matching lump swelled Jacqui's throat, too. The kitten’s eyelids fluttered slightly. Reviving it was the best deed she had ever done. It was a good work. A great work.

CHAPTER 14

The ring of the bell above the library's front door barely registered in Jacqui's brain as she scanned the overdues list on the screen in front of her. This was only her third month at work here and already she could see patterns. By the end of the first month, Jacqui knew the patrons who favoured Amish romance, who was on the wait list for the newest James Patterson thriller and the seven regulars who borrowed large print books. By the end of the second month, she knew the names of those who homeschooled, the guy who checked out books on necromancy, and those who were chronically on the overdue list. She couldn't help it. That's how her mind worked.

These laggards with overdues should be warned. After all, how hard was it to toddle over to the library and return your books on time? But Sheri didn't want her nicey-nice persona sullied by threatening late charges.

"We're here for people," she'd insisted when Jacqui had suggested making routine calls. "People are more important than a few books."

But those "few books" represented lost revenue, lost property and therefore wasted public funds. And for Jacqui, what rankled most was the lack of consideration for others who may wish to borrow the books. It simply wasn't right.

Since Sheri had foisted attendance at library board meetings onto Jacqui, she'd decided she would bring the matter up with its members. She was keeping a tally of the fines so she could show just how much money enforcement of overdues could bring in. People needed to be held accountable. Besides, she found it satisfying to mark books *Lost* and watch the patron's charges rack up. Back in Hamilton, the biggest single fine had been nearly a thousand dollars, but, of course, the guilty individual had never paid up. The person likely opened a new account under a different name at another branch. *How irritating.*

Jacqui was startled by the gravelly voice of someone standing before her desk.

"Weird."

Her gaze jerked upward into the face of the man who had spoken. *Another redneck, trying to be smart?* But the man's face was mild, his flushed cheeks girlish in contrast to the four coarse black hairs growing on the broad surface of his bulbous nose. *Honestly, would it kill you to rid the world of those four bristles? Do it for yourself. Do it for us all.*

"Double-u, double-e, r, d."

It took Jacqui another moment before she realized he was spelling his surname. How annoying that nobody around here presented their library card. Everyone expected she had nothing better to do than search their name, or worse, expected her to know them by sight. She typed in the name.

Weerd, Cornelius. While she typed, she scrutinized him from the corner of her eye. Wispy white hair topped a weathered face and scrawny neck ringed by a dotted navy bowtie that floated aimlessly above a collarless, formerly white T-shirt. Covering most of the shirt was a set of absurd denim overalls. Weird was closer to the truth, after all. She caught sight of the book he was returning. His hand covered the title, but the spine showed the writer was Noam Chomsky. The name of the prominent socialist author twigged something in her mind. Yesterday, Sheri had described a local character, Neil somebody, known for writing letters of advice to the world's heads of state. This must be that guy.

"If you could, dear, I'd like you to order these books." He handed her a grease-smudged list of hand-written titles. *The Case for Socialism* by Alan Maass. Two books by Chomsky, followed by Saul Alinsky's *Rules for Radicals*. The last on the list was a household name to Jacqui, as often as she'd heard Pops and his union mates quote from it over the years. She instantly felt at home with this Weerd fellow, having grown up around guys like him.

"I'll see what I can do." Jacqui took the scrap of paper from him by its cleanest corner and laid it aside.

Weerd hesitated then leaned across the desk toward her. "I'd like to know today if they're available. If not, I'll have to find a few others for something to read this week." His breath was funky with garlic, a haze which Jacqui, seated below where he stood, was unable to escape. "You don't know me yet, but you'll find I'm a vivacious reader."

As much to cover her laugh at his malapropism as to shield her face from the powerful smell, Jacqui coughed into her sleeve then began a search for the titles.

"And something else, dear."

"Mm-hm?" She glanced up without meeting his eyes, doing her best to banish the boisterous mental pictures that leapt to mind of what vivacious reading might entail.

"I wonder if you could perhaps help me learn how to use the email?" He clasped and unclasped his work-gnarled hands. "If you have time, that is. I thought it would save on postage for my correspondence." He leaned even closer and added with a confidential nod, "I write a lot of letters."

Jacqui reluctantly directed Weerd to one of the public computers and signed him in. She walked him through the setup of an account and the basics of sending email. Next, she did what little she could, helping him find email addresses he wanted for top government officials. Unsurprisingly, Russia's presidential contact information was especially elusive, and he was left disappointed on that score. She returned to her desk, shooting an amused glance at Sheri who was shelving books near the back of the stacks. Sheri rolled her eyes knowingly.

When Weerd finally rose and made his way to the exit, he turned briefly, nodding his thanks in Jacqui's direction.

On impulse, she raised her fist as she'd learned to do as a child. "Comrades, come rally!" she said. "Workers of the world, unite!"

The man brightened in recognition of the first line from the chorus of Communism's anthem, *The Internationale.* But the pleasant expression on his face gradually dissolved as his mouth fell open and he took a step back. His shoulders slumped as he buttoned his parka and pushed the door open to shuffle out into the late October cold.

Sheri's clipping heels headed Jacqui's way, followed by the startling hiss of her voice. "How could you?"

Jacqui's heart began to pound.

The irate woman planted herself close to Jacqui's chair, fists quivering on her bountiful hips. "Don't you ever speak to a person in my library the way you just spoke to Neil. We never treat our seniors with contempt here. Never!"

"Look, I didn't mean—"

"Never! Every patron is to be treated with dignity." A deep rose flush crept up Sheri's fleshy throat.

"But you were the one who told me about this guy and his crazy letters—"

Indignation snapped in Sheri's dark brown eyes, making Jacqui cringe "We may be simple country folks around here, and we may have our unique characters, but everybody has their quirks. We never disrespect them!" She turned on one spike heel and flounced to her desk, making a point of angling her chair away from Jacqui.

Jacqui clenched her teeth, feeling her own face heat up. *How many times have I listened right here in this library while you laughed with your friends about the faults and foibles of any number of the locals?* But Jacqui bit back the retort. She needed this job. *Besides, anybody who tangles with international leaders should be able to take a bit of good-natured ribbing.* And the teasing she'd dished out wasn't anything she wouldn't have done to her father's comrades. It had always gotten a laugh from them.

All afternoon Jacqui left the front desk to Sheri while she herself read shelves for alphabetic and numerical order. She fumed over the older woman's hypocrisy. *Let her play Miss Congeniality, pretending to be all community minded. All those schmaltzy thank you cards she has tacked to her computer, raving about how "warm and caring" she is. These poor folks have no idea that the minute they leave the front door, Sheri's gossiping about them to someone else behind their backs.*

Mentally, Jacqui added fuel to her inner fire by noting the woman's other inadequacies–the many mis-shelved books she found as she worked and the book spine labels that were so faded and tiny they were almost unreadable.

For someone so incompetent, this chick sure gets on her high horse in a hurry.

What rankled most was Jacqui's helplessness to prove she knew how to work with the public. She thought of the Hamilton library patron services awards she'd received three years running. Where were those plaques, anyway? Likely tossed in the trash like so much dead weight, due to her ferocious downsizing for the sake of the limited space in her car. Or maybe they were still in storage?

What difference does it make? Even if I could find them, what am I going to do—wave them in front of Sheri's face as an I-told-you-so?

CHAPTER 15

Three days later, Jacqui arrived at the library to find the lights on and the door unlocked. When she entered and turned toward her desk, she faced Sheri whose round fist was plunged into her amply padded hip.

"Did you hear the news?" Her flashing eyes insinuated something.

Jacqui wavered, mystified about what she might have done wrong. Mentally, she ticked off the steps in the library closing routine—tidy up, clear the shelving cart, shut down computers, turn off lights, flip the *Open* sign to *Closed*, set the alarm, lock both back and front doors. She'd done it all. Was the woman still angry about Jacqui's ill-advised quip to the local Communist the other day? But Sheri had already torn a piece off Jacqui's hide at the time, and by the end of that day, everything had seemed tickety-boo. So, what was this now?

"No," Jacqui said, peeling off her gloves and hanging up her coat. "What's up?"

Sheri's eyes narrowed further as she pointed her black patent pump a step closer to Jacqui's desk. "Neil Weerd was found yesterday, hanged to death." She paused for effect, leaning forward slightly, her eyes wide. "Jay and Sandy Duncan live across the road from his place, but they hadn't heard from him in a while, so they went over to check. Found him in his barn, hanging by a leather belt from a rafter." Another dramatic pause, as Sheri's eyes snapped and crackled.

She's blaming me! Jacqui realized in consternation. *Evidently, I'm to feel the full weight of guilt for this.*

"It was too late to save him." By now the familiar flush had risen to flood Sheri's face, leaving white patches only around her eyes. Her arms hung stiff and straight at her sides, hands still fisted. "You were mean to him!"

How could this possibly be my fault? Friday was the first time Jacqui had ever met the guy. How could a mere teasing comment be to blame for a man taking his own life? There had to have been a preexisting condition. In fact, the habit of regularly writing personal letters to worldwide heads of state was likely documented in the *Diagnostic and Statistical Manual of Mental Disorders*. Delusions of grandeur or something. It had nothing to do with her. Jacqui opened and closed her mouth a couple of times, but nothing came out.

"I'm sorry to hear this," she finally managed to murmur. Catching sight of someone's head bobbing up the steps outside the door, she added, "We've got to open up. I'll get us going." She fired up her computer, conscious of the dramatic flouncing of Sheri's black chiffon dress as she clip-clopped to the front to turn over the sign. Presumably, the black garb was meant as an indication of mourning. But the sexy cut of it, and the fishnet hose and heels seemed more apropos for a cocktail party.

The bell above the door chimed with the arrival of a woman in a melon-coloured print dress and a small black cap covering the back of her hair. By now, Jacqui recognized the distinctive dress of a Mennonite woman. She entered holding the hand of a small Asian girl with thick shiny braids and a matching print dress.

Before the woman had taken two steps inside, Sheri inclined toward her in a confidential tone. "Did you hear the news, Sarah? Neil Weerd has hanged himself." Jacqui watched Sarah's forehead wrinkle in sympathy. At the same time, the mother placed her hands gently over her child's ears.

Sheri's got all the subtlety of a foghorn.

Sarah whispered to the child, pointing her in the direction of the children's area at the rear of the library. Oblivious to the effect of her grim story, Sheri went on giving the gruesome details of the death in a voice of horrified outrage. And in case Jacqui hadn't caught it the first time, Sheri shot a glance her way while she spoke. Jacqui kept her head down, focusing on her computer and printing off the day's list of requests from other libraries.

“I never knew him very well,” Sarah asked. “Did he have a family?”

“Oh yes,” Sheri warmed to her role as news giver. “His wife left him years ago and went back overseas somewhere with their two daughters when they were quite young. I don't think they ever came out again to visit. They've been notified though, and hopefully they'll be able to come to make the necessary arrangements. I don't think there's much of an estate. Neil only had the one quarter he rented out and that dinky little house. And of course, the barn. But who's going to want to buy that place now this has happened?”

Sarah's eyes strayed to where her child played. “I'll let the ladies of our congregation know. We can put together a lunch as soon as we find out when the funeral is.”

Sheri smiled for the first time that morning. “Now that's always something to look forward to. You Mennonite ladies do know how to bake.”

Jacqui strolled the stacks, filling her arms with requested books. In the children's corner, Sarah and her daughter snuggled close, the glossy black and blonde heads bent together over a book. How annoying that Sheri's tragic news had intruded into such a picture of tenderness. Lingering nearby, Jacqui felt an unfamiliar pang of sentiment at the sight. Her own mother had never once read to her like that. Was it the devotion in the protective arm of the mother around the child that touched Jacqui, or the inherent trust in the spellbound little one? Perhaps it was the meeting of two races in such harmony. Jacqui shook herself alert and pulled another book off the shelf. The young woman read with warmth and dramatic flair, her wide-eyed child clearly smitten. *We should hire her for Read 'n Rhyme.*

Meanwhile, Sheri circulated throughout the building all morning like the Angel of Death, spreading news of the suicide to anyone who came through the door. Every time, she would hustle them over to the public computer desks where she conferred in low tones, occasionally gleaning new tidbits of information and invariably casting accusing glances Jacqui's way.

No doubt the story was gaining momentum, embellished with drama at each recounting. *Is she telling everyone I'm a killer?* Was it Jacqui's imagination or were patrons avoiding her desk when checking out their books? Sheri certainly seemed more than eager to take over the duty today.

By the time Sarah and her child arrived at the front, arms laden with picture books, Sheri had disappeared to the back, perhaps for one of her frequent coffee breaks. Jacqui hurried to serve Sarah, hoping somehow to salvage her tattered reputation. Not that it mattered, she didn't expect to be in the vicinity very long. *But still, it stings to be labelled the cruel cause of a local tragedy.*

"Anything else?" she asked the young woman, taking in the clean lines of her scrubbed face with its wide blue eyes and generous, smile-ready mouth. But rather than a smile, Sarah's mouth was pleated in worry, her pale eyebrows drawn together. From her purse, she pulled a scrap of paper and handed it to Jacqui.

"I read an article about international adoption in a magazine and they mentioned this book." She pointed to the carefully copied title and author then met Jacqui's eyes with anguished eyes. "I tried searching the non-fiction section here but couldn't find much of anything. Could you check for me and see if you have it?"

Jacqui found nothing in the regional libraries, but eventually located the title in a city university library collection.

"Okay, that's ordered for you. Should be in by the end of next week." She smiled up at the woman, who returned a bleak smile with her nod of thanks. After they left, Jacqui read the book description, curious about the cause of Sarah's altered tone. The author, herself a mother of an adopted Chinese daughter, had discovered that not all children in Chinese orphanages were voluntarily offered for adoption. Some of those children had birth parents who desperately wanted to keep them but, because of China's previous one-child government policy, they were coerced into giving them up. Jacqui stared after the brightly dressed woman and girl as they climbed into a minivan outside the library. What must it be like to fear that the child you have nurtured and grown to love is pined for and grieved by some other bereft mother on the other side of the world?

Should I cancel the request and simply tell Sarah the book was unavailable? But that would interfere with the woman's freedom of information. Meddling like that would cut to the core of Jacqui's beliefs. She could never do that. Still, something about wanting to preserve the bond between this mother and daughter battled against her better judgment. Jacqui had always been a good girl, a rule-follower, but was following the rules always right?

I am a good person, aren't I?

The thunder of condemnation thrummed in her head. Asking the question was laughable, given Sheri's current opinion of her.

CHAPTER 16

The minute Lewis came through Jacqui's door, he let his jacket slide to the floor and launched into a long dissertation on what had happened to the tractor loader the day before. Jacqui picked up the coat and hung it on a porch hook, waving C.H. off to drive to another grim day with Roslyn. She hurried to catch up with Lewis who had already reached the living room, the wisps of his monologue trailing behind him.

"I told them it wouldn't work. But no, they send out some first-year apprentice barely dry behind the ears and wouldn't you know it, he uses the wrong part. So, now we've got this mess with the loader arm buried up to the yin yang under a ton of compressed hay and no way can I get through on the help line. I really don't need this kind of stress."

Jacqui contemplated Lewis's thin face, at a loss for a response. "*You* were trying to contact the help line?"

But Lewis wasn't waiting for a response. He stared at a point above Jacqui's left shoulder, shifting conversational gears.

"My books were all uneven. I had to spend hours pulling them off the shelf and sorting them out. Tallest on the left, then the set of Johnny Tractor books, then the junior encyclopedia, then the animal books—whale sharks first, then sperm whale, beluga, narwhal. Next, elephants, bison, rhinos..."

Ah, I get it. The help line bit must be something C.H. was dealing with today, poor guy. And the animal books are sorted according to the animal's size. Makes perfect sense. Why didn't Dewey think of that? She giggled, picturing for a moment her library manager, Gwen presenting the new cataloging system and the groans of the staff as they contemplated the monumental task of implementing it.

"...and all the way down to kangaroo mouse. I don't have any animals between kiwi and kangaroo mouse." He cast a fleeting frown in Jacqui's direction then sat on the couch, pulling his backpack onto the seat beside him. Unzipping it, he withdrew a laptop computer and charger, along with several DVDs.

"Where's the kitten?" he asked without looking up. "You should call it Gandalf. He came back to life."

"Sure, we could call him Gandalf. He sleeps on my bed at night. I think he's still there. Want to see?"

But Lewis had moved on. "Where can I plug this in? I can use the battery, but I don't want to run it down. Why run down the battery in a place that has electricity? So, I can plug it in while I'm here." He held out the wall-plug end of the cord expectantly.

"I'll get you an extension cord." Jacqui rushed to the porch and back, caught up by the urgency of Lewis's agenda.

All five of Lewis's movies were nature documentaries. He fingered each one, examining the cover and the spine, before choosing BBC's *Life*. He squared the remaining four on the corner of the coffee table and placed the laptop to their left, leaving a hand's-breadth space between. This, as it turned out, was precisely enough space for the DVD tray when it emerged.

He's done this before.

Lewis loaded the disc and was enthralled from the opening strains of theme music. Feeling superfluous, Jacqui retreated to the kitchen. Her phone tootled just then with a message from Bree. Her girls had been home from university for fall reading week but had now left to spend the final day with their dad.

"I'm sure that will be a resounding success. Will Lonzo manage to pry himself away from his gaming long enough to recognize his own daughters? But the girls keep on trying. And I get to mop up the tears after the fact. Oh, well. They're big girls now. They'll figure it out.

"Did I tell you Gwen has been offered and has accepted management of the library in Halifax? Big step up for her. I put in my application for the manager position here, but there are others more qualified, as you know. Likely Dale will get it. And in the interest of full disclosure, you should know that Geoff and Dale are getting married. The invitation is on the staff bulletin board, so I guess we're all invited. Judging by all the wedding planning chatter around here, it seems like it'll be a big do. I won't go, if you don't want me to. On principle, I mean. Just let me know."

Married! The news was staggering. A scene from the past flashed on the screen of her mind, as clear as the day it occurred.

Geoff and Jacqui sitting in a tree

K-I-S-S-I-N-G

First comes love, then comes marriage...

Only they'd been sitting in a boat at their friends' cottage on Lake Algonquin, not up in a tree. There had been love, and kissing, and what she'd told herself, ever since, was the equivalent of marriage. Although they'd never referred to each other as husband or wife. By then, they had been together for five years. Not for the first time, Jacqui had tiptoed around the subject of commitment, shy of uttering the M-word. Geoff had always skirted the issue, scoffing at the insecurities of those who needed a piece of paper and a big expensive party to prove their love. Not only that, he argued, but who really thought marriage made any difference to the outcome of a relationship? From what either of them had seen, it worked the opposite way, killing love instead. And given what Jacqui had witnessed between both sets of their parents, and in their friends' marriages, she could hardly disagree.

On that day, during the drive up to the cottage Jacqui had ventured the topic outright. The silence that followed had made the trip tense and Jacqui vowed she wouldn't bring it up again.

But later that summer, on a warm afternoon, Geoff had killed the boat's motor, letting the lake lap against the hull to gently rock them. He leaned forward to grasp her hands in both of his. She had to scoot forward on the seat and separate her legs inelegantly to make way for the lifejacket. But her pulse raced as he held her hands tightly and gazed deep into her eyes.

"Jacqui, I love you, and I declare, by the earth and the sky and the water all around us, that you are the one for me." And he flashed her his dazzling smile.

Then Jacqui had swallowed the lump in her throat and the shame of her earlier miff at his lack of response on the last trip up. This surprise made up for it a thousand-fold. With a rapturous flush of affection, she responded, "I love you, Geoff. And by the earth and the sky and the water all around us, I promise to love you always."

Between kisses, Geoff had murmured, "There now, J-girl, what more could you ask?" Kiss, kiss. Then he pulled out a velvet box with a ring as dazzling as his smile. "Now we're married. Will that do?" And she was content with that.

Jacqui reread Bree's message. When it had been Jacqui with Geoff, marriage was an unnecessary formality, an archaic, obsolete encumbrance. But now Dale was worthy of a public commitment? And evidently a "big expensive party" too? Tears stung her eyes. Somewhere she had read there were only two reasons cohabiting couples got married: either their relationship was in trouble, or they wanted children. Whether that was still true, it had confirmed to her at the time that their relationship needed no formalizing.

But at forty-four, and with his avowed aversion to both pets and kids—the odious ruin of houses—could Geoff now want children?

Another scene rolled through her mind, this one more recent.

Pops was over for Jacqui's thirty-fifth birthday, along with a few of their friends, Bree and Dale among them. *Wait! Dale was there, even back then?* But yes, Jacqui's mind scanned the circle of faces, and Dale was definitely at the table. She tried to replay the banter, but her memory remained silent as an old movie.

Geoff's culinary masterpiece, a "tur-duck-hen" had come out perfect, the poultry flavours of the three birds mingling beautifully, enhanced by the many unique side dishes Jacqui had slaved over. Everyone had indulged aplenty, the wine flowing freely, and now each guest sat back lazily waiting for dessert. Geoff was plating wedges of mocha truffle cheesecake with a drizzle of raspberry sherry sauce when Pops clapped his hands together with a brisk rub.

"So, when can I expect a grandchild?"

A suffocating embarrassment filled the room like a blast of steam from the roasting pan.

Jacqui's eyes locked on Geoff's. Unfazed, he dribbled the last plate of dessert with an artful flourish of rich red sauce and handed it to Pops.

"There won't be any grandchildren, Pops. Jacqui and I have discussed it and decided it's irresponsible to bring a kid into a world so violent, so crowded and so uncertain." With a calm smile, he passed cheesecake to each guest at the table.

He was right, they had discussed it. For exactly the reasons Geoff expressed, and for others besides, they'd both agreed no children. Jacqui had her own fears about childbearing. How could she ever forget what had happened to her mother following the death of

Jacqui's baby brother? She had been seven when she was brought to the hospital to see him, a tiny mite whose features were somehow misaligned. She now understood he'd had a rare genetic condition "incompatible with life," as her subsequent online research had explained. The ominous word "genetic" gave Jacqui sincere misgivings about her own ability to have a healthy child. Then after the baby died, her mother's depression had gradually spiralled downward into alcoholism, promiscuity and divorce, a damning prediction of Jacqui's ability to cope with a traumatic loss. And besides, she and Geoff had always agreed—homes with children inevitably had sticky doorknobs.

But that day around her birthday feast, when she turned her smile on Pops, she was unprepared for the drastic alteration in him. The rare-enough joviality on his face from earlier now sagged into gray dejection. His shoulders and spine curled as though he'd been gut-punched and sudden tears glistened in his eyes. With a shaky hand, he reached for his wine glass and put it to his lips like a child with a pacifier.

Flustered at her father's unexpected reaction, Jacqui tried to catch Geoff's eye. But he had made his way to the far end of the table and was sharing a joke with one of his realtor friends, seemingly unaware of the blow their decision had delivered to Pops.

Well, really, Pops, what did you expect? I'm thirty-five after all—too old to have kids, anyway. And your own parenting track record was hardly stellar. My childhood of loneliness and chaos and confusion isn't exactly something to emulate. And having to be responsible for Mom was way beyond my years. What makes you think I'd be in a rush to follow that dismal example? Besides, it's nobody's business but our own.

Still, the aching disappointment on Pops' face haunted her. He had never brought it up again, but Jacqui had caught him one afternoon wistfully watching the schoolchildren tripping down the sidewalk past his house.

Swiping a weary hand across her face, Jacqui clicked off her phone. No, it was highly unlikely that Geoff would want children at this late stage of life. Which only left Jacqui with an even deeper cut of rejection. What made Dale more worthy of a public commitment than she had been?

CHAPTER 17

Jacqui made sure the row of books with their bold new spine labels was precisely aligned down the long shelf. She recalled the first time she experienced the piquant joy of bringing order to chaos—after the death of her brother but before her parents' divorce. Pops had been working the night shift, and Mom was out somewhere.

Where? Where did she go leaving a seven year old alone evening after evening? But really, Jacqui knew, eventually piecing the truth together as she got older. Pops must have known it, too.

On this particular evening, as usual, Jacqui had cried when her father left for work, then dried her tears and sat slumped on the ratty couch watching TV. But nothing good was on and she took the bold step of switching it off entirely. The unaccustomed quiet at first threatened, then grew tranquil. It was so peaceful, in fact, that it accentuated the tumult of her surroundings. She took in the darkened room, lit only by a dingy floor lamp. Chairs and tables threw long shadows with their heaps of papers, magazines, clothing, even food items. The floor was strewn similarly. The house was oppressively dark, stupendously ugly, and utterly overwhelming. Tears blurred her eyes and she kicked peevishly at the edge of the coffee table where she had stretched out her feet. A bevy of papers drifted off it. Jacqui stared at them as they settled on the one clear section of the stuff-scattered floor.

An intense distress immediately seized her. She'd made the mess worse.

Agitated, she gathered and straightened the pages, replacing them on the coffee table. Another page on the other end of the table caught her eye. She set it on the first stack. Then she sorted the newspapers and magazines into neat piles. The surface of the table beneath was laden with dust and crumbs. She found a cloth and wiped it, then emptied the overflowing ashtray. Around the room, one action led to another. She placed similar items together, edges aligned. Boxes too heavy to lift she attempted to straighten. Gradually, Jacqui made a discovery. The more order she brought to the room, the more she found her pain and loneliness diminishing, a narcotic more potent than anything that lured her mother away night after night. That evening she went to bed tired but feeling for the first time some control over her small and insignificant life. The work of a few hours became the habit of a lifetime. With her parents, she earned a reputation as a cleaner-upper, and whenever anything was missing, she was accountable. Strangely, even that level of responsibility elevated her in her own eyes and maybe theirs too.

The tinkle of the bell above the library entrance jerked her to the present. The spine label project was only a third complete, but the progress was satisfying. Jacqui returned to the front desk.

Two women in matching plaid jackets entered. The stocky, gray-haired woman accompanied by a heavily made-up girl began wandering the stacks. Minutes later, another woman entered, this one with a large briefcase in tow.

"Over here, Tannis," the older woman called out in a gruff voice.

"Oh, hey, Linda," Tannis answered, picking up the young girl's left hand to examine her ring. "Congratulations, Sierra. It's gorgeous!" She smiled eagerly then patted her briefcase. "I brought a bunch of samples we can take a look at."

Jacqui rose to shift chairs to a small table in anticipation of the women's need for a meeting place.

"Thanks." Tannis nodded, spreading out what appeared to be a variety of wedding invitations. The older woman and girl joined her, and Jacqui returned to her desk. Their conversation rang clear in the small building, informing her of an upcoming wedding.

"I hope this time she actually goes through with it," Linda said, doubt tingeing her words.

"Mom!" Sierra rolled her eyes and swatted her mother's arm.

"Last time she was engaged," Linda continued, "she made it all the way to three weeks before the wedding. The invitations had all been sent and then the jerk goes and breaks it off. After she'd gone and boughten her dress, and the altercations were already done."

Jacqui clapped a hand to her mouth to conceal a smirk. *If she's getting married, the altercations are just beginning!*

Tannis, apparently oblivious to the gaffe, murmured her condolences, then tried to brighten the mood with offers of rustic or formal invitations.

Jacqui spent the morning listening in on the wedding plans, inwardly mocking their earnest attention to the most insignificant of details and wondering what clue Sierra might have about the heartbreak in store for her. Another emotion lurked below the surface that Jacqui struggled to suppress. It went against her every modern, feminist principle, but she resented this young girl being found worthy of a wedding when Jacqui had not been.

Don't be ridiculous, she chided herself. Yet what prickled wasn't only the overheard conversation. After yesterday's news that Geoff was getting married, it seemed every book she came across today emphasized her unmarried state. *The Zookeepers Wife. The Time Traveler's Wife. The Perfect Wife.* The protagonists of these novels were all wives. She forced herself to concentrate on the labelling project, only to come across *The Girl with the Make-Believe Husband.* Jacqui stifled a groan. *That would be me.*

The entrance bell jingled again, this time letting in a pretty young mother with three children. Her long, highlighted curls bounced as she took in the room, glazing over Jacqui, a stranger. A spark of recognition lit up her face when she spotted the three at the table. She pranced over to the women with tiny, mincing steps, as though performing for a crowd. The children tagged behind her.

"Ooh! I heard the great news." Grabbing Sierra's hand, she glanced at the ring. "So sweet! It suits you. Nothing too big to lug around, just cute." She tipped up her own left hand, frowning at her large, flashing diamond in what appeared to Jacqui like humble bragging. "Mine is always snagging on things."

Unbelievable. What is this, the 1950s? Had the women's movement never happened here? Jacqui turned away from the group, focusing her attention on printing another sheet of labels.

But the newcomer's enthusiasm was difficult to zone out. The woman prattled on about her own wedding, advising, comparing. The others' bare toleration showed they were impatient to resume their business.

At last the children's unrest dragged their mother away to the kids' area. Shortly after, immersed in her phone, she tripped back to the front with her kids, who unloaded their books and movies onto the desk. They stared at Jacqui with solemn dark eyes as she waited for their mother's card.

Finally, the young mother raised her eyes to Jacqui. "Oh! Ha! I'm O'Dell Adrian. I never bother with my library card. I thought you were Sheri. She usually looks me up. Where is she?"

Adrian. Wasn't that Aunt Naomi's married name? This woman must be my relative then. Jacqui searched the name and checked out the books without acknowledging the relationship. "All she told me was that she needed the week off," Jacqui said, handing O'Dell her print-out.

"I wanted to ask her when the next kids' craft contest is going to be." The woman batted her ultra-long eyelashes expectantly.

Jacqui did her best to keep a professional expression and tone. "She hasn't mentioned anything to me about a contest. I'm sure it'll be well advertised, though."

"Hmph. C'mon kiddos." O'Dell turned on her heel and hurried her brood out the door.

You're welcome. What a piece of work. Jacqui pitied those kids.

The three women at the table departed soon after, leaving Jacqui alone with two more hours to fill before closing. She set to work on a stack of returns, opening a few books only to be overwhelmed by smells—these four were pungent with a perfume reminiscent of insect repellent, three others reeked like cigar smoke. *For Pete's sake, wash your hands, people.*

Next, she set to work on spine labels again, this time in the large print section. The extensive collection, on closer examination, Jacqui found to be mainly comprised of erotica.

What the—? Erotica, for seniors? Most of the books were by a single author unfamiliar to her, self-published by one Millie Sherona. That usually pointed to a local author, especially given the number of titles by the same name. *It's almost as though someone is writing this stuff specifically for certain local readers.* She carted a shelf-full of the books back to her desk. Her interest piqued, she opened one to search for an author bio only to stumble across a scene of scorching heat.

Whoa! She didn't linger long enough to evaluate the quality of the prose.

Jacqui snapped the book shut. *Must be some racy old folks around here.* Out of curiosity, she checked the book's circulation record for the number of lends. Five. And each of the other titles on her cart revealed a similar number of check-outs. *Probably the same few with an insatiable lascivious appetite.* Millie Sherona didn't show up on any author searches. Yet something about the name sounded familiar. Jacqui felt she should know it.

CHAPTER 18

Jacqui waited inside her porch, having slipped through the door just before Gandalf could follow. A wee kitten like him was not to be trusted out in the big frightening world all by himself. She was extra cautious with her pet because of the memory of the small animal in the talons of a hawk the day after she'd arrived here.

She squinted against the brilliant white world outside. Last night's snow had rounded the outlines of her yard with another thick layer of white. If it were up to her, she'd go nowhere in these conditions, but apparently Albertans thought otherwise. *As if C.H. is an Albertan. He's from farther south than I am but seems to have been here too long to have the sense to cancel in weather like this.*

Lewis's insistence was the only reason she'd agreed to this outing at all. "Miss Jacqui should come see Mom. Miss Jacqui will like Mom and Mom will like Miss Jacqui."

Before long, her neighbour's huge pick-up curved around the driveway, stopping in front of her door. Lewis's be-capped head was visible in the rear seat. Even before C.H. opened the door for her, she could see the boy talking, his jerky hand movements punctuating his words. He was back in his talkative mode again.

"Say good morning, Lewis," his father interrupted him.

"Morning, Miss Jacqui. T-Rex wouldn't win in a fight against triceratops because of triceratops' plated armour. The tyrannosaurus wouldn't be able to get its teeth into it, even though triceratops wouldn't be as quick on its feet as the other dinosaur."

Jacqui met C.H.'s wry glance. "You think T-Rex was nimble on those large hind legs then?" she asked the teen.

"Ha, nimble," came the voice behind her. "Not very nimble, no. But nimbler than Triceratops." Lewis dropped his voice but, in an undertone, continued comparing fierce creatures, with an occasional salient point rising to the surface. Jacqui made a mental note to order in a few library books on dinosaurs for him.

C.H. reached to adjust the fan for floor heat. "I should prepare you for Roz. She isn't like she once was. She's lost a lot of weight, and this last round of radiation has taken a lot out of her..." He took a breath, leading Jacqui to expect him to continue, but instead he fell silent.

"It's all right. I have no expectations because I never knew her when she was well." She loosened the scarf at her throat and fiddled with the zipper of her purse. "I'm not even sure I've seen a photo of her."

"Lewis," C.H. said, as he lifted his chin to be heard above the running commentary behind them. "Show Miss Jacqui your picture of Mom."

Without a pause in discussion, which had moved on to comparative rates of speed in the large cats, Lewis dug in his pocket for his wallet. He swung it open and thrust it ahead for Jacqui to see the photo. In it, a young grinning couple in wedding attire gazed rapturously at each other. The picture disappeared abruptly when Lewis snapped his billfold shut.

"You two were beautiful. I mean, she was beautiful. I mean—" Heat flooded Jacqui's face as she backtracked from her embarrassing comment, then fell into awkward silence.

"She's always beautiful to me."

The brave, simple sadness in the man's voice heightened Jacqui's discomfort. Was the hard lump in her throat only sympathy for him, or was there envy, too? Envy towards any woman who could stir that depth of devotion, a commitment that Jacqui hadn't experienced. Would Geoff have stood by her if she'd been struck down by cancer? He'd always been uncomfortable with illness; "leaving it to the professionals" was the way he'd put it when he'd declined to stay with her in recovery after her surgery a few years back.

At the hospital, Jacqui found more evidence of C.H.'s dedication. While she hung back outside the doorway, uncomfortable and not wanting to intrude, he entered the room with murmured endearments, followed by Lewis. A moment later, C.H. emerged from behind the pale green curtain searching for Jacqui. He beckoned for her to join them.

"Come in and meet my wife, Roz," he said, his eyes on the painfully thin woman forming only a slight bump in the bed. Lewis sat on the opposite side of the bed, holding her hand. C.H. gently took up her other hand as she raised deeply shadowed, trusting eyes to his. With apparent effort, she turned toward Jacqui. Lines multiplied beside her mouth as she smiled, her eyes travelling from Jacqui to C.H. and back again.

"Lewis has told me...about you," Roslyn said in a small voice. "Thank you...for taking care of him." She licked her lips and winced when she swallowed. "For understanding him."

"It's my pleasure." Jacqui's voice came out unexpectedly loud in the hushed room. She lowered it several notches. "I've really enjoyed him. He's an intelligent young man."

Roslyn's smile widened and she nodded slightly then said, "You have beautiful auburn hair."

What could she say to that? No glib "it's a wreck today," no superficial "needs a cut about now." No self-deprecation would do in the presence of this woman whose translucent scalp stretched thinly over every vein and bone of her skull. Yet Roslyn had offered the compliment without bitterness or self-pity. Jacqui shuffled her feet nervously.

Roz raised her head toward C.H with a faint glimmer in her eyes. "I had the dream again."

He pulled up a chair without releasing his wife's hand. Jacqui made a move to go, but he motioned for her to stay.

"Yes." Roz nodded at her then turned to C.H. "I was in the canoe again, but this time you weren't in the back with me. I was on," she cleared her throat weakly, "the most beautiful lake. The water, smooth as glass. You know how I've complained about this smell I always have. Well, that was gone." She laid her head against the pillow again, but the smile stayed in place. "So sweet, so beautiful. The music was all around me." She opened her eyes. "I wanted to go."

At a low moan from C.H., Jacqui pulled her fascinated gaze away from Roslyn. A vee had formed between his eyebrows and the corners of his mouth had tugged down.

Roz must have seen it too. She withdrew her hand from his and reached to smooth his forehead. "Now Charles, don't pout because you don't get to go, too." She used a teasing tone, but the effort appeared to drain her. Her hand dropped limply onto the flannel sheet.

Lewis rose to pace from the bedside table to the wall and back. When C.H. leaned toward his wife's ear to whisper something, Jacqui took the opportunity to suggest she and Lewis take a walk down the hall. She felt Roslyn's eyes trailing them.

"I'll show you the games room," Lewis said, stalking out the door. Jacqui followed, trying to keep up.

"You know I don't like it when you talk that way," C.H. told Roslyn. "You've beaten this before. You can do it again. We prayed for healing, remember?"

Roz regarded him with those melting brown eyes of hers. She shook her head ever so faintly, as though even that slight movement was an effort. “It's different this time, C.H. The dream was so real, more real than anything on this earth has ever been to me. I saw Jesus.” She made that difficult swallowing grimace before going on. “Well, not his face. But I knew it was him. And C.H., it was the most fabulous sensation. I don't really know how to describe it.” She paused, contemplating a spot where the wall met the ceiling. “I was so full. No, that's not the right word.” She nodded her head more firmly. “Yeah, so full. And at peace. Like when we first fell in love, only a thousand times better.” She gave a deep, rasping sigh.

C.H. glared a hole in the glossy, gray-tiled floor at his feet. She was giving up, slipping away, and he was helpless to stop it. It might be great for her, this wonderful destination. Listening to her descriptions, he could even enter into the dream with her, sense the anticipation, hope for a bright future. But for him, the one who had to plod on alone, the future got bleaker every time he lost another piece of her. And yet what kind of a heel was he, that he could sit here thinking about his own troubles when she'd been through so much for so long? How could he rob her of this deep joy that surged in her, flowing out of her even as she wasted away?

“I envy you,” was all he could croak out.

He felt her light hand stroking his hair and the sense of longing and loss became overwhelming. Then her hand stopped, and she tugged a bit on the top of his ear. “She's really good with Lewis. I like that.”

“What?” he raised his eyebrows enough to watch her through bleary eyes.

Nothing changed in her tender face when she spoke. “I believe you're going to marry her.”

C.H.'s head jerked. “What?” His chest started hammering. And then he was disgusted at himself for reacting. He'd kept all interactions with his neighbour platonic and above board, all of them had taken place with Lewis present. He had nothing to be ashamed of. Did he? God help his sorry soul.

Roz only smiled. "You're going to marry her."

"Why would you say such a thing? She's not even a Christian."

"But she will be. And I want you to know it's alright to marry again...In fact, do it as soon as you can after I'm gone. I won't have you... becoming a hermit. It wouldn't be good for Lewis."

Releasing her hand, he frowned. "You speak as one of the foolish women."

She gave a ghost of a giggle. "So, you've been reading the book of Job." She reached to muss his hair, but he pulled out of range, annoyed. "Keep reading it." She inhaled with a whistle "You'll see how Job kept on trusting God, no matter what." Roz brought their twined hands to her dry lips. "You do that too, okay? Please?"

CHAPTER 19

The best part of blowing clear across the country to relocate was that no one knew you, which meant you didn't have to worry about awkward accidental meetings with your ex and his new flame. The worst part of blowing clear across the country to relocate was that no one knew you. Which meant you didn't run into anyone you knew in the grocery store, or at the post office, or halfway to town like the two guys in trucks up ahead had done, stopping to chat in the middle of the road. If not this to hold her up, then a cattle drive. By now Jacqui was used to the relaxed pace around here and knew better than to lay on the horn. However, just once it might be nice to be recognized herself, to feel grounded, at home on this piece of turf.

And then her phone rang. *A telemarketer, no doubt.*

But it wasn't. Jacqui pulled over onto one of those short roads off the highway that led into a field.

"Jacqui? It's your cousin Beth. Remember me?"

A thrill of belonging, like a slender thread, tied her to this western world.

"Sorry you haven't heard from us for so long. Harvest time and fall work. But now that that's all done, Mom asked me to invite you over. You mentioned wanting to learn how to make pie?"

"I did. Your mom's was the best I've ever had. Is she able to talk a bit now?"

"Oh, that's right, she still wasn't speaking at all when you came by in the summer. Well, in the last couple of months, she's really been coming along." A child's voice sounded then Beth's voice grew muffled as she instructed someone with her. "So, I don't think I'll be able to join you, but can I let her know you'll be at her place some morning next week, say Tuesday?"

Tuesday was not one of Jacqui's library days. "Sounds good," she answered, promising to confirm the plan with Anna. She dropped her phone into her purse and moved back onto the road to town. She'd forgotten to ask what she should bring. Mentally, she added shortening and pie tins to her grocery list.

Aunt Anna answered Jacqui's knock at her door as though she'd been poised and waiting. When Jacqui stepped through the door, the older woman enfolded her into a lingering warm embrace, jacket, groceries and all.

"I brought my own pie pans and supplies." Jacqui disentangled her arms to hold up the bag. But Anna still grasped her with one hand, reaching up to stroke Jacqui's cheek with the other. The gesture was so gentle, fraught with the sense of time lost, that Jacqui's throat swelled with emotion. She kept utterly still, berating herself for being a baby, yet drinking in the affection and not wanting it to end. When had Jacqui's mom ever shown her such love?

At length, the older woman released Jacqui and motioned her inside. Jacqui slipped off her jacket and shoes and followed her aunt into the kitchen.

"Jesse's not home?"

Anna shook her head. "Out with his aide today." Her voice croaked slightly, as though from disuse.

Jacqui pulled a small bag of pastry flour, cans of shortening and pie filling, and foil pie tins out of the bag. "I came prepared."

Anna fingered the purchases, slowly smiling. She peered up into Jacqui's eyes. “Shall we begin?” She pointed out two baking stations set up side by side on her kitchen table, two mixing bowls, two hand-held pastry cutters, two rolling pins. “Just do what I do.”

Jacqui rolled up her sleeves to wash her hands then took her position at the table beside her aunt.

In tandem, they measured flour, salt and baking powder into the bowl, then cut in lard, not shortening. Apparently, lard was the only way.

Jacqui swallowed her low-fat misgivings. “The only time I tried to make pastry was when I was a kid,” she said. “I couldn't figure out what it meant to 'cut in shortening in until it resembles coarse oatmeal.'“

“Never mind oatmeal. Just go until the pieces won't cut any smaller.” Aunt Anna peered into Jacqui's bowl. “Looks about right.” She took her own cutter to slice a couple of the larger flour-coated lumps of lard remaining in Jacqui's bowl. “Now...”

Jacqui followed her aunt's lead, beating a couple of eggs with vinegar and cold water in a measuring cup. Together, they each dumped the contents into their flour mix. She tried to keep up, imitating Anna's practiced moves to combine it all into a single lump of dough. Anna placed a restraining hand on Jacqui's vigorous arm.

“Uh-uh. Not so hard. Pastry is the opposite of yeast dough. Use a gentle hand.”

“That must be where I went wrong the one time I tried this. I kneaded it like you would for bread.”

“Oh dear.” Anna shook her head, chuckling softly.

With her eyes on her aunt's every motion, Jacqui divided the dough into seven balls, placing the first on a flour-sprinkled sheet of plastic.

“I use the plastic liners of cereal boxes,” Anna explained.

Rolling from the centre outward, they formed and stacked seven flat, thin dough circles.

"Now I pop them into the freezer. When we want a pie, they come apart easily and thaw quickly." Her gray-blue eyes searched Jacqui's face. "But I see you were hoping to take one home today?"

Jacqui nodded, handing her the pie filling she'd brought.

"I'm afraid we've become cherry snobs," Anna said, setting aside Jacqui's tin. "Wait right here." She disappeared down the stairs next to the back entrance then emerged with a bag of frozen cherries. "We pick these every year at a local U-pick orchard. Nothing better."

Watching Aunt Anna's method closely from behind her phone, Jacqui recorded the making of filling, including Anna's commentary—the variety of cherries (bred specifically for the Prairies), the point at which to add the corn starch to the cherry juice and sugar (right before a rolling boil), a bit of butter to cut the starchy taste (about a tablespoon).

"Be generous with the fruit. No one wants jam pie," she gave a wry expression, "two crusts jammed together. Never skimp."

Bottom crust, filling, dot with butter, top crust pierced and sealed. Anna showed Jacqui how to crimp the edges with her thumb and opposite two fingers. They brushed the top with milk and sprinkled it with coarse sugar. "Bottom rack, don't forget," Anna said.

Jacqui set it in the oven

"Now, come and sit, my dear." Anna wiped the table and drew Jacqui to a chair, seating herself across from her. She took Jacqui's hand. "I feel our family has missed out on so much— our brother's wedding, meeting his wife, your birth and growing up." She tilted her head and gave a sad smile. "Tell me about yourself."

Where to start? Jacqui shrugged.

"I don't think there was much of a wedding." She forced a laugh. "I've only seen one photo, taken at the courthouse. Dad worked in the steel mills for years. He was pretty active in the steelworkers' union for a long time. Now he's retired..." *How much do I say? Pops had his reasons for cutting off connections with his family.* The warmth of her aunt's hand and the deep sincerity in her eyes broke through Jacqui's defenses.

"Things fell apart in our family when I was seven. That's when my baby brother died."

Anna gave a sympathetic squeeze of her hand but didn't appear surprised.

"My father only mentioned it once since then. From the little he told me it was a genetic anomaly. I researched it myself and I think it could have been a trisomy condition like Down syndrome but on a different chromosome. He only lived five days."

"Did you get a chance to see him?"

"Yeah, I saw him." She stared at a streak of flour on the table missed by Anna's wiping. "He seemed perfect to me. I don't think he ever opened his eyes, though."

"You know, the funeral home sent us a notice. That's how I got your father's address."

"Really? That couldn't have been Pops. My mother must have given them a list of contacts." Jacqui shifted in her chair, but the movement failed to lift the weight she felt whenever she dwelt on the past. "I don't remember much about what life was like before that happened. I only know things changed. My mother seemed to drop out of our family afterward. She was there but not there, if you know what I mean. I was left alone a lot when I was young." Jacqui's lips firmed as she recalled the years that followed. She snorted, remembering. "My mother's way of making up for wrongs was to buy me cheap and meaningless junk."

"Why must you judge her so harshly? She must have been deeply depressed."

Jacqui focused again on Anna's compassionate face. "I suppose.

But I was only a little kid. Anyway, one day she came home, put me in the car with a lot of our stuff, and we started 'a new life,' as she put it." With so few words, Jacqui had condensed a four-year gut ache of anxiety, of furtive dodging of her mother's moods and boyfriends, of school subterfuge to hide the grim reality of home. "When I was twelve, I called my Pops and begged him to let me live with him. He consulted a lawyer, but my mom didn't put up a fight."

"Was he... did your father drink?" Concern and doubt clouded Aunt Anna's eyes.

"No!" Jacqui jumped to Pops' defense. "At least, not much. And it never made him violent like— He was never abusive." She watched her aunt's face, somehow needing to convince her. "Things were good once I lived with him. I felt safe. Peaceful. He pretty much let me do as I pleased."

Anna's forehead registered a slight frown at this.

"But I was a good kid. I liked studying and I liked organizing the house. He put me through university, which is a lot more than most of the kids in my neighbourhood got."

A thoughtful silence rested between them until Jacqui ventured the question that had grown in her mind in recent years. "Why would your father make my father leave home so young? And what made my Pops never want anything to do with his family again?" Unexpectedly, it came out as an accusation. "I mean, you were probably too young," she said, hoping to soften her tone, "but do you remember anything about it?"

Anna closed her eyes, as though replaying memories. "The first one to plead his cause seems right," she murmured enigmatically, then allowed the silence to close in again.

CHAPTER 20

The kitchen stove timer ticked loudly in the quiet that followed. It seemed a long time before Anna spoke again. She cleared her throat, made a false start, then cleared it again.

"Your father was a very bright boy." She smiled faintly. "The rest of us children lived in his shadow a bit." Noticing a smear of flour on the table, Anna used the hem of her apron to polish it away. "Perhaps you've noticed that the very bright mind is often accompanied by a very stubborn will?"

Jacqui's shoulders rose. She hadn't noticed this in particular. It seemed old-fashioned, this reference to the will. Bree had referred to her oldest daughter as having "a mind of her own" which Jacqui supposed was what her aunt meant. But Bree had always chuckled indulgently about it, prizing the strength and sass of her girl. Aunt Anna clearly meant it negatively.

Pops, stubborn willed? The image of her stoop-shouldered father lifting a brown bottle to his sour-mouthed face was hard to read as willful or stubborn. But maybe. Maybe as a teen.

"If you said the sky was blue, your father would argue it was red, simply for the sake of resisting."

Jacqui chuckled. "That I can totally see."

"Our mother was very wise. She could bring him onside. She would patiently offer him choices, so he could feel he was in control. She praised his wit and encouraged him. But Father..." Anna shook her head sadly. "To Father, there was a right way of doing things. His way." She straightened in her chair, fixing an earnest gaze on Jacqui. "He loved us children. But he expected obedience. Prompt obedience. And that went against John's grain. He simply wouldn't give in."

The timer chirped, signalling the pie was ready. Anna rose to draw it out of the oven. She set the flaky pastry on a cooling rack, its golden aroma filling Jacqui's senses. "I'll make us some coffee to go with it."

While her aunt had her back turned to the counter, Jacqui couldn't resist catching a drip of the rich red pie filling on her finger from where it bubbled onto the table.

"I saw that."

Jacqui gave a start, pulling her guilty finger from her mouth, but when Anna turned around she wore a benign smile on her face. Soon, a coffee aroma complemented the sweet fragrance of the pie.

Anna served a generous slice for Jacqui and a narrower one for herself before sitting across from her.

"Mm." Jacqui closed her eyes, savouring the warm treat. "Better than any I've ever had."

"And you made it yourself." Anna used her fork to point out the bottom crust. "See, flaky even on the bottom. I'll send some cherries home with you so you can make one at home any time."

Something more than the heat of the pie warmed Jacqui as she enjoyed it. When they finished eating, Anna resumed her story.

"My boys were a handful, but when I think back to what Mother and Father had to deal with—I mean, John—I realize I had it easy. The trouble he got into. Or maybe trouble always found him."

"But he was only a curious little boy..."

Anna eyed her intently above the rim of her coffee cup. "Have you spent much time with children?"

Jacqui paused, then shook her head.

"You're right that your father was a curious little boy. But sometimes he—" she stopped, as though choosing her words carefully. "His curiosity had an *edge* to it. At times it bordered on cruelty." She searched Jacqui's face and must have read the disbelief there. "Yes, even as a young boy. I recall him hunting frogs in the springtime. He would flick a penny at their heads. At first it maimed them, so they hopped about in a crazy way. Oh, how it made John laugh! But eventually, it killed them."

Unbelievable. Resentment against this analysis of Pops began to burn inside Jacqui. She remembered his delicate touch as he held his baby son, with all of the tiny tubes and paraphernalia hanging from him.

Don't all boys do stupid things they later regret? But she couldn't escape another memory that surfaced. After her baby brother had died, a round, shabby lady from the Baptist church two streets over had arrived at their door. She offered a casserole and a plate of cookies with a sympathy card attached.

But Pops had shoved the dish back at her. "Thought you could bake us right into your stupid club of fools, did you?" he had snapped. Jacqui had watched the smile die on the lady's face before Pops slammed the door on her.

"John used to tease the life out of Priscilla and Naomi," Aunt Anna went on. "They were such obedient girls. He must have hated how they showed him up. Oddly, though, he was always good to me. At least most of the time. I think he thought I was like him. A bit of a rebel. Asking impertinent questions." Her eyes took on a distant look. "Once, when I was ill, Mother made a small bed for me on the kitchen floor. She liked to keep an eye on us while she was working. John kept sneaking around the corner, tugging at my blanket, teasing me. I told on him, and Father heard." Anna turned tear-filled eyes to Jacqui. "My brother got a dreadful beating that night. I can still hear Father's shouts and John's cries. I wanted to cry out, 'Not so hard!' But I was too afraid to interfere. We all were." She exhaled deeply. "I was so sorry I'd complained. I never meant for him to hurt so badly."

"That's what my Pops has talked about. It's called child abuse. Your father should have been criminally charged." Jacqui thrust her empty plate away from her in disgust. "If it happened today, social services would have removed him from the home."

"I know that, dear. But it was a different era." Anna paused, considering. "And there are times when parents are pushed to the limits."

"You're making excuses for him?"

"No... No, harsh treatment, abuse, is always wrong, The Bible says so."

Jacqui couldn't help snorting. "My father always said he'd heard enough God-talk to last him a lifetime. He never wanted to hear anyone speak about God again."

"I'm very sorry to hear it. Though it doesn't surprise me." The grief on Anna's face softened Jacqui's scorn. "What else did he say about it?"

"About the Bible?" Pops' contempt for religion, his ridicule of anyone who professed faith, grew in proportion to his blood alcohol level. The greater the number of empty brown bottles beside him, the more caustic his ranting became. Truthfully, he liked nothing better than to talk about God—in his own good time and on his own terms. In fact, the diatribes had grown longer and more vehement the older he got. *Why was that, when there was no one to argue the other side?* But Jacqui's loyalty to Pops forced her to resist divulging anything about that. And gazing into her aunt's kind face, she resisted sharing anything that might hurt her. "Mostly just jokes."

"I am very sorry for your loss."

This was unexpected. "What do you mean?"

"Something is missing when a child's spirit goes unnurtured. We can feed and clothe children, love them and educate them, but if we fail to introduce them to their Maker, we cheat them of something essential." The older woman's eyes reflected an unnerving perception. "And what did he tell you about our family?"

Cornered by the point-blank question, Jacqui demurred, swirling the last of her coffee with a tilt of her wrist. "Not that much. Nothing against you."

"And yet you seem well-prepared to charge your grandfather with abuse." Anna's sparse white eyebrows rose.

"Well, wasn't it?"

"Yes. I must admit it was. Father went beyond the bounds of acceptable and necessary discipline at times." She met Jacqui's eyes in a deep gaze. "But perhaps there is something about your father's stories that leaves you wondering? Why else would you come here? To the home of someone who collaborated with your father's abuser."

"I never considered you a collaborator. You were only a child."

"But from the first time you came here, I could tell you were searching. In fact, the need I saw in you changed something in me. God used it to remind me I was not the only one who might be hurting. After a long time in a dark pit, I began to come back up to the surface." Anna reached across the table and laid her hand on Jacqui's fidgeting fingers. "You were hunting for answers."

Was I?

"It may be a cliché, Jacqui, but things are not always as they seem. A father's parenting is best observed over time. A long time. Judging a person's life is not simple and cannot be done by sampling only a slice of it."

Was something expected of Jacqui? Descending into the murky depths of the human psyche didn't seem necessary when Anna herself had admitted her father was an abuser.

"The morning we discovered your father gone changed our family forever. Father came downstairs from the boys' bedroom with the note John left. I will never forget the anguish on his face. Or the sound of my mother weeping at her morning prayers. Our home was like a graveyard. Mother was ghost-like, though she carried on in spite of the tears. But father was a beaten man. It slowed him down, aged him years overnight. He was never the same."

Perhaps she's right. Maybe I wasn't only running away from something when I came out west. Maybe I was searching for something, too. But this other side of the story wasn't it. The unsettling confusion in it left Jacqui with too much uncertainty. Besides, what good did her grandfather's remorse do? It came too late. The damage to Pops had already been done. And that damage started a chain of detriment that affected Jacqui to this day.

She pushed her chair away from the table. "It's really time I got going. I still have a few groceries to get before I leave town."

Anna rose too, sliding the remaining pie in its tin into a plastic bag and following Jacqui to the door. "I am so grateful you came, dear. Do come again." She leaned close to hug Jacqui once again. "And please think over what I've said about your grandparents. They loved your father dearly. There's so much more I could tell you. Just know this: they never stopped praying he would come home." She squeezed Jacqui's shoulder. "In a sense, you're the answer to those prayers."

CHAPTER 21

Jacqui poured wine into her goblet, watching it twinkle its burgundy light against the glass. She replaced the stopper and padded to the living room to curl up in one of the resident green armchairs. When she started her playlist, Gandalf scampered over and shinnied up her leg as if responding to the music. The kitten nestled into Jacqui's lap, soon a reassuring, purring spot of heat. Why had she never had a pet before? She had no idea a living creature could be such a comforting companion.

Only problem is, I don't dare disturb him. But my right leg is falling asleep. These chairs are so stiff, and the lines are so boxy it's next to impossible to get comfy. The upholstery feels like a scouring pad. Jacqui tilted her head to examine the contours of the chair. *How hard could it be to re-upholster it? But none of that.*

She blew out a long breath and pulled her feet up under her. For tonight all thoughts of projects were out. She sipped the wine, swirling its flamboyance around her mouth, letting it warm its way down her body. With each swallow, she could feel it work its relaxation magic, banishing worries and fears and thoughts. She tipped her head back, readjusting it to avoid the chair's hard-welted piping, and remembered her divinely comfortable designer chairs at home. *Not home anymore.* But the thought of Geoff and Dale, and likely their friends, living and laughing and enjoying the home she had worked on, paid for, dreamed of, and compiled brought her head up with a jerk. The muscles at her mouth and eyes tightened in resentment.

She drained the last of her glass of wine and forced herself to relax again, floundering in memory for the relaxation techniques Bree touted. Empty your mind. She tipped back her head, staring up through slitted eyes. Become conscious of the beating of your heart.

I hate those stupid ceiling tiles. The irksome sight of them jarred her back to awareness.

Though Jacqui's efforts with the room—removing the loathsome carpet, painting walls, and clearing clutter—had brought a certain serenity, she'd never been happy with the way the ceiling ruined the look. The same was true of the bedrooms and kitchen. Brown marks like nicotine stains encircled the tiles near the wood heater pipe. *But what horrors hid above?* Re-drywalling the ceiling certainly was not a job she was capable of doing alone. She yawned. It had been a long day of cleaning out the contents of Uncle Russell's closet, and painting the room. For tonight, she would close her eyes to all of it.

Jacqui eased Gandalf off her lap to return to the kitchen. She was about to wash her glass and put away the wine when she saw only a small bit remained. She hesitated, her hand around the neck of the bottle. It had been her rule never to exceed one glass a day. Fear of her mother's fate, or her father's creeping dependence on booze had kept her true to that rule. *Bad enough I've been drinking alone. Not that I have any choice, anymore.* A wave of self-pity washed over her. She swirled the liquid in the tall, slim bottle. *Whatever.* She splashed the last of the bottle's contents into her goblet and downed it. *Only a swallow. I probably didn't fill my glass as full as I could have the first time, anyway.* She rinsed her glass, then headed to bed.

The next morning, Jacqui woke late, padded out of her room to the middle of the living room and stopped short, squinting at the dingy white squares of the ceiling.

You aren't going to let up on your ugliness, are you? She stood still, fighting the implications, dreading the work, but the answer was still no. It was unacceptable this way. She could at least investigate, perhaps at the attic stairway, and try to discover whatever hung above the hated tiles. Rolling her eyes, she returned to her room for her work clothes. *Nothing for it but to plunge right in.*

Sure enough, in the attic stairwell opening, the depth between the main floor ceiling and the attic floor above was greater than could be accounted for by joists. She hurried to the porch for a few tools then returned to pry and remove the first tile. It appeared a framework had been built to suspend the tiles. The gap was stuffed full of pink fiberglass insulation, obstructing her view into the dark depths between. Jacqui groped beyond the batting with a gloved hand and felt empty space and a solid ceiling above. She grabbed a flashlight and shone the light into the narrow space she'd uncovered. Her spirits rose when she detected some sort of decorative plaster work. Just then, a tickle in her nose led to an enormous sneeze, raising more dust and producing another sneeze.

It's going to be a colossal mess. Wavering in indecision, she thought with chagrin of the upheaval her earlier projects had caused, and the peaceful cleanliness she'd enjoyed for the past few months. But the grandeur of a higher ceiling captured her imagination. *Maybe if I'm careful...*

Jacqui pried another tile loose, careful to keep it level as she set it on the stairs. Gently pushing the insulation aside allowed a better view. Yes! The original ceiling featured plaster and what appeared to be a coved crown molding. *Let's do it!* She ran for the drop cloths, pushing the room's furniture together in the centre and covering it. After assembling her tools and setting up her ladder, she began removing the squares one at a time. As she went, she pulled out sections of the pink batting, which looked sickeningly like cotton candy with chocolate sprinkles. *Ew, gross!*

But progress was slow. Many of the pressboard squares broke as she loosened them, releasing years of settled dirt into the air. The possibility of airborne diseases made her flee to the porch for a dust mask and ball cap. On the way back through the kitchen, her heart sank at the sight of the counters and table covered with a fine film of black dust. And her shoes had left a distinct trail through the silt on the floor. *My beautiful floor!* Tears sprang to her eyes. She let out a groan only slightly muffled by the mask.

What have I gotten myself into?

Yet the gaping, ragged hole in the ceiling left her no choice but to finish the job. How much worse could a disaster get? With a hitch in her breath, and screwing up every last bit of courage, she attacked the ceiling with a crowbar, letting the pieces fall freely. *Now, that's progress.*

Near the heater, a cloud of fine silt showered down on her, bringing with it a large soft wad of something more solid. She coughed, desperately hiding her nose and mouth in her shirt sleeve while the dust settled. At the foot of the ladder lay a nauseating clump of filth permeated by all the black dirt blown in during the Depression dust storms—balled up insulation, bits of paper, grain seeds and even a few wrinkled strands of tinsel, mingled with decades of mouse droppings.

In disgust, she scrambled down the ladder. As her foot bumped the revolting mass, something clicked on the wood floor. To the side lay a small skull with razor-like fangs. That was no mouse.

Aeee! She raced to the porch, opened the front door, tore off her mask, and breathed deeply of the crisp winter air. It prickled her nose and she gasped and coughed. Pulling off a glove, she wiped her watering eyes, only to find a piece of soggy mouse poop on her fingertip.

She screamed out into the empty countryside, shattering the snowy stillness.

This is the absolute limit! I thought I was strong. I thought I was up to any challenge. But this is it. I'm done. Tears began to stream down her cheeks. Likely a reaction to the fiberglass. Jacqui's nose dripped onto the mask and she used it like a tissue. In furious frustration, she stamped her feet on the concrete step.

"I hate you!" She shook her fist at the wretched house. "And I know you hate me! What other hideous surprises have you got for me?" Though her jagged shouts trailed off, her body still shook in violent shivers from the cold.

How could you, Geoff? How could I not have known? And why wasn't I enough for you? The rejection tore at her, uneased by the passage of time. She kicked at the ugly gray siding of the house again and again. At last, the cold and her sore toes forced her indoors.

Face it, Jacqui. The house is simply a surrogate for your rage. Bree's voice sliced through her mood with calm reason.

Thanks for the analysis, girlfriend. Like that helps me now.

A ringtone sounded from the counter where her phone was plugged in. Maybe that was Bree now, calling because she had felt the evil vibes, and was offering a free psychotherapy session.

Jacqui splashed water on her face from the kitchen faucet and dried herself on a rag to keep the kitchen towel clean. She let it ring while she pulled on a sweater then took the call.

"I heard you were invited to the party tonight," Francie said, "and I figured I could pick you up on my way."

The party? Oh yeah, she'd forgotten about that. Wine and cheese in a clean, fragrant home while other women wearing nice clothes and make-up spent money on gifts for their families. No way could she face that. With bleak despair, she scanned the room, taking in the insidious dust and loathsome mess around her. Self-piteous moisture threatened to leak out her eyes again. Suddenly she knew what she had to do.

Stay sane. Don't let the house beat you.

"Sure, I'll be ready and waiting for you," she agreed, aware that her neighbour's offer was a lifeline of hope and escape from the misery surrounding her.

"OK, see you in a couple of hours."

Jacqui ended the call and squared her shoulders to the catastrophe in the next room. *The only way past it is through it.* Avoiding the mound of horror that had fallen, she shifted the ladder and resumed demolition. It wasn't her first renovation calamity.

Keep working. It can all be cleaned up and so can I.

CHAPTER 22

Jacqui rode with Francie up a curving evergreen-lined lane to a sprawling ranch house with a central gable vaulted high above the roof line on either side. Chandeliers sparkled in gold and white through its vast front windows. An ear-muffed, red-nosed young man directed them to the left where a cobbled pathway led to a separate small white cottage trimmed in icicle lights.

Inside the cottage, though it was early for a Christmas theme, country carols and smells of cinnamon and pine greeted them, along with perfume and toasted cheese.

Jacqui hung her coat on a hook in the shoe-crowded entry. As she'd expected, the rooms were filled with cheerful women who all knew each other. A quick scan of the room revealed a few women who stood out for their sense of style, but for the most part, these were Walmart shoppers. She could at least hold up her head in her designer sweater and jeans.

Francie introduced her to the milling guests like a pedigreed puppy "from Ontario." Everyone was fascinated by where she'd come from, which, since few out here seemed to know the location of Hamilton, she'd simply described as "near Toronto."

Gratefully, she accepted a glass of excellent chardonnay from the buffet table in the tiny kitchen, glad for the wine's fortifying warmth. Several faces were familiar. Perhaps they'd been in the library? Or maybe they merely resembled someone she'd known back east.

Complete strangers surprised her with questions on her local family connections, about which they already seemed to know far more than she did. And all wanted to know what she thought of the West. That's how they said it, The West, as though it were an entity all its own. Jacqui murmured vague compliments, not wishing to bring on a political diatribe. Mostly, she sipped at her wine, listening.

This small cottage, Diana the hostess explained to the guests at large, was the original farmhouse which had long been neglected but which she'd slaved over for the past two years.

"I come here now when things get hairy on the ranch to get away from everything. But you can't imagine the disgusting mess this place was."

Oh, yes I can. What's hard to imagine is you, with your perfect hair and fingernails, dealing with the atrocities I dealt with this very afternoon.

Diana laughed. "And it had to get a lot worse before it got better."

The house was about the size and era of Jacqui's own home, minus the misguided 1970s renovations. Loads of the period trim Jacqui had hoped for in her own place surrounded the windows and doors. All the messy and miserable work was complete here. The place was furnished with Victorian antiques and charmingly decorated. Jacqui experienced a deep pang of envy. The woman had money, obviously, but everything else too. A handsome husband who even now, was bringing in firewood to stoke the adorable potbellied stove in the corner of the living room, the jaunty son who directed traffic, a gorgeous home, a cute hobby house.

Jacqui worked her way to the kitchen buffet for another glass of wine. She needed to relax. Beside her, a woman nodded in greeting. She was at least Jacqui's height, with beautiful eyes and a substantial nose that veered off to the left.

"I'm Amanda," she said, shifting towards Jacqui and steering her glass out of reach just in time to avoid someone's purse swinging by. "Whew! Close one."

"Wouldn't want to lose any of that precious nectar." Jacqui giggled. "I'm Jacqui. Nice to meet you."

Amanda grinned, then picked up a small plate and surveyed the table of appetizers. "Bacon, bacon, bacon."

Ah, a vegan like Bree.

"I know, right?" Jacqui said. Already this woman made her feel at home. She had never taken the plunge into veganism, but thanks to Bree, she knew all the arguments in favour. If it hadn't been for Geoff, she would have switched long ago.

"I'll take one of each," Amanda decided. "Anything is improved by bacon."

Jacqui stared in surprise as the woman loaded her plate with bacon-wrapped water chestnuts, potato skins sprinkled with bacon, bacon-flavored crackers and a dollop of bacon-dotted cheese ball.

The woman raised her eyebrows at Jacqui. "Aren't you going to have anything?"

Jacqui opened her mouth to speak but couldn't think of an answer. Instead she nodded and placed a few vegetables and a spoonful of dip on her plate.

"Load up, there's plenty. I'll bet this is supper for most of us who had to feed husband and kids and still try to make ourselves presentable before we left home." Amanda winked, piling more onto her plate. "And don't forget dessert. Life is uncertain—better grab the sweets while you can."

About now is when Bree would start in on the evils of sugar. Guiltily, Jacqui added a dainty square with smooth chocolate topping.

"Oh, not those." Amanda shook her head. "They're store-bought. Here, compare that to these homemade Nanaimo bars." She took a piece from another tray, handed it to Jacqui, then popped one into her own mouth. "Mm, no contest," she said, chewing with her eyes closed. "C'mon, let's find a seat."

They wended their way through the crowd, Amanda introducing Jacqui to a stream of faces that were starting to all look alike, then sat near the woodstove.

"Do you curl?" Amanda asked, watching at Jacqui over her glass of wine.

Jacqui swallowed the snow pea in her mouth and wrinkled her forehead in question.

"You know, curling." Amanda made brisk sweeping motions with her free hand.

"Oh. No, I've never tried it."

"Too bad. We need a new lead this season. Ours is down with super bad morning sickness." She munched away on her bacon treats.

The idea of joining a group of women was appealing. *How hard could it be gliding down the ice after a rock?* "Actually, I wouldn't mind trying it if you're open to a newbie."

"I'll talk to the skip. If they can train me, they can train anybody. Give me your number."

The gathered women gradually settled onto one of the many pieces of furniture. Francie smiled at her from across the room. Next to her was a table with wares and their seller clearing her throat for everyone's attention. As the saleswoman began her spiel, Jacqui tuned out, reminding herself of the condition of her bank account. Rather than listen, each time the saleswoman picked up an item and explained it, Jacqui took a sip of her wine. The sales pitch continued long after she swallowed the last drop. At length, the women began to stir again, some to place their orders, others returning to the buffet. Jacqui joined them. She poured another glass of wine then wove her way through the throng to sit farther away from the hot stove, fanning her neck with a folded paper napkin. She scanned the milling room for her new friend. Amanda was seated with an older woman across the room now, deep in conversation. Before Jacqui could mourn the loss, however, another woman sat next to her, balancing her full plate on her knee while quaffing a mug of hot apple cider.

"Hi Jacqui, I'm Linda. We met at the library awhile back, remember?" Linda's flushed cheeks and rounded body did seem vaguely familiar. Jacqui leaned toward her, peering more closely at her. Right. The two in the plaid flannel jackets discussing wedding invitations.

"Oh yeah, you're the one who was at the library with your daughter, planning a wedding, right?" Jacqui was fascinated by the way the woman's Santa elf earrings danced jerkily whenever she spoke.

"That's right." Linda looked pleased to be remembered, and even more pleased to be offered a segue into a favourite topic of conversation. "We're in the final countdown to the big day, New Year's Eve." She set her mug beneath her chair. "Though why it had to be scheduled for a time when there are so many other events happening is beyond me." Crunching a phyllo pastry, she caught the flurry of flakes with her free hand then gave an indulgent laugh. "But you know, kids in love..."

"Yeah, I know kids in love," Jacqui muttered, taking a long drink from her goblet. "I used to be one."

"Used to be?" Linda's face was all sympathy. "You too, eh? I know all about marriage gone bad."

"Yup," Jacqui said, encouraged by her companion's understanding. "I gave him twenty years of my life. I *thought* we were good. I *thought* he loved me. I *believed* all his promises."

Linda shook her head sadly, murmuring at the injustice. Jacqui nearly purred at the comforting feeling that someone understood. Here was a woman who had been through the same betrayal, listening to Jacqui's heart.

"Now, all of a sudden, he's changed," she continued, warming to her new friend. "He's found his soul-mate—my friend from work. The cheater." The hurt of it, the outrage, the utter incomprehensibility of it flooded through her, raising her to her feet. "Now he says he truly knows what real love is. For the first time, he says." Heat and emotion bubbled up from her core, making her dizzy. "I mean, what am I? Chopped lover?" Jacqui burst out with a bitter laugh. "Lover, liver. Ha ha!"

Others were laughing too, which emboldened her to go on. She gestured expansively around the room with her empty glass. "I mean, what's a girl s'posed to think when her man takes up with the office floozy?" All eyes were on her. To Jacqui, every woman in the room was a sympathetic sister, united against the wicked, oppressive, double-crossing male sex. "'Specially when the office floozy is a man?"

All voices in the cottage ceased. All movement stopped. Eyes widened and chins went slack. Then, as though choreographed to cover a belch, the women rushed back into conversation again. Linda rose quickly to pull a snuffling Jacqui down onto the chair next to her, handing her a napkin to wipe her nose. Francie, too, materialized at her other side.

"Probably time we got you home to bed, honey." She propelled Jacqui to the bedroom where coats had been laid on the bed. Jacqui submitted to being relieved of her wine glass, bundled into her coat and guided out to the cold car.

CHAPTER 23

Jacqui knew it was late when she woke to daylight streaming through her window. Slowly she oriented herself, wondering why she lay on top of the covers, still fully clothed. Her bra cut into the skin around her ribs and her pants had ridden up uncomfortably. At her side, Gandalf purred in a furry ball, a warm, living example of a good deed she had done. She turned to look down at him and the boulder rolling around in her head thunked to one side. With a moan she recalled the party, the wine and her disastrous disclosure of the night before. Cringing, she pulled the covers over her head against the merciless light of day. Hopefully, everyone else had had a bit to drink too, and would forget all about it. She was counting on the mercurial community news cycle to work in her favour. One thing was sure, never again. She wouldn't be letting her guard down that way anymore.

Vaguely, Jacqui had a memory of Francie's help getting her to bed last night. Somehow, they had navigated through the debris-strewn, furniture-clumped living room, prior scene of the Attack of the Attic Weasel Skeleton. She cringed at the thought of her neighbour witnessing the squalor she was living in. *But is it any worse than seeing the fool I made of myself spilling my guts all over a bunch of strangers last night?* Not only would the outside world be waiting to ridicule her but thinking about the disaster awaiting her on the other side of the bedroom door made Jacqui shudder. She would stay in bed forever. Yet while the prospect of getting up was dreadful, the discomfort of sleeping fully clothed forced her out of bed. As she rose, the kitten stretched extravagantly.

Jacqui shucked off the rumpled outfit and changed into clothes for the day's rough work ahead. Hand on the doorknob, she took a deep breath. She'd give anything to avoid facing the mess out there, but the only way past a dreaded job was through it. She opened the door.

To her immense surprise, the floor was clear and shiny. Jacqui shuffled through with wondering eyes. Dirt and bits of insulation still dotted the drop cloth covering the furniture bunched in the centre of the room, but the floor was swept clean. She exhaled in profound relief.

First, she took a couple of painkillers, then she made coffee and drank half a cup to clear her head. Finally, she hunted down Francie's phone number.

"Good morning!" Humour winked in Francie's greeting. "And how do you feel this morning?"

"Not the greatest," Jacqui admitted.

She heard a chuckle.

"I'm laughing at you, not with you," Francie said.

"Very funny." Friends ridiculed one another like that, Jacqui realized. She felt cared for. "I'm calling to thank you for doing a major clean-up here. How long did it take you?"

"You mean you didn't hear me? I thought for sure I'd wake you, making all that horrible racket, trying to find your broom and dustpan and then hunting for more garbage bags. Didn't take long to sweep it up, though. I figured no one would want to wake up to that. How come you tore down your ceiling?"

"I couldn't stand those ceiling tiles. Didn't you see what I uncovered? Really nice texture."

"But you've lost your insulation. It'll be awful once the cold weather hits."

Jacqui hadn't given that possibility any thought. Deflated, she said, "You mean it hasn't yet? It's November." How much worse could the weather get?

"Oh, it can get pretty bad at times. There are still four or five months of winter to go."

"Five months?" She heaved a sigh of discouragement. "Too late now. I guess I can always insulate the attic some more."

"I guess." The hesitation in Francie's voice gave the impression she doubted the good sense of the recent work. "So, are you all recovered from last night?"

Jacqui moaned inwardly. She had hoped to consign her outburst to the past. When she didn't answer immediately, Francie plowed ahead. "I'm real sorry for your loss. Divorce is such a bummer. What's got to be the worst is being thrown over for a guy!"

Jacqui could add nothing to this, nor did she want to. And yet, for the first time, she soaked up the sympathy from someone who seemed to understand the peculiar edge of Jacqui's misery. Bree, whose husband had split for the sake of computer gaming, had never understood the uniqueness of Jacqui's hurt. Her throat contracted ominously.

"I mean, how's a gal s'posed to compete with that?" Francie went on. "And then, you've got all this kerfuffle about gay rights going on now. If you raise a stink about it, everybody calls you a homophobe or a bigot or something. No wonder you've never said anything. Well, I just want you to know, what happens at the hen party, stays at the hen party. I can't guarantee the news won't get around, but I can promise you, we're on your side, hon."

Jacqui swallowed hard. "Thanks. And thanks so much for sweeping up the mess in here. I really wasn't looking forward to that job."

"Any time. I really mean it," Francie said, before she hung up.

Laying her phone gently on the table, Jacqui dropped onto a kitchen chair. Francie had hit on the source of Jacqui's raw pain with the precision of a brain surgeon. That was exactly it. Jacqui despised the low-class, country-music image of "fighting for her man," but the way Dale had supplanted her, nudging her out and showing her up until she was practically forced from her own home, was unbearable. It made her roller-derby-mama fighting mad. Only a lot more helpless. Again, for exactly the reason Francie had identified. If you were gay, you were born that way, right? No one should be forced to live a lie. Jacqui had always believed a person should stop fighting his inborn nature and embrace his inner truth. How could she expect Geoff to deny his true self, his real identity any longer?

Oh, she knew the rationale all too well. In college, she'd attended gay pride parades, had expressed support for friends who had come out, approved of increasing freedoms and recognition for LGBTQ people to be who they were meant to be. Isn't that how the reasoning went?

Then why did it hurt so terribly when it touched her personally? By all measures, she knew she should be happy for Geoff, finding himself the way he had. Self-actualization and all that. So, why did it strike at the very core of her as a woman, make her feel she was inadequate, a lesser being somehow, rejected not only for being the wrong woman for him but for being the wrong sex? She hadn't simply been rejected for a better model; she'd been discarded because she was the *wrong* model.

Maybe Bree did understand. She'd been thrown over in favour of video games, something inanimate preferable to a flesh-and-blood person. But Jacqui's pain was different. Society at large didn't hold celebratory parades for the man-computer union.

And on top of it all lay the utter humiliation of having been hoodwinked. Why, oh why had it taken Jacqui so long to catch on to what was happening?

Dale, the assistant manager at work, now her friend. Such a funny guy, with his understated British wit, his satirical comments on politics, his love of fine cuisine. In fact, their mutual interest in cooking had made them friends in the first place. Then she'd introduced him to Geoff. "You guys will definitely connect. He's crazy about jazz, too." Soon Dale was attending concerts with them, jumping right in to work with them on the condo renovation, increasingly present for dinner, overnighting in the guest room, the guys staying up late for whiskey and deep discussions on philosophy, culture, economics...

And then one morning, Geoff's side of the bed was empty, untouched. Weird. Jacqui tumbled out of bed, padded to the kitchen. Dale in Jacqui's barbecue apron, making biscuits, Geoff frying bacon, both of them beaming joyfully at her, at each other. Everything great. They'd got talking so late, Geoff said, he hadn't wanted to disturb her by coming to bed in the wee hours. Scrumptious breakfast. Dale's biscuits lighter than any Jacqui had ever made. The secret, Dale explained, was in souring the milk before adding it to the dry ingredients. Geoff slathering a biscuit with butter, raving over it.

Had that been the first time something seemed strange? Why didn't I see what was going on right under my nose?

Because how could that even be possible when Geoff and I had been together for nearly twenty years?

As time went on, I simply refused to see.

"Dale has this great idea for opening up the master bedroom to the ensuite."

"Hey Jac, would you mind sleeping in the guest room? It's farther

from the living room where we're listening to music. We don't want to keep you awake, laughing too loud." Glances exchanged between the two of them.

Dale and Geoff cooking together, Dale and Geoff taking a Spanish language course together on Wednesday nights, Dale and Geoff choosing paint colours for the bathroom.

Isn't Geoff amazing? Dale's eyes shining with adoration at Christmas after opening his gift from Geoff.

That was finally the tip-off.

Seriously Jacqui? That was the first time you understood?

But the truth was unthinkable. And I had so much invested—years of loyal commitment, a shared mortgage, a merged life, the life-altering, permanent decision Geoff and I made together not to have children.

How could I ever have known Geoff was gay? Why did I hide from the truth for month after month?

CHAPTER 24

Steeling herself against possible talk about her gut-spilling scene at Diana's party on the weekend, Jacqui arrived at work Tuesday in a defensive mood. She went through the library-opening routine with grim efficiency, hoping not to see anyone who had been at the party that night.

To her relief, the place was empty all morning, allowing her to make serious headway on weeding out discards. Shortly before noon, Amanda, her new bacon-loving friend, came bursting through the door with a preschooler in tow.

"Oh, hey," Jacqui greeted her, "I haven't heard anything from your friend about curling yet." She stopped short.

Amanda's jaw had gone slack when her eyes fell on Jacqui.

"You're here." Smoothing the static from her hair, Amanda searched Jacqui's face. "You don't know, do you?"

Jacqui blanked out, at a loss.

"Maybe you should sit down," Amanda suggested, drawing a chair from the computer desks and pulling her son onto her lap. The wary apprehension on her face made Jacqui's stomach plummet.

"What?" Jacqui edged toward her own chair and dropped into it.

"I was afraid somebody would say something stupid to you before you heard the news," Amanda began, rolling her eyes, "and now that stupid someone is me!"

"What are you talking about?" The words came out shrill.

Amanda levelled a grave look at her. “There was an accident early this morning. Three local men were killed on their way out hunting.”

Was one of them C.H.? The possibility wrung Jacqui’s heart. Before she could examine the reaction, Amanda went on.

“Deer season started today.” She dropped her gaze, fiddling with her boy's parka zipper. “They were your uncle and cousins. Eli Adrian and his sons, Chet and Mac.” She flashed a quick glance at Jacqui's face, as though to gauge the effect of this news. “I'm so sorry for your loss.”

Jacqui breathed again, yet she hardly knew what to say. Without question, the loss was tremendous... for somebody. Just not for her. She struggled to recall the family tree. Would these be Pops' sister Naomi's husband and sons? Relatives she hadn't even met yet. She was embarrassed at her lack of emotion, but faking grief at the news would be more awkward still.

“What happened, exactly?”

“From what we can gather, a semi hit them when they were turning onto the highway. Al Barry drove past the scene not long after. The passenger side of their pick-up was badly smashed in.” Amanda's son climbed off her lap to get to the children's area. “Getting ready for such a big funeral might take longer than usual. I s'pose you'll be taking time off to go?”

The thought made her skin crawl. Jacqui had never been to a funeral. *But why? Had there even been a funeral for her brother?* “It's a lot to take in. I'll have to call my aunt.”

Amanda rose, keeping her eyes on Jacqui as she slowly moved toward her son. “Sorry to bring the bad news. I didn't expect you to be in to work today.”

At that moment, Jacqui's phone rang. Anna’s number showed up.

Jacqui had no good reason to be late arriving at the church for the funeral. Only the kinds of excuses she had no patience for when anyone else used them. Like procrastination and stalling over facing the unfamiliar, and indecision about what to wear. She'd settled on her black leather blazer and black dress slacks with a cream cashmere sweater, hoping she wouldn't stand out. Her hands, dry from the low humidity and rough from sanding baseboards in preparation for paint, kept snagging the soft knit of the sweater. *Hand lotion companies must make a fortune out here in dry Alberta.*

She found the church without difficulty but had to park far from the building. Slipping past a pair of black-clad ushers through the already-closed doors of the sanctuary, she searched for a seat. The building was packed. Who were all these people?

She retreated to the foyer, following other latecomers to another crowded room where a large video screen was set up. There she spotted C.H., clean-shaven and in a tweed jacket, and sidled into an open spot beside him. Before she'd settled, a woman in black with a brass name tag whispered in her ear, "The family is gathered in the lower level." She beckoned Jacqui to follow.

Family?

From a cluster of people talking in low tones, Aunt Anna came to embrace Jacqui, murmuring something about introducing her to everyone later. Clearly, she had continued to emerge from her mute depression even since Jacqui's last visit with her. She seemed to encircle everyone in the family, caring for them and enveloping the outliers.

"The family's all here now," she told the funeral director, and the group began filing up the stairs to take their places in reserved pews at the front of the church.

Family. Jacqui embraced the unusual sensation of belonging. She felt as though she could face anything, even the eyes that followed their progress up the aisle, even the unsettling presence of those three oak boxes at the front. In the pew in front of her sat the three widows, ashen-faced Aunt Naomi, tall Ruthie with the lustrous dark hair and, separated from the first two by her three young children, O'Dell. Jacqui knew she should feel sympathy for them, but what kept intruding was envy. Clearly, they'd had husbands who loved and stood by them. Cruel as their loss was, could it be worse than being thrown over for a man?

Jacqui took surreptitious glances around her, overcome by the sheer numbers of people in attendance. They couldn't all be family, so what interest did this many people have in these men? Farming associates? Neighbours? Church folk? She saw glistening eyes and heard sniffles and suddenly wondered who would show up at Pops' funeral.

The service wasn't the dolorous dirge she'd envisioned. She heard kindness, comfort, and surprisingly, humour. From the simple, heartfelt comments of friends and relatives, Jacqui caught a glimpse of men who took care of their families, their animals, their land, their neighbours. By the end, she keenly felt their loss and wished she'd known them. Which is what she said to her aunt Naomi when Anna introduced them after the service as they waited to be seated at tables.

Naomi blinked back the moisture in her eyes. "Thank you for your kind words. I'm sorry I haven't gotten around to meeting you yet."

The woman has just lost most of her family and she's apologizing to me for not reaching out?

In the crowded church basement, Aunt Anna suggested Jacqui sit at her family's table. Her daughter Beth was already a familiar face and now Jacqui met Beth's husband Steve and Anna's youngest son David. The lean young guy sported a unique leopard print hair-dye job and sat drumming his thumbs on the table in a complex rhythm. Clinging to his right side was his girlfriend, a waif-like young woman who seemed as ill at ease as Jacqui felt.

A short, barrel-chested man arrived to take a seat beside Anna as though he were part of the family. With lively eyes beneath bushy white eyebrows, he brought an almost palpable verve to the table.

"Jacqui, this is our pastor and my dear long-time friend, Tom Townsend." Anna set a hand on Jacqui's arm as she introduced her to the man beside her.

He cracked a wide smile that paralleled his square jaw, rising from his chair to pump Jacqui's hand. After offering pleasantries, he set to eating.

Sitting next to him, David spoke first. "Remember that time Uncle Eli brought an old canoe along when we went to some lake, Beth?"

His sister nodded, aligning two slices of cheese on a bun. She gave a soft chuckle. "He brought it for the older kids, but you were being such a pill, bawling about not getting to go for a ride, that he rigged up an old life jacket just for you."

David curled his lip. "How come all these stories make me sound like a brat?"

"Uh, 'cause you were?" Beth goggled at him.

He flicked a pebble of cheese her way. "All I remember is Uncle Eli spending time with me, just the two of us out on the water. He never said a word the whole time." David swallowed hard, then went on. "But I felt like I really mattered to him."

"Hm." Anna mused, shaking her head. "You couldn't have been more than three years old at the time. That would have been the time we all went berry picking and had a picnic at the reservoir."

"I'm trying to wrap my mind around the word 'picnic'," Beth said with a wry smile, "in the same sentence with Uncle Eli and Aunt Naomi."

Jacqui grasped at this intriguing thread. Pops had frequently complained of his upbringing being one long sentence of hard labour, relieved only by dismally boring Sundays. She cleared her throat. "They weren't picnickers?"

Beth turned to her. "Hardly. The Adrians were known for never taking vacations, or even a day off now and then. What was with that, Mom?"

Before Anna could answer, Jacqui murmured, "Chips off the old block, I assume."

She instantly regretted her words when she sensed the silent question in the eyes around the table. "I mean," she stammered, feeling a flush rise up her neck, "the grandparents were pretty intense, right? Hard work all the time, no fun allowed..."

Anna steepled her fingers in thought. "Naomi and I grew up in that home too, dear. And you're right about the hard work. But I remember our parents making it interesting and even fun. Father would start singing in his beautiful tenor voice when we picked berries or husked corn and we would all join in. It made the job go more quickly. And Mother—she had a wonderful gift for mimicry. While we washed dishes or hung clothes on the line, she'd tell us stories, often funny ones. As we think back, those are some of our best memories. And don't forget, working together was simply how we used to live. We were like other farm families that way." She stopped to sip coffee, eyeing Jacqui over the rim of the cup.

Her words were gentle, but Jacqui felt the reproach in them. Could it be that Pops' version of his past was simply the myopia of adolescence, one-dimensional and perennially stuck in a quagmire of resentment and rage? Anna's memories were opening Jacqui up to a wider view, but at the same time she struggled to keep hold of her trust in Pops and everything he believed in. *And everything he didn't believe in.*

Anna set down her mug and turned to Beth. "As to why Naomi's family took so little time off for recreation, especially in later years when there was more labour-saving machinery, I've wondered about that myself..." But her voice trailed off, her attention caught by someone rising from the next table where the bereaved family sat. Jacqui followed the direction of her gaze and saw Ruthie, one of the young widows, hurrying through the fringes of the crowd. Anna excused herself and left the table.

Wait! What? That can't be all there is to it. I want to know more. How could Jacqui accept that the pain her father carried was simply a case of skewed perspective, a mere misinterpretation of his parents' intentions? On impulse, she pushed out from the table and pressed her way through to the ladies' room.

But Anna wasn't in sight. Instead, Ruthie bent over the sink, splashing water on her face, and fumbling for paper towel. Even in her grief she was a beautiful woman with cheekbones to die for.

Flustered and suddenly tongue-tied at the magnitude of her young relative's loss, Jacqui ducked into the first available stall. Before long, she heard Anna's soft words of comfort to her other niece.

"Everything hurts right now—the memories, the sympathy, the thoughtless comments."

How does she do that? How does she know exactly what to say? Jacqui herself felt heartened by the words. What might have been different if her parents had had such kind support when her baby brother died? What if her mother hadn't gone off the deep end and ultimately disappeared, at last report anyway, into the dark netherworld of crime and homelessness? What if Jacqui could have grown up with two parents, maybe even siblings? And the safety net of cousins and uncles and aunts?

She cleared her throat and came out of the cubicle.

"Ruthie, have you met our long-lost relative yet?" Anna asked, reaching for Jacqui's arm. "This is Jacqui, my brother's daughter, which makes her your cousin. She moved to this area in July from

Ontario. Jacqui, my niece—and your cousin—Ruthie."

Jacqui dropped her crumpled paper towel to briefly clasp Ruthie's hand. She averted her gaze from the raw grief in her cousin's deep-set dark eyes. "I'm sorry for your loss," she managed to say.

"Thanks."

Later, as they moved toward their cars for the procession to the cemetery, Jacqui noticed Chet's widow, O'Dell approach Aunt Naomi. She caught alarming snatches of the sharp-toned message, not at all in keeping with the day's tender solicitude.

"...not really my mother... not going to pretend anymore that you are."

Jacqui stared in shock as O'Dell snatched the hands of her two small children, snapped at the other daughter to follow her, and clipped briskly on spike heels to a nearby car without a backward glance. The grieved shock on Aunt Naomi's face was a pitiful sight.

CHAPTER 25

The candy pink plastic tile in the bathroom didn't pop off the wall as easily as had the tile in the kitchen. Jacqui worked with painstaking effort to avoid damaging the wall behind it. Still, she found it energizing to relieve the tiny room of its lurid pink and burgundy. A pile of debris on the floor gradually grew. Then she reached the end of the tub where the faucets were. As she pulled off the panel of tile surrounding the taps, she found an ominous thick, dark substance clinging to the wallboard behind it. It had a musty, earthy smell. She clamped her sleeve to her face.

Black mold.

Jacqui well knew how dangerous the stuff was. Hadn't Geoff nearly been sued along with the owner of a house he'd sold? The buyers had been inexplicably ill for months until they uncovered extensive black mold in the walls. In the end, Geoff had escaped the lawsuit because the original owner had failed to disclose what he knew. But Jacqui had read the complainant's lengthy list of ailments.

She rushed out of the room, slamming the door behind her. *What else could go wrong? That room will have to be gutted to the studs and everything replaced.* A sick feeling shrivelled her innards. The time. The expense. The hassle. Where would she use the toilet or shower while the work was in progress? And how would she ever afford to have it done? Her breath came faster as panic set in. The house was going to defeat her.

Grabbing her phone, she followed her first impulse and called C.H. But doubt set in while waiting for him to answer. *His wife is terminally ill, and he has a high maintenance son and a farm to keep going. He's got enough on his plate already. Besides, what's he going to do about any of this? He's not a plumber.* She should never have phoned.

"'Y'ello!" came his cheerful voice before she could quietly end the call.

How does he keep that buoyant attitude with all the adversity in his life?

Embarrassed, Jacqui described her bathroom walls, downplaying her fears, asking only for pointers on what her next steps should be.

"It's only in the area around the taps?"

"Well, yeah."

"Were you planning on gutting the whole room anyway?"

"Not really. I don't have the funds for that." Admitting this brought back the squalid childhood Jacqui thought she'd left behind. She hated that.

"Tell you what. Lewis'll be home from school in about an hour. We'll be over as soon as I can stuff a snack down his gullet."

"Okay, thanks." *But why not now, before he gets home? I only asked for a bit of advice. It's like they're joined at the hip or something.*

Jacqui started a pot of coffee, then Googled what to do about black mold. This stuff was not on a hard surface where it could be scrubbed and disinfected. She would have to remove the affected wallboard. Squaring her shoulders, she reentered the bathroom. To be on the safe side, she put on a disposable face mask then spritzed the black blemished wall area with bleach. For good measure, she covered the spot with hair spray, hoping to seal in the fungus. With her handsaw, she carefully cut out the section of wall, then gingerly placed the moldy piece into a trash bag and sealed it with packing tape.

That feels better already.

Behind the opened wall were the same thin, wide boards she knew lined the living room ceiling and the walls of the attic. A splintery hole had been hacked in the dry fir to allow for plumbing fixtures. *That accounts for the mold. The fittings weren't sealed properly.*

A firm knock at the back door sent Jacqui picking her way through the demolition rubble to answer it. C.H. and Lewis breezed into her porch on a frozen gust of air. They stepped inside, shucking off their jackets and boots that Jacqui surreptitiously hung and straightened.

"Thanks for coming. I think I've solved the problem, but I'd like to know if you think the mold might be anywhere else." She turned to Lewis. "You can see if there's anything you want to watch on TV."

Lewis made a beeline for the living room but C.H. snagged the loop on the boy's backpack, pulling him to a stop. "Uh-uh. Let's see what you've got there first." Lewis strained forward while his father reined him in, producing a selection of books and movies from the pack. C.H. scanned the titles, mainly animal and dinosaur junior books and nature shows, from what Jacqui could see. He pulled one movie out of the bunch, sneered as he examined it, and stashed it into the sleeve of his own coat. "We'll give this one a pass, buddy." He released the lad, who seemed unperturbed by the confiscation of his movie.

"Did I just witness an act of censorship?" Jacqui asked.

Quirking an eyebrow, C.H. said, "Some material requires a level of discernment that Lewis doesn't yet have."

"What about freedom of information?"

He fixed Jacqui with a solemn gaze. "I have a responsibility to teach and protect my son from all kinds of harm, including harmful ideas." He craned to see past her. "So, let's see what kind of damage we've got here," he said, sauntering toward the bathroom.

Jacqui grabbed a disposable face mask. "Here, I don't want to be sued."

C.H. rolled his eyes but took it from her, shoving it into his shirt pocket.

She held back in the kitchen while he "hmmed," inspecting up and down the surface of each wall, sniffing at the faucet area.

"Looks alright to me. I'd give it a good spray with bleach, scrub the walls and pray for the best." He leaned against the doorjamb, handing back the unused mask.

"I'll have to bring in a plumber though, to get that faucet flush with the tile I was planning to install," Jacqui said, holding up a coffee mug and raising her eyebrows at him.

"Sure, I'll have a cup." He sat with an elbow on the table. "I didn't bring any tools with me today, but I could probably do the job for you. I redid the plumbing in our bathroom a few years back."

She poured his cup. "Would your work pass inspection?"

He laughed before raising the mug to his lips. "I reckon so."

His rueful response made her feel as though she shouldn't have doubted him. But this was her house. "Sorry. But my ex was a realtor. We saw way too many do-it-yourself disasters that cost more to fix than it would have cost to have a professional do the job in the first place."

"You can call a plumber if you want."

But the expense. "I'll think about it." She sat down with her own cup. From the TV in the living room, David Attenborough's cultured voice narrated the flight of birds. "What was that movie you vetoed?"

"Zeitgeist. He's brought it home before." He watched her over the rim of his mug. "Did you ever see it?"

"Oh yeah. That one was a favourite of my dad's."

"What did he like about it?"

"It fit perfectly with a lot of beliefs he already held. I could tell the stuff about international banking was just classic conspiracy theory. Unverifiable. I tried to refute some of the worst ideas in it, but I don't think I convinced him. It fit too well with what he believes about the little guy against The Man."

"The problem is, it's so earnest, so certain," C.H. said, taking a sip from his mug. "It's kind of appealing the way it dots all the i's and crosses all the t's and brings everything around full circle, letting you know who to blame for everything that's wrong with the world."

"You got that right. All those typical propaganda techniques," Jacqui said. "Move fast so the viewer never gets a chance to think over the claims you're making, let alone decide if they're supported by evidence. Use humour and animation to soften us up so we buy into the film's ideas."

C.H. grinned. "I mean, who can resist a George Carlin one-liner, right?" He pulled one leg across the other knee. "So, your father liked the financial conspiracy parts. Was there anything else that appealed to him?"

"Well, he was pretty pleased to find scholarly confirmation on the whole religion thing."

"Scholarly?" A smirk unbalanced his face. "If the other topics were full of propaganda and conspiracies, why would you think the points about religion were sound?"

"I don't know. It seemed to make sense."

"What did?"

"Hm," Jacqui said, wishing she had better recall, "I guess the parts about how the early Christians came up with their teachings by borrowing from other mythologies."

"You know, it's been a few years since I watched the movie, but I do recall it raising questions for me. When I checked into it though, I found exactly what you found about its financial claims. It moves fast, so you don't have a chance to refute anything. The producer probably figured no one would bother to verify, anyway."

"Like what did you find?"

"Man, I'm trying to remember." He ran his hand around his stubbly jaw. "That cult with a myth about... what was that other god's name? The one they were comparing to Jesus?"

Jacqui gave a wry smile. "It's not exactly something that's on my mind all the time." She grabbed her phone to look it up. "Horus. Apparently, he was born of a virgin, on December 25, visited by three kings guided by a star, etcetera, etcetera..."

"Oh yeah, that's right. The Mithra cult." C.H. leaned his elbows on his knees. "I read about that. Turns out, the real story of Horus is quite different from what the New Testament tells us about Jesus. Plus, the New Testament predates it, so you have to wonder who copied from whom. Historians contest a lot of points the film made. But what I came away with was the question of why Jews in ancient Palestine, who were absolutely steeped in the idea that there's only one God, would suddenly copy this idea from polytheism and start peddling it at the risk of their lives. That'd be kind of a tough sell. Because all but one of Jesus' followers were tortured and killed for their beliefs. They'd be nuts to do that, wouldn't they?"

Jacqui stared at her neighbour as a memory surfaced. She was at home alone on a Sunday afternoon, maybe nine or ten years old, her mother out with one of the guys she strung along. Aimless and bored, Jacqui started paying attention to the always-running TV, an archeology show talking about the discovery of the Dead Sea scrolls. The narrator described how these were copies of the Bible far more ancient than anything people had before. But except for a few differences in spelling, they were the same as a modern Bible. The feeling that came over her then was the same feeling she had now—a guilty tingling that made her legs tremble and her jaw stiff with tension. Guilty, because even though she rarely saw her father in those days, she knew without a doubt he would have switched the channel away from such a show. It shook her to think Pops could be wrong. He was the only one in her life to offer her roots, the only one she'd ever trusted. Yet the ideas in the program fascinated her. Until that time, she had never heard anyone talk as if the Bible was real history. Now here was C.H. calmly discussing religion like he believed it.

“Uh, Jacqui?” The scrape of his chair as C.H. stood brought Jacqui back to the present. “We've got to get going.” He leaned toward the door to the next room and boomed, “Lewis! Let's make like the trees and leave.”

No response came from the living room couch.

“C'mon, buddy!” he called again, setting his chair under the table and moving to the porch in search of his jacket. “Where art thou, 'O troubler of Israel'?” C.H. shot Jacqui a silent plea. “I've got chores to do and dinner to rustle up. He'll have a royal fit if I go in there and shut down his movie. Would you mind doing it?”

“Oh thanks. I get to be the bad guy.”

“I figured, being a librarian, you'd be good at it.” He grinned. “No, seriously, he'll do anything for you.”

C.H. was right. When Jacqui stopped the show and told Lewis it was time to go, the boy meekly gathered his belongings and headed for the door.

An hour later, Jacqui received a text from C.H. “Fun fact: the Mithra cult was a Roman military thing. Men only.”

CHAPTER 26

"The roads were okay on the way out here?" Jacqui asked Aunt Anna as she closed the door against the blustery winter wind.

"Bare and dry," Anna commented, unwrapping her winter scarf. It snagged on her lapel pin and she struggled for a minute before turning to Jacqui in exasperation. "Can you see better than I? I can't seem to unwind."

"You need to relax. You're like the guy who thought he was both a wigwam and a tipi," Jacqui said as she worked on the tangled yarn.

"What?" Anna smiled in anticipation.

"His psychiatrist said he was too tense." She released the scarf and stepped back.

Anna's eyes widened, then crinkled as she broke into a laugh. "I love puns."

Jacqui took in the older woman's unfettered mirth, wishing she could have seen her father's eyes light up like that more than they had. She ushered her into the living room where Anna gazed around in wonder. "You've done amazing work here. It's so fresh and clean."

"Thanks. I have more plans than cash, but I enjoy it."

They settled into the living room chairs near the fire Jacqui had built. She offered her aunt a mug of cocoa and took a sip of her own. "My dad loves plays on words too. He and you both would have loved what happened last week at the library. I had to call this guy about three books that were overdue: *The Case of the Missing Books* by—"

"Oh, go on!" Anna said in laughing disbelief.

"No seriously, that's a real title." Jacqui grinned. "The others were, *Gone Too Long* by Lori Roy, and here's my favourite—*You Will Pay* by Lisa Jackson."

Her aunt lapsed into gales of giggles. When she calmed, a smile lingered on her face. "You know where we all get this from, don't you dear? This love of word play?"

"It would have to have been your mother." Jacqui couldn't imagine her tyrannical grandfather enjoying anything.

"That's right! She had the most amazing gift for mimicry. Sometimes her impressions of local folks were so spot on my father would frown and warn her, 'Not in front of the children.'"

"What a spoil sport."

"Well, he had to make sure we kids didn't make a repeat performance in front of those very people. But I know he found them amusing too, because more than once I caught him and Mother later snickering to themselves." She sipped her hot chocolate. "Tell me more about your father. I was so young when he left home that I never really got to know him. What did your father find funny?"

Jacqui sobered as she recalled Pops' jokes. How could she tell her aunt, for whom faith was so vital, that her brother's favourite sport was ridiculing the very religion she held dear?

Anna's face grew sombre as she answered her own question. "Let me guess. He poked fun at religion, didn't he?"

Jacqui squirmed in discomfort.

"I can see I'm right. But never mind, I understand. It is hard to kick against the goads. We fight with whatever feeble weapons we have."

"I don't get what you mean."

Anna paused. "Sorry. A biblical reference." She shifted in her chair. "So, tell me something else about your upbringing."

Jacqui hesitated as she always did at such a question. All that she wished to forget, all that she was ashamed of and felt had disadvantaged her in life flooded her mind. She decided to tell the scrubbed version. “Things were good before I went to school. My mom worked part-time in retail and my dad was on shift work at the steel mill, so one of them was almost always at home for me. When my baby brother died... things changed. It's kind of a sorry tale that I don't love to tell.” Jacqui stared at the unfinished upholstery of the empty chair beside Anna, running her finger around and around inside the handle of her mug. Her aunt sat quiet, evidently waiting. Finally, Jacqui gave a summary of her mother's downward spiral after the baby's death, ending where she always ended, with Pops taking her to live with him.

Setting down her mug, Anna leaned toward her. “I'm curious to know what John was like as a father because ever since you came you've had questions about your grandfather's harshness. I guess I want to know if your dad did it better.”

“Of course he did. Pops was never abusive. He never laid a hand on me.”

Anna offered no response to this, which somehow Jacqui interpreted as doubt. “He was a really easy-going dad. I guess he could trust me to pretty much do whatever I wanted. Go to bed when I liked, eat what I wanted, go to friends' places.”

“Not all children would do well under those conditions. You never tested the limits?”

“Well, there really weren't any limits that I remember. Pops never had to tell me to do housework or anything, we kind of fell into a routine when I found out I liked cooking and cleaning. I always got my homework done and didn't get into trouble at school. I was a pretty good kid.”

“Sounds like he had a dream child. Of course, no one is entirely good,” Aunt Anna leaned her head to one side, “which is why we have a guilty feeling when we see the flashing lights of a police car behind us or experience a bit of fear when someone tells us they have something they wish to speak with us about."

"Well, I think Pops was proud of the job he did with me." She drained the last of her cocoa and set the mug on the side table. "I guess my father did have one rule. He told me I could believe whatever I wanted to, but I was never to mention anything to do with religion."

The older woman made a muffled hum. "How was that for you?"

Jacqui scrutinized her, checking for some clue to her aunt's opinion on this. "Okay, I guess." She thought of the occasion when she'd broken that rule.

"I remember one time I wished he would have said no to me." She put her feet up on the round vinyl hassock she'd kept for its utility rather than its style. "After I went back to live with my dad when I was about twelve, my friend Melanie and I were invited to this birthday party for twin boys a year older than we were. Her parents were quite strict, and she knew they wouldn't let her go so she got me to invite her that night for a sleepover knowing that my dad wouldn't object. Pops dropped us off for the party and told us to call him when we wanted him to pick us up." A shudder ran through her at the memory—black candles in the corners and the strange cloying smell of the place, the barrenness of the rooms but for a couch and a table with a couple of chairs, the weird symbols and words on posters on the walls. The look Melanie had given her when they walked in showed she felt the same way. But then the boys came downstairs and a couple of other kids arrived.

"You were saying?" Anna raised an eyebrow.

"Right. Yeah, we spent a couple of hours just hanging out, goofing off, listening to music. But then the twins' mom came home. Uh, she was like nothing we'd ever seen before. Almost like she was in costume, except this was nowhere near Hallowe'en. She was a tiny woman with long, kind of poofy hair dyed jet-black, a ton of eye makeup, black lipstick, black fingernail polish. She wore this airy-fairy black dress with lots of dangling beads and fringes all over, and thigh-high black suede boots that laced up the front. I'm sure our mouths were hanging open at the sight. But it wasn't only her outfit that freaked Melanie and me out. She had this guy with her, kind of a big guy who seemed way too young for her. He seemed like her henchman or something, the way she ordered him around." She lifted her arms from her sides in a hulking impression of him, but Anna didn't laugh. Instead a deep vee had formed between her eyebrows.

"So, she gives each of us this piercing look, smiles without a word, then heads off up the stairs. She comes down a while later in a different black outfit with a game box under her arm and tells us to gather in a circle on the living room floor. Then she sets the Ouija board in the middle of our circle. All at once Melanie jumps up and blurts out that she has to go to the bathroom. She takes off and the boys' mom makes us close the circle and play this dumb game. I was convinced she had some sort of sleight of hand going on to make it move the way it did. But soon she got Igor to light the candles and starts a séance. That's when I started to feel uncomfortable."

"Why?" Anna probed.

"I don't know. Maybe it was only the scent of the candles, but the air started to get heavy and hard to breathe. I felt as though I needed to get into the daylight... I don't know, it just gave me the creeps. I can't explain it." Jacqui picked at a hangnail remembering the eerie atmosphere and unexplainable noises, the unnatural twitching of one of the boys. "I went to the bathroom to find out what was up with my friend. She said that what was going on was evil and we should have nothing to do with it, that she should never have gone against her parents to come. She begged me to sneak to the phone and call my dad to come get us. I was about to do that but when I opened the door of the bathroom, I nearly ran right into the boys' mom. She seemed irritated and even irate when I told her we wanted to go home. She said the aura around me was very bright and promising and she needed more time to assess me. I told her Melanie wasn't feeling well and we had to get home. Finally, she let me make the call and Pops picked us up.

“And that's when you broke your father's rule about mentioning God?”

“Well, technically I didn't but going by his reaction I might as well have. On the way home, I told him what had gone on, what a weird and spooky atmosphere it had been in the house that night. I was trying hard to work it out in my mind and the best I could do was a question. I was careful how I worded it, but I remember asking him if there was evil, wouldn't there also have to be good? I'll never forget his response. I was expecting him to just pat me on the head and pooh-pooh it all with some rational explanation. In fact, I was kind of hoping he would. Instead, he slammed on the brakes on a side street, turned to me with the worst anger I'd ever seen on his face and said, 'Don't you ever, *ever* get involved with anything supernatural like that again! It's very dangerous.' And that was it. We rode the rest of the way home in dead silence.” Jacqui waited for her aunt's response.

“And he specifically said 'supernatural'?”

“That's right. I remember because it surprised me, since he'd always said the supernatural world didn’t exist.”

Anna waited a long time before responding. Twice she appeared to be about to speak, then closed her mouth. Finally, she asked, “What did you make of it all, dear?”

Jacqui pondered the experience she'd nearly forgotten. “I guess I lost respect for Pops. I mean, he usually had these scientific and philosophical-sounding arguments that answered my questions, but that time I thought he really dropped the ball with his emotional reaction.”

"He was right, you know," Anna said. "Getting involved in the dark side of spirituality is extremely dangerous. And you were right too—just as the absence of light equals darkness, if there's a force for evil, there must also be its opposite, a force for good. I believe he is a person, not merely a force, and that he entered this world to provide a way for those of us who aren't good people to be forgiven of the dark deeds we've done."

"Yeah, well, I don't have any dark deeds hidden away." To keep from fidgeting in her seat, Jacqui rose to pick up the empty mugs. "I hope you're hungry. I've planned a frittata for lunch."

CHAPTER 27

Driving the freshly snow-powdered roads to work, Jacqui asked herself the question she had asked every day since she'd decided to leave Geoff. *Was I even married?*

They had been a couple since she was twenty, and they'd moved in together less than a year after that. Four years later, they had spoken their vows on that beautiful lake in Algonquin Park. After that, she had always considered herself married to Geoff. Of course they were. What difference would a piece of paper have made?

And yet, an odd hesitance to refer to each other as husband or wife had persisted. They'd referred to each other as partners. Like a business transaction.

But surely they had been more than that. She ransacked her memory. What was it Geoff had actually promised? It seemed like such a long time ago, and she had no one to ask—no one had witnessed the vows, no nostalgic video had recorded it. She strained to remember.

Ah, yes.

"I love you, and I declare, by the earth and the sky and the water all around us, that you are the one for me." That was it. A statement, and rather a self-satisfied one, embellished by the nature imagery. Which was strange, considering Geoff's general distaste for the outdoors. But certainly, there had been no promise or vow. What kind of spell had she been under that such meaningless words had satisfied her? She clearly remembered following his lead with the earth, sky and water hooey but with one difference. She, at least, had promised to love him always.

What was it that made two people married? A legal document? For tax purposes, she and Geoff were the equivalent.

Or was it a carefully choreographed party? They'd hosted plenty of special dinner parties. A promise? They'd made one, or at least, she had. An emotional bond? She'd learned the hard way it was no easier to end their relationship than to dissolve a traditional marriage. No easier, and just as agonizing. She'd been subject to all the same feelings of betrayal at the cheating and the hassles of division of property. So, what was the difference?

She stomped up the steps of the library, entering with an emphatic slam of her purse and books onto her desk.

Today Sheri had decided to make an appearance, which only worsened Jacqui's mood. During Jacqui's first weeks on the job, the older woman had hovered, teaching and reminding Jacqui of the most elementary procedures with the most annoying condescension. Then for months, Sheri had left the running of the library entirely to Jacqui. It didn't much matter—she was glad for the income and preferred not having to maneuver around Sheri's brassy persona. However, today the chubby bunny was in high spirits for the season, wearing a tight red, fur-trimmed sweater and long glittery earrings.

"Merry Christmas, Jacqui!" Sheri chirruped in her most irritating baby-voice. She thrust a large crisp white envelope under Jacqui's face, her name in large looping curlicues on the front. Sheri twinkled her brilliant acrylics at her. "I've made some wassail for anyone who comes by and there's lots of baking over by the coffee station, too." She thumped a ghetto blaster onto her desk and started a Christmas playlist. Elvis, no less.

Jacqui sighed. As Bree would say, it was fixin' to be a long day. She stationed herself at her desk, firing up her computer to check in her personal books.

The bell above the door chimed and a young child raced in followed by his parents. The heavy-featured woman stopped in front of Sheri's desk, her man at her side.

"You'd think," the woman began in an aggrieved tone, "with two kids to get ready for school and chickens to feed, this Bozo here could at least manage to figure out what's wrong with the furnace." Throwing an annoyed glance at him, her lips thinned in a grim line.

Shocked at the reckless accusation, Jacqui's eyes slid towards Sheri, who gazed mildly at the two patrons. "Merry Christmas, Norma." She nodded at the man. "You too, Norm."

"So, not only do I have to get everyone's breakfast," Norma went on, warming to her topic, "take care of my son, and wash three dozen eggs, I also have to call a repair guy. 'Cause you know, the guy who *lives* in the house wouldn't want to lift a finger to make a phone call."

Jacqui watched Norm for signs of outrage or offense, but the man's face remained impassive. How could he stand it?

Sheri cut short the berating by steering the woman to a movie recommendation. Jacqui had to admire her quick thinking.

After they left, Sheri chuckled at Jacqui's open-mouthed stare. "Oh, never mind her. She's always on about him. She makes the rounds, the hair salon, the tearoom, even the seniors' center. Anybody who will listen gets an earful about dumb Norm. I figure, if he's that bad, why doesn't she just leave him? They're not married, after all." She rose and hurried down the large print aisle.

Norma's supposed to leave simply because they don't have a piece of paper? Sheri's comment revealed a low regard for the common-law relationship that offended Jacqui. Yet why didn't disgruntled Norma leave? A better question might be, why didn't Norm leave? Obviously, he endured the verbal abuse for the sake of his children.

Sheri scuttled back to Jacqui's side with an armload of books. She gave a soft tap on Jacqui's shoulder.

At that moment, the bell above the door rang again, and a couple of seniors entered. With a poof of perfume, Sheri instantly dropped to an awkward crouch.

"Check these out to Misham Pete," she whispered.

Jacqui threw a glance her way, noting the deep flush on Sheri's cheeks. Typing in the name brought no results. "How do you spell Misham?"

"M-I-S—" Sheri began, then craned her neck to peer up at the screen. "No, silly! Pete's not his first name, Misham is."

Silly? I'll give you silly! What kind of a silly name is Misham Pete? She remembered names like that back east—Windsor Brett, Fraser Kenneth, Taylor Annabelle. *How sadistic do parents have to be to saddle their kid with a lifelong problem like that?* She typed it in and handed the checked-out books back to Sheri, who put them in a bag. The woman stuffed herself into her faux-fur coat, grabbed the book bag and said "ta ta" before leaving through the rear door.

Jacqui breathed a sigh of relief and promptly rose to put an emphatic stop to Elvis's Blue Christmas crooning. Back at her desk, she was about to leave Misham Pete's borrower page, then paused. Sheri's surreptitious stealth with those books was weird. Jacqui took a closer look at the patron record. Each of the seven books listed bore a title like *Sweaty Knights* or *Sweaty Daze.* Erotica. That accounted for Sheri's juvenile sneak mode. Each book was written by the same author— Millie Sherona. *Why does that name sound so familiar? And why does Sheri feel she has to hide this guy's taste in books?*

The bell above the door chimed again, ushering in a young man in low-hanging jeans, followed by the young Mennonite woman, Sarah and her Asian daughter, who had been in weeks earlier. The mother seemed sombre and paler, even for her fair complexion. She took slow steps toward Jacqui, finally setting down a short stack of children's books and one non-fiction title heavily on the desk as though their weight was unbearable. She reached to retrieve the adult book. As she stood in front of Jacqui's desk, her eyes made a slow circuit of the small library, and she shifted her weight from foot to foot.

"May I speak with you," she glanced around again, "privately?"

Jacqui watched a senior couple round the end of a book stack and vanish down the row. The young guy of the baggy pants was still ensconced at a computer, wearing headphones.

"Sure," she said. "Why don't you come behind the desk and sit here?" Her pulse accelerated as she pulled Sheri's office chair toward her. *Have I done something wrong?* She searched her memory of the woman's last visit. Nothing came to mind, except... Jacqui tried to catch a glimpse of the title in Sarah's hand, but she held it close against her chest while she sent her little girl to the children's section.

"I am Sarah Bergen. You've seen my daughter, Ava?" She pointed to where the child had skipped around the corner.

"Yes."

"Ever since I laid eyes on her in the orphanage in China, I knew she was meant to be mine." She searched Jacqui's face through ice-blue red-rimmed eyes. "You know what I mean?"

Jacqui didn't. But then she thought of her desperate feat of will-power, reviving the wee kitten, Gandalf. She knew it wasn't the same but gave an understanding nod anyway.

A brief glow of pride suffused Sarah's face. "She was the most beautiful baby there. Such huge dark eyes and lovely creamy face. Her hair was so thick and long that even at two months she could wear hair clips." She smiled. "We were finally able to bring her home when she was eleven months old. Waiting until all the paperwork went through was the hardest thing I've ever done." The smile faded as Sarah gazed off through the winter-white window. "Much harder, even, than the long wait we had after our wedding, hoping for children." Sarah met Jacqui's gaze. "I only had the one small picture that the orphanage gave us. Our people don't take photos, you know. But I couldn't help keeping that one and nearly wore it out with staring at it all the time."

She heaved a deep sigh. "When we first applied to adopt, the agency told us the children were orphans." She blinked and moistened her lips. "They never told us anything about the children's birth parents. But every year, the orphanage staff in Zhengyuan invites adoptive parents and kids to visit. It's expensive and we thought the trip would be too long for Ava when she was very young, but finally, last summer, it worked out that we could go. We enjoyed the trip so much. Ava was old enough to understand, and she asked so many questions. But I noticed something unusual. A number of the local Chinese people attended, too. None of us adoptive parents knew who they were..." Her eyes swam above blotchy cheeks and she reached for a tissue from Jacqui's desk.

"Was it the police checking up on you?"

Sarah shook her head, the wisps of baby-fine blonde hair escaping her dark cloth head-covering and floating around her face. "No, not that. Those people acted so... strange. They seemed to be searching for certain children. And one of the ladies came to Ava and hugged her again and again. I was confused with so many people there—the orphanage staff, the Chinese government lady, the interpreters. The Chinese interpreters were hard to understand even when they spoke English. And then all the different languages spoken by the adoptive parents from other countries." She dabbed at her eyes and cleared her throat. "But at the airport, we spoke to an American couple who said they felt sure some of those non-staff people were the real birth parents of our children." Sarah clutched at Jacqui's arm. "That was exactly what I was afraid of, but I didn't want to even think of the idea." She squeezed the arm tighter. "But now this book," she said as she held up the volume she was returning. "I wish I'd never read it. It says a lot of the children adopted internationally weren't given up voluntarily. Many have parents who really wanted them but were forced by the government's one-child policy to give them up." She searched Jacqui's face as though seeking contradiction to what she'd read. "What if my sweet Ava has a mother over there, a mother who is crying for her baby at night, missing her? Missing her child for five and a half years now!" Tears now streamed down Sarah's cheeks. "I can't sleep, I can't eat, and I can't stop thinking about it. But how can I give up my precious little girl?"

CHAPTER 28

Jacqui smeared peanut butter on a sandwich for a rushed lunch on the way over to her neighbours'. C.H.'s voice had been taut with anxiety when he called a few minutes ago asking her to come stay with Lewis. Roslyn was in crisis. What would that mean for Lewis?

I hate dead. Those were the boy's own words a few months ago when together, he and Jacqui had discovered the frozen kittens. Would his mother's critical health cause him to retreat into a remote shell, or would it make him high strung? Either way, it would be up to Jacqui to somehow talk him down. And strangely, she relished the task.

The rear end of her car fish-tailed a bit as she made her way up the sloping, snowy drive to the Legrands' home. From the cab of his idling pick-up, C.H. raised a hand at Jacqui in greeting while she headed for the house. Inside, a woman with bobbed, steel-gray hair was buttoning her winter coat. "You're Jacqui Penn. I've heard a lot about you." She scrutinized Jacqui unsmilingly from under the creased lids of her gray eyes.

Jacqui nodded, sensing hostility, and noted the woman didn't bother to introduce herself.

The woman inhaled deeply then gestured through the porch door to a kitchen beyond. "Lewis and I have been baking Christmas cookies. There are still a few pans left to go into the oven." She tilted her head in question. "I'm told you can handle Lewis?"

"I think so." *I hope so.*

"Alright then." Her lips were firmly stitched in a rippled seam. "I have no idea how long we'll be at the hospital. My daughter—" Her voice cracked and Jacqui released some of her defensiveness. This was Roslyn's mother. No wonder she was on edge.

"You may have to make a bed for yourself on the sofa," the woman went on in a husky voice. "Lewis shouldn't be left alone. Whatever you do, don't talk to him about his mother's health." With that, she left the house.

Jacqui hung her jacket and padded through to the kitchen. An expansive island resting on over-sized, turned oak pedestals appeared to be part of an ongoing renovation. Against the outer wall, a bank of dated cupboards and sink awaited a matching update. The oven was on, but nothing was in it.

An unfinished strip on the ceiling revealed that a wall had once separated the kitchen from the living room. Through the open space, she could see Lewis at the living room window, watching the tail of his father's truck glide out of the yard. For the first time, she saw him without his ball-cap. A quarter-sized spot of dark hair sat like a lone leopard's spot, slightly off-center at the back of his white-blond head.

"Hey, buddy. I think you've still got a few of these cookies to decorate before I can put them in the oven."

The lad remained motionless at the window.

"Okay then, I guess I get to decide whether to use blue sprinkles for these angels, or red sugar." Jacqui reached for the small packets of decorations across the island's dark granite, so similar to what she'd had installed in her dream kitchen back east. The battered metal edges of the worn counter tops in her current place were a far cry from this clean, smooth surface and she could feel her gut twist in resentment at Geoff's stalling on the sale of their home. With effort, she forced her mind back to her purpose here.

Slowly, she began sprinkling the cookies, hoping Lewis would join her. From the corner of her eye, she sensed movement. “Hm. I think this one needs a little sprucing up. How about one of these silver balls on each wing?”

Silently, Lewis joined her and resumed his careful work of ensuring each tidbit of sugar was placed equidistant from the others. He corrected the ones on Jacqui's cookies as well. Snatching glimpses of his face, she found his mouth was set in a grim line, a corner of it caught between his teeth in concentration.

Must be in one of his silent modes.

“You like baking with your grandma?”

Lewis nodded.

“Anything special you're hoping for this Christmas?”

A slow smile spread across Lewis's face. He stepped up his pace spreading sugar crystals on the last angel cookie before motioning to Jacqui to slide the tray into the oven. Then he sped down the hall where Jacqui heard rummaging while she wiped up sugary remains. Lewis returned, arms laden with computer printouts and brochures which he spread across the countertop. And he was off, detailing every model of farm machinery toy, which ones he owned, which he hoped to acquire, which size scale he preferred. He pulled her by the hand to his room where shelves held his collection of tractors and implements, all green.

“It's my long green line,” he explained in a confidential tone.

Jacqui took in the John Deere bedspread, neatly smoothed, the barnboard trim and deep green walls, while Lewis tossed tractor numbers about like kernels of wheat. *So, he's not on mute after all.* Was his earlier silence an indication he knew something serious was happening with his mother?

Abruptly, he turned to leave the room, twitching his head for Jacqui to follow. She switched off the bedroom light as they rushed back to the kitchen. He led her to the Christmas tree where he knelt and began shaking one of the few gift-wrapped packages beneath it.

"Just a sec, Lewis," Jacqui said, hurrying back to the kitchen. "The timer must have gone off by now." She drew the cookie sheet out of the oven and placed the remaining two pans inside.

"So, what do you think is in that one?" she asked him between shakes of the box in Lewis's hand.

"It's the 9620R!"

"Oh, yeah? How do you know?"

"'Cause that's what I asked for. And it's just the right size for the 1/32 model, I can tell. It's the biggest R tractor Deere's got. Nine hundred and sixty horse-power, e18 TM power shift with efficiency manager, Hydra Shift TM suspension." Lewis stopped to catch his breath.

Jacqui grinned. *Did the kid memorize factory data from owner's manuals?* "Do you know what TM means?"

"Trademark," the boy answered, without missing a beat. He went on rattling off tractor specifications that were meaningless to Jacqui. Her attention strayed, drawn by a book-lined corner next to the tree. Among the books, she noticed a set of classics, *Marlowe to Shakespeare, Milton Poems, Tennyson to Whitman* and other volumes of poetry, too. Poe, Leonard Cohen, T.S. Eliot. *Interesting reading material for a farmer.*

Lewis must have caught her gaze. He beckoned her to the cluttered desk nearby and began riffling through papers. Hung above the desk were two framed certificates acknowledging Charles Haddon Legrand—a bachelor in biblical studies and an agronomist level II. *Kind of a weird combination.*

Lewis thrust a few loose pages into her hand.

"What's this?" she asked, unsure whether they were his to share.

"Dad's poems. He writes cowboy poems all the time and I help him. He asks, 'What rhymes with snow?' And then I go through the ABCs telling all the words that rhyme with snow."

Jacqui glanced at the verses on the top page.

She's a prairie Canuck and I'm from the south
And we met at a college half-way
We studied together, the words from her mouth
Held me captive that very first day.

So, C.H. writes poetry. A schmaltzy ballad recounting how C.H. and Roslyn met. The predictably rhythmic lines seemed personal, yet curiosity drew her in.

Before she could read on, Lewis cut in. "He doesn't always use the words I say. And sometimes they don't rhyme at all." He slid out one of the pages Jacqui held, laying it on top of the stack. "Here." He tapped the page in front of her. "Read this one. It's my favourite."

Jacqui focused on deciphering the deeply indented print.

"Out loud. I want to hear it," Lewis insisted.

She cleared her throat.

Wind knifed through my Carhartts, I squinted to see
Through the blur of the swirling dry snow.
Old eight-forty-two, the first cow to calve
Had been missing at feed time, you know.

She'd always been faithful, a good calver, good mama
And usually had given us twins.
But I didn't like the weather this mornin'
And figured I'd just coax her in.

Spur huddled behind me, his tongue tucked inside
Too blustery for both dog and man,
I combed the far pasture and up close besides
But could barely tell white sky from land.

Spur gave a sharp bark and leapt off the quad
So, I followed the dog to a copse
Where old eight-forty-two bent her head to the ground
A'nudging and licking her calf.

I cut the motor, swung my leg off the quad,
And fought through the wind with its sting.
In a wallow of snow melted slick with red ice
Lay a hushed, still, dark, wet little thing.

The mama kept licking with powerful strokes
But the poor critter just didn't move.
My heart felt like ice as I stared at the scene.
I'd counted on eight-forty-two.

I'd counted on twins, perhaps even three
Not this pitiful waif lying still.
With Roslyn expecting and due any day
We were hoping our ship had come in.

But wait, there was life. I saw its ear twitch.
I scrambled ahead with my towel.
It flinched as I rubbed, then I cuddled it close.
The cow let me take it, then followed.

Back at the barn, I worked the poor calf
Let his mama lick him and nose him.
He strained to get up with his forelegs braced stiff
But the rear legs were too weak to hold him.

It came to me then I could save us the bother
Of bottles and all of that bit.
There was always next year for old eight-forty-two,
I could give up and that would be it.

But the cow wouldn't stop with her nuzzling and bunting
And the wee calf's great will wouldn't give.
With her nose, mama lifted the calf's floppy rear
Reminding me, Life wants to live!

I sighed, shook my head, shrugged at Spur's puzzled look
Searched the barn walls for something I might
Make into a sling for the gimped little critter
I'd be in for some long, wakeful nights.

In time, that brave dogie found his feet, front and rear
And could keep up with Mom like the rest.
It cost me some sleep and some old-fashioned ribbing
But I saw it as some sort of test.

'Cause you see, not long later, my Roslyn gave birth
To a baby the doc said wasn't right.
He had seizures and trouble and moments of terror
When his breathing would stop in the night.

They gave us the forecast of deafness and blindness
And never a step would he take
They laid out before us the ominous choice
To cut short the pain for his sake.

But I thought of the sling I had rigged for that calf
All the effort and love I had given,
Looked my bride in the eyes, stroked the babe's velvet face
And answered them, Life wants to live!

Jacqui finished reading and slowly lowered the hand-written page, her throat tight with feeling. Whether the poetry was good or not, it evoked all Jacqui's tender memories of her baby brother, his soft completeness and her helpless feeling at his inevitable slipping from life.

"That was me!" Lewis intruded on her thoughts with a grin, his eyes on a spot near the top of the Christmas tree behind her. "Dad said I was like the runty calf that was so weak. And they said I wouldn't walk, or talk, or hear or be smart. But I am!" He jumped up and attempted a heel-kick, his long amphibious legs flailing wildly.

Jacqui swallowed the lump in her throat. She couldn't help laughing, relaxing, as he made a few more leaps around the couch. "You're smart, all right, Froggie!"

CHAPTER 29

The dreaded prospect of spending Christmas Eve alone turned out not to be as traumatic as Jacqui had expected. Aunt Anna had called a week ago asking her to spend Christmas day at her house, so that was something to look forward to. Anna said she regretted she couldn't ask Jacqui to stay over, but she was expecting a full house.

The twenty-fourth went much like most of Jacqui's Saturdays did. She set her phone to a jazz play list to work by, deliberately avoiding the seasonal music that might evoke too many memories—dismal ones from childhood or happy ones with Geoff. None of those were an appealing reminder now. Besides, jazz always drew Gandalf to come sidling up to her. She headed purposefully to the waiting bathroom project.

Somehow C.H. had found the time last week to re-plumb the tub faucet and even help her patch the wall around it. She felt confident she had the skills for the rest. Today she meant to tackle the last of the drywall finishing. Her plan was to clear up the mess of dust, prime the walls and hopefully still have time to start on the tile around the tub. She'd splurged on the tile, thanks to Pops' curiously generous Christmas cheque this year.

Probably feeling sorry for me. But was it the break-up Pops pitied her for, or was the gift prompted by her ongoing chatter about the house project during her calls to him? She limited herself to projects she'd already completed. Whatever she expressed an idle wish for, he would offer to buy for her. Even in the past, complimenting him on some household item he'd acquired at a garage sale resulted in his appearing at her door with a new version.

Then a different thought occurred to her. *Maybe he meant for me to fly back to Hamilton to spend Christmas with him.* Jacqui stopped stroking the walls and her sanding pad went slack. Pops had made no hints or suggestions about that, but still a twinge of guilt fluttered through her.

Too late now. And I'm not ready to face all that. I'll phone him tonight, though.

But while waiting for the dust to settle, she decided not to put off the call.

"City morgue," came Pops' gravelly voice when he picked up. "Tell me who you want to speak to, and I'll check the tags."

"It's that bad, is it Pops?"

"Ah, the daughter speaks at last. How're things?"

Jacqui related the latest mishaps and advances on the house, downplaying how often the furnace was running now she'd removed the insulated ceiling. She thanked him for the gift and described the bathroom tile she'd bought with the money.

"Sounds good," Pops gritted out. "You up to setting the tile on your own?"

What? Pops was actually asking something about her house project? Ever since her move out here, he'd changed the subject when she talked of the family, or even people in the community. And the same was true of the reno. He seemed determined to steer clear of any discussion of the home where he'd grown up.

"You do remember I've done a fair bit of tiling on my own since you and I worked on my first place?" But she was grateful for even his slightest interest. She went on to describe her progress in the bathroom, told him how Gandalf the kitten loved music, gave a weather report, then ran out of conversation fodder. What she was tempted to ask him was whether he'd seen Geoff at all. As soon as Jacqui informed Pops about the state of her relationship, he would have cut off all contact with Geoff out of loyalty to her, but perhaps he'd run into him somewhere? Yet she couldn't quite bring herself to ask.

"So, are you keeping alright?" she asked instead.

"Just about well enough to sit up and take nourishment," he said.

Jacqui fidgeted on her chair. "OK then. I should get back to the grind. Thanks again for the cheque and Merry Christmas!"

"And a Ho Ho Ho to you, too."

Oh right. How could she have forgotten? No Christmas according to Pops. Out west here, the expression was so common she'd let it slip without thought.

Hours later, Jacqui ran her hand across the wall of cool, glossy tile in satisfaction. The more she completed, the more motivated she became. Finally, she was seeing some transformation in this house. By the time she finished setting the tiles on the third wall, her lower back and right shoulder were aching. But the tub area had turned out fantastic. She snapped a few photos to send to Bree, cleared away the mess and tools and had just enough energy to throw together a quick sandwich before washing up and heading for bed.

It was still dark the next morning when Gandalf began kneading her arm in a wake-up call. Despite the early hour, Jacqui found herself eager to get to Aunt Anna's. She savoured again the novel sensation of belonging she'd experienced when she sat with family, her family, at the funeral in November. And while it seemed wrong somehow to have so thoroughly enjoyed herself at a time when others were reeling with shock and grief, that was the plain truth of it.

The car headlights flashed a thousand sparks of light off every frost-feathered branch and twig as she left home. From behind her, the wintry fuchsia sunrise tinted even the shadowy western clouds with blush. On the way to Red Deer, she met only two other vehicles. Except for her, all the world was snug at home, opening gifts. The melancholy thought made her doubly grateful for a place to be this morning. She was expected.

At Anna's modest duplex, the driveway was full of vehicles, so Jacqui parked on the other side of the street. Sounds of merriment whistled from inside the door before she even rang the bell.

A tall muscular man with "cop" written all over him answered the door. Jacqui recognized an understated wariness also written on him, likely a hazard of the job. With one arm, he grasped the door, effectively barring her way in, while a little girl in fuzzy pink pyjamas perched on the other arm.

"I'm your cousin Jacqui."

"Don Fawcett," he said, relaxing into a wide grin that transformed his face. He let the door swing open for her. "C'mon in!"

Jacqui stepped inside, surveying the buzz of activity from every quarter.

"Everybody," Don called out, commanding the room, "meet your cousin, Jacqui!"

Such a list of names and connections followed that Jacqui couldn't quite remember who belonged to who. Don must have sensed her confusion. "Just remember the five of us—Burk, me, Beth, David and Jesse. You'll figure the rest out eventually."

Jacqui had already met Beth and her brother David at their uncle's and cousins' funeral in the fall, "Is Aunt Anna baking pies?" she asked, craning her neck to peek into the kitchen.

Rising from the floor where she was engaging young Dusty with a brightly-coloured toy, Beth approached Jacqui. "No, something came up and she had to leave for the day."

"She took off as soon as we finished opening gifts," Don said, backing farther into the room and waving a hand at the whirlwind of Christmas debris. "Sorry you missed all the excitement. Kids, you know."

From behind Don, Jesse approached to give Jacqui a squeeze. Her heart melted with the love he offered. "Your coat," he said, holding out an expectant hand. Jacqui unwound her scarf and began unbuttoning her coat.

"The past few days," Beth went on, "Mom couldn't get an answer from Aunt Naomi, so she called Cousin Ruthie. Turns out Aunt Naomi fell and broke her ankle last night and they kept her in hospital overnight. So, Mom skipped out on us after our gift opening to help her get home and to spend a little time with her." Beth searched her face. "Don't worry, she'll be here tomorrow, and she asked if you could come then."

Jacqui glanced from Don to Beth, slowly pulling her coat back up onto her shoulders.

Beth laughed and laid a hand on her arm to stop her. "No, no! She meant spend today with us and come again tomorrow so she can see you, too." She swept a path through toys and ribbon and cleared a space on the sofa. "Why don't you join the fun here while I finish clearing away breakfast?"

"Or I could help..." Jacqui moved to follow her.

"Not enough room in the kitchen. But next time, for sure."

A preschooler in pink sidled up to Jacqui as she sat at the end of Anna's couch. Jacqui smiled down at her, which prompted the tiny girl to climb onto her lap and lean against her chest. While Jacqui tuned in to the middle of her cousins' conversation, the kid's bunny-ears hair-do tickled her neck with her every fidget.

"Right," Burk, the scholarly cousin, said with a smirk. "The cause of everything that's wrong with the world."

On the floor near him, David shifted to cross his legs, leaning his chin on his fist. "So, what would you have said to that?"

Burk inclined his head to his brother. "First I'd have to figure out if he was serious. A lot of times people beak off about stuff they've seen online, but really have no intention of defending the ideas. Half the time I wonder if they know what they're talking about."

David didn't respond, only stared at the pair of Lego wheels he was twirling in his free hand.

"Somebody hit you up with that one?" Burk probed. "That religion is the cause of everything wrong in the world?"

"Not that, but a few others I didn't know the answer to."

Burk stretched his legs out in front of him, clasping his hands behind his head. "We live in a meme world now. Politics, theology, culture. It's as if there's no concept too profound that it can't be reduced to a Kermit the Frog meme."

Don made frantic typing motions. "Someone is wrong on the Internet!"

Burk nodded, chuckling. "I've begun to think it's pointless to even try to answer people who communicate that way."

A gangly young boy appeared at the door to the kitchen calling David to join him downstairs. Jacqui was left with the two oldest brothers, Burk and Don, who stared at each other in wonder.

After a few moments, Don said, "Can you believe little bro asking questions like that?"

Burk shook his head with a bemused smile that piqued Jacqui's curiosity. What made it unusual for David to be asking questions about religion? Was he a younger counterpart of Pops, the misfit in this family?

Jacqui fixed her mind on the question that had caught her attention initially. "So, what *would* you say to someone who says religion has caused all that's wrong with the world?"

Burk's drooping eyes widened, and he sat up straighter. He scratched his stubbly beard. "I guess I'd want to know what they meant by 'all that's wrong'."

Jacqui shifted the now-sleeping child's chubby legs so they stretched across her lap. "Let's say they brought up all the millions throughout history that have been killed in wars fought in the name of religion." She tried to keep Pops' belligerence out of her tone.

"Hm. I guess you could take that in a couple of different directions. Like, on what basis does your hypothetical questioner decide that wars are wrong? Judgments like that require a moral law-giver, right?" He eyed Jacqui for a moment, then continued. "But here's the thing. If you study history, often what's called a religious conflict isn't bottom-line religious at all. Take Northern Ireland, for an example. Or wars in Eastern Europe or the Middle East. There are religious differences, yeah, but at the root, those have been all about ethnic hostilities. They would have occurred, regardless. In fact, you could make a case for conflicts being shortened because of the pleas for peace by religious people."

"What about the Crusades, though?" Jacqui asked.

Burk leaned her way. "What about them?"

"The Crusades were instigated by the Church, so definitely religious wars."

"No question, that was some misguided thinking. But initially, they were defensive wars. Christian pilgrims to the Holy Land were being slaughtered and the pope wanted to make the region safe for them. Of course, he had no business promising heavenly rewards to people for participating. That was way out of line. But honestly, Christianity holds the key to evaluating history."

"What do you mean?" Jacqui stuffed a cushion under her arm, feeling the weight of the child's sleepy head.

"That there's something bigger—an objective standard by which to measure both church as a whole, or individual Christians. So, we can evaluate current events or history to see how some of these decisions stack up by God's standards. Of course, there's another important component to your question." He paused. "Has atheism fared any better? Nazism, communism? Hasn't the greatest evil always come when people deny there's a God they'll have to answer to?"

Don raised his eyebrows and held his hands out toward Jacqui, as if to take his daughter from her arms. She shook her head, enjoying the soothing warmth of the child.

"Yeah, I'd have to agree," Don said, settling back in his chair. "Check out the stats on massacres and genocides. In just a few decades, atheist ideologies produced over a hundred million dead in the Soviet Union, Germany, China, and Cambodia. Seems like humanity does a pretty good job of wrecking the world all on its own."

"So, Jacqui," Burk began, lacing his fingers behind his head. "You're obviously a deep thinker. I'd be interested in knowing what's behind these questions."

Jacqui busied herself straightening the soft pyjama folds of the child in her lap. She felt protective of Pops, though she wondered if he'd ever heard a well-considered response to his questions. Or had he simply refused to listen? "Oh, nothing really. When I heard David ask you that question, it reminded me of someone I know."

"Well, pass on the truth to your friend. And maybe add this: Christianity's real legacy is a radical transformation of whatever society it has touched. Hospitals, prison reform, the status of women and the disabled, literacy of the common people and hence, modern education." He enumerated them on his fingers. "Christian abolitionists were relentless against slavery and finally won. Wherever Christians went, they fought against abuses like child marriage, immolation of widows, polygamy, foot-binding, abandoning of babies, addiction and corruption." Burk took a deep breath, dropping his arms to the recliner.

Don chuckled. "Yeah, what he said. And no offense to your friend, but he or she should maybe know what they're talking about before sharing memes online."

CHAPTER 30

It felt strange to be heading to Anna's again the next morning. But late last night, when Aunt Anna still hadn't come home and Jacqui had reluctantly left, everyone reminded her to return and spend the next day with them, too. Christmas with the cousins had been fun, playing games, working puzzles but having to retrieve puzzle pieces swiped by crafty toddlers, listening to the older kids play their instruments, eating and talking and teasing. Somehow, they had made Jacqui feel she was at the heart of everything, almost as though she'd grown up with them. No arm-twisting was necessary to induce her to come back today.

Besides, she'd been promised a breakfast of Aunt Anna's famous deep-fried sour cherry fritters, made only at Christmastime. Of course, they'd warned her she'd have to recite the obligatory poem to get her share. "In Low German," Don had said, bursting out laughing. "Don't worry though, we all butcher our way through it. Anything for Loefelkuchen." It was good to see Aunt Anna free of her deep depression. In a way, Jacqui took credit for the transformation. Anna herself had said Jacqui had motivated her to return from the brink.

Today, traffic on the highway was back to normal too, perhaps even heavier than usual. Boxing Day sales, Jacqui suddenly realized. For an instant, her mind went back to Christmases past when she and Bree would brave the crowds on December 26 for an exhausting day's shopping. It had always been a tradition, but did she miss it? Curiously, she didn't.

When she arrived this time, Aunt Anna pulled her in out of the cold and greeted her with a prolonged hug.

"We got the whole mountain done," one of the older kids called to Jacqui from the dining room table spread with puzzle pieces. Before Jacqui could get her coat off, the little girl who had slept on her lap yesterday ran toward her now with arms upraised.

Jesse silently appeared at Jacqui's side with a bow and an offer to take her coat, and Jacqui scooped up the cuddly toddler.

"Beth told me you spent yesterday with Aunt Naomi," Jacqui said as she followed Anna into the kitchen. "How's she doing?"

The older woman offered a grateful smile. "She's hobbling about in body, but... soaring in spirit." She searched Jacqui's face with a meaningful expression.

What's that supposed to mean? Jacqui decided not to pursue it. Instead, she said, "I've been thinking about her and Ruthie and O'Dell, the daughters-in-law. What a blow that's got to have been to them, losing three men in one day. And that weird scene where O'Dell disowned Naomi right after the funeral."

"It's a tremendous sorrow, you've got that right. Grief is something that takes years to get used to. But I'm encouraged to see my sister understanding God's grace, at last. She'll never be alone now." She made for the kitchen counter where a large bowl held a lofty mound of dough dotted with spots of dark fruit.

"We've got the oil heating on the stove," Beth told her mother.

Anna began scurrying, with her daughters-in-law and Beth setting up for the deep frying. Jacqui withdrew to the kitchen table, enjoying the soft child on her lap. Soon warmed platters of golden fritters glittering with sugar were arrayed on the kitchen counter.

Jesse leaned in through the kitchen doorway. "They ready yet?"

"You bet." Beth said. "Get everyone lined up!"

Jesse wasted no time gathering the family. They paused while Burk prayed.

"Now," Anna said, directing a mischievous smile at Jacqui, "the moment you've been waiting for... Kids first!"

Line by line, she led the children in the German poem, translating as they went.

"Ek sau die Schorstein rucke
Ek vist nicht vaut Sie mucke
Ek dokt Sie mucke Loefelkucke..."

"I saw the chimney smoking,
I didn't know what they were making.
I thought they were making Loefelkuchen,
Give me one and I'll stay standing
Give me two and I'll start going,
Give me three and four together
And I'll wish you all the world's blessings!"

"Burk, show Jacqui how it's done." Anna held out a plate to her son. "His father and I always used to say we could sell him down the river, for all the Low German he knew," she explained to Jacqui. Burk mangled the words to much ribbing by his siblings but was rewarded with his portion.

"Now it's your turn, dear," her aunt said to her.

"No escape," taunted Don, who waited in line behind her. "And hurry it up, they're getting cold."

Only a bit self-conscious, Jacqui gamely stammered her way through the recitation, twisting the unfamiliar syllables much the way the others had. When she finished, she carried her plate to the extended table where a clear vinyl tablecloth covered the incomplete jigsaw puzzle. One by one, her cousins recited the ritual poem and joined her, while Anna finished frying. She arrived with her own plate just as the youngsters were leaving the table.

For a time, the table was quiet as everyone concentrated on eating the crispy sweet treats bursting with tart cherries, murmuring sounds of enjoyment. Anna offered seconds. “No poem required.”

Jacqui shook her head, laying her knife and fork on her plate and pushing it away. “Very tasty, though. Thank you.” She toyed with the rim of her plate while Aunt Anna pressed more fritters on the others, then cleared her throat. “I keep meaning to ask something, but I always forget.”

“Oh?” Anna turned to her.

“There's an old car at my place. People I meet ask me about it all the time.”

While the others left the table to attend to their children, Burk and his wife Katie began gathering up empty plates and removing the vinyl so work on the puzzle could proceed. Anna nodded her thanks. Swallowing, she wiped her mouth with a cloth napkin. “The Bel Air.”

“Yeah, someone told me they've seen it in a couple of town parades. Apparently, it's in almost new condition. Why did Uncle Russell never drive it?”

Aunt Anna gave her a lingering look. “Well, it wasn't his car, you know.”

“What do you mean?”

The older woman focused on sliding her fingers down the length of the handle of her fork several times before answering. At last, she raised her eyes.

“Let me start at the beginning. It'll make more sense to you that way.”

From his lounging spot in the nearby recliner, Don caught Jacqui's eye and winked. “Sure sign there's a story here.” A hush settled over the adults in the room. Anna's stories appeared to have a reputation.

“I remember it as clear as day. I was only a girl at the time, maybe ten or eleven years old, but it made a big impact on me and in our family. It was a '61 Chevy Bel Air. A snazzy convertible."

The oldest grandson, Caleb snickered. "Snazzy. Gotta remember that one."

Anna smiled. "The snazziest! The local Chev dealer in town had the demo on the lot and brother John had had his eye on it for months. It was the colour of turquoise that you see in pictures of the Caribbean. Seemed like that car was all he could talk about all winter. He'd just turned sixteen and he nagged Father to take him to town at the first opportunity to get his license. For months, we heard little else from him at the supper table. Now you've got to remember, farming was tough in those years and money was scarce, so the Bel Air sat on the lot long after the next year's models came out.

"But the way John acted at the time, you'd think there was a mad rush on cars. He'd walk from school to the dealership nearly every day at noon hour, to make sure 'his car' as he called it was still there, and to sit in it for a while. I know that because one time he let me come with him when he took it for a test drive. I still remember how smooth those beautiful white vinyl seats were and how proud I felt as we drove slowly past the school. I was hoping the kids in my class would see me in such a nice, new car."

She frowned, her fingers polishing the fork handle more rapidly. The eyes of the older kids at the table were fixed on their grandmother.

"Did they notice?" her granddaughter Sabrina asked.

Anna's furrowed forehead cleared, and she chuckled. "People are generally far less interested in us than we think they are.

"Well, a year passed, and John stopped talking about it. I think he gave up. He may have still gone to see it sometimes, but probably not to sit in it. Whether he found it too humiliating or the dealership wouldn't let him do it anymore, I don't know. But shortly before John's seventeenth birthday, Father got a big grain cheque. He paid off a few bills then went to town and bought that car. The farm and the house had other needs, but Mother insisted they spend it on the Bel Air.

"Now understand, I was only a child then and all this is pieced together from what Father and Mother told us years later. But yes, he bought the car with cash. I believe that was the first time, maybe even the only time, that Father bought a car so nearly brand new. He arranged to have it delivered to our farm the day before John's birthday, while John would be away working at a neighbour's. Mother planned John's favourite breakfast for the next day, a Sunday that year, and their plan was to send him out on some errand where he would discover it for himself on the other side of the trees."

Don't say it. Please don't tell me that was the morning they found Pops missing.

But Anna did say it. She clasped her hands on the table in front of her and with sorrow in her voice, continued. "I remember the smell of saskatoon berry sauce that Mother had made that morning to go with the special birthday Blintzen." She turned to Jacqui. "You would call them crepes. I can't recall if we ate them; we were all so stunned and heartsick. But I can never forget the shock on my parents' faces when Father came down the stairs to say that John was gone. Just a few clothes missing and a note on the nightstand. Even though he'd been late coming home the night before, and had missed supper, we knew he'd been there because he'd made his bed. Mother had often chided him about leaving it unmade, and that morning he had done it perfectly." She paused, her eyes filling.

"My parents never shared with us what he'd written in the note but the Bible he'd received for Christmas years earlier was left, carefully centred on his pillow."

The young teens at the table stared at their grandmother, open-mouthed. A heart-wrenching silence filled the room. And Jacqui felt responsible. Not simply because she had asked about the car, but because she had believed her father's stories. She had ingested his bitterness, even finding ways to blame his family for the ways she had suffered because of his moroseness. It had never occurred to her there might be another side to the matter.

Dabbing at the corners of her eyes with the napkin, Anna took a deep breath. “Father kept the car hidden with a cover Mother made from scrap fabric. None of the rest of us ever drove it, and we never asked. It simply wasn't spoken of. But at mealtime prayers our parents often pleaded with the Lord to bring their boy home to them.” She raised her face, looking Jacqui directly in the eye. “You see, my dear, although at times my father was much too harsh with your dad, he did love him. We all did.”

Jacqui turned her eyes up toward the ceiling, blinking rapidly. *The lost years. The wasted years. The lost family.* All the angst swirling in her soul made her heart hurt.

CHAPTER 31

Gabrielle Sammett had been hanging out at the library for the four and a half hours since school let out. Now Jacqui was beginning the library closing routine and the chunky girl with the braid like sisal rope sat at one of the public computers. Jacqui was running the place alone, as she usually did. Although she never expected Sheri to show up anymore, the woman still called or texted to explain her absence—she had to babysit her grandchildren, or she had obligations at the seniors' home where a member of her family lived. Whatever. Jacqui was hungry for the income and was just as glad not to have Giggle-Barbie at her side.

Other patrons and the teens who had been hanging with Gabrielle had left for home and dinner some time ago. By the girl's frequent anxious glances out the darkened front window, Gabrielle appeared to be expecting a ride. Jacqui stopped shelving books to watch her.

Except for her size, that could have been me at ten or eleven years old. Once Jacqui discovered the refuge offered by the world of books, she hung out as much as she could at libraries, either at school or the public library downtown. Enfolded in the embrace of a book, no heroine's dilemma could be greater, no monster more fearsome than Jacqui's own life with her mother. And in books the heroines could always figure a way to solve their problems, with the monsters inevitably defeated. The library became her safe place, a haven in which to hide, to escape, to rest from her constant vigilance. Was

Gabrielle hiding here, too? She was certainly a regular. Her borrower information stipulated no phone calls to the number on file. This wasn't necessarily suspect, but it could mean someone had something to conceal. She wove her way through the stacks to approach the girl.

Gabrielle jumped when Jacqui came up behind her and softly cleared her throat.

"I'll be closing in a few minutes. Are you waiting for someone to pick you up?"

"Yeah."

Jacqui hesitated. "You could call from the library phone, if you like."

Gabrielle raised unreadable eyes to her. "I guess," she said without enthusiasm. She trailed Jacqui to the desk where Jacqui handed her the phone.

Retreating to the bookshelves, Jacqui kept an ear tuned for the outcome of the call. It wasn't urgent she leave here on the dot of closing time; it wasn't as though she had anyone expecting her home at a certain time. She could wait with Gabrielle as long as it took for someone to come pick her up.

The girl only listened for a few moments then raised a hesitant voice in the quiet library. "Um..."

Jacqui peeked through the books, catching sight of Gabrielle searching down the rows for her. She hurried up front.

"Did you need me for something?"

"Uh, yeah. My guardian wants to talk to you." Avoiding eye contact, the girl handed the phone to Jacqui with a slump of her shoulders, muttering, "She's been drinking. Again." She took a few steps back as though to distance herself from the drama that was her life.

Guardian, eh? Now there's a cold, remote relationship. A gust of past incidents blew across Jacqui's mind bringing a cold front of emotion. Abandonment, loneliness, neglect. Too often, she'd been one of the few kids at a school event without a parent attending. More than once, she, too, had been left after closing time at a library without a ride home. The memory of a store manager's irritable scolding at having to stay late because of Jacqui, before Pops had finally come to pick her up still stung.

Jacqui pressed the phone to her ear, but she had a feeling she knew what she would hear. She spoke brusquely. "Yes?"

A short laugh prefaced the breezy voice of a woman giving her name, which Jacqui missed. She did note that the surname was different from Gabrielle's. "I was supposed to come get Gabrielle," she slurred, "but I was out with friends and I've had a few drinks, so I can't drive." Mumbled words that Jacqui couldn't make out followed. "She'll need you to bring her home."

Are you serious? No apologies, even? You neglect your kid and assume a stranger should do your job? What if I'm a child molester? Now I've got a young girl in my clutches for enough time to seriously damage her.

How familiar the scenario was. How many close calls with her mother's predatory boyfriends, how many compromising situations had Jacqui's mother been responsible for in the time she had lived with her? As if it were happening this very moment, she felt herself tense behind a locked bathroom door, heard it tried, shaken, and tried again. Heard anew the murmured voice through the rickety door, crooning, promising, and finally threatening. At eight or nine years old, she'd cowered all night long in that tiny, windowless bathroom, clutching her mother's razor in pitiful and futile defense, too terrified to sleep.

That dark, perilous souvenir of her childhood gave Jacqui a powerful feeling of urgency now. Only, this time, Jacqui was one of the adults in the scenario. A dozen options popped into her mind.

Should she call Social Services or drive the girl home and confront the woman herself? Should she take the girl home with her? All the options were fraught with risks, and none of them solved anything for Gabrielle. Jacqui considered the girl, who was doing her best to appear nonchalant, fingering teen magazines on the display rack.

Jacqui's hand had grown slippery with sweat on the receiver. "I'll get her home *safely*," she said, hoping the emphasis conveyed her disgust then worried she might have made things worse for Gabrielle. People without conscience sometimes took out their guilt on the children. The girl herself was the one who had to do life in that home, after all. Still, Jacqui reminded the woman, "She'll be needing her dinner."

Replacing the phone, she softened her tone with Gabrielle. "I have to do a few last jobs here before we can leave, if you don't mind waiting."

Gabrielle leaned toward her with an eager light in her eyes. "Can I help?"

Poor kid. Jacqui tried to recall what library policy said about non-employees working, then decided Gabrielle was a volunteer. The way Sheri made up her own rules and arbitrarily appointed someone as staff, Jacqui figured it wouldn't hurt to do the same. "Sure. If you could go down the rows making sure every display rack has a book on it, and then shut down the public computers, that'd be great."

Feeling an ominous tickle in her nose, she grabbed a Kleenex and hurried to the washroom at the rear. What a lousy time for another nosebleed. Ever since fall, she'd been getting these without warning. At first, she'd been concerned, but when she'd commented about it to a nurse checking out books one afternoon, the woman had said she'd had the same problem when she'd moved here from the coast. "It's the dryness. Your body adjusts to the low humidity after a while. There are times in winter when we're drier than the Kalahari Desert."

It was a nuisance, though. Jacqui doctored her tender nose, impatient for it to stop bleeding. By now, Gabrielle must be wondering if Jacqui had deserted her, perhaps suspecting she'd taken off through the back way. As if the kid needed more abandonment in her life. The thought of adding to the girl's sense of aloneness made Jacqui rush through cleaning up the mess and washing her face.

She scanned the library as she returned up front where Gabrielle perched on the edge of the desk waiting for her. "Everything looks good, thanks. You ready to go?"

"Uh-huh."

Outside of town in the moonless dark, a sense of isolation on the snow-packed roads accompanied her and this child who travelled the world alone. She was drawn to the girl and suspected the feeling was mutual, as Gabrielle grew more talkative in the intimacy of the car. Jacqui learned the girl's dad worked on the oil rigs up north for weeks at a time. Her guardian, an unemployed woman who binged-watched horror movies had moved in with them only a year ago.

"I don't like her," she said, "but who listens to a kid anyway?" *Who indeed? What say does a child have when parents go their separate ways—set up house elsewhere, introduce new parents and siblings? Where is home?* The girl slid both bare hands between her knees as if to warm them. *Where are her gloves?*

"I know exactly how you feel."

"I miss my mom," Gabrielle snuffled, then swiped her sleeve across her nose.

"Do you ever get to see her?" Jacqui felt the girl's eyes on her and met her gaze. The shocked dismay on Gabrielle's face told Jacqui she'd made the wrong assumption. She'd stepped on an emotional landmine. "I—I'm sorry. I shouldn't have asked that."

Jacqui bit her lip in the tense pause.

"She died three years ago."

"I'm so sorry."

More silence.

"But I like talking about her. Everybody at school tries not to mention my mom to me, or Mother's Day, or even anybody else's mother. I hate that."

Jacqui took a chance. "What was she like?"

Gabrielle gave a small sigh of fond memory. "She was funny. And kind of crazy at times. I mean, pulling pranks and stuff. One time on April Fool's Day she baked a cake with these small pink and blue make-up sponges in it. Sponge cake."

Jacqui chuckled, and Gabrielle joined in.

After a hush, Jacqui said, "So, you escape from the awkward conversations and the loneliness into books?"

"I guess so. I've always loved reading."

Jacqui reached over to squeeze the girl's arm. "Me too."

Driving home after dropping off her charge, she pondered Gabrielle and the memories the girl had evoked. Her extra pounds could very well be a reaction to the uncertainties of her life. In Jacqui's case, she had kept her eating under strict control, feeling tremendous pressure to have her own life together because the rest of life was so unstable. If she hadn't persuaded her father to let her live with him when she did, who knows what eating disorders might have developed?

Could she be the stabilizing influence this young girl seemed to need so desperately? It came to her that here was another good deed she had done.

I am too a good person, Sheri Mueller. So there!

CHAPTER 32

One January evening, Jacqui answered the library phone with her standard spiel.

"Hey, Jacqui," a smooth male voice asked without introduction. "Can you give me the words to the Scooby Doo theme song?" The man spoke with a breezy familiarity, as though Jacqui should know him.

"I beg your pardon?"

"I'm doing research into popular music and I need the lyrics for the Scooby Doo song."

You have got to be kidding! "Have you tried Googling it?"

"Unfortunately, I haven't had any luck with that. That's why I called you. Could you do it for me?"

"Actually, I'm pretty busy right now. Why don't you come into the library and you can use the public computers to find it for yourself?"

The voice, so pleasant, so reasonable, so needy, explained his limitations. "I'm not able to get there. Vehicle issues, you know."

Next, you'll tell me you're bedridden. Perhaps you don't have arms and are using a voice-activated phone? Despite the ridiculous request, Jacqui dutifully searched online for the song lyrics.

"How about I email them to you?" she offered.

"Well, to be honest, my computer's been acting up lately. What I was really hoping was to have you read them for me."

Seriously? That's a first. Over her eighteen years and various roles as a librarian, Jacqui had given book recommendations, revised resumes and returned left-behind personal effects to their owners. She had jostled a fussy baby so a mother could work online, mediated children's disputes, and even cleaned up vomit. But reading the Scooby Doo theme song to some creepy dude over the phone? It was a bit much. Was she too suspicious?

"Tell you what. I'll print this off and you can come pick it up next time you're in town. Or you can send someone by to pick it up for you."

"The truth is, Jacqui," the guy continued with his disconcerting familiarity, "my study has to do with the effects of the female voice, preferably a pleasant young voice such as yours. I really need you to read it."

Jacqui glanced at the cartload of books she had yet to shelve before closing time. "OK. Grab a pen and take notes, 'cause I'm only going to do this once." Rolling her eyes, she rattled off the simple words. She felt ridiculous even though the only other person in the library was Albert Fanshawe, the scrawny English gentleman in the far corner armchair, lost in the depths of his news magazine.

"Scooby Dooby Doo,
Where are you
We've got some work to do now..."

She read it fast and without expression to the final stanza, followed by a long silence on the line. "Hello?"

The man's voice was softer now and breathless. "Uh, I was wondering...could you read it again, only slower?"

Okay, you're done buddy! This is too weird. "Sorry, I'm quite busy," she snapped, then hung up. Her hand still held the receiver in a tight grip as she glanced out the front window. From where she sat, she could see around the corner to the end of Main Street where the highway ran through town. Down the street, snow crystals in the air sugared the seasonal lights like Christmas candy, but nothing else was open, and even the street by the hotel bar was empty. She had an hour to go before closing and a bit of a walk to her car. A sliver of foreboding slid up her spine.

Don't be dramatic. It's only one of the local weirdos. But every true crime book she'd ever read rushed to mind. Scenes of unutterable torture seemed all too possible in this out-of-the-way town without a police presence. She was vulnerable as a field mouse to a hawk.

Forcing herself to get moving, she grasped the book cart with sweaty palms, guiding it to the stacks to start shelving books. The front doorbell rang, making her jump. Adrenaline shot through her. She shot a sharp glance at the entrance, shifting herself into the shadow of a bookshelf. But C.H.'s large, familiar frame filled the doorway. Jacqui's whole body sagged in relief. He ushered Lewis in ahead of him.

"Am I glad to see you!" she burst out, moving towards them.

C.H. raised an eyebrow as she emerged from behind the shelves. "Business is slow tonight?"

Jacqui flushed as she came toward him, describing the bizarre conversation she'd just had. "The number display on my phone had already faded by the time I realized the guy was off his nut."

"Man, I'm sorry I wasn't here to help. I might have had a few suggestions for where a character like that could direct his search." He smirked then glanced at her trembling fingers clutching the handle of the cart. "Seriously, I don't think you've got anything to worry about. Someone like that is likely too cowardly to come out into a public space. But if it'll make you feel better, Lewis and I can hang around while you close up and follow you home."

Bree would scorn her for finding comfort in a man's presence. She would quote Germaine Greer about superfluous men and fish with bicycles. But with heartfelt gratitude, Jacqui agreed to C.H.'s offer. *Better to be thought a pansy than to be prey.*

While Lewis scanned the junior non-fiction section, C.H. settled himself in the empty armchair across the room and managed to coax Albert out of his magazine. *How does he do that? Make people open up like that, so genuine and personable?* No doubt he and Lewis had stopped in here on their way home from an afternoon with Roslyn, which had to be a stressful and draining experience. How could he then show an interest in others and appear so relaxed and upbeat? Geoff had had a knack for that too and later he'd entertain their friends with outrageously funny accounts of the quirky people he met selling their appalling homes. But observing C.H.'s rapt interest in his companion, she somehow knew he wouldn't be using the man as story fodder. C.H., she decided, was one-of-a-kind and Roslyn was a lucky woman.

Jacqui's jitters dissipated as she listened to the political banter between the two men and wrapped up her inter-library ordering. Was *everyone* here in the west on the right side of the political spectrum? Certainly, Neil Weerd had not been. Not that it mattered to her. She'd never cared much for politics, but the comments she was overhearing now were foreign to the heated talk she'd grown up hearing from Pops and his union mates. Even Geoff used to adapt himself to fit the leftist narrative when he was with Jacqui's father, tossing out socialist slogans as handily as any of them. Despite his real estate career, he would simply laugh off their snide contempt for his obvious capitalism.

"I'm all about getting the working man into home ownership," he'd say with an apparent sincerity that pleased Pops and his buddies. So, even when Geoff switched to commercial real estate it hadn't seemed to matter to them, as long as he agreed with their resentment against the greedy rich. Privately though, Geoff poked fun at the fervor of Pops' comrades, calling them out-of-touch losers.

"...Another sad example of government overreach," C.H. concluded, rising as Mr. Fanshawe gathered his books and magazines to leave.

Jacqui checked the items out for him and saw him to the door before turning the *Open* sign to *Closed* and finishing her evening routine.

With a spurt of mischief, Jacqui hummed the Communist theme song while she tidied the magazine area. C.H. showed no signs of recognition.

"Comrades, come rally..." she began singing, waiting for his reaction.

Now he tilted his head at her.

Jacqui broke off the song and laughed at his quizzical face. "I heard your conversation."

"So is that from some musical?" he asked

"You've never heard 'The Internationale'? I cut my teeth on songs and slogans like that."

"No kidding." C.H. said. "Let's hear the rest of it."

Self-conscious now, she recited rather than sang the words that easily flowed back into her memory.

"No saviour from on high delivers,

No faith have we in prince or peer.

Our own right hand the chains must shiver,

Chains of hatred, greed and fear."

She finished and crossed back to her desk.

C.H. turned to where Lewis stood holding out a stack of books and motioned with his head to move the boy toward the checkout desk. "Do you believe that?"

Jacqui pulled the books across the desk toward her. "What? You mean the communist manifesto?" She processed the items and handed them to Lewis. "I try to stay neutral on politics as much as possible."

"How about the religious part?"

"Religious? I think you mean irreligious. My father knew Marx's philosophy well and he always prided himself on having no religion."

"All that talk of saviours and faith and deliverance sounds pretty religious to me," he said with a twinkle in his eyes. "And if you ever get a chance to talk to an immigrant from the old Soviet Union like my college roommate was, they've got a somewhat different perspective on those 'chains of hatred and fear'." He zipped his jacket. "We'd better get moving. I'll walk you to your car."

They made fresh footprints on the snow-blanketed sidewalk, Lewis following silently behind them. Jacqui felt safe in their presence, despite the eerie vacancy of the town. She clutched her scarf close to her neck against the cold.

"Do you have to spend a lot of time outside with the cattle when it's cold like this?" she asked him.

"Just feed them in the morning, but I do that in the warm cab of my tractor. And then we go out and check on them every once in a while, too."

"On snowmobile?"

"Usually, yeah." He peered at her from under his hat brim. "Why do you ask?"

She blushed despite the subzero temperature. "The cold reminded me of something. When I was at your place to watch Lewis before Christmas, he showed me some of your poetry. In fact, he made me read one to him." She fumbled in her pocket for her car keys and hit command start.

"The one about the lame calf, right?"

"Mm-hm. I take it that's his favourite?"

He sighed. "Oh, Lewis. Well, I wouldn't exactly call it poetry. At least not the kind I like to read. But it's been fun to write something up for cowboy poetry nights here in the winter."

"You and poetry...hm." They reached for the door of her car.

His shoulders were dusted with snowflakes. "You find that hard to imagine?"

"Sorry, I just—"

"You just didn't expect a redneck rancher to have a clue about literature, did you?" She could barely see his face as he blocked the streetlight behind him, but his tone mocked her assumptions.

Shuffling her feet partly from cold and partly from embarrassment, Jacqui floundered for a response.

Before she could answer, C.H. touched the brim of his hat. "Drive safe, Miss Jacqui," he said, turning back toward his own truck with a hand on Lewis's shoulder.

How was it possible to inject that much ice into southern charm? She told herself it didn't matter, but his stiff formality bothered her all the way home.

CHAPTER 33

On a sparkling morning in late February, Jacqui set her brush on the edge of the paint tray and fished her vibrating phone out of her back pocket. Sure enough, Aunt Anna's number appeared on the screen.

"I was wondering, dear...would you like to come with me today to visit your Aunt Naomi?" Anna's cheerful voice asked. "I like to stop in and check on her as often as I can in these early months of her grief. But I remembered you've never been out to her place and since you live so close to them, I could stop in and take you along."

Jacqui surveyed the dishevelled living room, its furniture shoved aside yet again, and the floor protected from paint by Aunt Priscilla's old linens. Fed up with the dated built-in china cabinet, over the past few days she had removed its upper doors and faux-wood trim on the lower doors, filled the holes with wood-filler, and sanded, wiped and covered the dark-stained plywood inside and out in primer. Today she'd counted on finishing the transformation with a couple of coats of white paint. She checked the time, wavering. Despite her eagerness to see this project completed, the thrill of being included in the life of a family still hadn't worn off for her. Besides, with both her aunts together, it would also be an opportunity to compare Naomi's memories of her father's upbringing. "I work at three, but I'm free before that."

"Okay if I pick you up at ten then?"

"Sounds good."

Jacqui had finished putting away her tools and cleaning herself up by the time Anna drove up. The sun dazzled, while her boots sank into the wet snow of the driveway. As they pulled onto the road, Jacqui asked, "How are Aunt Naomi and Ruthie and O'Dell doing?"

Anna tipped her head toward Jacqui. "Losing the men of the family all at once that way has been a terrible blow to them as you can imagine." She faced the road ahead with pursed lips. "And there have been other complications that have added to their sorrows. But I'm encouraged at the changes and growth I'm seeing, especially in my sister. There's a strength in her now that I've never seen before. You know, the two of us grew up in the same home, yet she took from it an entirely different notion..."

Jacqui shifted in her seat. "You mean she was abused too?"

"No, dear! She was not." She smiled and gave a bemused shake of her head. "Not everything is about abuse. What I meant was, she misunderstood the message of the Bible. Whenever parents teach their children to do what is good and right, there's the risk that children will grow up thinking they can actually *be* good or earn God's favour, or that they can do enough good deeds to make up for something they've done wrong."

In the silence that followed, Jacqui pondered this. *What do you mean 'actually be good'? There are good people and bad people and it's simply a matter of choice.* But she had a feeling Anna disagreed and questions of upbringing and life's hardships came to Jacqui's mind that undermined her hasty assertion. She needed more time to think it over before she questioned her aunt on the matter.

A few kilometres later, they drove into a yard sheltered by trees where a cottage-style house sat smugly settled in the landscape. The snowbanks were low and small, and with the recent unseasonably mild temperatures, patches of damp black soil in flowerbeds awaited the spring sun.

Naomi met them at the porch door and welcomed Anna and Jacqui into her tidy kitchen. "Ruthie's resting at home right now but said she'd be over to join us for lunch." The house appeared to be from the same era as Jacqui's, but in original condition. Everything from flooring to counter tops was worn but immaculate. The plywood cabinets reminded Jacqui of her own before she'd painted them.

A younger woman in stiff new jeans and a red sweater came through the kitchen door just then. Static in the dry air made strands of her thin, blonde hair float around her wide, pale cheeks, inexpertly dusted with blush. She came toward them with an outstretched hand.

"Jacqui, this is my niece Bertha," Naomi said. "She's from the Adrian side of the family, so no relation to you. She moved here from up north a couple of months ago and is staying with me until she can find her own place." The older woman turned to Bertha with a smile. "Come and sit." She gestured to seats at the old kitchen table. While she scooped coffee into the basket of the coffee maker, she said, "Bertha and I have been talking lately about what is involved in caring for her aunt Carol. It's been on my mind a lot lately that I could bring her here and take care of her."

"Carol is in a wheelchair as a result of a brain injury as a teen," Anna explained, picking up on Jacqui's blank expression. "Until recently, Bertha was her primary caregiver." She turned to address Naomi as she took a seat at the table. "You aren't thinking of it as some sort of—"

"A way to punish myself? Not at all. Carol and I were friends as girls, and now I have time and room in the house. I expect Bertha will be finding her own place soon, right?"

Bertha beamed, displaying the small, friendly gap between her front teeth as she sat at the end of the table. "Today Ruthie said she would take me to practice my driving again." She spoke with a faint accent, broad and somehow country-like, but not one that Jacqui had ever heard before.

"Her driver's test appointment is in two weeks," Naomi told her guests, setting a plate of raisin oatmeal cookies on the table.

"We set up some straw bales for parallel parking practice." Giggling, Bertha confessed, "I hit them a few times yesterday, but today I will not hit them." Her juvenile behaviour seemed oddly out of step with her age, which Jacqui guessed was somewhere around thirty. But it was hard to tell. Genuine blondes tended to look young. "I do not want to upset Ruthie, because," she made a rounding motion at her stomach, "you know..."

Jacqui took in Naomi's face, glowing with pleasure. "She's pregnant?"

Naomi nodded. "The baby will arrive sometime in July. We are so thrilled about this!"

"A little piece of Mac." Anna's forthright mention of the deceased made Jacqui cringe and glance quickly at Naomi, but the older woman simply smiled.

"Yes," she agreed,

"The Lord brings beauty out of ashes, doesn't He?" Anna pushed the empty chair toward Naomi who took a seat.

"I came to that very verse in my Bible reading this morning. I took it as a promise from God to me. Honestly," Naomi said, reaching for the small black Bible on the table, "I don't know how I missed the wonders of His love and goodness all these years."

Abruptly, Bertha's chair scraped the floor as she quickly rose. "I have to go now." She hurried through the porch door for her coat, letting the wooden screen door bang closed behind her.

A meaningful look lingered between the aunts.

"What was that about?" Jacqui asked.

Anna turned to her. "It's understandable that Bertha is not interested in hearing anything about God right now."

"What was it you were going to read, Aunt Naomi?"

The older sister withdrew a pair of reading glasses from the pocket of her apron and read, "To comfort all who mourn, To console those who mourn in Zion, To give them beauty for ashes, The oil of joy for mourning, The garment of praise for the spirit of heaviness..." She raised watery eyes from the book.

Jacqui was surprised to find the words of comfort moving her strangely. "Why would Bertha object to that?"

"She's only recently come out of a home where all her life she was mistreated and used," Anna said.

Alarm bells rang in Jacqui's head. *Another case of abuse? What is it with this family?*

"But worst of all," Anna went on, "she was taught some very wrong ideas about God and the Bible. I don't think it's too much to call it spiritual abuse, do you Nomi?"

"No, that's what I would call it."

"And you helped her escape? You're her safe house?" Jacqui asked Naomi with an urgent need to know.

"Well," she answered slowly, her face wary. "Leaving her father's home was her own doing, but yes, Ruthie and I are providing for her until she can get on her feet."

"Then why don't you think my father needed protection when he was in danger? Obviously abuse runs in the family."

Both the older women startled at her outburst.

"Naomi already said that Bertha is not related to our family except by marriage, Jacqui," Anna told her.

"Still, I don't understand why your mother, or any of the rest of you, didn't stand up for my father against the abuse."

"How do you know that Mother didn't 'stand up against the abuse' as you say?" Anna asked with a sad smile. "As I've told you before, we don't deny that our father was too harsh with your dad. But there are many ways to approach someone who is sinning, dear. And I believe our mother, over time and in her gentle way, was persuasive with Father. Even John would have to admit that before he left home, the physical abuse had stopped."

"It only stopped because Pops grew strong enough to fight back!" Agitated, Jacqui pushed off her chair to pace the short distance across Aunt Naomi's patched kitchen floor.

"Do you think direct confrontation is the only acceptable way? Isn't it possible, after all, to win the battle and lose the war?"

"What do you mean by that?"

"Let's imagine for a moment that Mother had 'stood up' to my father, as you suggest. Perhaps she would have given him an ultimatum—shape up or ship out? Or perhaps she might have simply taken us children and left. Is that what you think would have been best?"

"Yes!" Jacqui felt defensive, yet this was what all her advocacy training for at-risk individuals recommended, separating the abused from the abuser.

"To you, this would mean she had won the battle against the abuse of your father?"

Jacqui nodded, her hands balling into fists as she mentally prepared her defense.

"But what about the long-term effects?" Anna asked. "First, Mother would have faced the logistical difficulties of trying to set up a second home with next to no money. Then somehow, she would have had to provide for a family of five children. And don't forget the stigma our entire family would have endured, including your father. Times were different back then. Not only that, but with Mother off to work, we children would have lost both parents, possibly setting us up for all sorts of trouble children can get into when left to themselves."

Jacqui stopped her pacing abruptly. She knew all too well the hazards of being left to herself. But she landed her palms on the kitchen table leaning in on the other two women. "*No* father would have been better than a *terrible* father!"

"Would it though?" Anna returned her gaze mildly. "I'm afraid statistics do not bear that out. A father in the home, even a mediocre one, is one of the most important predictors of the stability and success of the children."

"Pff, statistics." Jacqui rolled her eyes and sat down again.

Anna's voice softened to a murmur. "You know, the real question you may be trying to answer is how do we know there's an ultimate standard of what a father should be like? Every parent falls short, yet isn't it odd we have this innate sense that a father must be unfailingly loving and good?"

Staring a hole in the worn Arborite tabletop, Jacqui brooded over this. Did she know even one ideal father?

Naomi broke the silence with a gentle question. "If I may ask, dear, why does this matter so much to you?"

Jacqui stared at her for a moment. "Because he's all I've got left," she blurted. "He's my anchor. He's the only parent who cared anything about me all the time I was growing up. It *does* matter. I have to know he was right. I have to know he didn't just run off in a teenage snit, that he had legitimate reasons for leaving." She burst into tears, covering her face with her hands.

Until that moment, Jacqui hadn't realized this was her quest. The move out here wasn't simply her own desperate escape from a failed relationship. It was more, far more than that. Retracing Pops' journey from home and family was a search for her roots. She was following the kite-line of his life down to a grounding she'd never even known she lacked.

She clenched her teeth against a sob. The more deeply she'd searched since coming here, the more she recognized all she had missed because of his cutting off family ties. The more she found herself rootless, the more she longed for a solid foundation. And as that longing grew, so did her doubts about his side of the story. Now she found that if she couldn't validate him and his youthful decision, she'd end up having to blame Pops—the one person who cared about her—for the gaping void in her life. Then who would she have? Who would be her family?

"You might not think so, but he's a good person!" she insisted.

"But aren't our categories of good and bad a little flawed? I think your dad had the idea a life of faith was all about being a good person. But none of us is good. There's only ever been one perfect person, Jacqui. And He died to take the punishment sinners like you and me deserve."

Anna's words were becoming a jumble to her. She could understand why Bertha wanted an escape. Confusion whirled like a cyclone in her head

Peering out from between her parted hands Jacqui found both her aunts watching her with concern. Their deep blue eyes, so alike one another, were uncannily like Pops' the way they drooped at the outside corners. But where his usually conveyed cynicism, even bitterness, with only a rare twinkle of wry wit, these held compassion and a strange sort of insight. She could feel it emanating from both of them, as though they could see her thoughts and motivations. Yet she sensed love, too, a love that made her resentment dissipate. Love, and a tissue that Anna was offering her.

"Look, I'm sorry. I shouldn't be going off on you two." She reached for the tissue.

"All is forgiven," Anna said.

"Think nothing of it," Naomi said at the same time. In unison, they patted her arms.

Jacqui couldn't help chuckling. "Have you two always been peas in a pod?"

The older women exchanged glances and broke into a laugh.

“Not always,” Anna said. “But when we were children, oh yes!”

Jacqui released a long breath, relaxing in her chair and basking in the presence of her aunts.

After a pause, Anna said, “Well now, would it be inappropriate to offer some happy news at this point?”

Both Jacqui and Naomi stirred in their chairs.

“I'm sure you can guess,” Anna teased.

“Do tell!” Naomi's spreading smile showed she had some inkling of the nature of the news, but Jacqui had no clue.

Anna stuck out her left hand, for all the world like a blushing twenty-something. “Jacqui, you met my dear friend and pastor Tom at the funeral last fall. Well, two nights ago he proposed, and I said yes!”

CHAPTER 34

The china cabinet turned out every bit as fabulous as Jacqui had envisioned it would. Each time she walked by it, she took a moment to enjoy its transformation from a hulking dark monstrosity lurking in the corner to its bright and sleek new look as a bookshelf. Leaving the glass doors off had been a good decision. Yesterday before work, she had finished the subtle tone-on-tone damask stenciling behind the shelves. The piece was now an elegant feature of the room.

Out of the blue, she felt an instinctive urge to snap a picture and send it to Geoff. He had always been so good at admiring her work. He'd had a thousand unique ways of voicing approval, which was what made him such a successful realtor. She caught her breath. *No more of that.* With a rush of pride, she realized she hadn't had the impulse to contact him for months now. She was growing stronger. Bree would be impressed. But then, she hadn't been in touch with Bree as often as she used to either. Life here had become fuller.

Touching the inner corners of the shelves and a few other places where paint might have built up, she found them perfectly dry. Now she was eager to style the piece. She set herself some upbeat jazz and, true to habit, Gandalf leapt off the sofa to come and rub his fuzzy sides against her ankles. "This is the fun part, my music-loving pussy-cat!"

Last night before falling asleep, she had puzzled over what she could fill the shelves with, a pang of bitterness running through her at the thought of the many valuable pieces still in storage in Hamilton.

But this morning Jacqui had woken determined to search the attic for special items. The marbles she'd found in the box of Pops' keepsakes might be playful in a glass Mason jar. She pulled on a sweater and headed up the stairs.

Setting aside the makeshift insulated cardboard barrier she'd fashioned last fall to keep from losing all the heat through the attic, Jacqui shivered. The air was chilly up here, making her momentarily regret removing the false living room ceiling tiles. But Gandalf scampered past her up through the opening, the cold only seeming to bring him to life. She paused to watch him skating and skittering across the old blue linoleum in an ecstasy of kittenish exuberance.

"Any mice you find, Little Wizard, do your magic and turn them into dollars for me," she ordered, then hurried to the row of cardboard boxes along the south wall. Opening the one marked *John*, she pulled out the hand-carved wooden tractor. It would be perfect alone in all its vintage glory on an upper shelf. Next, she hoisted the syrup can full of marbles out of the box and then the ice skates. They, too, would be great on a shelf by themselves if she stuffed them with something to hold their shape. Her plans for the unit were rapidly shaping up to become a vignette of her father's childhood.

Reaching beneath the stack of school notebooks to the bottom of the box, Jacqui's hand touched a book. She drew it out and discovered her Pops' Bible, likely the very one he'd left in silent scorn on the pillow for his family to find after he'd left home. If he hadn't forbidden talk of God while Jacqui was growing up, would she be as drawn to this book as she was now?

She flipped through its pages, pausing in places where sentences were underlined.

This book, she couldn't help perceiving, was of vital importance to her father's story. It would go on the very centre shelf, propped open on a stand.

She carried the items to the edge of the stairs, then set them down. Other boxes might hold treasures she could use. She rummaged through them, finding a white hand-knit baby romper, a miniature blackened silver mug, an odd metal sailing ship that appeared to be a table lamp, and a box of books and papers. The books were a thrilling find—grade school readers from the 40s and 50s. But what made Jacqui sink to her knees in wonder was a stack of slim notebooks with pages covered front and back and up the margins by a closely written hand. She gathered these and the other finds into her arms to take downstairs.

"C'mon kitty," she called over her shoulder on the way down the narrow steps. She heard the cat galloping away across the attic floor and knew it would be tricky getting him back downstairs. Once she deposited her found items in front of the shelves, she discovered she was right. No amount of reasoning or chasing or trickery succeeded in luring the high-strung creature down. Gandalf was determined to go his own way even at the risk of being cut off from food and water. Was this what her grandparents were up against with Pops? Wanting his own way even if it meant taking a much harder road?

In the end, though it felt cruel, she closed the attic door, hoping Gandalf would come to his senses when he was hungry. But then a different idea came to mind. She turned up the volume on her play list and held the phone to the attic door. Sure enough, the fuzzy jazz lover began scratching at the opening. She pushed the door a crack, reached in and brought him down. Then she set to work, cleaning and arranging the everyday decor on the shelves. Standing back to survey the results Jacqui was pleased. Enough that she felt compelled to phone her father to bring his voice into the home along with his past.

"Pops?"

"Lolli-, Coco- or Corn, take your pick," Pops quipped in reply. Clearly, he was in a good mood, remembering her old variations on his name.

"So, how's it going?" she asked, pacing between the living room and kitchen, tweaking the skates or the jar of marbles, rearranging the old books on the shelf as she passed by. What would he think of this gallery of his early life?

"It goes." The loud TV voice in the background snapped off abruptly. "What's on Little Girl's mind?"

"I'm wondering how you feel about a trip out here for a wedding this fall?"

A pause meant Pops was thinking. "Out west? That's a fair piece to hitchhike at my age."

"Pops! Uh, welcome to the new millennium. I meant buy a plane ticket."

"Hold on a minute. I must be hearing wrong. Did you say a wedding? You're not marrying some hick from out west are you?"

"I wondered when you'd click in. Yeah, a wedding. But not mine. Though it is someone you know."

"Oh, yeah?"

"Yeah." She paused for effect. "Your baby sister, Anna." After at least a minute, Jacqui asked, "You still there, Pops?"

"I am indeed." His voice had lost its breezy tone. "When shall I polish my shoes?"

"Seriously? You'll come?"

"Wouldn't miss it."

What? He had missed every family event for over fifty years. What made the difference now? Could my talk over the last few months about life out here and the family be pulling him back? Jacqui didn't dare ask. Instead she forced a casual voice. "That would be great. The wedding's set for October 7th. I have room for you to stay with me. I'm about two hours from an airport, though, so make sure you don't book your return trip too early in the morning."

"I know where the old place is, girlie," he groused. "You want to do all that booking crap for me? I'm not too handy on the inter webs."

"Sure, no problem."

When Jacqui ended the call, she sat down dazed. Anna and Naomi would be thrilled to have their brother come to visit. But did Pops really mean to return after all these years and after so much poison had flowed under the bridge since he ran off as a teen?

She rose slowly and wandered to the couch again carrying the notebooks along with her. She tucked her legs beneath her and picked up the topmost book. Its small, yellow-edged pages were coming loose in spots and were so densely written they were hard to figure out.

Leafing through them, she found they were her grandmother's thoughts written partly in what appeared to be German and partly in English, a diary of sorts. Very few of the entries carried a date, but the rhythms of seeding and harvest and winter were evident. Reading what she could understand, Jacqui soon was engrossed in Granny's life.

> Snowing today, but we needed clothes for Sunday, so laundry had to be done. Hung them on the lines in the basement. Nehemiah 8:10 "Do not sorrow, for the joy of the Lord is your strength." Oh Lord, how I need your joy, and I know you promise to give it (John 15:11) Thank you, Lord! Finally tackled the mending basket. Too tired to get more than three pairs of socks mended this evening but went to bed joyful.

Jacqui flipped a few pages in another volume.

> Thank you, Lord for a promising garden! Peas and carrots flourishing, all the beans are up and tomatoes I started indoors are starting to blossom. Today, little Anna asked me why I speak in "round sounds" to the Avon lady who came calling. I confess I was reproached. The dear girl

noticed the difference from the way I speak to the children. Oh Father, make my words sweet (Proverbs 16:24) for I may have to eat them.

"The greatest of these is love. Love covers a multitude of sins." Lord show me how to love the unlovable. Give me patience with those who seem to want to deliberately hurt others. Finished Priscilla's Easter dress and half of Naomi's. Must take time to teach the girls to sew some rainy day soon. Went to town for upcoming election meeting. We treasure the privilege of voting, recalling our parents' stories of Russia. Sign in the window: 'Saw's Sharpened Here.' I dearly wanted to pencil in beneath it – 'Saw's what?' Restrained myself.

Ha! Seriously, Granny? I must get that love of grammar gaffes from you. The only difference between us is that I wouldn't have restrained myself.

She read on. Jumbled together as the ideas were, it made for engaging reading, transporting Jacqui to another era. She caught a glimpse of the thrifty, hard-working woman as faithful wife, loving mother, generous neighbour. More than that, the writing revealed a woman who documented her struggle to be patient with the children, kind to her neighbours; one who, even in something as personal as a diary, was unwilling to name the names of those who had offended her, yet whom she longed to forgive.

"Canned 32 quarts of peaches today. Golden reminders of summer. Priscilla preferred helping the threshers, but Naomi was a tremendous help. Father, Russell and John (and P. too) finished threshing the last of the wheat before a late supper of 'rofe beast' as John used to call it when he was three. Used the last, badly bruised peaches for cobbler

> for dessert. Premier Manning's radio sermon this evening - Matthew 6:25, Jesus says, 'do *not* worry.' If He commands it, then to go ahead and worry anyway is *sin*. Instead trust Jesus in all things. I need to trust Him with the worries that plague me, esp. about J. Slept poorly last night fearing for his future if he doesn't get his anger under control.

Intuitively, Jacqui knew the worry was over her own father, John. The knowledge that Granny had suffered on his account sliced her heart. Had he ever considered the grief he caused? Could that have anything to do with his willingness to come out west for Anna's wedding?

CHAPTER 35

Jacqui had barely gotten the library lights turned on when the phone rang. The smoker-voiced woman on the other end of the line wanted home delivery of a long list of suspense novels.

"But Sheri always brings my books right to my home," she said. "She just pops by on her way out of town and sticks them in the barbecue on my back deck. Why can't you? Let me remind you, young lady, that my taxes pay your salary!"

It was a rough first ten minutes at work. In rapid succession, Louise Ecklig had threatened Jacqui's job because she declined to provide home delivery of books and Karl Oster had insinuated Jacqui was lying about Sheri being unavailable. He refused to leave a message, as though Jacqui were somehow sequestering the other librarian bound and gagged in a back room somewhere. When Jacqui had made a phone call, the voice mail message had been screamed by an entire family, leaving her ears ringing. Then an irate Hutterite father demanded she do something about the disgusting *Cosmopolitan* magazines his daughter had brought home. All this was punctuated by explosive "I'm gonna kill you!" outbursts from the boys at the public computers not far from Jacqui's desk.

She was almost relieved when Sheri breezed in through the library back entrance to make one of her rare appearances at work. And what an appearance!

When Sheri emerged from between the book stacks, Jacqui did a double take. No, the woman *was* clothed below the waist but she was decked out in form-fitting flesh pink that from a distance...

Is it possible she's unaware of the impression she's making in that get-up? A frilly sheer blouse splashed with huge stylized flowers that unpleasantly resembled giant infected pimples topped the tight leggings. She tottered to her desk, sitting down hard with a poof of strong perfume.

Jacqui did her best to ignore the outfit, filling Sheri in on the latest from the library board meeting the previous week. They had given Jacqui the okay to proceed with a book sale once she had finished weeding through the entire collection for outdated and damaged volumes. Sheri gave no response, not even to defend why there had never been a sale before. She merely sat motionless, staring at the large floral purse on her lap.

Is she offended because I had an idea she hasn't tried? "Is everything all right?" Jacqui ventured at length.

"I don't want to talk about it."

"Okay then." Jacqui turned to her work. She sorted through a cartload of books while Sheri kept silent at the next desk. The atmosphere began to feel uncomfortable.

"Ha, check this out!" Jacqui shifted her computer screen to show Sheri the internal note on the western novel she had checked in a few minutes earlier. She pointed to the words, *Book in wrough shape.* "Someone's spelling appears to be in rough shape," she quipped.

Sheri offered no responding laugh. In Jacqui's experience, literary types had always enjoyed a sense of superiority laughing at the spelling mistakes of the hoi poloi. *But this is Sheri we're talking about here. It's a wonder such a dimwit ever found her way into the library life.* Jacqui took a moment to scrutinize her colleague's round face, noticing her unusually scanty make-up. The wind in her sails had gone slack.

Sheri finally let out a mournful moan. "You know Doreen Sanders, right?"

Doreen Sanders. Jacqui searched her memory. Family library membership. Not usually on the overdues list. Avid borrower of Harlequin romances, gardening manuals and diet cookbooks. "Yeah, I can place her, I think."

"We've been best friends since junior high. Been through everything together. And now, all of a sudden, she turns on me. Says I've got the hots for her husband." She snorted. "As if!"

"What makes her think that?"

Sheri tried to cover a lopsided smile with one manicured hand. "Well, I'm sure you must have guessed by now why I'm hardly ever here? I write books."

"Oh yeah?"

She gave a sheepish smile and slapped her hands to her knees. "I'm Millie Sherona!" She giggled as though it were the punchline to an old joke, then dug in her capacious bag and with a triumphant flourish, and handed Jacqui a glossy red business card. "I wish I could put my picture on these and hand them out all over. But, you know, all the prudes around here."

Sheri Mueller. Millie Sherona. Duh. I knew that sounded familiar. The flaming card bore the tag line "Bringing the Broads to Broad Valley." *How clever.*

"You know all the erotica we have in the large print section?"

"I noticed that, yeah. It's a bit unusual."

"Well, they're mine. I self-publish. It was my Uncle Wally's idea. He's super generous. He pays for all the publishing costs and makes sure I make a profit too, the sweetie. Him and a few of the old-timers at the personal care home don't get out much but they sure do love my books. Can't get enough! They just eat up everything I write."

So, that's how you can afford to pass all the library

responsibilities onto me. Rich Uncle Wally has you on retainer so you can provide him with that crap. What a pervert! Jacqui felt one nostril lifting in disgust, but Sheri was oblivious. She had slumped back into a shapeless mound and sat staring into her lap.

"Turns out," she continued bitterly, "Doreen's niece, who works at the Lodge, found a copy of one of my books on my uncle's bedside. And he went and told her I wrote it. So then, Doreen got hold of it and decided she knew who I was writing about. She figured it was about me and *her husband.* But I swear, he never tied me up on a stack of hay bales and did things to me." She gave a bitter scoff. "Like he's some hot stuff. All he's ever been is a big oaf. I've never told her this, but he asked me out back in high school long before he ever asked her. Come to think of it, I should tell her that." She looked up with plaintive eyes. "And now she's going all over town saying I'm some kind of floozy or something. So much for best friends. The worst part is, I'm afraid it'll get around to my daughter. And if Mia finds out, she'll keep my grandkids from me, like I'm a bad influence or something." She covered her face with her hands, wailing, "Oh, what am I going to do?"

Jacqui was finding it hard to drum up sympathy for the woman. "I'm still stuck on the news that you'd give pornography to—"

"It's not pornography! It's erotica." Sheri's brown eyes crackled with resentment and the corners of her mouth pulled downward.

"Whatever. Isn't it a bit cruel to give it to old guys who can't, as you say, get out much?"

"They're old," Sheri snapped, her expression turning cold, "not dead. And they have every bit as much right to read what they like as anyone else."

"But what about the women who have to work around them? What if they're being sexually harassed because of something you're feeding those dirty old men?" As a librarian, Jacqui was all for freedom to read, but she'd also heard what porn did to the brain, how sex crimes were inevitably linked to porn use. She was confident she was on the moral high ground here and was aghast at the woman's low standards, her lack of solidarity with other women. *I mean, hasn't she ever heard of the MeToo movement?*

"They're not dirty old men!" Sheri huffed. "They're lovable old guys who need a little something to spice up their boring lives and I'm giving it to them. They deserve to enjoy something, too." Sheri rose abruptly from her chair, then leaned down to hiss, "I thought you, of all people, would understand, what with your gay boyfriend out east."

And there it was. Clearly, what went on at the hen party last November had not stayed with the hens. In the months since then, Jacqui had imagined every possible scenario of how her drunken disclosure might be thrown in her face. She had braced herself against the day it would come back to bite her, but now that it had, she felt unready. Sheri's dig wasn't against Jacqui's deplorable party behaviour. It dug at the cut that had hurt her the deepest, had slashed to the core of who she was and over which she had no control. It punched her in the gut and left her gasping.

She turned back to her computer in rigid silence, not trusting herself to speak. Her fingers trembled above the keyboard and the inside of her cheek might have been hamburger where she bit back her rage and indignation. The galling fact that fuelled her frustration was that she was backed into a corner and had to hold off giving a response. After all, it might jeopardize this stupid two-bit job in this lousy hole-in-the-wall in this double-crossing, boondocks community that she needed because she had nowhere else to go.

With a pronounced sniff, as though she was the one who'd been offended, Sheri flounced out to the rear entrance. Jacqui could hear her stilettos clicking up the back stairs to Sheri's residence on the upper floor. A door slammed.

In the ensuing quiet of the afternoon, while Jacqui kept her hands working, two thoughts surfaced from the morass in her brain. *It'll be a cold day in hell before I ever again trust the women around here to keep a secret. And if it were the last option on earth for making a living, there's no way I would ever stoop to doing what Sheri's done.*

CHAPTER 36

Whenever Jacqui closed her eyes lately, visions of dead wood, rotted tree trunks, or dry branches and twigs crackled before her.

Even before the snow began to melt, she'd been itching to clear out the dead falls and underbrush from the woods around the pond down the slope in front of her place. She wanted a view of the water below her living room windows. She envisioned a park-like forest, free of undergrowth, with perhaps a pea-gravel path meandering down to the pond where a bench would wait invitingly. It was a matter of hard work, she reasoned, not a big financial outlay. And she'd never shirked hard work. That was something Geoff had never understood about her, this penchant for hard manual labour. And Pops had sometimes teased her that this was something inherited from her Mennonite heritage. Whatever. She found working on a project rewarding. And besides, she could get what she wanted on a tight budget.

While Jacqui was shut in by the winter snow contemplating the plan, removing the crisscrossing fallen trees leaning against one another had seemed a simple matter. But the area was bigger than it seemed and tangled with more branches and tree trunks on the ground than she'd bargained for. For weeks she'd been hard at work in every spare moment, trudging through the thinning snow, snapping branches and dragging wood to the burning pile.

Yesterday, Lewis had come over and put in a good two hours with her before fleeing to the safety of the house as soon as he saw her pull out matches. She was left to light the fire alone, spending the rest of the day gradually reducing the pile they'd accumulated in the open area beyond the driveway. A primitive satisfaction in the work, breaking branches and feeding the flames, almost let Jacqui imagine she was content, that she could forget all her confusion and hurt as though she and the fire were all there were in the world. Having control over an element of such latent power was strangely gratifying.

This morning, in the crisp early stillness, she started across the frosty grass hoping to put in a few hours before noon. Once again, Sheri had called on her to take the afternoon shift at the library, allowing Jacqui only a few hours to work. She would need a quick shower before then to wash away the smell of smoke.

Pushing the blackened remains of yesterday's burning into the centre of the fire circle, Jacqui crumpled some newspaper, threw on small twigs and struck a match. Adding larger sticks from the pile nearby, she took the time to get a good blaze established, finally positioning a couple of full-length saplings across the middle so they would burn in half. She'd found that sped up the process. Then she turned back to the woods to drag out more deadwood. Her back and thigh muscles were protesting yesterday's work, but she pushed through the pain. A couple more days of work would clean up the last of it. Then she could start on the walkway. Now that the snow was gone, she knew exactly where she would trace the curves of the path.

In the dell where the pond lay, she first gathered thin branches into handful-sized piles, then loosened fallen trees from the thatch of dead grass in which they were buried. Once they budged, she hoisted a tree trunk under each arm, filled her hands with the sticks and began dragging her way toward the fire. Something stopped her short. Behind her, the fork of her left tree trunk had caught between two close-growing trees. She groaned, setting down her handfuls of sticks. It took the full weight of her jumping on branches to break off the ones caught. Finally, after repeated tries, she was able to free the deadwood from the narrow opening. The rising breeze cooled her sweaty neck and she peeled off her jacket, hanging it on the nub of a small branch before lifting her load again.

The last stretch to the fire circle was uphill and steep. Out of the shelter of the trees, the wind tousled her hair, blinding her to the way ahead. She plodded on, one of the boles under her arm slowly slipping out of her grip. Setting down the logs and handfuls of kindling, she raked the hair out of her eyes then picked up the wood to resume her trudge upward.

When she crested the rise to the fire pit, for one terrifying second her heart constricted in alarm. She dropped her load and ran closer to the fire. Beyond its circle, a renegade trail of flames raced hungrily down the length of the sapling that had rolled off her carefully constructed firebox. Already it had eaten a trail of black grass beneath it.

Jacqui hunted vainly for something to beat back the flames. She was reluctant to stamp the red-glowing curls of burning grass while wearing her expensive running shoes, but she had no choice. The swirling smoke choked her as she crushed the embers.

Through squinted eyes, she saw tongues of fire licking at the nearby large pile of branches still to be burned.

"No-o-o!" she wailed.

She had been careful to keep that pile well away from the fire pit. Now, with dismay, she watched flames devouring the dry wood. Faster and faster they spread, fanned by the persistent wind. She raced to the far side of the pile, hoping to head it off, scatter the branches or something. Could there still be enough snow beneath the few trees to the west to put out the fire? Anything to quench the flames? It was useless. The smoke was thick and rising higher.

Jacqui staggered back from the fire in defeat. And really, what did it matter if the pile burned up? She would have preferred to keep the blaze and the area of burnt residue as small as possible, feeding the branches to the flames gradually. But the whole pile was all destined to burn. This would simply get the job done quicker.

She turned back down the rise to retrieve her jacket.

When she came back, an area of grass beyond both the fire pit and the wood pile was aflame and rapidly moving west. For one indecisive minute, Jacqui stared. Then she took off for the house at a gallop. From her porch, she grabbed a couple of buckets to fill at the water faucet on the side of the house. She cursed the slow-filling inefficiency. Hobbling back to the scene with her unwieldy pails as fast as she could, she emptied them onto the pile of wood near the fire circle. But her meagre efforts were far too little and much too late. In an agony of helplessness, she watched the blackening earth reach the nearby fence posts and trees to consume them.

Standing by, watching the destruction was intolerable. She started for the house again then stopped in frantic fear. She spied a trail of black devouring the dry grass southwest beyond the fence line like some voracious serpent. In horror, she watched it spread in width, gaining speed with each passing minute. It breached the fence, leaving its flank to consume a fencepost.

Pursued by the drunken wind, it crept across the open field like a ragged road, veering haphazardly. It grew nearer to the outbuilding on the other side of her trees. She held her breath. The building was metal, but could it withstand fire? Pops' fabled car was stored inside.

She sped to the fence between her yard site and the pasture beyond. In her haste to slip between the strands, the barbed wire scraped her back, catching her shirt. She stopped short. Feeling for the snag, her fingers came away bloody. *Never mind that now.* She gave an impatient tug, hearing the rip, and pulled her leg through the wires, setting off at a run again.

If I can just get ahead of the flames, I can beat them back. Then I can get all this under control.

She ran in a deadly race with the fire. The hungry blaze lashed ahead, laying waste to the overgrown pasture in its path.

Heat from the scorched ground reached through her shoes even as she ran, forcing her to make a wide circle around the path of destruction which slowed her down. Finally, she faced the flames, only to realize her helplessness. Gusts of heat overwhelmed her. She could do nothing but scream in frustration, even as she fled to the side, out of the way of the speeding blaze.

Chased aside by the heat, Jacqui pounded back to the house, now aiming for the open gateway. She propped the empty buckets under the outdoor faucet while she rushed inside. The situation was out of control. She'd be forced to ask for help. She hated to admit defeat, but visions loomed in her mind of the fire spreading throughout the neighbourhood, perhaps even putting someone's home in jeopardy. She called the first number that came to mind—C.H.'s. Her breath came in rasps.

Wonder of wonders, he answered.

“Fire!” she gasped out. She could say no more.

Even so, he understood immediately. “Be right there.”

Back to the pasture she charged, still hoping to head off the flames, fanned by her enemy, the wind. But it outran her. She could only heave the water that remained in her sloshing buckets in a useless arc after it. *Where are you, C.H.?* The ache in her throat from smoke inhalation was made worse by her hammering pulse.

What do I do now?

CHAPTER 37

Jacqui hitched her way from the house with another futile round of small but heavy buckets. With every step, she gasped and listened for the sound of C.H.'s truck or ATV chugging up her driveway. She pinned her hopes on him, willing him to come. He could solve the mess she was in. Closer to the pasture, she could see the fire had grown. Even from this distance she spied orange tongues of fire devouring last year's uneaten grass. A billowing cloud of yellow-gray smoke announced Jacqui's folly to the neighbourhood. She cringed.

A vehicle turned in the driveway. But it wasn't C.H.

Al Barry swung stiffly out of his truck after it rolled to a stop. "Saw the smoke and called the fire department." He hurried toward Jacqui and grabbed her buckets. "Go soak some old blankets!"

Uncertain of his meaning, she stood immobile, staring in dismay. *Fire department?* She groaned. *No! Don't get them involved. Surely it's not that big a deal. Can't just a few of us handle it?*

"Go on! We can smother the flames with 'em."

She stormed back to the house to rummage for blankets. But what did she have that would work? Whatever they used to fight the fire would surely be ruined. Jacqui racked her confused brain. Then she remembered the bedding that had been left in the house when she arrived. She stumbled up the steep attic steps in search of the right box.

She found it quickly. Aware now of every aching muscle, she seized the blankets and raced to the bathroom. Poor Aunt Priscilla. Her dainty ruffled mauve bedspread was about to be sacrificed for the greater good. Under the bathtub faucet, Jacqui soaked the coverlet and a couple of others, then lugged them, dripping, back to the fire.

By this time, C.H. and several others had arrived, their vehicles parked haphazardly around the yard. She could see a few men out in the open field, running west, trying to catch up to the surge of flames.

A woman rushed toward her. "I'll take those!" she yelled, grabbing the bundle from Jacqui's arms. "Go soak some more."

Wheeling back toward the house, Jacqui heard more vehicles drive up.

How embarrassing! Why does the whole neighbourhood have to show up?

She emerged with another bundle of wet sheets, jogging toward where the men worked. They flung blankets and sheets at the fire from behind, not in front of the blaze. This put them at the back of the wind, allowing them to get closer to the flames without being overcome by smoke or blowing heat.

Why didn't I think of that?

Picking up the covers again, they spread them on other spots. Jacqui followed suit, repeating the smothering motion and finally beating the diminishing flames with the blackened bedding. The others kept on, energetically stamping out glowing curls of grass with their work boots and crushing stray sparks at the outer edges of the burnt area until every last flame was out.

Jacqui breathed a relieved sigh that ended in a coughing fit. She was about to thank the others for their help when a huge red fire engine pulled into the yard, lights flashing. From where she stood, she was annoyed to see yet more neighbours trailing behind it.

Exactly what I need. A whole posse of ambulance chasers coming to gawk. Can't they all just mind their own business?

Several of the new arrivals leaped to direct the fire engine. Firefighters in protective gear set to work spraying her fire pit and the fire's blackened wake, thoroughly drenching it. Jacqui's heart sank at the sight. *Whoa! Not so much. Now I'll never get it going again.* There were still plenty of deadfalls from down by the pond that she wanted to burn up.

They progressed through the opening in the west fence and out to where she and C.H. and the others were stamping out the smoking edges. She followed the engine with her eyes, resenting the excited chatter of those around her. Arriving in the field, the fire chief jumped off the truck, yelling orders at the other firefighters. He motioned for those on the ground to clear the area. Soon a gush of water was spraying the charred ground, drenching it far beyond the obviously burnt part.

C.H. appeared at her side. "Kind of surprising how much that tank holds, isn't it?" He lifted his cap to wipe his forehead, leaving a smudge of black. Al and a few others joined them, watching the machinery at work.

"We had it pretty well under control," Jacqui said, watching them spray everything in sight. Long after the danger was past, the firefighters kept up the dousing. "This seems like overkill to me,"

C.H. responded with a silent frown. When Jacqui glanced around the circle, she saw caution and incredulity reflected in the eyes of the others.

"Nah," he finally said. "They've got to give everything a real good soaking. Even the smallest ember or spark could smolder for quite a while in the thatch under the surface. All it needs is a bit of wind and we'd be back at it."

Al sauntered closer to her. "You were pretty lucky this time. But maybe don't do any burning for a bit, eh?" He gave a grim nod.

Jacqui's gaze moved from one smoke-smudged face to another in disturbing recognition.

They're blaming me. "It could have happened to anybody, you know. The wind just picked up too suddenly."

No one came right out and argued the point, but the group gave indistinct murmurs as they shifted from foot to foot or scratched heads in discomfort.

It could have! There wasn't a breath of wind when I came outside this morning.

"Well, I guess I should get back," C.H. said. "I left Lewis on his own." He turned to Jacqui with a bit more cheer. "You know how he is about fire."

She turned to him, relieved at the change of topic. "Yeah, why is that?"

He gave her a curious look. "Sort of the same story as this morning's. We had a scare a few years back in harvest when his grandpa parked the grain truck exhaust too close to a swath. It scared Lewis pretty bad."

"Poor kid. Well, thanks for coming to help out." Jacqui swept her hand to include all the neighbours gathered. "Thank you, everyone. I couldn't have done it without you."

"No worries."

"It's what neighbours are for."

"Anyone want to come in for a drink?" she asked them.

"Not me," Al said. "I've still got chores waiting at home."

The rest averted their eyes and declined Jacqui's offer too, heading for their trucks.

Weary to the bone with the efforts of the past hour, Jacqui trudged back toward the house, still smarting from the disapproval of her neighbours. Directly in her path a decrepit pick-up truck was parked crosswise on her driveway. An unknown local leaned against the door, talking with whoever was at the wheel. Her ire rose like a wind-fanned flame at the inconsiderate clod who claimed her space in this way. She hadn't noticed these men among those who fought the fire with her. She stopped short before they noticed her.

"I get what she was trying to do," the man on foot commented, his plaid flannel jacket hem curled up at the back like a duck's tail. "Got a few piles of brush I'd like to set a match to myself."

The driver had no sympathy. "It's no excuse. Remember that grass fire south of here a few years back? Great swath of scorched earth for seventeen miles. Started by sparks off a burning barrel. Some fool woman just had to burn garbage." Jacqui could see only the greasy visor of the all-knowing man's ball cap wagging as he shook his head in disgust. "Middle of a drought! You gotta wonder what's wrong with some people."

"Heard this one's a city gal. Probably didn't know any better."

From the pick-up, Jacqui heard Clever-Boy snort. "We've had five months of snow cover to get your burning done. Some people have got no common sense a'tall."

Jacqui's necked burned with indignation.

Don't they have anything better to do than come snoop at someone's misfortune? I didn't see them lifting a finger to help. And besides, the idiot's parked his lousy heap of a truck on my grass. The minute he pulls forward, he's going to drive through my lilies. But I s'pose rednecks don't know any better. 'No common sense a'tall.'

She stormed forward. "Excuse me." She forced ice into her words.

Plaid-man gave a start and lowered his elbow from the truck window to make way for her.

"You're going to have to clear my driveway," Jacqui said as she passed between them, "so the people who've been *helping* here can get their vehicles out."

Unmistakably, she felt their frowns on her back, a condemnation that stung far worse than the scratches from the barbed-wire fence. She stalked past them and into the house, slamming the door behind her.

CHAPTER 38

At a sound from her phone, Jacqui hurried to the circulation desk and pulled the device out of her purse. Currently, the library was empty, but schoolkids would be charging in sometime in the next half hour.

The name on the message made her pulse leap. *Geoff!* She took a deep breath and exhaled slowly before reading it. In nearly a year, there had not been a word from him. The momentary pang of excitement she'd felt on seeing his name pop up disgusted her. She reminded herself of his casual rejection and steeled herself to read the short message.

Hey, Jac! Hope you're doing well. Could you take a minute (or an hour) to sign these papers so we can proceed with this? Sorry it's this long. Legalese and all that. As ever, Geoff.

Was she finally going to get her share of the house? It was about time, but she couldn't help tasting the bittersweet flavour of it. Yes, the cash would be a welcome injection to her strained renovation budget, but there was also a bleak finality to that chapter. She'd given Geoff half her life. *As ever, Geoff? As if.* Evidently to him their break-up was no big deal. Had she meant nothing to him? Business as usual?

She opened the document. Funny. It didn't seem like any sale agreement she'd seen before. But the image on the screen was tiny. Jacqui turned to the computer at her desk, bringing up the seven-page document on the larger screen.

It took three readings of the opening lines before the truth struck home. Staring at the words, she bit her lip and her hands balled into fists.

> "Dear Jacqui Penn," The name was handwritten in Geoff's strong block printing.
>
> "The Stiles family has provided your name as a friend who can attest to their suitability as adoptive parents of Quinnley Arielle.
>
> "We would appreciate your response in a timely fashion to the enclosed questionnaire. Please be as thorough as possible, citing examples of your observations if appropriate. We can assure you that any information given on this form will remain in the strictest confidence. You will not be named as the source of any information which you provide, and your confidentiality will be carefully protected."

Jacqui knocked back in her chair, her face to the ceiling. She fought to contain welling tears of fury and frustration. *Stiles family? So, Dale changed his name and they're a family? How come I didn't rate? I was always just a "partner." And now all I am is a "friend"?* Jacqui slammed her shoe on the edge of her desk, propelling her chair and the back of her head into the wall behind her. Somehow the pain of the collision felt good. Like lashing out at the pain she'd endured to go through a tubal ligation all those years ago, a permanent birth control measure that Geoff had convinced her "made the most sense." And she had agreed. In what universe had that dark decision ever made sense? She couldn't remember now.

She leaped up to pace the short distance from desk to window, her breath coming in shallow bursts. *Why did I agree to that? What was I thinking?*

First the surgery, then a slow and painful recovery. Then a year and a half of never feeling quite right again. Finally, a second operation to correct the first surgeon's mistake. Oh yes, Geoff was outraged and at the time she took that as protectiveness, that he really cared. He showed it by going all gung-ho, suing for negligence and winning. But was that genuine love? And what could a few thousand bucks do to repair the emotional damage, the regret?

Jacqui's insides churned in misery at the memories, the betrayal. But even more, she was furious at her own gullibility in letting Geoff make decisions of life and death for her. She returned to her desk chair and leaned forward again to glare at the computer screen.

"What observations have you made as to this person's ability to care for a child?"

I could ruin this for you, Geoff, and I should. You may have been able to charm your realty clients by gushing over their kids, but I could tell Social Services what you used to say in private. How you've always called kids "guttersnipes" and "urchins." Should I describe your reaction when a kid in a restaurant with spaghetti sauce all over his cheeks and hands leaned over the back of his seat and reached for you?

"Do you have any concerns about the applicant's ability to parent a child?"

Should I write about your dread of having kids enter our home? I knew you weren't joking when you used to say, "Kids are a mess on one end and a noise at the other." Or maybe I should describe how you have a hard time making commitments, how you can breezily dispose of someone who loves you the minute you "find your true self." Hm? How about that? What's going to happen to this little girl if you suddenly go on a new "journey of self-discovery" like you told me you did when you found out you were gay? What if someday you decide your true self has always been "childless at heart"?

The computer mouse slipped from her moist fingers and she

purposely slowed her breathing. With a weary rub of her temples, she slumped in defeat. No vindictive denouncements, no matter how much Geoff deserved them. Jacqui couldn't risk her share of the house. To keep the peace, she'd give him his glowing reference. Nice, reliable Jacqui. Once again, Geoff would get his way. Hopefully, when the house sold and she got her pay-out she could forget all about him and his new "family." Or somehow attempt to do so.

The library doorbell chimed. Three boys came in to use the public computers, followed by Sarah Bergen, whom Jacqui hadn't seen since before Christmas. The sight of the devoted mother blew a fresh gust of emotion through Jacqui, feelings of envy and irreparable loss.

Sarah directed her daughter to the children's section then faced Jacqui with a warm smile. "I want to thank you," she began. "Remember you found that book for me, the one about Chinese adoptions? And then you listened to my troubles when I really needed someone to talk to." She gave a small shake of her head. "I was wondering, would you like to come to our place for supper tonight or tomorrow night? My husband and I would love to have you."

Jacqui was unprepared for this down-home, get-to-know-you hospitality. Especially since her reputation as an arsonist in the neighbourhood surely must have spread as fast as the fire had. She almost refused, still choked with bitter thoughts of childlessness and her own ruined and dead future. But how could she turn down the open friendliness on the face of this woman?

"Yeah, I'd like that," she said, and as she checked out a stack of children's books the little girl brought to her mother, Jacqui found herself hungry for Sarah's warmth and friendship.

Sarah's directions for finding their farm were simpler than they seemed at first. Jacqui drove up the winding lane over-arched by tall cottonwoods not yet leafed out. She arrived in front of an older, two-story home rising above the green-hazed lawn still scattered with puff patches of snow in the shady spots. Order and symmetry reigned in the park-like setting just beginning to awaken from winter's slumber. She recalled Francie Barry's comment, "Instead of watching TV, Mennonites keep their yards perfect." Hours had been spent here, creating interesting nooks and hideaways amongst the carefully trimmed plantings. She took note of a few ideas to incorporate in her own place, and with a start realized that she'd stopped viewing her life on the Prairies as temporary. When had she taken root here?

Sarah met her at the door with a warm and unexpected hug. She introduced Jacqui to her husband Andrew, a tall, thin man with thick glasses and streaks of gray at his temples. Ava rushed toward Jacqui with a large picture book in her outstretched arms.

"Not right now, Ava," Sarah said, taking the book with a gentle laugh. "Maybe after supper Miss Jacqui can read it with you."

Jacqui braced herself for the child's tantrum, but Ava accepted this mildly and they all moved into the dining room. The table was simply yet beautifully set, centred by a tiny arrangement of grape hyacinths. and fleeting whiffs of their fragrance teased at her.

Over roasted vegetables and barbecued chicken, Jacqui responded to her hosts' interest in her library career and her ongoing house project. She learned they raised feed barley, oats, and chickens.

"How many chickens do you have?"

Her hosts exchanged glances. "Thirty thousand. Would you like to hear their names?" Andrew deadpanned.

Jacqui widened her eyes, but Sarah shook her head with a smile. "He's teasing."

After the laughter, Jacqui pointed to the wall opposite her where a rustic painted wood sign read, "Rooted and built up in him, and stablished in the faith, as ye have been taught, abounding therein with thanksgiving." "Did you make that, whatever it means?"

"She did," Andrew said quietly as he helped Ava cut the last bit of her chicken off the bone. "Sarah sells baking and crafts at the farmer's market in summer."

Sarah blushed. "Not all the signs I make are this big, and I don't make only Bible verses."

Jacqui mulled over the phrases in stylized script as they ate. *Rooted...in the faith...with thanksgiving.* Did that account for the palpable peace she felt under this roof? Husband and wife, smiling over their small daughter's first attempts at cutting and serving the dessert brownie? Jacqui accepted her lopsided piece even as a sad envy tugged at her, sharpening the fresh betrayal of this morning's message from Geoff. How was it that suddenly something she could never have was what she wanted most?

Later, while Andrew took Ava off to prepare her for bed, Jacqui helped Sarah clear away dinner.

"We both wanted to thank you again for finding that book for us," the young woman said, setting a dripping clean platter in the dish rack. "It pained me to find out that a mother in China might be missing her child, our Ava, but..." Her mouth worked, appearing to fight a downward pull at the corners.

Andrew returned, encircling his wife from behind and finishing her thought. "But we've come to a decision." He reached to place a hand on Jacqui's shoulder. "We have contacted the orphanage in China, and we are going back to see if we can find Ava's birth mother."

You're thanking me?

"We've decided we'll take Ava to visit her every year so she can spend time with her family, maybe learn the language and understand her people," he said. "If it works out and we feel it would be safe, we might even let her go on her own and stay for a few weeks when she's older."

Jacqui thought immediately of the totalitarian government, the dangers of kidnapping and human trafficking and even the cultural barriers. Did these kind people have any idea of the risks?

But Sarah nodded through tears. "She means everything to us, but the other mother loves her, too. How can we be selfish about God's gift to us?"

CHAPTER 39

"I'm going over to the shed to do some cleaning, Lewis," Jacqui told the boy, soon after the school bus let him off at the end of her lane one early April afternoon. "I'll be on the other side of those trees if you need me. I won't be long." To be certain he heard her, she lifted his earphone out of his ear and peered into his face over the dinosaur book he was reading. With the glazed eyes of one returning from a visit to the deep prehistoric past, he stared back at her, before nodding solemnly.

Again, C.H. had left the boy in her care for the day so he could stay with his wife. Clearly, by the increase in the amount of time he spent at the hospital, Roslyn was deteriorating. Yet C.H. gave unfailingly positive answers to polite questions: "She's fighting hard" or "saw some improvement in today's blood work" or "God's got this."

But Jacqui read the grave truth of Roslyn's decline on C.H.'s haggard face and in his strained tone.

On her way through the kitchen, Jacqui picked up her phone. Lewis was currently in his silent phase so he wouldn't need it. Then again, there was no Internet service in the outbuilding where she'd be working and she didn't expect to be out there long. At the last minute, she left it on the counter.

A gust of wind nearly snatched the porch door from Jacqui's grip. She grasped the handle tighter, pressing against the invisible force to close it. For days it had blown like this, making the sunny weather unpleasant, the nights a sinister howl. Why did it have to blow continually? Again, she felt that insecure weightlessness as though it would catch her up and scatter her beyond Earth's grip. For a moment she thought of tying a long rope to the house and clinging to it until she reached the far building. Fingers of air current grasped at Jacqui's hair, whipping it against her face. *It's been too long since my last haircut. Now I need a ponytail.* She dashed back indoors for an elastic, almost losing the determination to face her planned project.

Finally, as she often had, she pictured Bree's withering gaze at Jacqui's weakness. Her girlfriend's messages had prodded her on in the work on this place more than once. She picked up her gloves and supplies, stiffened her backbone with resolve and made her way across the yard and through the chartreuse-leafed poplars to the home of her father's unclaimed gift. She fought to keep a tight grip on the empty rubber tote she carried that acted like a giant sail against the wind.

The double doors of the machine shed were fastened shut by a simple wooden arm on one door resting in a metal slot on the other. She lifted the arm upright, yanking on the door to open it. After her initial prying, the wide door swung open well enough despite a sharp creak. The interior was dark in contrast to the day's bright sunlight and smelled of mechanical substances—gear oil, transmission fluid, diesel fuel? She had no idea. Those were only words she'd heard Pops mutter. There was an earthy smell, too, reminding her of the cramped garage in Pops' city back yard. It had had a dirt floor too.

Jacqui couldn't escape the sense she was entering her own version of prehistoric times. Other than the first brief glimpse into this building last summer, she'd been too busy with projects in the house and immediate yard to pay much attention here. Slowly her eyes adjusted to the gloom, lightened only by the open door and a long strip of translucent fiberglass corrugated like the metal walls, high on each side of the building.

In the centre sat the precious '61 Chev Bel Air convertible, the talk of the community. She ran her hand over its covering of patchwork fabric made by Granny. Briefly, the thought of selling it to raise cash had crossed her mind, but how could she now that she knew its story? No, the car rightfully belonged to Pops and she hoped that he would come out to see it in person when he came in October.

Today, she had another purpose here. Jacqui had been thinking about the possibility of tools out here ever since C.H.'s suggestion that there might be some of value. She was beginning to wish she had tried to sell Aunt Priscilla's kitschy ornaments and those dozens of salt and pepper shakers. They might have been worth something. The tackiest of knick knacks on the local social media marketplace would often induce a bidding war. Conversely, what Jacqui knew to be of actual value inevitably failed to produce any interest. Still, in the hope of raising some cash, it was worth a try. And she hadn't dismissed Francie's suggestion to auction off the contents of the old wooden granaries lined up along the fence line south of the house.

Inside the building, a workbench ran most of the length of the building under the strip of daylight. Nuts and bolts and unknown metal parts littered the wood surface, interspersed by mouse droppings and covered by a generous coating of dust. She barely paused at the sight of the rodent feces and the thought of possible disease.

I'm becoming a country girl. I laugh in the face of hantavirus.

Working with her back to the dim rear of the building, she let the daylight shine on the workbench, doing her best to sort trash from treasure. She chose one of the least greasy rags on the bench to clean tools and hardware, hoping the items collecting in the bottom of the tote were worth something. Outside, the wind howled, creaking the bones of the building and puffing up the car's fabric cover as though it were a breathing entity. The wide doors squawked with each gust.

The work grew mind-numbing. Wire and screws and gaskets and all manner of unknown items began to swim before her eyes. In frustration at the still-scattered surface of the long counter, Jacqui finally took a short piece of plywood and plowed the debris into a pile at one end. She was about to use the wood to shovel it all into a garbage bag when a swirl of movement caught the corner of her eye. Something white had flown past the door. Turning, she watched the patch of daylight framed by the open door. It grew hazy and dull. Her hands stilled. A whirl of dust rose from the patch of gravel outside the shed. Beside her, the car cover flapped and snapped against the vehicle beneath it. Outside, more dirt gathered, rising higher and higher. Particles of sand pelted her face.

All at once, the open door slammed shut with a bang. Jacqui froze in the sudden darkness. A muffled clang made her heart plummet. The wooden arm on the outside of the door must have fallen into its slot. She was locked in.

She clung to the corner of the workbench as her eyes adjusted to the dusk. The high strip of translucent panel still offered a murky light from above. But the closed doors now amplified the mocking scream of the wind. It echoed against the metal walls of the structure, filling her ears with the groans of its wooden frame.

Jacqui's hands grew clammy inside her gloves. She ran to the doors, hoping she could somehow slide something up between them to lift the metal arm outside. But the inner door overlapped the outer one and allowed no access. Panic rose within her. She scanned the high walls, catching sight of the strip of light at the top. The space was too small for a body to get through.

At least I could break through to yell for help.

She rushed back to the bench for a heavy tool. A large overturned metal bucket allowed her to climb onto the workbench. But the fiberglass stoutly resisted her frenzied banging. On tiptoe, she peered through the blurry fiberglass ripples. She could just make out her house beyond the trees.

"Lewis!" she screamed as loud as she could. "Help! Come open the door!" She called repeatedly but the screeching wind and creaking building drowned out her cries. She climbed down from the bench. Did she really want Lewis to venture out into this wind, anyway? Would he even know what to do? She thumped down onto the overturned bucket. If only the howling outside would quit. She could barely hear herself think.

Without her phone she was hooped. Lewis was back in the house, dead to the world. How long would it be until C.H. came to get him? Last week, it had been after ten p.m. And today, Lewis was in his silent mode. He'd be unable to explain where Jacqui was. C.H. would conclude she had abandoned his son and think her neglectful and irresponsible.

But surely, he'd see her car still home and start searching? That was her one hope. Yet the prospect of waiting that long...

Get a grip! Jacqui covered her ears against the shrieking wind, forcing herself to breathe slowly. Sitting on the bucket, she stared at the dirt floor below her. Images of digging her way beneath the footings of the wall played through her mind.

Yeah, right.

She should finish the work she came out here for. But a glance at the pile of junk on the dusty bench produced zero motivation.

Why? Why am I trapped in a stupid cave like this when all I wanted to do was clean up? Why does everything I hold in my hands blow off the way all that dust is blowing away out there? Ever since I was a little girl, I've tried so hard to be good and do what's right. And when I thought I was getting my dream come true with Geoff, all it did was blow up in my face, too. Even out here in the middle of nowhere, every stinking project I try somehow flies apart—the living room ceiling, the kitchen cupboards I haven't been able to afford to replace, black mold in the bathroom. Still, I soldiered on.

But Sheri thinks I killed that guy, Neil Weerd, because I poked a bit of fun at him the day before he offed himself. The community women think I'm a drunken fool. And then there was the fire. No one around here will ever forgive me for nearly burning down the whole neighbourhood. But how was I to know the wind would pick up like it did? It wasn't my fault!

Wasn't it? One voice crashed through her protesting self-pity. Was anything your fault? The force of it stunned her.

"I'm a good person. I had a lousy childhood and I still won the high school English award three years running. I got scholarships in university. I got service awards at work. I'm a responsible daughter, a loyal friend and a faithful partner. I recycle and I compost and I've never had a speeding ticket or even a library fine. I am a good person!" Her shout left her throat raw but was powerless against the accusing wind.

Jacqui dropped her face into her hands and stormed along with it in a howling cry. These were not the first tears she'd cried since that horrible morning when the truth about Geoff and Dale had dawned on her, but they were the most violent. She wept from frustration at this horrid predicament. She wept for the rejection and the loss. More than anything, she grieved the irretrievable past.

CHAPTER 40

Doubled over in sobs, Jacqui wiped her nose across the knees of her jeans. She'd worn herself out. Her stomach muscles were tender and aching and her mouth dry as dirt. She kept utterly still, listening to the ferocious wind. Next to her, the multi-print fabric of the homemade car cover gave a great snap when a sudden gust burst from under the shed door. The material folded up on itself and caught on the rear-view mirror, revealing the bright turquoise of the Bel Air. Jacqui wiped her eyes with the back of her hand. She had never carefully inspected the car.

Why not? She peeled the fabric away from the door enough to open it, tugging where the underside's frayed seams clung to the convertible roof.

Cute, and still in pristine shape with not a trace of rust marring the turquoise paint. People said that Uncle Russell had begun allowing the car to be used by non-profit groups in the local Sports Day parade and C.H. had told her there might be any number of interested buyers for the car. But it belonged to Pops. And he should at least know the story behind it.

Pressing the handle with her thumb, she opened the driver's door. Inside, the bench seat was a smooth invitation to her panic-weary limbs. She slid inside and closed the door. Jacqui let out an involuntary sigh at the relative quiet, a sweet unexpected reprieve from the din of the howling wind. Stretched the length of the seat, her legs still had to bend tightly. She closed her swollen eyes against her troubles and against this intrusive, troubling new voice, the one that dared to question her goodness.

But her eyes shot open. There seemed to be no escape from the insistent accusations. Agitated at the trajectory of her thoughts, she sat up, folding her legs beneath her. An inner wind was blowing, sweeping away her defenses, winnowing, husking, sifting her, leaving only a kernel behind. And the kernel of her that was left lay hard and parched, rankling within like a pebble in her shoe, forcing her to find someone to blame.

She remembered one of the books she'd been reading that winter. As a Jewish boy in a Nazi concentration camp, Elie Wiesel came to believe a fellow prisoner was right in his bitter denouncement of God. How could there be a good God in the face of the evil and suffering that surrounded them? Jacqui, too, had simply taken Pops' word that the suffering he'd endured meant there was no God.

"We're on our own," he would often say. "This lousy life is all there is, so you've gotta make the best of it." That's what he'd taught her and that's what she'd always believed.

All my life I've been the good girl, trying to make the best of what life threw at me. But what of that unexpected ending of Wiesel's *Night*? Forced on a starvation march, young Elie tried to save himself by escaping the burden of caring for his father. In doing so, he discovered he was no better than the God he'd condemned.

With a jolt, that earlier relentless voice intruded again.

Good? What makes you think you're good? Compared to who? How can you be the judge of your own life? If the truth were told, would your every action, word and thought be found good, every motive pure?

Jacqui shrank from this strange inner inquisition, squirming inwardly. She rubbed her hands across the fluted vinyl of the car's seat hoping to escape the probing searchlight by rooting herself in the present. With more and more effort she pressed the plastic seat as though to force her thoughts onto something, anything else.

Only four months ago at Christmas, Aunt Anna had said their father had bought this car for Pops with cash, the only time he ever bought one new. Taken back to the story, Jacqui envisioned the muted excitement of her grandmother, preparing Pops' favourite breakfast, anticipating his thrilled reaction when they sent him out on an errand, and he would discover the car.

As it had when her aunt told the tale, her stomach gave a sickening flop at the knowledge of what happened next. She imagined the whole family, heartsore and stunned when Grandfather told them Pops was gone. Her young father's vacant room, the uncharacteristically made bed, and the cruelest insult of all, the Bible they'd given him defiantly left on his pillow. His rejection was thorough, so final and complete it had permanently altered the family he left behind.

How could you do it, Pops? Didn't you ever regret it? Jacqui knew her father couldn't have known about the gift or he would have mentioned it to her with some acidic explanation. What had his headstrong bitterness cost him? And what had he missed? More than just the magnificent surprise of his dream car, he'd missed the chance to see his father trying to make amends. How clearly she saw what he had been blind to—the life and heritage he'd turned his back on and everything that she, his daughter had missed out on because of his youthful rebellion. Over the years, his stubbornness became a rut worn so deeply into his will that not even the natural urge to show off his child to his parents could pull him out of it.

She sat clutching the steering wheel, wondering about the life that never was. What if Pops had stayed on the farm, received this generous gift from his father and the attempted apology it represented? What if he had let it soothe the wounds of his soul?

What would that John Penn have been like? Of course, he would have kept the name Penner. Would he have been cheerful, optimistic, openly tender-hearted? Strangest of all to picture, would he have been faithfully religious? Jacqui gave a rueful smile. That image was impossible to imagine. Perhaps that positive young man would have attracted some motherly local girl and they'd have raised a family here in the safety of rural Alberta, taking them to church as Jacqui's cousins had been, encircling them with family and community and traditions.

Of course, the conjecture was moot. If Pops hadn't run away to Ontario and changed his name, if he hadn't married Sylvana Mareno, there would have been no Jacquelyn Margaret Penn. Pops' farm child would have been an entirely different person from Jacqui. Who knew? Maybe a whole passel of Penner kids would have been raised here, growing up like Aunt Anna's kids, knowing their way around farm life. No doubt none of them would ever have got themselves ridiculously trapped in this metal and wood tomb on this uncivilized wind-swept prairie, forgotten and forsaken by everyone.

The light had shifted. It came now from below the wide slit of translucent fiberglass across the top of the western wall and it tinted the inside of the shed ceiling a lurid red.

Which means the sun is going down. Oh God! I can't stay here all night. If you're really there, get me out of here.

Jacqui froze in mid-agitation. *What did I just say?* Was her cry for help simply a meaningless epithet, the panicked plea of helpless frustration? Even to her that seemed a cheap trick, the kind she'd experienced more than once from fair-weather friends back in grade school. But no, the words sprang from a crack in the deepest part of her. With a sense of wonder, she admitted her cry had been a genuine prayer. She knew instinctively that ordering the Almighty around was as laughable as defying the power of the incessant wind out there. Like the wind finding its way through every crack and fissure in this building, God was sweeping through her soul, loosening thoughts, fears, remorse, and now even raising prayers.

Okay. Jacqui held her breath then said it aloud in a croaking, quavering voice. "Okay. Pops is wrong." She cleared her throat. "You win. I believe you're there. Here. Everywhere. Inescapable, really. I think I've always known it." She exhaled, half sobbing from a tremendous sense of release. "You've done a number on me. I get it. I'm not a good person like I've always told myself. But I—I believe what Aunt Anna says, that you are good." Inexplicably, saying the words cemented them in her soul, making her more certain of their truth than of anything she'd ever known.

"You are always good. I see that now. Is that why everything happened? Were you my good Father, bringing me here? And me running the opposite direction the way Pops ran from home?" Her voice caught and broke, but she forged on. "I want to believe it all, the whole shebang about Jesus and how he died to pay for my sins the way Anna once said. And I want you in my life, I really do. I want to be rooted in the faith, like Sarah Bergen's sign said."

When she inhaled, the air that filled her was fresh and cold.

At that moment, a tremendous shriek tore the air. Jacqui jerked in terror. Her head snapped back and forth searching for the shriek's source. Then it came again, longer this time. The fabric car cover tore from the back windshield only to tangle on the radio antenna at the front. And suddenly the building was opened to a shaft of daylight. Facing the rear window, Jacqui cowered in horror as the shed roof began to peel away from the walls with a long and terrible screech, lifting, lifting its rafters and metal sheeting like the lid of a tuna can. In shock, she watched the wind tip the front end of the roof higher and higher. Dust particles pelted the windows of the car. A flurry of feed sacks from the corner swirled up to plaster themselves against the rising roof. Finally, it towered straight up on the edge of the back wall, then with a final burst, the gale took the huge structure of roof and rafters like a plaything and sailed it away.

The shrieking continued until Jacqui recognized it as her own voice. She shut her mouth, but her body still trembled violently. Tears streamed down her face. For a long while, she crouched tightly with her forehead pressed onto the seat back.

CHAPTER 41

Like a child exhausted from a tantrum, the wild wind was reduced to a mellow breeze that now lazily puffed Granny's patchwork car cover still bunched around the aerial of the Bel Air. Along the top of the shed's west wall, sunset's glow silhouetted a row of curved nails like tree trunks bent by the wind.

But I can see sky. There must be a way to climb out.

Jacqui unfolded her legs from her tight crouch, stiff and sore as though after a workout. She let herself out of the car. If she could find a way to get up there, she could hammer a few of those nails flat and climb over the wall. She stood, calculating its height. From here it looked to be about eight feet above the workbench, which meant it would be about a twelve-foot drop to the ground on the outer side of the wall.

How bad is that going to hurt? It didn't matter. She had to risk it. Thirst was cleaving her tongue to the roof of her mouth and by now, she urgently needed the bathroom.

Finding another empty five-gallon bucket to match the one she'd climbed on earlier, she placed them side by side upside down on the workbench. Next she hunted for a hammer but found only an unwieldy sledgehammer. She dragged it to the bench, set it beside the buckets, and hoisted herself up. But they still didn't raise her high enough. She could see only enough through the rippled fiberglass to know that the house was dark. Was Lewis so engrossed in a movie that he'd forgotten to turn on lights? And would he have thought to scrounge something for dinner? Or had C.H. already come for him and taken him home? Anxiety curled its tentacles around her insides.

She'd need to stand higher to surmount that wall. Stepping off the buckets, she jumped down from the bench and hunted in the dim corners of the building for something to increase the height. The best she could do was a pile of scrap lumber which she lugged piece by piece to stack on the work bench. She fought the warp of the odd-sized pieces to produce a makeshift platform on which to place the pails. This gave her more than a foot of extra height, but the buckets wobbled perilously. Lugging the sledgehammer, she climbed the tower. Now she could see over the wall and to the ground outside.

That's an awfully long way down. Jacqui squinted ahead through the trees to the house with its darkened windows. If C.H. came for his son and found the boy all alone in a dark house, how could she explain her negligence? But it occurred to her that C.H. was a Christian. He would understand and forgive her. Jacqui's mood lightened by degrees.

With tremendous effort, she managed to heft the huge tool high enough to crush down two pairs of nails. This smoothed a way for her to get over the wall. But again, the drop below made her stomach flutter. And the sharp metal edge of the corrugated tin would surely snag her clothing and gouge her flesh. She stalled at the prospect, her gaze roaming the area around her feet, searching below for something to use as padding. The workbench, still littered with dust and hardware, offered nothing. But something else caught her eye. Hanging from a nail on the side of the workbench was a collection of bungee cords. Never had such a homely device sparked such joy in her.

"Oh, beauteous implements of hope!" she cried, clambering down from her tower as quickly as she could, almost giddy with their promise.

She snatched the thick black rubber bands, testing their elasticity. Satisfied they would hold together, she fastened their hooks in a line to make a long, springy rope. But she would need gloves. In the aftermath of the storm, she was disappointed to find only one of the pair she'd brought with her, but it would have to do. Now for something to cushion her from the sharp edge of metal.

With a flash of inspiration, she gathered the bundled car cover from where it was looped around the side mirror and made the tedious climb up the bench and blocks and buckets again, this time certain she could manage the jump. She wedged the first hook into the space between the corrugated tin panel and the wall's wood frame. The bungee cord rope clattered against the outside of the metal wall as she let it down. It reached about half-way to freedom. Then she arranged the fabric cover thickly over the top plate of the wall at her point of escape. Murmuring another hopeful prayer, she hoisted her legs one at a time over the wall. For a moment she teetered on the height, the bottom dropping out of her belly. Then she lowered herself to hang on the top of the wall by her armpits. With her gloved hand and then the other, she grabbed the length of bungee cord, sending its lower part swinging. Her weight stretched the cords alarmingly. Breathing hard, she groped with one foot, trying to trap and grasp the cord between the soles of her shoes. She dropped rapidly downward, twirling out of control and bumping against the metal wall of the building.

But that's the idea. I'm trying to get down.

Bit by bit she lowered herself. With her right hand, she used the length of fabric as padding to grasp the cord. Finally, she was near enough to the weedy earth beneath to release her line. As she did, the hook end of the bungee cord sprang up, narrowly missing her face. She landed on her rear with a jolt. Flexing her arms and legs, she found she was intact and stood shakily.

She felt drained of energy but started for the house as quickly as she could, calling for Lewis as she charged through the door. There was no sign of him anywhere.

After using the washroom, she poured herself a tall glass of cold water from the fridge. It went down so smoothly, moistening her sandpaper-lined throat, she could have cried. She hunted the fridge, stuffing her face with hummus on a pita, then sat back in her chair for a moment, satiated, surveying the kitchen. There sat her phone, useless on the counter where she'd left it.

What if C.H. has tried to reach me? She grabbed it to check for messages. Sure enough, he'd sent a couple of curt lines, first letting her know he was leaving the hospital, then an hour and a half later when he must have found Lewis alone, asking where she was.

What kind of a slacker will he take me for? I never meant to abandon Lewis for that long. I only meant to be outside an hour or two and then come back in to make Lewis a nice meal. Instead, did C.H. arrive to find his son sitting in a darkened house, still watching television at ten p.m.? Worse, had he taken the boy home hungry? There wasn't a crumb anywhere in the kitchen to show Lewis might have scavenged for something to eat. *Oh, what must his father think of me?*

Conscious-smitten, Jacqui rushed to the bathroom. She was grubby as a street waif, but she had no time for a shower now. She had to see how Lewis had made out. Hurriedly she washed away the silt and grit on her face and hands as best she could, changed into clean jeans and a sweater and did what she could to tame her wind-tangled hair. While she was brushing and re-twisting her curls, her phone rang. The display showed her neighbour Francie's number.

"Hello?" She tapped her foot in impatience.

"Jacqui, are you okay? Al saw a great big piece of something flying out from your place. Couldn't really tell what it was, but with this terrific wind, we were afraid it might be from your house."

"That huge something was my shed roof. It peeled right off and sailed away. Did it land at your place? I hope it didn't damage anything."

"The trees north of our place stopped it. At least it wasn't your house roof, though. You could have been seriously hurt."

"Francie," Jacqui said, trying to convey the intensity of her fear, "I was locked in the shed when the wind tore the roof off."

"What? How in the world..." Muffled sounds of conversation followed as Francie repeated the story to whoever was with her. "Look, you said you're okay right?"

"Yeah, I'm fine now."

"Seems like your place got the worst of it in this area. We'll be over to check out the damage tomorrow. Al says we should be able to put together a work bee to get your new roof put up."

My place got the worst of it? Was it punishment for what her foolhardy burning last month might have done to the neighbourhood? But Jacqui immediately cut short that line of thought. She knew instinctively that wasn't what had happened. The wind of God had immobilized her so he could perform heart surgery on her.

She focused on what Francie had promised and, as she did, a deep feeling of gratitude welled up inside Jacqui. After the risk she'd put her neighbours in with her careless fire, now they would repair the damage to her building? Tears welled in her eyes, choking her voice. "Thanks, Francie. Thanks so much." If her insurance didn't cover the cost of materials, she'd use her credit card and pay interest, if only to experience the kindness of her neighbours.

She hopped into her car buoyed by this added joy. Though it was late, she felt duty-bound to explain her predicament to C.H. He was a relaxed sort of man. She knew he would understand.

And besides, she had something exciting to tell him. Jacqui had a feeling he would be as overjoyed at whatever had happened to her that evening as she was herself.

CHAPTER 42

C.H. gave his son a wooden hug. He hadn't told the boy the fearsome news. He couldn't because he didn't know how. For now, he clung to the homely rituals of bedtime, performing with painstaking attention to detail each step of the routine that Roslyn had established for Lewis from the time he was a toddler. Snack, drink of water, send him to put on pyjamas and brush his teeth. Turning back the covers at a precise forty-five-degree angle, C.H. let Lewis crawl into bed and tucked the blanket just the right distance under his chin. Then he sniffed Lewis's breath to be sure he had really brushed his teeth. He had. That was a relief. C.H. wasn't up to playing that game. Not tonight. Maybe never again. Next came the reading. Except for the Bible story. C.H. skipped that, simply ignoring Lewis's reminders about it. Instead, he read from the latest National Geographic and a chapter of *Little Britches*.

He switched off the light in the boy's room and pulled the door to within six inches of the jamb the way Lewis liked it. Before he turned off the hall light, he made sure the night light was on in the wall outlet. He switched off the overhead light but stood immobile in the doorway of the master bedroom for unnumbered minutes, staring at the luminous digits of the clock on the night table beside his bed.

His bed, now. Not theirs.

He trudged through the door, closing it with a gentle click. Moving softly to the bed, he stared down at the intricate design of the quilt Roslyn had made with her mother a few years ago. He even remembered the name of the pattern: Double Wedding Ring. His eyes strayed to the large wedding portrait of the two of them above the bed. What kids they were, confidently repeating the words "in sickness and in health, 'til death do us part." How beautiful she was, with glowing eyes and gleaming hair.

Roslyn. His throat constricted against whatever surged within him and had been seeking to burst out for several hours, or was it years now?

A malevolent power coursed through him. It forced him to pull his fist back and wordlessly plunge it into the pillows. He did it again and again, and then with both fists, like a pile-driver, methodically punching hollows in the accursed pillows that slowly and stubbornly kept filling the holes. Something needed to suffer the strikes he was compelled to inflict. In a frenzy now, he beat the bed wherever his blows landed, breathing hard but silently. He caught a glimpse of himself in the dresser mirror, his face purple with pent-up rage, his neck bulging with throbbing veins, hair falling in lank shocks onto his forehead.

The doorbell rang faintly from the other end of the house.

Panting, he paused in his rampage to listen. It sounded again.

Go away. He willed the person to give up trying.

Probably Roslyn's mom. She would be home from the hospital by now too and checking up on him and Lewis. She would want to cry with him, pray with him, pore over memories, discuss the best way to tell Lewis. *Sorry, Ma. Not interested.* Another long ring of the bell. *She'll never give up.*

He released a long, slow breath to steady himself then roamed out of his room and down the hall. When he opened the door, it was not who he expected. His neighbour Jacqui stood poised to press the ringer again. Seeing her there was like one of those switches of scene in a movie, from gloomy twilight to the broad light of day. Her smile was wide, something he'd never seen her wear before, and he caught a hint of raspberry fragrance in the movement of air as she straightened. Her cheeks were flushed and under the porch light the ripples of her flaming hair shone.

Bitterness filled his veins as he took in her vibrancy, so sparkling and alive. His mind returned to the memory of his wife's gray face as he had last seen it, only hours ago, the sunken eyes, her drawn mouth, thin dull hair and the cloying smell of sickness in that wretched hospital room. The contrast was cruel. Worse, he remembered Roslyn's prediction last fall that he would, should marry this woman. The conflict in his chest was like two tomcats in a sack.

"Oh, there you are!" Jacqui was bubbling with something new, barely able to contain her excitement. "Guess what? I've got something fantastic to tell you." She searched his face, her smile dimming at what she saw in it. "I mean, I guess first I should apologize that I wasn't there when you picked Lewis up. I just got your texts a few minutes ago. I hope he wasn't too panicked when I didn't come back from cleaning up one of my outbuildings. Was he? I sure hope not. But I'd left my phone in the house and I got locked inside the machine shed by that big wind. Wasn't that horrendous? I didn't notice, did you have any damage here? 'Cause it totally lifted the roof off my shed and carried it away. Francie Barry called to tell me it went clear over to their place. But I was awfully worried about Lewis, so I figured out a way to scale the wall and get out of there to check on him. You should have seen me. He was okay, wasn't he?" Her eyes wandered past him as though trying to see for herself.

C.H. remained planted in the doorway, making no move to invite her in. "He's fine."

"I didn't see any sign in my kitchen that he'd made himself anything to eat."

"Never mind. He got fed."

She watched him warily now. He didn't have the energy to explain.

"So, I wanted to tell you what's happened to me..."

C.H. was aware he wasn't making this easy for her. Why couldn't she see he didn't care about her day? She dropped her head to concentrate on her shuffling feet, sending out that puff of scent again. Its freshness made him grit his teeth.

Up came her luminous blue eyes. "All that time I spent locked up in the machine shed, I was thinking..."

He waited.

"I couldn't stop remembering what my aunt said, you know, about Christ and that. Something was reminding me of wrong things I've said and done all my life, how I'm not a good person like I've always thought. I wanted to tell you," her voice faltered. "I mean, I know you're a Christian, and since we've talked about religion before, I thought you'd want to know," she said with a rising warmth, "I believe in Jesus now. That he paid with his life for all that I've done wrong"

For long seconds, he stared at her, barely focusing. Her eyebrows pulled together in doubt. Finally, he said, "Nice for you, but Roslyn breathed her last tonight while I held her in my arms. I'm not sure I believe in anything anymore."

Jacqui's frown deepened.

He shifted his gaze away from her face, staring at the satin skin at the hollow of her throat. He felt himself drawn to peer closer. The steady, almost imperceptible pulse throbbing there mocked him with its vitality. Her lips parted, forming an O. Then she did the last thing he expected.

She clamped her hands on his biceps, searched out his gaze, and spoke with a deep fervency, "But I *need* you to be sure. You've always been this bedrock of faith for everyone. Lewis needs you; I *need* you to believe and... and you need it too. Now, more than ever."

Jacqui bit her lip at C.H.'s unwelcoming silhouette, his shaggy hair and imposing posture backlit by the yellow porch interior.

He jerked his arms out of the grasp of her hands. Finally, he spoke in a voice streaked with the acid of resentment. "Last spring a woman in our church stopped Roz and me after the service, told us she'd had a word from the Lord. Roslyn wasn't going to die, she said. I believe her exact words were: 'Your illness is not unto death.' Roslyn told me at the time that was nonsense. 'The Bible's only guarantee about suffering is that we will go through it,' she told me on the way home. But I hung onto what the woman had said. Whenever the situation was grim in this last round of the fight with cancer, her words came back to me. They kept me hoping. I guess I wanted to believe it. More than anything, I was desperate to believe it was a message from God."

"'Life wants to live,'" Jacqui murmured.

C.H. gave a derisive snort. "Yeah. Life wants to live. Except when it doesn't."

"I don't understand very much about God, but one thing I do know: God is real. Roslyn knew it and now I do too. And since he's real, we know Roslyn is with him. Right this minute. That's something amazing to hang onto, don't you think?"

He swiped his hand across his weary face. "All I know is my wife is not with me. She's dead and I've somehow got to figure out a way to break that delightful news to Lewis. Look, it's late and I'm beyond exhausted. I don't want to talk about it now. Good night." He closed the door in front of her so quickly she had to step back to avoid it slamming on her toes.

Jacqui backed slowly down from the porch door in stunned silence, turning and stumbling toward her car. She had never seen her neighbour like this. Tonight, she'd come here bursting with newness, eager to share with him, confident he would be thrilled for her. The hollow place inside her now made her realize she needed his stamp of approval. She needed to tell him the story of what had happened to her in the windstorm and she needed to have him explain it to her, tell her he'd had the same experience. She'd been counting on him to teach her what it all meant and where she was to go from here.

And something else, something strange. She could have sworn for a second there that C.H. was about to kiss her.

CHAPTER 43

Through blurring tears Jacqui drove up her own driveway, her emotions verging on hysteria. As soon as her suspicion of a kiss had surfaced, she scolded herself for a fool. This man was the most faithful person she had ever met, and he had just lost his wife. *Get a grip, Jacqui!*

But still, her insides swung in a violent arc between hurt, confusion and giddy exhilaration. She switched off the car engine and sat still, allowing her emotions free range until she felt ready to burst with the commotion. C.H.'s indifference to her news had shaken her. For nearly a year, his faith and unfailing good humour had been an ever-fixed mark to her. Watching his devotion to his suffering wife and vulnerable son proved him reliable and safe, a beacon of masculine trustworthiness that proved such men were still to be found. Oh, she knew he was married but that was part of what was appealing about him and Lewis. They were neighbours and friends without any of the relationship weirdness that might arise if he were single. Why then did his dismissal of her tonight sting this badly? She could never have dreamed he would turn out to be shifting sand.

At the same time, her stomach flip-flopped at the memory of the transformation, the upheaval that had happened to her in the machine shed. She wanted to contemplate it, the way a new mother might do with her baby, marvelling at the newness and freshness, examining it from every angle, savouring the new life, thrilling at the hope. She was a new person, one who belonged to Someone utterly perfect and perfectly reliable. She drew a sharp breath, flinging off the seatbelt. Suddenly she needed fresh air.

She slammed the car door, leaning for a moment against its cool metal, as she breathed in the spring night. High above her, a heavenly glory leaked through uncountable perforations in the velvet sky. If she raised her arms from her sides for a moment, would she float up and up, and be able to peek past the pinpricks to the vast light behind the curtain? That was no longer a terrifying thought; it invigorated her. She laughed at her fancy then shivered. The spring air still carried a chill. She headed indoors.

Wide awake, Jacqui longed to share her tumbling thoughts with someone who would understand, someone who could define and explain them to her. It was far too late to call Anna. Instead, she brushed her teeth and aimed for bed, knowing sleep was unlikely. As she passed her father's Bible, sweetly displayed on the living room shelf, she ran her fingers over the onion-skin paper. Assailed by a small pang of betrayal toward Pops, still she lifted it off its stand and carried it with her for a long-overdue introduction.

Summer's warmth arrived before spring had finished her lavish blossoming. Granny and Aunt Priscilla certainly had gone crazy in the flowering shrub and tree department. The yard was bursting with lacy white spirea, deep-pink flowering plum, and fragrant apple blooms. But more spectacular than these were the extravagant lilacs. White and magenta and mauve, they encircled the yard sending waves of scent on the breeze. Jacqui kept her house redolent of them with armfuls in vases and pitchers in each room. By hammering their woody stems before placing them in rainwater she found she could make a bouquet last a good four days, something she learned from one of Granny's journals. The notebooks, the Bible and Aunt Anna herself had become a triad of truth and learning for Jacqui in the past few weeks. By consulting these sources of wisdom, she found answers to questions on everything from the meaning of biblical terms to household hints like sprinkling ashes around her delphiniums for protection from worms.

Months ago, desperate to boost her income, Jacqui had appealed to the library board for more hours of operation. No guarantee that Sheri wouldn't suddenly decide to work and use up the extra funding, but in June the board had finally approved Jacqui's request. That first clear answer to prayer had signaled a revolution in her thinking. Praying for daily bread, she learned that ultimately everything comes from God and she began a gradual unlearning of her lifelong habit of independence.

"Self-reliance is another form of pride," Anna had reminded her. "And worry is sin. Trust in God's providence."

More hours at the library, however, also meant less time to tackle home and garden projects. Still, her pathway down to the pond was taking shape, edged by round red rocks that Francie let Jacqui pilfer from the pile of stones cleared from their land. As she lugged the most recent load of rocks from the trunk of her car down the trail, she glimpsed the wide strip that marked the site of her disastrous fire. Shame continued to hound her at the memory. But the grotesque black scar on the landscape had soon filled in with a fresher, more verdant growth than the surrounding field. The reminder was not as ugly now, and she was gradually accepting the truth that, in the same way, her failures were gateways to grace. For her pride and selfishness, she'd found forgiveness, both human and divine. She could almost be grateful for the blot on the land that matched the far graver scar on her soul. Both were scars now healed.

Of the forgiveness from humans she had ample proof. Eight of the neighbours had shown up for three days running to rebuild the roof of her machine shed. Aunt Naomi and even Cousin Ruthie wearing her newborn son in a sling had been among the women who helped with meals for the workers. *Such an old-timey feel.* During that work bee, Jacqui met Bowen Redime, who was plainly smitten with Ruthie. Watching the two of them made Jacqui feel keenly C.H.'s absence. But why should that be? He owed her nothing.

Occasionally, she had driven past her neighbour's fields and seen C.H., or at least his tractor at work. He would have been seeding the soil and later spraying then haying, as she heard others in the community reporting. On one long May evening, she found herself slowing to a stop on the road to watch him in silhouette on the brilliant horizon, working late. The outline was so sharp that at times she could see two heads in the tractor cab. It smarted, knowing he now kept Lewis with him instead of bringing the lad to her house as he used to do.

There had been no communication between the two of them in the months since Roslyn's death. C.H. seemed to have dropped even his infrequent interaction on social media. The thought of initiating contact had grown to become an awkward thing, like stuffing toothpaste back into the tube. Jacqui missed their comfortable conversations, tucked in the crevices around Lewis's stays with her. She missed Lewis too, and found herself worrying about how he had coped with the loss of his mother. Did he even understand what had happened to her? Was he able to continue with school? Had grief made his periodic silences longer or more frequent?

His words from last fall haunted Jacqui and revealed that, on some level, Lewis did understand. *I hate dead.*

At the memorial service for Roslyn, the boy had silently shadowed his father's every move and seemed calm enough. But that was from the distance where Jacqui sat, having slipped in late to the rear balcony of the crowded church. What had Lewis thought as the photo slide show told the story of his mother's life, from pony-riding toddler and gawky teen to radiant bride and beaming mother? How had he borne the sight of her saddle and sewing machine on display next to her portrait, or the loving words of tribute by cousins and friends? Jacqui's heart squeezed in sympathy for her young friend.

One piece of the puzzle she'd discovered by accident, C.H. had stopped attending church. She knew this because by contrast, she had begun. Anna had suggested the tiny church down the street from the library, the one Aunt Naomi and Ruthie Adrian were part of. Jacqui had come to anticipate each sermon by the deep-thinking Bowen Redime who usually spoke on Sundays. The tall, red-bearded man had a knack for pulling his listeners along on the same quest he'd followed while studying the previous week. He would open by dropping a perplexing question then take the congregation along on a biblical treasure hunt to find answers. Before her spiritual awakening, Jacqui never could have imagined how thrilling the chase could be, or how satisfying the conclusion.

One Sunday, Jacqui had overheard Francie tut-tut to another woman, "Al and I have dropped in on C.H. a couple of times, but he won't engage. You'd barely know he's the same man with those hard eyes he's wearing now."

Jacqui knew what she meant and shuddered, remembering all too well the effect of that hardness the last time she and C.H. had met. She was glad to hear the other woman promise to pray for him. Ever since their last meeting, her own mind had turned from one dramatic intervention to another, scheming ways to bring her neighbour to his senses. None of the ideas she came up with seemed likely to work. How could he do an about-face like that? How was it possible to simply throw off something—no *Someone*—as wonderful as the One who had rescued her? But perhaps C.H. had never truly known and been known this way. She pictured the college theology diploma on his wall, his cheerful confidence in the face of his wife's illness that "God's got this!" What had it all meant?

Round and round went Jacqui's befuddled brain calmed only by her regular nighttime Bible reading and her new practice of praying about what was beyond her understanding.

According to the online phone photography tips Jacqui had been studying, the light from the ebbing sun was perfect right now. The minute she got home from work, she stashed her purse and books inside the porch door and hurried out to capture the beauty. She rummaged for shears in the small garden shed and grabbed a broken basket, then cut a sheaf of the best purple and blue delphiniums and arranged them to hide the basket's hole. Digging into her pocket for her phone, she backed away from the flowerbed and dropped to her belly to get the idyllic shot, blurring the riot of colour in the background to focus on the bouquet in front. *Bless you, Granny and Aunt Priscilla, for planting all these perennials.*

She was lying in the cool grass, playing with filtering the pictures she'd taken when the buzz of an ATV grew louder up her driveway. Jacqui scrambled to a stand.

Even before the machine came to a full stop, C.H. leaped off it and was beside her in a few bounds. He was haggard, with over-long hair and a thick, unkempt beard, but more than that, she was shocked at the panic in his face.

"Have you seen Lewis?" he demanded, panting as though he'd run the distance to her place on foot.

"N-no," she stammered, bewildered by the question. "What's—"

"He didn't come over here?"

"No, at least, not since I got home from work a few minutes ago."

C.H. groaned, tugging at his hair with both hands, making it wilder than ever.

Jacqui dared to reach out and touch his arm. “Let me help. What’s happened?”

His deeply shadowed eyes pleaded with her. “We were out cutting hay on the three acres east of the house. He needed to take a leak. I stopped close to the yard to let him out, figuring I had time to finish one more round before he’d be done in there. When I got back to the house, he wasn’t there. Searched inside, the yard, the outbuildings, everywhere!” His voice rose to an unnatural pitch. “He’s gone.”

CHAPTER 44

"Have you called around to any of the other neighbours?"

C.H. scowled, giving the grass a vicious kick. "I can't keep anything," he muttered.

"C.H.!" Jacqui stepped forward to confront him. "He can't have gotten far just walking. I'll call Francie, get her to alert everybody. We'll round up a whole bunch of people to go out searching. We're bound to find him. You keep driving wherever that thing will take you, I'll keep to the roads in my car."

He paced in short, jerky steps.

"Go!" she shouted, finally prompting him to move toward his quad. "We'll find him."

She phoned Francie while hurrying to the house to grab her keys and purse from the porch door.

Francie assured her that a crew of neighbours would be driving the roads and back trails for miles around. Jacqui could see some of them crisscrossing the prairie road grid as she did the same, scanning every clump of trees and slowing in trepidation alongside each slough. She shuddered, wondering how deep the ponds in the area were, willing her eyes to detect the slightest ripple in the water's mirror-still surface. But she found no sign of the boy, no scrap of the blue plaid shirt C.H. had described on any wire fence or tree branch. Her earlier confidence gradually gave way to dismay, then real worry as the sun puddled on the horizon.

She waved down an approaching silver pick-up. The driver rolled down his window. Jacqui thought she recognized his weathered face as one of those who had come to stamp out her fire in spring. Sweeping aside a momentary pang of shame over her carelessness then, she reminded herself this man had also been one of the volunteers who had shown up later to repair her shed roof.

"Any sign of Lewis?" she asked.

The older man shook his head. "Hope we find him before dark. Kid like that, there's no telling where he might have gone or if he even has sense enough to find his way home."

"He's got plenty of sense," Jacqui said, feeling defensive. "He just gets focused on something and loses track of time."

"Well, I hope we find him before dark. Been hearing about cougar sightings in the vicinity."

Not to be outdone, the man's wife leaned her bulk toward the driver's window. "Just last week my brother's family drove into their yard west of town to find a black bear messing around by their garbage cans." Her round face shone as she delivered this cheering news.

Yeah, thanks for nothing. Don't you dare fill C.H.'s head with horror stories like that.

She hadn't seen C.H. since around five. That was nearly four hours ago and not only was she famished, she needed the washroom. For at least the fourth time, she rounded the two-mile block south of her place, still alert for any sign of Lewis. Frequently, she stopped, turning the engine off and listening to the twilight. Only the occasional bawl of a cow, and a steady cricket-chorus greeted her. The long shadows mocked her imagination. Every tussock of grass, every irregular fencepost was the spindly figure of a youth, only to turn out to be nothing. There had been no exultant texts from Francie or C.H. With a leaden heart, she drove up the rise to her house.

The porch door creaked shut behind her as she tossed her purse and keys onto the kitchen counter. She imagined C.H. still combing the pastures and fields, his stomach churning in anxiety, and she felt guilty tearing off a piece of flat bread and spooning antipasto onto a plate. She told herself she'd be more useful if her stomach wasn't growling. Fully intending to continue the search, Jacqui swallowed the last of her hurried dinner and rushed to the bedroom for a sweater. She tugged it on as she passed through the darkened living room, thinking she should bring a snack for C.H. in case he hadn't eaten.

Suddenly, from the corner of her eye, she caught movement on the couch. Jacqui lurched to a stop, her chest banging an alarm. Breath caught in her throat.

"Miss Jacqui?" Lewis rose to a sitting position, his lanky knees splayed.

"Lewis! You scared me half to death" She puffed in relief.

The boy covered his face with both hands. "I hate death."

Way to go, Jacqui. She dashed toward him, wanting to fling her arms around him. But knowing his discomfort with touch, she settled for kneeling at his side. "Where have you been? We've been searching all over for you."

"Here." He rubbed his eyes with his fists, the way a much younger child would, then moved his arm to press tightly against her knee. "I wanted to see you."

Jacqui kept still, realizing he was leaning against her on purpose. Watching his innocence, sensing the fondness for her behind his words, Jacqui dared to lay a hand on his shoulder. He bent to touch his cheek to her hand. She swallowed a lump in her throat. Oh, the maddening, precious, oblivious boy. "I'd better call your dad. He's been really worried." Jacqui ran for her phone and punched in C.H.'s number to give him the great news. "Yes. I couldn't believe it. He must have slipped in quietly while I was out in my yard taking pictures of my flowers... I'll bring him right over."

Jacqui bustled about the kitchen putting together a bento box meal for Lewis and another for C.H. "Come on, Froggie. Let's see if we can get you home."

Lewis strode through the kitchen without stopping and headed for her car.

Jacqui sent a brief text to Francie, snatched up the food and her keys and followed the boy. They rode in silence, a sharp contrast for the talkative kid. Was this the beginning of his silent phase?

Under the darkening summer sky, made darker by the rustling trees of the Legrand driveway, Jacqui suddenly felt bashful, thinking of the last time she was here. They stopped in front of the house. "Go on, Lewis, your dad's waiting."

But Lewis tugged on her arm. "You come, too. Then Dad won't be mad at me."

She'd hoped to make an unobtrusive getaway. Instead, she climbed out and trailed after him planning to stay in the shadows below the step. But Lewis pulled her into the porch with him, calling for his father, then nearly collided with him when C.H. charged out from the kitchen. He engulfed his son in a giant bear hug. Jacqui could see C.H.'s Adam's apple bobbing violently below his deeply coloured face. She turned to slip away from the emotional scene.

"Don't go!" he croaked from behind her.

Lewis squirmed free and disappeared into the house. That left his father staring at Jacqui, his arms hanging apart from his sides, somehow poised.

For what? Jacqui willed herself not to fidget, digging her hand into the pocket of her sweater then pulling it out to brush the hair out of her eyes. She inched backward half a pace, holding out the boxed meals to him.

"Thanks," he said, without letting his eyes leave her face. He set them on a shelf and took a step toward her. It brought him within arm's reach, but Jacqui stood still, all too aware of his nearness. "You ..." He swallowed. "Thank you for finding him. For bringing him home." He waved a hand, taking in the neighbourhood. "For organizing everybody to search."

"Not at all, C.H. I was worried, too."

"You like Lewis." He made this an observation, not a question.

Jacqui gave a nervous chuckle. "He nearly gave me a coronary tonight when he popped up from my couch in the dark, but yeah, I love that kid. And I've missed him."

C.H.'s face softened with the hint of a smile. He took a deep breath. "I owe you an apology."

She stilled her hands and waited.

"I was rude to you the night your roof blew off, and I'm really sorry. I was only thinking about myself."

"Hey, that was completely understandable, considering what you'd just gone through." Jacqui avoided the light in his intense gaze. "And I've never had the chance to tell you in person how sorry I am for your loss."

"Thanks, I appreciate it. But it brings up something else I regret. For the last few months, I haven't given anyone a chance to get close. I've ignored everyone, especially you..."

"Especially me?"

"Yeah."

She raised her eyebrows, hoping for more, but C.H. didn't explain. The silence expanded with her unvoiced questions.

"I've missed you, my friend." He reached to smooth a strand of hair from her forehead and let his hand trail down her cheek. Jacqui closed her eyes at the whispered touch, holding her breath. In all the months she had lived here, a little over a year now, she hadn't let herself think of him the way she was thinking of him now. But in some way, this was exactly where she knew she wanted to be.

Suspended in time, neither moved. Only their warm breath mingled between them. Jacqui opened her eyes to find C.H. still watching her. He made no move toward her, but his old familiar smile brightened his face.

"So, you'll forgive me for my curmudgeonly ways?"

"Yes," she breathed, not wanting the moment to end.

"And you'll tell me now what you wanted to tell me that night?"

"Yes."

"Not that I can't guess." He gestured toward the bright kitchen doorway, welcoming her inside and pulling out a chair for her at the island. "But I'm curious to know how a flyaway roof makes such a dramatic change in a person."

Jacqui told him her story, adding in a lot of what she'd learned in the following months. He listened with interest, asking insightful questions and laughing in the right places. She paused, suddenly shy, and fingered her coffee mug handle. "So, now it's your turn. Are you going to tell me why you were avoiding me, *especially*?"

C.H. averted his gaze, appearing uncomfortable himself. Then he raised his eyes to meet hers. "It's been a struggle, loving my Roslyn but at the same time feeling a growing, uh, friendship with you." He scrubbed his beard with one hand. "I mean, I know what God calls that and I take my vows seriously..." He shook his head, covering his face with both hands now. "After she died, I felt like it wasn't fair to her if I... I don't know, simply up and replaced her."

Jacqui sipped her coffee, her pulse thundering in her ears. She willed herself calm, then said slowly, "I think I get it." She cleared her throat. "But we're still friends, right?"

He pulled his hands away from his face. "Yeah, we are." And he grinned.

CHAPTER 45

For months, every time Jacqui left work she averted her eyes as she passed the Days of Your antique shop. Solely on principle she refused to enter. Anyone who couldn't bother to spell the name of their business correctly didn't deserve her patronage. Besides, the jumble of kitschy bric-a-brac in the window of the place sent her spare contemporary self running the opposite direction in revulsion. Places like that inevitably smelled of mildew and unwashed socks.

But today she was haunted by Pops' random question on the phone last night after they'd confirmed the logistics of his flight tomorrow for Aunt Anna's wedding.

"Ever come across a pair of salt and pepper shakers shaped like a hen and rooster?"

Guiltily, she thought of the contents of Granny's curio cabinet which she'd stuffed into a box last year without paying attention to individual pieces and hustled off to the local thrift store at the first opportunity. When he asked, she'd put him off with some airy excuse about boxes she'd packed away. How could she ever confess to having bundled the whole works off that first week after she arrived? None of the junk had been valuable—no crystal or china or even Depression glass or milk glass. Just a whole bunch of dust-collecting, mismatched knick-knacks. Or so she'd thought.

What possessed him now, of all times, to need suddenly, urgently to know the whereabouts of those salt and pepper shakers?

"Mother always had them on the kitchen windowsill," he said, an odd tenderness in his voice. "I gave them to her for Christmas when I was nine or ten years old. Just wondered if she kept them."

Ah, that would explain it. With all the back and forth of the past few weeks countering Pops' endless excuses to cancel the trip, Jacqui had been on tenterhooks. She had to find those chickens.

A frantic call to a sleepy Aunt Anna later last night confirmed that the precious fowl indeed had been kept in the kitchen window and later, in the china cabinet for decades. And no, she didn't have a picture of them. But she gave a detailed description of what Jacqui should search for. And look for them she did, ransacking the boxes in the attic without results. Today after work, in addition to putting the guest bedroom back together for Pops now that its final coat of dove-gray paint was dry, stocking up on some of his favourite foods, and baking a pie for the wedding rehearsal dinner, she needed to come up with the shakers, or a reasonable facsimile. Somehow, she had to manage it all before Pops showed up at the airport tomorrow and she brought him out here to the old home place.

Pushing the door open emitted the shop's predictable smell and the loud radio pontifications of an opinionated talk show host. Jacqui entered and paused to let her eyes adjust to the dim light. She scanned the room, daunted by the jumble of crammed shelving and heaps and piles of oddments in no particular order. Would there be a salt and pepper shaker section? Brain fatigue soon set in as she tried to sort through the visual clutter of ornaments: a pair of faded Pinkie and Blue Boy paint-by-number portraits, a Chatty Cathy doll in its original box, old-time flour sifters, a vinyl record of The Monkees, a couple of iron cattle brands—one shaped like a happy face.

She approached the woman behind the old-fashioned upright cash register, engrossed in a romance. "Do you have any salt and pepper shakers?"

The woman peered over her reading glasses at Jacqui. "Do we ever! A whole wall full of them. Right through that green curtain and to your left." She returned to her novel.

Jacqui followed the trail, sidestepping a stack of old suitcases and several metal milk cans as she made her way into the back room. The clerk was right. The entire wall was covered in shallow, closely spaced shelves laden with shakers of every description. Checking the time, impatience welled up in her. It would take days to scan every pair. And then she spotted them. Near the top left, between a pair of tiny cookstoves and a miniature Humpty Dumpty and wife, there stood the hen and rooster. From Anna's description, these had to be the same ones. She scanned the floor of the room hoping to find a step stool. In lieu, she overturned a metal bucket to reach her find. Grabbing the pair, she hurried to the till without checking the price. She'd pay whatever it cost if only she could have it in place on the kitchen windowsill before heading to the airport to pick up Pops.

John Penn paced the width of his front window, watching down the street for the airport shuttle bus. Had he turned off the coffee pot? He shuffled to the kitchen to check. He would only be away for five days, should he turn off the water supply? He stumped down the steep basement stairs only to discover he'd already shut it off. Back at the living room window, there was still no sign of the shuttle five minutes after the appointed arrival time. *Sure. Charge the little guy a fortune for lousy service.* If the government wasn't cronied up with big business, it would put a stop to this kind of exploitation and provide the service for free.

The itinerary Jacqui had sent specified being at the airport at least an hour in advance of departure. To be on the safe side, he had allowed two hours plus the time needed to get from Hamilton to Toronto.

Resuming his pacing, he decided if the bus didn't show up in the next five minutes, he'd cancel the whole venture.

Immediately upon making the decision, a sense of relief washed over him. It was just as well he wouldn't be going. He'd lived seventy-three years without risking his life in a aluminum tube hurtling through the air at inhuman speed; he could go on the same way till he died. He stepped outside to putter among the tomato plants in the garden bed beneath the window. John checked his watch. One more minute and he could unpack his suitcase and relax. But at that exact moment, the van pulled up to the curb. *Lucky devil. You get to fly after all.*

At the airport, he held back, watching those ahead of him in line at every stage of the process, trying to learn what to do when he arrived at the check-in kiosk. Then a well-fed girl in a navy uniform stepped up beside him and all but took over.

"Go ahead," he said, stepping back from the screen, "I'm only a doddering old fool."

She gave a merry laugh and took his passport from him to type in the information. "Any carry-on?"

"I prefer my meat freshly killed," John growled.

The girl's face went blank.

What a dingbat. "Never mind," he said, grabbing his papers and turning away.

In the end, he managed without having to grovel for any more help from the airline toadies. He handed out a few contemptuous looks to the bourgeoisie in first class before finding his seat toward the rear of the aircraft. Stowing his bag, he settled into the cramped seat between two young women. He'd specifically asked Jacqui to make sure he wasn't in a window seat, but from here he could still see outside. He listened studiously to the safety demonstration, making special note of the emergency instructions, and for the next four hours, averted his eyes from what he felt sure was a stomach-turning view. He kept his seatbelt fastened even though he sorely needed to use the facilities. Not until the plane finally came to a complete stop, did he release his vice-grip of the armrests and breathe a shaky sigh.

"Have a nice day!" The flight attendant said, all sugary-sweet, as he approached the exit.

"No thanks," he said, scowling. "I have other plans." He paused just long enough to watch her fake happy face slump and dissolve before she pinned it back in place for the next sucker in line. He found it enormously entertaining to strip the veneer off these corporate types with a few deft words. Then he turned on his heel and went in search of the nearest men's room.

With that pressing need attended to, he was ready to find his Little Girl. John was surprised at the stinging in his eyes when he picked out her red hair and waving arm from the throng on the other side of the sliding doors. The two of them had never been given to displays of sappy emotion but... Dropping his suitcase with a thud, he enfolded her in his arms and held on, not trusting himself to speak.

"Pops!" he heard her say, half laughing. "Easy."

Finally, swallowing hard, he released her. "Well, let's get this over with," he told her, reaching for the handle of his bag.

He caught the scorn she gave his old black suitcase. "Nothing wrong with it," he grumbled. "No need to buy a new one just to line the pockets of capitalists."

Jacqui shook her head with a grin. "C'mon," she said. "I'm parked over there."

He'd forgotten how dry the west was. The early October day was warm and sunny as they drove through a city he no longer recognized as Calgary. Out in the country, though, the open road and golden fields of stubble under a cobalt sky brought a flood of memories he thought he had obliterated. The vastness, the clear air, the miles-distant horizon—he was unprepared for how it moved him. Harvest was nearing completion. On one field there were multiple combines, big ones, and trucks catching the bronze stream of wheat even as the combine moved on gathering the swathes. Everything was bigger now, more efficient than when he left farming.

"Lotta changes in fifty-five odd years."

"Yeah?"

He jerked a thumb to the right where four identical gleaming combines devoured the standing field in diagonal precision as though choreographed. "All this corporate takeover of agriculture pushing out the family farm. Pretty soon big business will have a stranglehold on the food supply."

"I don't know about this land here, but around where I live, the family farm is alive and well. Some of them have legally incorporated for the tax benefits, is all."

"Sell-outs," he grumped.

That made Little Girl clam up and he berated himself for a clod. They sat in silence while her small car ate up the miles and before long he began to recognize some of the countryside. South of where he'd grown up, they came over a rise to a panoramic view of low hills of pasture, like bumps under gray-green carpet laid out before them. They were getting close. He cleared his throat and shifted in his seat, then noticed Jacqui picking at a hangnail. *What's she got to be nervous about?*

"Quit that gouging," he ordered in his old dad voice.

She gave him a sheepish smile and rubbed her hand against her leg as though to erase her habit.

"I've got Uncle Russell's bedroom ready for you," she told him. "But there's still only one bathroom. I don't know how all of you ever fit in that house with just two bedrooms back in the day."

"People weren't so greedy back then. No need for umpteen bedrooms and bathrooms."

"Aw, Pops," she said with a chuckle and patted his knee. "I've missed you."

"Missed you patronizing me, too," he muttered. She only laughed.

Now the road had flattened, open to the vast cerulean dome puffed with pillowy clouds. The way home had remained essentially unchanged over all these years, taking him back in time. John felt by instinct the nearness of the turn to the old homestead. He tensed up despite himself. And then Little Girl was turning, and they were creeping up the old familiar rise to the house that had cradled his youth. He fought the claustrophobic sense of captivity, telling himself it was ridiculous after nearly five decades. He reminded himself that his father was long gone.

CHAPTER 46

John got out of the car with effort, standing motionless for a moment, letting the circulation flow to his extremities and staring at the house as he listened to the silence. Not even crickets chirped. In the warm stillness, you could isolate the faint rustling of dying leaves from the distant drone of a throbbing diesel engine.

"I've been busy fighting with the inside of the house," Little Girl told him, "so I haven't done anything with the exterior yet, but I've got big plans. I can't wait to get rid of that ugly fake brick. Why don't you take a stroll around while it's still light." She hoisted his suitcase out of the back of the car and headed for the house.

"I'll have you know I worked hard to help put up that ugly fake brick," he said to her retreating back. "Looks perfectly fine to me."

John roamed the old place from the wooden granaries he'd had to endlessly shovel out to the pond down the slope where he and Russell had built forts. That is, when they weren't busting their backs loading bales or cleaning stalls. He noticed Little Girl was civilizing the pond with a stone-lined pathway and a stump-legged bench. He circled back to the driveway and turned to the west where something glinted beyond the trees. Passing through them he found an up-to-date machine shed that he didn't remember as part of the original buildings.

"Wanna have a peek inside?" Jacqui's voice sounded behind him.

Together they pulled back the creaky door which Little Girl propped open with a concrete block. They stepped inside its cool depths.

She hurried forward toward a vehicle in the centre that was cloaked in some sort of quilt. Sweeping the large fabric cover partway off and bunching it in her arms, she watched him expectantly.

At first, John hardly knew what he was seeing. Shiny turquoise paint. A gleaming chrome bumper. *They don't make chrome like that anymore. Has Little Girl gone and got herself a classic car?* He raised an eyebrow at her, but she only watched him, saying nothing.

He'd taken just two slow steps around the side of the car when a rush of memory overwhelmed him. The Bel Air. His teenage dream car. It seemed to be the very one, right down to the rag top and white interior. A gush of emotion heated up his core. He stroked the sleek paint job, raising wondering eyes to his daughter. How could she have known? Where did she find it? How could she afford it?

"It's the one you always wanted," she said with a tentative smile. "It was supposed to be your birthday present. They were going to send you out on an errand to discover it for yourself, but then you didn't come down for breakfast..."

"They?" He gaped at her, a seeping awareness of her meaning beginning to dawn.

"Your parents." She straightened the patchwork cover and folded it across the hood of the car.

"You mean you didn't..." He jerked his hand away from the cool enamel even as a ball of lead began to grow in the pit of his belly. "How long has this been sitting here?"

Jacqui pitched a frown at him. "Since whenever you left here, 1960-something." She shook her head in sudden understanding. "Oh, I didn't buy it, if that's what you're thinking. I only discovered it here."

The weight inside him expanded.

"It's still got really low mileage," she said, talking fast while she kept folding and fussing with the fabric. "Apparently, Uncle Russell loaned it out a few times to local non-profits for parades, but other than that, it hasn't been driven." She gestured around the building. "I think they built this shed later to store it."

He had to move before his legs petrified. He lurched toward the open door and stumped blindly in the direction of the house.

Jacqui froze in the act of reaching for the folded cover. *Now I've done it.* Pops' face had been formidable. She braced herself for an unpleasant few days' visit. What if the old boy got so belligerent that he backed out of attending the wedding? Jacqui had only been to two weddings, both beach destination events that were more focused on vacationing than on a ceremony. She didn't want to miss her first Christian family wedding ever. She knew all too well how stubborn Pops could be. Yet he had been awfully glad to see her, surprisingly so. Jacqui released her pent-up breath. What was the worst Pops could do? Hitchhike back to Ontario? She smiled and hummed as she replaced the cover on the Bel Air and closed up the machine shed.

She burst through the door to the kitchen to find her father slouched at the table nursing a beer. His battered old suitcase sat on the floor next to him, but he'd made himself at home.

"Have you toured the house yet?" she asked him while washing her hands.

"I know what it looks like."

Evidently, it was going to be that kind of an evening. Jacqui cleared her throat. "Aunt Anna invited us to the family dinner they're having after the rehearsal tonight. We thought it might be nice to reunite everyone privately before the wedding."

It took such a long time for Pops to reply that she finally sat down across from him.

He met her gaze with faint defiance. "What?"

"Well, do you want to go? It's early yet and there's plenty of time to get there."

"Haven't you got anything around here to eat?"

"Yeah, of course." Disappointed, she got up to search the fridge. "Okay then, dinner will be ready pretty quick here. I don't know about you but I'm starving."

As she worked, Pops seemed to perk up at the aroma of chili and warm buns. Predictably, he turned up his nose at the salad she set in front of him, but he munched away at it without comment.

While they ate, Jacqui asked about his famous tomato plants back home, his cronies from the steel mill, any of his neighbours she still remembered—whatever she could think of to get him talking and improve his mood. She wasn't surprised by his refusal to see family tonight. After all, the old boy had already faced one major fear today by getting on that plane. *But Lord, would you keep him from backing out of the wedding tomorrow?*

For dessert, she was proud to offer him pie, and soon a second piece when he polished the last of the pastry flakes and plum filling off his plate in a few minutes.

"Don't mind if I do," he said, holding out his plate. "Your pie has improved. I remember the first one." One corner of his mouth quirked in amusement.

Jacqui rolled her eyes at the memory of that unfortunate concoction from her high school days. Without a rolling pin, she'd been reduced to pushing and prodding the stubborn dough into the pie tin. The result had been a lumpy, tough crust that defied chewing. His praise now warmed her. "Aunt Anna gave me lessons." She rose to start clearing dishes. "I'll clean up here if you want to take your suitcase to your room and get settled in."

She noticed he winced and paused for a couple of minutes after rising, just as he had when getting out of the car earlier. Was it merely stiffness, or was there something more serious? Whatever the cause, she realized anew that Pops was getting old. Would he even tell her if something was seriously wrong?

After folding the dishtowel and hanging it on the stove handle, she peeked through the doorway to the living room. There was no sign of Pops, though she was sure she'd heard his step in there. When she came through, she found him up close to the shelf unit, scrutinizing the display. She leaned against it, watching him, and the sound made him start.

"Where'd you find all this old junk?"

"In boxes in the attic."

Pops moved to the middle section, coming face to face with his old Bible. His eyes narrowed and he drew back, then abruptly turned his face to the next section of shelf where he fingered the laces of his old ice skates. "Had a lot of fun on these old bombs."

"So, do you like what I did with all that?"

He took a step back, his gaze making a circle of the shelves and avoiding the central feature. "Most of it."

Jacqui decided to come right out with it. "I read your Bible every night now."

He fixed a glare at her that somehow morphed into a succession of unfathomable expressions, none of them pleasant. She met his look, forcing herself not to flinch.

At length his shoulders dropped, and he sighed. "You said you were going west for only a short while, remember? You wanted to give yourself a breather, yeah? But I was afraid something like this would happen." He shook his head slightly, fixing her with an aggrieved stare. "Where did I go wrong?"

CHAPTER 47

In a stunning sapphire dress, Anna's daughter Beth poked her head from a side door of the church foyer to scan the gathering guests. Apparently, she'd caught sight of Jacqui. She beckoned with a finger.

Jacqui nodded at her but glanced uncertainly at Pops, half afraid he'd disappear out the open church doors through which they had just entered. She searched the small crowd for C.H. Weeks ago, she'd pushed aside her uncertainties about their relationship to ask him to attend the wedding with her. She'd explained she would be arriving on her own because of Pops. Still, if C.H. was here already, she hoped to introduce the two of them. He would be able to keep Pops from bolting if anybody could. But there was no sign of him yet. Then she spotted a quiet corner and tugged on Pops' arm.

"Wait here," she said, depositing him on the available chair. "I think Aunt Anna wants me for some reason. I shouldn't be long. Don't go anywhere."

The small anteroom was a frothy muddle of flowers and make-up and florist's boxes. Among the women who were attending Anna, Jacqui recognized Beth and her twins and Anna's two daughters-in-law who turned from hair and nails to greet Jacqui. Aunt Naomi stood behind a woman in a wheelchair who wore a pink floral dress and flip-flops decorated with silk daisies. Her brown hair had been carefully curled, but her eyes stared vacantly at a corner of the ceiling. This must be the sister-in-law, Carol, whom Naomi had brought to live with her.

Anna turned from the mirror in front of her to welcome Jacqui. Her snowy hair shone, and her lined cheeks were rosy with joy above the cape that protected her powder-blue dress from product and spray. Jacqui caught a glimpse of lacy sleeves beneath it.

"You're gorgeous, Aunt Anna." Jacqui bent forward to give her a careful hug.

"Thank you, dear. And you're lovely in that dress, too. I wanted you to join us girls for a short prayer time before I walk the aisle." She lowered her voice to whisper confidentially, "Did you bring my brother?"

Jacqui nodded, keeping to herself her misgivings about Pops' staying resolve.

Anna squeezed her arm, but then her smile dimmed. "There's only a few minutes before the service is to start and my Tom hasn't shown up yet."

"What? Where is he? Not a case of cold feet is it?"

"No, no. Nothing like that. But we got word on Wednesday that my dear old neighbour, Joan Klug had passed away. She had gone downhill rapidly with dementia these last couple of years. It seems some folks must lose some of their faculties before they can enter the kingdom of God like a little child. Back when she was still lucid, she'd insisted Tom was to preach her funeral and of course, this morning would be the only day her whole family could come together." The older woman chuckled. "Ah, well, my first taste of the pastor's wife life. You know, she said he was the only pastor who ever made sense to her. So, off he went this morning. I'm sorry to have missed it myself." She motioned the women to gather around her. "Girls, let's pray my prince will come."

Returning to the emptying vestibule, Jacqui heard violin music softly playing as guests filed into the sanctuary. She sought out the corner where she'd left Pops but as she had feared, the seat was vacant.

For the first time her annoyance with her father grew to anger. Why couldn't he cooperate for once in his life? Determined to drag him back indoors if necessary, she hurried towards the exit as fast as her heels would allow. As she reached for the door handle, she heard his raucous throat-clearing and pivoted to find him standing behind her with arms crossed and foot tapping.

"Where were you?" She tucked her hand in his arm. "Never mind. Let's find a seat."

Cousin Beth had said there were family pews reserved near the front but as Jacqui was about to steer Pops that way, she caught sight of a set of familiar broad shoulders. C.H. sat third from the rear wearing a suit, his recently trimmed hair showing white skin above his deeply tanned neck. She paused uncertainly, wanting to sit next to him but feeling drawn to the family pews. In sudden resolve, she bent to lay a hand on his shoulder.

"Join us up front with the family," she whispered in his ear, inhaling his soap-clean smell.

He turned toward her, a slow smile lighting his face at what he saw. The three of them followed the usher to the front, Jacqui conscious of the small gap between her and C.H. She itched to take his arm but held back, feeling the many eyes watching. An eagerness to cling to him teased at her while at the same time uncertainty hovered. What was their relationship? Friends, he had said. But he'd also mentioned his angst over "replacing" Roslyn. Jacqui understood his hesitation and conflict in not wanting to dishonour his late wife by quickly starting a new relationship. But how long after Roslyn's death was long enough? Jacqui felt sure C.H. had feelings for her as she did for him.

She ignored Pops' critical eye appraising C.H. It had been her hope to introduce the two of them before now. When they reached their seats, she whispered a quick introduction. The two men shook hands across her lap as the pianist paused and softly began a new piece of music. From a door to the right of the platform, Anna's minister son Burk entered carrying a Bible. He was followed by a flush-faced Tom and a young man who, by the resemblance, must be Tom's son. Tom's shiny pate glistened, and he was breathing as though he'd hurried to get there.

Pops checked his watch and gave a snort. "Doesn't look like much of a catch to me."

Jacqui cringed at his volume in the subdued sanctuary and gave him a hard jab in the ribs.

"What?" he said, without lowering his voice.

Behind them, someone tittered.

The music changed again, and heads turned toward the back. Jacqui craned to see as a pair of adorable four year olds came shyly up the aisle sprinkling flower petals. They were followed by Beth who directed the girls to her husband in the front row.

"Friends and family, we are assembled here in the presence of God," Burk began, "to join Tom Townsend and Anna Fawcett in marriage. Let us reverently call to mind the institution, purpose and obligations of the marriage state."

Jacqui found herself enthralled by the majesty of his words. What makes two people married, she had wondered last year after the Geoff debacle. Now her cousin's rich and solemn words declared the answer.

"Moreover, God said: 'It is not good that the man should be alone; I will make a helper suitable for him...Therefore a man shall leave his father and his mother and shall cleave unto his wife; and they shall be one flesh.'"

The ancient lines sent a thrill of certainty through Jacqui. True marriage was something far greater and grander than she had ever imagined—a covenant before the Creator and other people. It carried a stately importance that she had unknowingly craved, beyond the casual arrangement she and Geoff had had.

"Marriage, then, is a divine ordinance intended to be a source of happiness to man, an institution of the highest significance to the human race, and a symbol of the union of Christ and his church. We may, therefore, as Christians look with confidence for grace in the discharge of our mutual responsibilities and for guidance and help in our common perplexities and trials."

The minister asked the bride and groom to join hands. Anna handed her bouquet of mums to Beth and turned toward Tom. Jacqui could see the older woman smiling into the face of her loving groom.

"Tom, do you solemnly declare that you take to yourself and acknowledge as your wife Anna, here present, and do you promise that you will, with the gracious help of God, love, honour, and maintain her, live with her in the holy bonds of marriage according to God's ordinance, and never forsake her, as long as you both shall live?"

At those words, Jacqui felt C.H.'s great hand engulf her own. Startled, she stared at it, then at him. His head was tipped back and from the corner of his closed eye a tear trickled down the side of his face. Jacqui's heart was already brimming with emotion, and the heat of his hand and the sight of this man weeping beside her was her undoing. She fought the swelling in her throat and blinked back her own tears. No doubt his emotions were caused by the reminder of his own vows taken those years ago. Or maybe he was in anguish over the part about as long as you both shall live. *Then why is he holding my hand?*

"I do," came Tom's deep affirmation. Next came the bride's vows and the exchange of rings, while throughout it all C.H. clung firmly to Jacqui's hand.

Finally, Burk said, "According to the laws of the land and the ordinances of Christ's Church, Tom and Anna, I now pronounce you husband and wife. What therefore God has joined together, let not man put asunder. Henceforth, you go down life's pathway together, and may the Father of all mercies, who has called you by His grace to this holy state of marriage, bind you together in true love and faithfulness and grant you His blessing."

After an expectant pause, the young minister broke into a grin. "Tom, you may kiss... my mother."

Laughter erupted and faded again as Tom gazed into Anna's eyes, motionless. As the quiet fell, he slowly raised his hands to gently hold her face. Then slowly, slowly he kissed her lips. The tenderness was achingly precious.

Full-hearted, Jacqui watched them, acutely conscious of C.H.'s presence beside her.

His warm breath tickled her ear. "Life's pathway together," he whispered.

Now she was sure he intended something toward her, but what? She met his eyes with a question of her own. But he only squeezed her hand and smiled.

The newlyweds marched down the aisle to a triumphal tune, guests were ushered out, introductions were made in the receiving line, and the family was reunited with Pops. And all the while, C.H.'s hand kept returning to hers. Jacqui was conscious that people were noticing they were together, some even whispering, and still C.H. persisted. Not that she objected, but what did it mean? Then she noticed that whoever planned the reception seating plan had paired the two of them at one of the family tables. *Am I the only one in the dark about this relationship?*

She tugged on his arm, hauling him to an empty corner of the church basement and whirled to face him. "Are you going to let me in on what's happening here?"

With a wide grin, he pulled her to him. "Surely you know, girl. I've loved you since the day you came rampaging out against my cattle on that broom of yours with your hair all wild and hell-fire in your eyes."

Whether from the thrill of his embrace or the ridiculous memory, Jacqui felt the blood flow into her cheeks. "Not one of my better moments."

C.H. laughed, his arm tightening around her. But he sobered again, pulling back slightly. "That's been part of the problem. I made vows to my wife and I truly loved her until the day she died. But I had this confusion because of the feelings I was beginning to have for you and..." He averted his eyes. "I mean, I tried to guard my heart. I made sure I was never alone with you, but the feelings kept growing. I hated myself for it. And when Roz died, I felt..."

"...like it was too soon?"

"Nah, more like I had to punish myself." His smile returned. "Then I had a good talk with my father-in-law. He straightened out my disappointment with God that Roslyn wasn't healed. And once he found out Roz had predicted I would marry you I couldn't believe how understanding he was. He actually encouraged me to pursue you."

"She what?"

"Yeah, last fall when I took you to the hospital to meet her, my wife predicted I was going to marry you." He pressed her against him again. "And since I love you with all my heart, that's what I'm going to do." He gazed deep into her eyes. "I mean, if you're OK with that?"

Jacqui stilled, the giant lump in her throat preventing her answer. The depth of sincerity on C.H.'s face, the integrity she had seen in him firsthand over the past year, the love he had for his son, and the solicitous care he'd shown for his wife—all of it had secured her trust in him long before.

He loosened his grip on her. "You gonna keep me in suspense much longer or what?"

The worry in his eyes made Jacqui smile. "Sorry, just savouring the moment." She laid her hands on his solid shoulders. "Yes, I'm OK with that. And yes, I'd love to marry you."

A thrill raced through her as he wrapped her in his arms. When he lowered his lips to hers, Jacqui found herself grounded in the certainty of his love and permanence. Their kiss started out warm, fusing them together as it grew more heated like two live wires. From the vibrations at her core she was enraptured, knowing that in so many ways over the past year, she had finally found her roots. She was tethered to the land, to a family she never knew she had, and to this excellent man.

They parted, breathless with wonder.

"And just for the record, I wasn't *on* the broom," she said, "I was *wielding* it."

EPILOGUE

Five years later, Anna:

My heart is full to bursting. Listening to the swelling lilt of more than a hundred voices singing *I'll Fly Away,* this funeral for Naomi's sister-in-law, Carol, is more like a celebration. My precious Tom, bless him, preached such comfort and joy to us here that even Naomi has dried her eyes and is smiling. Free at last, he reminded us. Carol is free of every hindrance to her brain working properly, free of pain, free of limitation and indignity. Free of all her years imprisoned in an unresponsive body since that terrible accident decades ago. Face to face with Jesus. All joy!

The way poor Nomi has taken Carol's passing so hard, I must admit, has surprised me. I was taken aback at her extreme grief these last few days. Ever since she brought Carol to live with her five years ago, I was concerned the workload would be too much.

When Carol's pneumonia returned for the third time since Christmas and she died, I thought Nomi would be focused on Carol's release from her difficult life. I was sure my sister might feel a bit of relief from the constant burden of care she took on when she brought Carol to live with her. After all, like me she's not getting any younger. Instead she was inconsolable. The depth of her grief has astonished me.

Could it have been what I experienced years ago at the first funeral

I went to after my Gerry died—a fresh reminder where all the pain revisited, the magnitude of this life's sorrow accumulated? But this afternoon when Tom spoke of God providing Carol as a life-saving purpose to Naomi after the loss of her husband and sons, she raised her head with recognition on her face. As Tom so often does, somehow he hit on the truth and I think she realized it in that moment. *Please God, fill my sister with your joy and keep her from despair.*

When she brought Carol home less than a year after her men were killed, I feared it was too soon for such an enormous undertaking. But she took to the task with such zeal and joy that I had to change my mind. The results were noticeable. Naomi played worship music for that dear girl, took her on field trips, to concerts, to massage therapy, brought her to the swimming pool and even went with her every year to that special camp out west for folks with disabilities. So many wonderful experiences. I know she's been proud of Carol's every response, no matter how small. How she did love her music! Her hands would wave, her whole body would quiver. Well, now she'll be rejoicing with the angels, whole at last. *A thousand thank yous, Lord, for the promise of resurrection.*

For someone who'd been unable to communicate, Carol was greatly loved. This small community church is full and her family fills three long church pews. Beside Naomi sits her faithful daughter-in-law Ruthie with her husband Bowen, and precocious young Davy. He stood up front, adorable in his red cowboy boots and plaid shirt with the bolo tie, reciting the twenty-third psalm for us all, word perfect. Such earnest brown eyes so like his mother's. How lovely it would be if Ruthie and Bowen could have another child. But from comments Ruthie has made, Naomi doubts that will happen. Like me, she would never pry into such matters. Our mother often warned us to mind our own business. Instead, we pray.

On the other side of Naomi is O'Dell, her pretty face all lopsided from

Bell's Palsy. Although at times she still manipulates Naomi, she's settled down considerably since marrying Big Bart Neufeld. What a pussycat he has turned out to be, for all his fearsome biker looks. He's a fine, upstanding husband and father. He is the one who makes sure the children spend time with Naomi each week and I don't doubt that he was the force behind taking them out of school to be here at the family funeral this afternoon. His devotion to O'Dell is obvious, in spite of her appearance now. Perhaps the palsy is an unexpected blessing to temper her vanity and willfulness. *Lord Jesus, pull them to yourself.*

And who could ever have imagined that at the end of our reserved family pew would sit Naomi's brother-in-law, Jake? A much-tamed Jake, too. Now he's the one in the wheelchair. I suppose it's uncharitable to think it, but it's probably for the best that his speech was destroyed by that stroke two years ago. Now he must be the one to listen, instead of preaching his outlandish brand of homegrown, cobbled-together heresy. Perhaps the Lord has silenced his tongue for a purpose. *Oh Father, give him ears to hear and a heart to learn.*

On the opposite end of the pew is Bertha, still keeping as much distance as possible from her father, I notice. She's almost unrecognizable from the gauche but cheerful girl who first came down from the north country five years ago. Here she is, finishing up her last semester to become a licensed practical nurse and about to be married to a nice man from Naomi's church. She's downright stylish now too, in her short hair and up-to-date outfit. Beneath the polish, though, Naomi tells me Bertha is still wary of anything biblical. Not that she openly rejects God, but I still see an ever-so-slight hard edge to her friendliness. It's as though you can circle the building and see the lights are on, but she won't open the door to let you in to talk about what really matters. *Lord, heal her from her father's false teaching. And would you break down the barriers she has set up against You because of it?*

Beside me, like another daughter, sits my Jacqui. I'm overjoyed that she finally married C.H. And I'm ever so glad she was able to put to rest her feelings of obligation that plagued her for a while there to return to that boyfriend Geoff. When his relationship with another man didn't work out, he began calling her again, guilting her into thinking she should return. It caused a year of unnecessary delay to her marriage which seemed grossly unfair. I was outraged! As I suspected, he was only using her to gain sole custody of the daughter he and his partner had adopted. Naturally, I was heartbroken for that poor child, but I'll confess I pushed rather hard for Jacqui to consign that selfish man to the past. He treated her abominably and only coughed up her share of the sale of the home they bought together when she threatened to take legal action.

And besides, I wanted her near us. I wanted to enfold her in our family and in some small way to make up for all we missed in her growing up years and all she missed with us. It would have given Father and Mother such joy to see this lost granddaughter of theirs belonging to Jesus and at the heart of our family. She's more insistent than my own children that we get everyone together for any excuse for a party. *Bless their marriage, Lord, and make them wise and faithful parents to Lewis.*

How often she used to come to me, burning with questions about the Bible or the challenges of life, back and forth trying to unlearn the biases her father instilled in her, never afraid to reexamine her preconceived notions. What a girl! I'm thrilled to see her so happy. Now that C.H.'s boy is off to college on a modified program, they're filling their empty nest with people. Neighbours, stray young people Jacqui meets at the library, lonely seniors and misfits, their home is open to all. Today, she even has one of them with her, a lovely young lady named Gabrielle whom Jacqui has taken under her wing for years now.

Despite the joy I have in knowing and loving Jacqui, there's a sadness, too. If only Mother and Father could have known her. If only they had seen the answer to their prayers in their lifetime. How God brought John back home, as Nomi and I have seen. I was surprised enough when John showed up at Tom's and my wedding, but to have him make the move back to Alberta after all these years, and live in the very house he grew up in, all beautifully renovated by Jacqui... It seemed, oh, I don't know, impossible to believe somehow, a miracle. It grieves me still that Mother and Father never had the chance to reunite with John, but perhaps on the other side? After all, we do see him softening and even attending church with Jacqui and C.H. occasionally. There's nothing like aging to focus our thoughts on what is most important in life, for now and for eternity.

Loving Father, thank you for answering my parents' many prayers over the years. You are a God of great and good surprises. I can't wait to see what happens next.

A NOTE FROM THE AUTHOR

For each of our unique personalities, God has a unique way of getting our attention. He tailors our lives to pull us to Himself, whether through conflicts from the past or circumstances like windstorms.

Poor Jacqui. As the author, I felt sorry for her, putting her through the storm she had to endure. Yet God knows exactly what it will take to bring us to repentance. "When you cry out, let your collection of idols deliver you. But the wind will carry them all away, a breath will take them. But he who puts his trust in Me shall possess the land..." Isaiah 57:13

Have you experienced the "winnowing wind of God" as Jacqui did? I certainly have, and while it is painful and uncomfortable in the storm, I'm so grateful He lovingly brings me to the end of myself so I will cry out to Him.

While I always hope to engross my readers in a story, I pray the deeper truths of God's pursuing love, His kind guidance in our lives and His amazing way of working things together for our good and His glory will encourage your trust in Him long after the story ends.

Your friend,
Eleanor Bertin

ACKNOWLEDGEMENTS

Every writer is the product of many influences, teachers, and helps along the way. I'm especially indebted to my sister Becky Magill who has been a godly example to me and mentored me from childhood. It is through her I have learned the truths of the depths of my depravity and the deeper reach of God's grace.

I'm thankful to my beta readers, Janice Dick, Angela Meyer, Deb Elkink and Sara Davison for their insightful comments and corrections.

As always, a heartfelt thank you to my husband, Mike and most especially to my Lord, Jesus Christ. May this work glorify Him.

Eleanor Bertin

ABOUT THE AUTHOR

In a fit of optimism at age eleven, Eleanor Bertin began her first novel by numbering a stack of 100 pages. Two of them got filled with words. *Lifelines*, her first completed novel, was published in 2016, followed by *Pall of Silence* in 2017, a memoir about her late son Paul.

She holds a college diploma in Communications and worked in agriculture journalism until the birth of her first child. The family eventually grew to include one daughter and six sons (the youngest with Down syndrome) whom she home-educated for 25 years.

Eleanor grew up on a Manitoba farm, spent 20 years in cities and towns, and in the past 16 years has come full circle to embrace country life again. She lives with her husband and youngest son, Timothy, amidst the ongoing renovation of a century home in central Alberta where she reads, writes, sweeps up construction rubble and blogs about a sometimes elusive contentment at www.jewelofcontentment.wordpress.com.

LET'S CONNECT

Find Eleanor online at www.eleanorbertinauthor.com, and on Facebook and Goodreads.

For news and encouragement about upcoming books, contests, giveaways, and other activities, subscribe to *Leaf & Blade,* Eleanor's monthly newsletter.

If you've enjoyed *Tethered,* please consider leaving a review on Amazon and Goodreads. Your words bring hope and encouragement to the author, as well as other readers.

Coming soon to

THE MOSAIC COLLECTION

Heart Restoration by Regina Rudd Merrick

For interior designer Lisa Reno things go from bad to worse when her contractor brother falls off a ladder and breaks his leg. Now she has to deal with the past coming back to haunt her, an old house with a corpse in the creepy cellar, and everybody in town trying their best to fix her up with any man that moves.

Nick Woodward is willing to do his old college roommate a favor – especially since it involves renovating his own inheritance. The last thing he wants is to get involved with anyone. When he lost his wife and unborn child so suddenly, he had made the decision to keep God and everyone else at arm's length.

So far, so good.

But what a difference a trip to a dingy basement makes.

Made in the USA
Middletown, DE
20 August 2022

71042642R00186